—WHERE THE—
WILD LILIES GROW

To my beloved daughter
Fiona

Love Mamma.

WHERE THE
WILD LILIES
GROW

A NOVEL

SHEENA SUMMERFIELD

This book is a work of fiction. Names, characters, places, and incidents are either the product of the author's imagination or are used fictitiously, and any resemblance to actual persons, living or dead, business establishments, events, or locales is entirely coincidental.

Printed in the United States of America

Cover illustration: Audrey Carver
Interior and Cover Design: Ghislain Viau

Preface

It was, as records tell, a long time ago.

In 1620, two English naval men who had landed at The Cape audaciously proclaimed, in true British pomp, the Sovereignty of James I, and hoisted an English flag on Signal Hill, Cape Town.

However, the king did not agree, having Southern Africa to his claims and domains, and so it did not occur. The English came to South Africa, Cape, many times before they established themselves there.

The Dutch East India Company had established its re-victual station at The Cape, and many nations visited Table Bay: the mountain was shaped like a table, and when it was covered with white clouds it looked like the table was covered with a white cloth. Hence the name "Table Mountain." The Station was thriving.

War broke out between France and Holland, the result of Napoleon's Campaign Toward the East. Immigrants arrived—Dutch, French, German—and settled industriously and successfully, so much so it caused the conquering English to capture the Cape and undertake a government.

These were the peoples who gave birth to a fantastic rich and beautiful new country. Their story has been reported in several ways—documents, books, diaries, chronicles and publication: not for in-depth research scholars, it's merely a glimpse to satisfy curious persons interested in knowing more about these pioneers.

In 1820, the Cape of Good Hope, as it was named, had as the governor the son of the Duke of Bedford. He was considered ignorantly unsuitable, as an English Aristocrat, to explore the Terrain and dark mystery of land unknown. He was Lord Charles Somerset—hardly able to assess accurately agricultural potentialities of such a wild, wide undeveloped country.

Somerset journeyed bravely for weeks, inland by ox wagon travel, down through the frontier region. He observed a sprinkling of farmers who inhabited the Land who were well established—where the air was clean and fresh, people walked, horses were transportation, ambition was to survive, and true accomplishment was building a successful farm, with eggs from the chicken coop and milk from hand-fed cows. From the udder to the pail!

He was extremely impressed and smitten, especially by the park-like beauty and space of a town named Graaf Reenet. The great fish river and its green banks, at times a fordable trickle and at other times a 40-foot-deep flow of water that crushed before it every living or stationary object. The river fails to provide a barrier; it has eccentric bends at a critical point, it makes a right turn. More blood has been spilled near this river than anywhere else. It has been the area of nine wars and constant discord.

Lord C. Somerset returned to England, leaving Rufus Donken, a young and sad man, mourning the death of his beloved 28-year-old wife (who died in childbirth) in charge, during his absence.*

---

* Lord Charles Somerset was the original founder, creator of what became the hated "apartheid" in South Africa. Rufus Donken eventually committed suicide.

The world was floundering from the consequences of the Napoleonic Wars, revolution flooded Europe. Beethoven was writing his
Ninth Symphony, Greeks were plotting to fight the Turks: Britain
was in political morass, passing new acts and laws, from the pits of
poverty and distress. At this time this idea was born:

Send the landless to become landowners all
along the frontiers of the Cape, in South Africa!

In 1819 they set sail, dreaming of a paradise, against overwhelming challenge: the vagaries of climate, constant life-and-death
threats by marauders, multitudes of wild animals and fearful
wilderness. Steep mountains, no roads, fordable rivers (drifts, as
they are known), tensions between peoples with similar aims
of living, similar qualities of bravery with hardihood, to fight to
survive—on horseback and in wagons.

The reality was, they brought constitutional reform, cleared
and spread out land into sheep farming country, into new colonies
into the Boer Republics, into diamond mines and gold fields, and
into the rapid changing South Africa.

O n e

Frederick Heath McCabe scanned the warm comforts of his living room. A cheerful fire flickered and glowed in the hearth and his hand rested on the loose antimacassar over the arm of the chair. He looked down at his daughter: Indeed she was a true beauty. His girl, her red gold hair tumbled down her shoulders like an avalanche.

Long lashes brushed her beautiful amber eyes. Smooth clear skin, like an ivory cameo, and a full smiling sensual mouth.

She was silently reading, her lips moving as she read out loud, "soldiers and sailors were on half pay, mechanical inventions, particularly in the spinning trade had displaced many people who became out of work and all were still in shock by the Peterloo Massacre. (Where British troops fired on their own dissident countrymen.) Lord Charles S. pressed for his emigration scheme (1819)."

She jumped up from her reading, almost flung herself upon her father. "Oh Father this is the worst October ever! Why don't we go away to this Cape of Good Hope? Outside the parish today, people were falling over each other they were so excited and dozens are

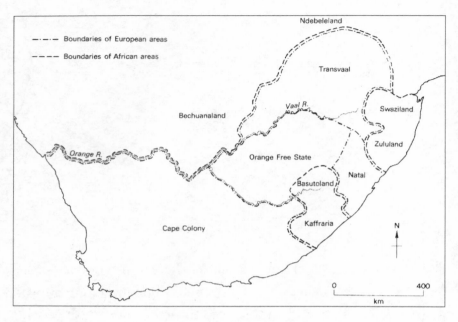

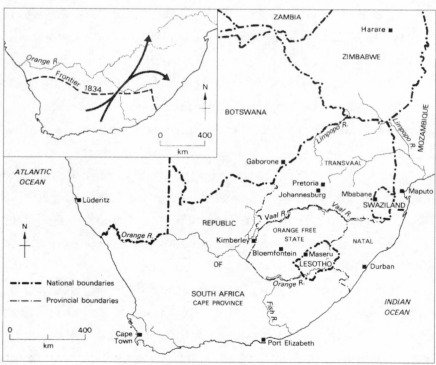

planning to take all their belongings and go out and start a brand new life."

She placed her tapered fingers on his lips. "Listen Darling Daddy!" She said, "Here in our home it's all a pathetic testimony of mother, we can't live with all our smothering memories." She hesitated, "I loved her dearly, neither of us will ever forget her. How could we? But we are here on the earth to live, we have life! Daddy, this endlessly tiresome weather, the sight of able-bodied men and their families in the workhouses, people hungry, political unrest add to it our own grief, it's just too much to bear."

She looked at her father. "Can you not see?" she said. Her father reached down and picked up the Times. He slumped back into his chair and read through the details of the Lord Charles Somerset immigration scheme. The article ended on a curious note of warning. "Emigrants might soon discover that an African climate was injurious to their health, detrimental to their life's little comforts. By bargaining with the Parish officers, they must remain where located, for, to return is not merely a serious work and labor, but a practical impossibility. They may die if they remain. They may starve if they return."

They simply looked at each other. "I would never have thought of this; you, my girl, have planted the idea."

She flung her arms around her father. "We have each other Daddy, we will take care of each other all the way, come what may."

She chuckled, perhaps nervously, but not without excitement!

The thought of moving had never entered his mind before. He felt a small tingle of excitement and wonder. Something moved within him—inspiration, maybe? "Why not?" he thought. "Different, exhilarating." He had an adrenaline rush. He took the paper from her hands, and at that moment, a positive decision drowned out all other thoughts.

Frederick McCabe put his arm around his daughter. The thoughts of her wondrous, fresh ideas, were infectious. Prospective emigrants only had to pay the deposit to the authorities, of ten pounds. He knew there would be little doubt about his selection. The terms of the emigration plan were comparatively simple and involved the selections of individuals into parties under selected responsible leaders.

A deposit was to be paid! There was a promise of a free passage by ship? Once there, free rations whilst the first crops were growing, and a hundred acre holding allocated to each family, plus transport from whatever landing place, would be provided. It was ox wagon transport, but settlers would have to pay for it. The whole dazzling prospect of adventure conjured visions of escape from the depressing conditions of the Industrial Revolution.

The present was not a good time for Frederick McCabe, he lost his wife, a lovely gentle woman. She died from a strange fever, all so quickly: The Honorable Rosanne, a granddaughter, of the Viscount and Vicountess of Traubridge. His was a happy marriage. He was stricken with grief, and loneliness and now he was living in a world still floundering from the consequences of the Napoleonic Wars. Europe was undergoing a ferment of ideas, inventive and political, and the pungent feel of change hung heavy in the atmosphere.

Queen Victoria was born, so was Karl Marx. The Greeks were plotting the overthrow of the Turks, Beethoven was composing his Ninth Symphony, frustration gave precedence to creation, literary works began to sparkle, but the most marvelous new breath of living, was this musical flow of words and chatter that came from the mind of his beautiful and beloved daughter Kathleen! He and

Kathleen would emigrate, partly by independent means but on the same ship!

Almost 90,000 persons were anxious to leave England and depart to the unknown dangers of a new and untamed land, but because of funds only 4,000 were finally chosen. The administrators of the scheme selected leaders and dealt with them by selection and heritage, education, experience and knowledge. Their committees were formed and the chosen persons were those of good and fine character, persons who were considered to be contributory to an infant colony.

The thought of traveling on an emigrant ship seemed less daring: alone was a daunting image. Nevertheless, he was prepared to pay for his requisites and perhaps, with luck and persuasion a little more space! One had to be selected of course, but it did not occur to him that he would not be. It was an opportunity, and he would accept with gratitude. He would go as an independent individual and pay his own passage, but perhaps claim the land grant.

There was no sadness as Kathleen and her father tirelessly sold many of their possessions. The excitement and eagerness of Kathleen was contagious. He was filled with enthusiasm each day they waited for news of where the vessels awaited them. Excitement reached fever pitch when they were told the vessels awaited in Cork, Portsmouth, Bristol, Liverpool and Deptford-on-the-Thames.

In the media, pessimists depicted the horrors and hardships emigrants could expect. Cartoonist Cruikshank drew cartoons of "wild beasts and Kaffirs," killing settlers at the Cape of Forlorn

---

*The term "Kaffir" Caffres, Kafirs, Caffers, has been used in speaking of the natives of SA. Black skinned natives distinct from light skin Bushmen Hottentots who confronted white men when first landed at the Cape.

Hope." Undaunted, her composure unaffected, Kathleen was very busily packing in little items she felt would withstand the journey. "A toolbox, Daddy, I always said if I had one thing I could be allowed to take on a desert island it would be a well-stocked toolbox." And they chose every tool in the fashion of the day.

She had a large ungainly box, strongly put together, she had numerous spades, scythes, pitch forks, short forks, hay forks and hard forks, harro-teeth, axes, bill hooks, hinges and nails—hammers of solid steel, levers, triangle set squares, a spirit level and 2 steel English ploughs.

The weather was bitter, below freezing point, and the newspapers wrote that one vessel was frozen in a fathom of ice. Kathleen was seemingly totally calm, not discouraged; rather, she was very pleased that her father was proclaimed the group leader. Roads to London, Liverpool and Cork were thronged with travelers in all types of conveyance, some on carts, in stagecoaches, even walking. It was midwinter, bitterly cold, but spirits were high, church bells were ringing and the townspeople gathered to bid farewells.

Kathleen and her father were to travel from the Thames on the "Belle Avant Garde." There was no restriction on the trunks and boxes one could take so Kathleen McCabe had a distinct advantage. She had a large consignment, including a carriage, beds, porcelain, silver, feather covers and pieces of fine old furniture. They included the ploughs and innumerable tools and implements.

Finally, they boarded the ship, just as darkness fell. The wicked weather had persisted and travelers were tortured by the excruciating conditions. When Kathleen arrived, she was forced to discard her heavy cape to help direct operations. She hated the idea of pewter mugs and took care to carefully place her long coffin-like trunks of china. Pewter mugs and plates were what the burghers used at the Cape, she heard, often melting them down to make bullets.

She shuddered at the thought. It was not the bullets that made her shudder, but drinking from a pewter mug. Thank God she had seen to that. Weeks she had spent lining her wooden trunks with wallpaper and then covering them with slightly tarred canvas.

The ship was "The Belle Avant Guard" said to have been built in Calcutta in 1799. It had been acquired by the British Navy around 1804. A wooden ship—tall masts—powerful, 3, across the tops of the ship, and a mass of rope ladders at the base of the masts leading up towards the sails. A long ship, 295 feet long, 18000 ton bark ship—and it could carry 450 passengers. Most wooden ships had no heating—top deck, lower deck and in between where the Dining Saloon, the Captain's Cabin and a dance floor were. Rope ladders dangled down the sides. There were 13 portholes, or windows rather, and wooden railings all round for safety.

It was the 26th of December, 1819. Twenty-one ships carrying 4,000 people were sailing to Algoa Bay and the journey would take three months and three days, 90 days, most people said. Frederick McCabe had charge of a party of 220 people. The rules were fairly rigid: emigrants of varied ranks and occupations, a motley multitude of wheelwrights, ex-soldiers, plumbers, millers, lawyers, farmers, clerks and carpenters, but, all of one mind, and all traveling by the same means.

There were various boats, snowed in, semi covered in the fog. Ranged from whalers to a 70 gun, man of war. The docks were wet and dirty, ice chunks and broken ice melting, scattered and slippery. Thick wet ropes tied to the lanyard. Tethered in an ungainly manner and left in positions where people tripped and tumbled over them. The wind brought sprays of icy water up over the wharf.

It was sorely ugly. Cold, wet, and dangerous slippery: with icy winds blowing and bewildered people moving everywhere with uncertain expressions, and tiny tinges of wonder.

On arrival they were all shown to their quarters. Party heads in a saloon on the upper deck, some on bunks and others into small cabins leading off the saloon. Party members were packed between decks on wooden bunks, tables and benches. They had very little space, hard and uncomfortable.

Though emigration is a leveler, of course, some privileged persons had private cabins, privacy, one or two had brought a grand horse carriage on board, as well as provisions. For the ordinary settler, there was hard, salt beef, moldy ship biscuits, oatmeal, sago cola and sugar. Water was rationed.

They dressed behind curtains which were their only privacy. Here in this cramped space, they ate, slept and vomited, and were up at five in the morning. All screens and curtains had to be removed by eight. No one was allowed a late sleep unless certified ill by some medical gentleman. A measure of military discipline prevailed. All bedding had to be brought up on deck to be aired.

Other ships were chopped out from the ice of the frozen Thames which that year was frozen so hard, booths and stalls were erected in the middle of the river and bonfires flamed. The ice bound emigrant doubles, danced with zest around them. Indeed, a queer last glimpse of their beloved land, for people committed as they were, to a land so remote and little known, among savage tribes way out onto the very outposts of uncivilized lands. They were aware of the glare of public interest in them. They haughtily felt they were making history.

On a Sunday in early February they sailed downstream to Gravesend, the entrance to the Port of London, where incoming vessels cleared customs. Suddenly there were tears streaming down cheeks. All passengers felt they were leaving England, never to return, yet all seemingly rejoiced to begin after a wearisome wait.

Hardly had the ships left the mouth of the Thames when they encountered rough weather. The sea smashed and broke in all directions, churning chairs, tables, plates, dishes, boxes, men, women and children, all mixed together, dreadfully and groaningly seasick.

Fred McCabe was up helping the sailors. Kathleen was below holding a basin. All able-bodied people were rallying to do their best. The ship tacked backward and forward twice along the coast before she could safely follow a steady course close to the English coast as far as Cornwall and then out into the open sea. They were to sail southwards, keeping close to the coasts of Africa, until they reach the equator, and then in a wide westward sweep, take the prevailing winds, finally eastwards, toward Table Bay.

Once the captain was clear of the English Channel his first thought was to cleanse the ship. All hatches were closed and the ship fumigated for rats and cockroaches with nitrous fumes, a sore discomfort to the passengers. The hope was to prevent epidemics, but it was a vain hope.

Every day at a regular time, fresh water was distributed. This was one of the greatest hardships of the journey. The water went foul after a time. Each family was issued with a wooden tub or kid holding two or three quarts which had to be used for drinking, cooking and washing. And it was a disaster, if, by rolling and pitching the tubs capsized.

Each family had its own crockery and cutlery and teapots were taken to the galley for boiling water. One evening just before midnight, a message came to the saloon that Mrs. Font's child was ill. Mrs. Font, between decks, had three children. McCabe and Kathleen were in a tiny cabin off the saloon on the upper deck.

He filled his hip flash with rum, placed it on his hip, and taking Kathleen by the elbow, went down toward the bunks. Boxes, packages, bundles and bins were everywhere about the ship. Bodies were hanging in hammocks suspended on rings from the beams of the ship; there seemed to be no fresh air and no space! And to make it worse, the noises of the sea were at times ear shattering; women's hysterical high-pitched voices and miserable crying of dozens of children.

Someone called out "It's Mrs. Font's Angela," and they headed for the cramped bunks on port side. The child's mother was in a state of hysteria and her husband, stunned by fear, seemed to have lost the power of speech. McCabe took a cup from the small bench and half filled it with rum, handed it to the poor man forcefully.

"Drink this, man," he ordered, but Kathleen withdrew. The man swallowed the rum and wiped his mouth with the upper part of his right thumb. The mother kept hysterically repeating, "What shall I do, Mr. McCabe?" Kathleen removed her cape and slowly placed it over the little girl. She was crazed with helpless pity, but the fear of contact was so great she didn't offer playing a role of a dedicated nurse.

It was each man for himself in this world, she thought. God only knows what diseases these people were afflicted with. There was no medical inspection before sailing. She would have liked herself more if she had the courage to help more. She watched as her father summoned the bosun and then some person who had been designated the position of Ship's Doctor. The child had measles. Both children died on successive days and were buried at sea, wrapped and sewn into their contaminated bedding.

The captain, a short, freckle-faced bosun, cupped his hands around his mouth and bellowed, "All hands on deck!" His voice echoed across the icy fog-wet decks and men came scrambling up ladders and at companion ways up the rigging, swarming 150 feet above the deck, loosening the furled sails. "Loose the fore royal, loose the main royal, man the fort gallants, sheets and halyard. There, look alive deck." The sails began to drop like curtains at a play's end. Men hauled furiously on the sheets to trim sails to the wind.

Men grabbed the hemp lines, thick as a man's wrist, braced their feet on the deck and hauled hand over hand, faces purple with frantic effort. "Heave, heave, heave," they shouted as the sail was winched home. The wind met it and the ship heeled over slightly as the sails billow and fill. Out in the swollen ocean, there was ship and sea and sky. All anxiously watched for signs that speed on one's way, or bring delay and doom. There is witchery in the seas and its stories, and in the mere sight of ship.

As they sailed south, the weather became warmer and men were able to sleep on deck in fresh air and listen to the seafaring tales told to them by the sailors. Also this alleviated the congestion and mothers and children had more room and comfort. Their progress was often leisurely, sometimes becalmed, but always with infinite time for thinking.

One morning Kathleen was on deck very early, it was warm and not yet daylight. It was calm and only a slight breeze whistled through the sails. How wonderful it all seemed, so full of promise and wonder. The Eastern horizon was gray-pink, suggesting the coming of day. The air tasted salty and the water looked black and swollen, huge swells rising and falling endlessly, like time.

Suddenly, there was a loud noise, something cracked like a whip over her head, and there were great flaps and screeches and men calling. Oh God, they had caught a huge bird. It was tired and was resting on the ship. She slid from the box she was sitting on and got up with a prodigious leap. The sailors had killed an albatross, a huge, sleek and magnificent creature. "No, no, no" she screamed, "let it be, please let it be," but the face that turned up to look at her, an unheeded appeal as he held the great dying creature, told her how futile it was to beg.

The albatross weighed easily 20 pounds and the sailors of the Belle Avante exchanged the carcass for rum, which the settlers drew from the ship's stores. It was the first fresh meat they had for seven weeks. Men caught sharks that swam around the ship, and one man, having baited his hook with a lump of salt pork, tied the line around his arm. This confident gesture nearly cost him his life, as the shark was the stronger of the two. It was only the prompt action of his friends that stopped him from being dragged overboard.

The captain, though a short man, was an aggressive person with an ardent desire to assert himself. He was a good sailor and an equally good captain. He showed Kathleen great courtesy and attention. So did every other man. This pleased Kathleen for she was used to being spoiled and pampered. On one of these wondrously calm mornings there was great excitement. A school of whales was sighted. It was all so beautiful. Their vast gleaming bodies rose up out of the water, then glided smoothly back down into the deep marine water. One of them, as if curious and wanting to be sociable, came alongside the ship with its back 10 or 12 feet out of the water, a monster gentle and curious.

At that moment Captain shot at it with a ball, and it made a sad noise and swam away slower than the others, for it was wounded. "Oh dear God, Captain. It was trying to befriend us," cried Kathleen. "How hateful of you to have hurt it." She caught up her skirts with one hand, holding the other hand over her heart as though she felt the pain. "What manner of creatures are we, we men," she semi-sobbed. And the whole exciting diversion stopped with her words.

At Palma in the Canary Islands, the Nautilus, a fellow ship of settlers, caught up with the Belle Avante and they sailed in a sort of convoy for the rest of the voyage. It was an eventful journey. One baby was born and there were not many complaints despite the privations of the emigrants in the airless ships.

Flying fish were a source of great interest and discussions, as were the phosphorescence of some of the tropical waters when the ship was becalmed. The settlers rowed around and feathered their oars which seemed bathed in liquid illuminated silver. People danced on deck while someone played a fiddle, and often sailors danced the hornpipe for the passengers.

By the first of May, 1820, eight of the ships anchored off Simonstown (named after Simon Van der Stel) to replenish supplies and only the party leaders were allowed to land because of the outbreak of various diseases during the long monotonous course of the journey.

The acting governor at the Cape, Sir Rufane Donkin, was acting governor in Lord Charles Somerset's absence. Sir Donkin was known to be a kind, humanitarian man, some leaders called on him, but he soon left for Algoa Bay.

One of the passengers, a gregarious chap named Wilson, managed to obtain a couple of sheep and some onions, which he shared among his friends. But passengers were given fresh fruit, black, white and red grapes and sweet silver figs. They loaded with fresh water and provisions then after a tantalizing lie out in the Bay where they only saw the hills and valleys in the distance. Tempers

Lord Charles Somerset

frayed and impatience was intolerably increased. They once again put out to sea.

On May 15, the Belle Avant Guard anchored near the shores of Algoa Bay. No harbor, nothing; it was too shallow to go closer. Algoa Bay itself was calm and sea gulls and seabirds were everywhere. Hills rose up from the sands, green hills and tallish milkwood trees, contrasting the white sands void of palms and coconuts. Why did she expect to see coconuts, palms and dates? No roads, no traffic. She felt happy that at least the hills were green.

Sir Rufane had left his comfortable quarters at Governor's House in Cape Town, traveled down to come to Algoa Bay to personally supervise the landing and to see what he could do to see that all needs were met. He was a tall, sad, lean man, as only a few months previously he had suffered the grievous loss of his own young wife (after whom Port Elizabeth got its name). The tremendous activity which the settlers entailed distracted his own feelings of self pity and depression. His spirits livened and he was a great help to many.

Captain Francis Evett, military commander at Fort Frederick, also oversaw the landing, his soldiers carrying the settlers through the final surf.

ALBANY

High up on the hill overlooking the Baakens River where it flowed into the sea was Fort Frederick—a fortified barrack built by the British in 1799. This served as Sir Rufane's quarters. Colonel Ayler, the Landdrost of Graaf Reinet, was responsible for providing food and transport for the settlers. He assembled many ox wagons, all waiting and ready together with live rations in the form of oxen and sheep.

Seed ploughs and implements were held in readiness for these prospective new farmers, who in turn were to put them to immediate use. Temporary shelters were erected on the beaches before they departed to their allocated lands. Sir Rufane extended the boundary of the colony from the great Fish River to the Keishama and reconstituted the Albany district to include all the neutral territory, the Zuurveld and part of the district of Utenhage. A few forts were built in what was formerly the neutral area for settler protection and the area was called Bathurst. This small fortified hill of marquees and tents were occupied by officers of administration was all the habitation the settlers were to see.

Back on the ships, decks were crowded with eager passengers scanning the landscape. Gloom, tears, and disappointment reflected on their faces as they first glimpsed the land of their future homes. It was a sort of desolate shoreline: The Naked Beach, banked by windswept sand hills, against steep hillocks, some dry and some brown but most covered in green bush. In the distance were bluish mauve shapes of mountains: as far as the eye could see from the

Southwest to the northwest were beaches and sand hills. The earth seemed pale, sterile, and a lot of the beach without verdure.

It was at once dull and frightening and the effect upon the minds of the passengers was discouraging indeed. Some began to contrast this new wilderness with the beautiful green shores of England and wondered whether they had been lured away by false representations. As Kathleen screened this land through the misty pounding surf of the beach, and the beating of her heart, her thoughts were stricken with sudden apprehension.

The ship Captain marshaled his passengers into groups, and with their hand luggage, put them into flat-bottomed boats, hauled alongside. Heavy luggage was transported separately. Men, women and children clambered down rope ladders at the ship's sides and the flat-bottomed boats were warped towards the beach by ropes fastened on the beaches, on sharp rocks, or trunks of trees.

As the boats neared the shore, men jumped out and waded, and women were carried by men of the 72nd Regiment stationed at Fort Frederick. An obliging Scots officer, seeing Kathleen, splashed forward, arms outstretched and scooped her and her baggage up in his arms. When Kathleen was placed, laughing, on firm ground, she looked around for her father. He was wading through the water, wet to the thigh. Her heart was pounding wildly with the excitement of adventure. Her fears and qualms were allayed and blown away on the strong southeast wind.

It was a powerful wind, which carried the settlers landing to halt for four days, and drove the surf beating around the shore to a height of 10 to 12 feet. Now that her feet were on this new land, Kathleen looked at her pale-skinned father, and then gazed wide-eyed at the huge wagons with their broad-horned oxen and silent men smoking long stemmed pipes. Rugged, brown, suntanned men in short blue coats and trousers made of softened leather, wide-brimmed mesh hats of woven rush, and velskoens made and hand sewn from softened hide.

She gazed all around at the naked Hottentot servants, pale yellow faces, with peppercorn hair! Her father, so sedate a gentleman, his quiet dignity and conservative taste. Thank God he was a successful man and well able to pay for additional food. She thought of the new land. The rugged antithesis. Yes, this earthy Burgher was a symbol of Africa, and her father, soft, like soft, green England.

She wondered when and where the supply ship had piled all their many boxes and articles for their future home. Where was their hansom cab, the token of her aristocratic rank and an obvious part of her refined home life of England. She looked at her hands, small, lovely hands, utterly unfitted for the course farmer habits, for rough life, but she wouldn't think about that, some other time—tomorrow—would do.

Fred McCabe was in consultation with Colonel Cuyler, landdrost of Uitenhage, to ascertain from him the plan of his exact location and the land allotted to him. Once through with the business of settlement he now wished to purchase a fine horse, yes, and more land. Captain Moresby was a captain of a sloop of War the "Menai." He offered to come to help the British settlers to construct sheds and cover. etc. upon landing. Captain Moresby who seemed to be everybody's friend, had enlisted the help of the admiral in command at the Naval Base at the Cape, to sponsor a "fund" for the relief of the settlers. He also knew of a Dutch burgher who had a most suitable horse.

The process of disembarking 4,000 people and settling them all on new found land inland was fairly lengthy. Some sought food and work. Some just occupied the days of waiting as best they could. All paid respects to the Marquee* of Sir Rufane Donkin.

Everything was sold to the settlers at reasonably low cost. But many were dismayed that they were allotted locations so far away. Many complained, but the young enjoyed the beaches waiting for the return of the wagon trains which had left with the first parties. Because of the house purchase of Fred McCabe and his daughter, the delay gave them more time. He awaited the return of the wagon train, for with it he expected the promised horse.

Kathleen delighted in the novelty of camping, living under the stars, fascinated and thrilled by the strange sights and sounds. She wandered out into the night, listening to the night jars, crickets, frogs and night owls—always aloof. She declined to sail out beyond the three-mil limit with Captain Mosely to witness the marriage of the gregarious passenger John Wilson to Jane Donald, members of her father's party.

In the evening, she was invited to accompany her father to dine with Sir Rufane Donkin and Captain Evatt arranged a dance by putting down a floor in his marquee.

What was happening was the organization of these 4,000 passengers from one ship, their possessions and all their implements and equipment. Government officials, the burgher farmers and settler all bustled about busily, in an anxious effort to assure the combined departure of every settler. Each burgher's wagon had to have its own Hottentot "voor loper" to lead his span and each wagon carried a huge load of goods. Tents, axes, spades, hoes and saws, trunks, chests and household belongings. Beside the wagons, loose oxen were driven to ensure a regular meat supply. The wagons

---

* A marquee is a large field tent or outdoor canopy.

would travel in single lines, each taking thirty yards of the route, which stretched in a long wagon train a strange cavalcade procession of carrying and parade, caravan or wagon train and would cover almost three miles.

On the day, before the McCabes' wagon train was due to depart, Captain Morseby rushed up to Fred McCabe with Mr. Dawson. They had found a suitable horse for Kathleen's cab. There was no exchange for money. Fred McCabe handed over a solid gold bracelet still in its Bond Street box. He had quite a collection of his wife's jewelry, which he intended to keep for his daughter. He felt no grief or guilt; it was a good exchange. He felt it was for his daughter despite the fact the horse was priced at costing 10, enough for two horses. He was thankful for his part of the wheat rations, and for food for the horse, corn, which had been delivered from Cape Town. He thought about the deteriorating effect of moist sea air and wondered how the horse would fare. There was green graze along the route.

Taking the horse by the halter, he led it down towards the open where the carriage stood, a 4-seater. It had traveled well and the tough British leathers had weathered the seas bravely. Patches of mold had formed here and there, like blue white meal, and the buckles showed signs of rust. He was pleased it was a four seater, and he noticed Kathleen had filled the underseats to capacity. Two pails and a scythe were sticking up above the footman's seats.

The girl had thought of almost everything. He took his time to harness this strange newly acquired horse, but it was gentle, with a kind eye, he thought. He led it up towards the carriage; it seemed calm and willing even though he was unused to it. He led it up to where Kathleen was loading the wagon. Her excited, happy laughter rang out, bright and rippling like a busy stream. She was trying to make conversation with a burgher busily packing all her boxes and kicking them into place with her feet as well as her gloved hands.

The horse gave a shrill whinny, which brought Kathleen back to earth. She suddenly appeared from out of the wagon. She was stunned, her amber eyes wide with wonder. She lifted her skirt and sprang down onto the ground. "Good Lord, Daddy, where did you get him, where, Daddy?" She patted its neck and ran her gloved hand over his muzzle and it blew into her face with wide nostrils. "Not a him, darling, it's a her, a big chestnut her," he said. "Once she had an Irish hunter relation, but now she has become a well trained Boer Horse."

Everyone gathered around and everyone was patting and gazing at the quiet chestnut. She was well fed and sedate, but moved lively enough when she felt the tug of the harness and the reins beside her cheeks. Everybody was sighing almost with envy. A private Democrat was just the thing for Kathleen. She felt she already knew this mare, like a friend to share some of the magical moments of her life. She felt the camaraderie and she wished for magical days!

Finally, order prevailed over the chaos of the settler camp. It had reached a climax and all was in readiness for the convoy to set out towards their land, allocated to the parties. The long wagon train set off. One of the burghers drove the carriage and Kathleen, tucked up beside her father, squeezed her hand through the back of his elbow and held his arm.

Their other guides chose a track away from the shore into sandy bush, dense in places and covered with the most extraordinary plant life, a weird and wonderful landscape quite alien to the knowledge of these Englishmen. The great loaded wagons cut deep furrows into the earth and the trampling hooves of the oxen turned the track into loose dust, which rose in the air like a misty ribbon denoting its course.

The weather was fine, but Kathleen was distracted by a myriad of strange sights and sounds. There was a din of shouted orders, yells and screams. The wagons creaked and groaned, and the lowing and bellowing of the oxen as the burgher cracked his long Riempie* whips calling the strangest names of every beast, in the span.

The McCabe's were fascinated by the short yellow man at the head of the span pulling and straining to get the team moving, as they moved forward slowly. By their facial expressions, they all seemed to wonder if they would ever be free of the jolts of transport, and the violent and uncomfortable movement which now seemed inseparable from their lives.

Across the undeveloped, somewhat bleak flat land between the hills, sliced by the knives of erosion, driver helped driver, through ravine kloofs** and dongas*** to the Swart Kops River, until all wagons were safely across the sandy water. Here they out spanned and the camp organized and settled for rest.

The carriage driver made a hobble for the mare and in no time at all Kathleen had found a wholesome wheat meal which she damped in a pail and fed to the horse. Mind there was graze as well. The hills were cutting off the sun's rays which seemed to rise and fall and the long shadows soon fell into darkness. Soon, rows of twinkling fires sparked beside the wagons, lighting up the weather-beaten faces of the kindly farmers who helped the settlers

---

* softened leather strips like ropes.
** ravine.
*** ditches caused by erosion.

cook. Meat was roasted and children were excited and noisy. It was difficult for the burghers to answer questions in a language the settlers did not understand. The Hottentots, separated from the settlers, made their own fires and cooked their own rations. It was found that some were terrible thieves and stole whatever they could. They slept under sheep skins and were not at all clean.

Pangs tore at Kathleen's heart when morning came. She saw they were moving into thick vegetation and bush, away from the sea. Huge, strange, often grotesque plants reached angular arms to the sky. Lush, suffocating creepers, also parasite plants twined around the trees, at times passage was difficult. Flashes of color, orange candelabra aloes, cheerily blazed forth on the dense and defiant bushland. The land seemed vast and empty, perhaps even lonely.

The wagons loaded salt from the pans beyond the Swartkops river. The day's trek became wearing and by night Hottentot drivers chattered away in their odd language. They seemed to mingle among the oxen, the night held mystery with strange cries of the African veld, and the men looked to their guns.

In places the trees were so thick they had to chop a road, hack it, rather, before the wagons could even think of passing. They encountered many hindrances and difficulties, but the amazing skill of the burghers prevented many accidents as they lumbered along. Near the Sundays River, the country began to change. Good rains left the deep ravines running freely. Several species of buck bounded into the bush as the wagons disturbed them. There was ample spoor of wild animals, massive herds of Trekbokken,* patterned in the earth, where no coverage occurred. Beautiful

---

* Trekbokken in great herds. Impala, flooded the lands. These antelope or buck herds, migrated when grazing demanded.

birds sang everywhere. Kathleen looked forward to the nightly encampment. The soft mauve light of evening was so beautiful it stopped one's speech. Things lost perspective in the roseate glow. Things seemed to creep nearer.

The smoke from the cooking fires circled upwards in plumes and feather-like columns and in the quiet of night somewhere not so distant, a jackal called with a haunting cry. Ostrich, lions and hyenas lurked and called. Sounds came from everywhere.

It took nine days to reach McCabe's location. Then suddenly his burgher driver, looking at papers, called the oxen to halt, putting on a brake. The cab driver at the back of the wagon brought the horse trap up under a huge gwenya tree. The burgher had become more relaxed and talkative with Kathleen. His name was Moolman. The driver of the carriage was the son of his neighbor on the next farm. The son, a superb guide, was well-versed in bush craft and the secrets of the wild.

The vegetation changed as they moved. They now all looked at this acreage of land before them. It was beautiful really, with large green painted gold wattle trees and vast yellow mimosa, splashes of vivid vermillion Cape honeysuckle scented the air and tall spiky aloes flamed ahead of the scrub all up the hill in the background. At the foot of the hill was a ravine, where a stream murmured in the thicket. Within the denseness of the bush, it was rich and exciting, permeated by Dung middens, and the smell of wild, green patches of grass, pasture, grazed short and open, and spread before them.

The old Boer driver, pipe sticking out from his bearded, prophet-like expression, removed his pipe and smiled, showing yellowish teeth. "Sonnestroom Mevrou,"* he said. "Sonnestroom,"

---

* Mevrou means Mrs.

repeated Kathleen. She frowned. "What" she said out loud, "is that?" He looked up to the sun, screwing up his blue, weather beaten eyes. "Son", he said, and then pointing to the water, "Stroom." He then put the words together, "Sonnestroom." "Sun stream," said Kathleen. "Daddy, did you hear what Mr. Moolman said? He said it's a sun stream, and this is our land." The younger of the two men was busy placing a halter on the horse's head and then a knee halter on her front legs. Beneath his wide brimmed hat, he too repeated with a flash of a smile, "Ja Mejuvrou.* Sonnestroom." It was a small tributary.

The Hottentot was lifting and dumping boxes and parcels cursing and smiling at the thought of what he could escape with before he left. The Burghers were strong men, and helped them until the very last box and tin was placed outside of the wagon. They helped to gather wood for the fire and helped to erect the tent, which suddenly, would be home for the McCabes. Home, in a wild, new, untamed land, surrounded by beasts and snakes. With only five oxen, 13 sheep, a cab and a mare. Suddenly shock took over!

"Please Meneer, before you go," Fred struggled to indicate what he wanted. Yes, he wanted the burghers and his Hottentots to fell bushes in order to make a kraal to fence in his sheep. He unfolded some money, and an agreement was reached for a few days of labor and help: much shopping and dragging until a small circular kraal of thorn bush was ready. The trunks of the trees facing inward, and the brush on the outside, like the shape of a wagon wheel, the stems and trees' trunks, like spokes.

The sheep were herded in, all huddled together. Then the same thing was done for the oxen that were fastened to their yokes.

* mejuvrou means miss.

"Even in the wilderness," thought Kathleen, "money has power." She took the pail from the hansom and followed a game trail to the stream. There was no time to ponder on fear and sentiment. Soon the burghers would depart and she and her father would be left to their own resources—alone. Once the tents were erected, all the things and household equipment was carried inside. Thank goodness they had several tents.

Fred McCabe had drawn no solace from Col. Cuyler's parting words, "Gentlemen, when you go out to plough, never leave your guns at home," he had repeated. This was one thing he personally supervised. Fred McCabe had two silver circa revolvers and hundreds and hundreds of rounds of ammunition, pistols of the East India Cavalry, boxes of ammunition and besides those he had a choice of 13 muskets. No way would he have come to Africa less armed. He did take comfort in the fact that he was a splendid shot and so was his daughter. Then it had suddenly occurred to him that he had almost forgotten to secure some help, staff, from the native servants. He would surely find one or two workers before the wagon train convoy left them.

He immediately set about bribing the burghers and with surprisingly little effort, he and Kathleen for a coat and several Rix dollars and a porcelain jug, obtained the services of an aged brown man and his less-aged woman. The little yellow Hottentot also wanted to stay, but the burgher needed him as a voerlooper.* Kathleen took the horse to drink, put two pails of water to the sheep and pondered about the oxen for their first night on Sonnestroom. Things had not gone too badly. 100 acres away was Mrs. Font. Kathleen wondered, and how had the Fonts fared? She

---

* voerlooper = heads the oxen in the wagon train; forewalker.

had lost two children on the ship, and when last she saw Mrs. Font, she was sitting on a wet head chest at the beach camp, subdued, pale-faced and dull. Her husband seemed like a beaten man and their surviving son was desperately trying to convince them it was not "the Cape of Forlorn Hope." Mr. Font had visions to bring the word of God to the savages in Africa. So now he had to have it out with his God. The tragic death of his children; "suffer little children," he mumbled through closed eyes.

Kathleen wept with frustration during the first eventful month in the veld. Great strides had taken place. A thousand conflicting ideas swept through her fertile mind. She had heard her father speaking in his sleep. It was disturbing she had to summon her courage, and go and sleep in the hansom, one time! It was not a handsome—but somehow everybody referred to it as a handsome!

"Jesus Kathleen, this is no life for you my darling," her father often said. "You're so young and so alone, sometimes I feel I'm on some strange sort of holiday and we will be going home to England, home to the security one earns from life, to our home and privacy, protected! Springtime and daffodils and English ale."

Perhaps he was gullible. Perhaps he had allowed Kathleen to persuade him, in his weak moments. Surely, he was still grieved from the death of her mother. Look at him now, his hands were brown and rough with new callouses, his neck was red and his nose cracked and burned from the sun. "He was such a fine man," thought Kathleen, "not an old man, goodness no, he is 46 years old, a man is not old at 46," she thought, screwing up her brow, "well a little old, perhaps." Perhaps she did the wrong thing. Perhaps he should have remarried and even had some other children. She smiled. She enjoyed being an only child and loved the care and attention she always received. "No," she thought, "maybe she would even resent a sister or brother, there's something special about being the only one." She would fix his skin! She looked down at her lovely long legs. They were brown already starting to tan. Yes, perhaps she would enjoy a little company, but it was useless dreaming of what one has not got. Here she is with father in a land almost devoid of communication and ravaged by constant wars. Here they were almost deposited: after almost half a year of exhausting travel, then into the wilds, the dense zuurveld, alone in the bush in the keen cold air of evening, surrounded by land never touched by spade nor plough. Perhaps they were resented by man and beast, but it mattered not now, here they were, and there was no time wasted for regrets. Here in the zuurveld they must now take root or rot!

Where exactly on the map were they? Somewhere near Somerset farm, not far from Cradock, on a creek, maybe a spring? Almost a little tributary to the fish river that flowed into the great Fish River. Neither were great rivers! She jolted herself into action. A small dead buck, with tiny sharp horns, hung limply across a homemade stile. Her father had shot it. While they could survive on wild meat they would. She had erected the stile together with Moerskind. The old native Moerskort, she learned, was meant to mean "murdered child"; there were reasons for the names given to children, and often they were named after an event that happened or took place nearest the moment of the child's birth "Moerskind," (child of murder), whatever it was, it hinted of tragedy—he was a kind, gentle and helpful soul. His quiet gaze and common sense were quite obvious, to anyone who possessed a smidgeon of human understanding. It was reassuring, Kathy sensed already, after only days, here was reliable relationship; she felt she could trust this wrinkled man of the bush veld who carefully taught her how to cook. She found solace in his comforting gestures.

He led her to a flat-stoned fireplace shaped in a triangle. The stones were built up in such a way that anything cooking, did not touch the sand. She took the flint and steel from her tinderbox. She then lit the fire, instructing in semi-sign language, to the old maid "Tante"* to skin and disembowel the buck and roast it. Tante gathered pieces of dried cow dung, feeding it into the fire to get glowing embers, and cutting the venison into smaller portions, she carefully sprinkled it with salt.

Her father had erected a large enclosure by tying poles together with all the string and ropes from the packing and whatever he could lay hands upon. They had felled hundreds of tree poles, saplings, and huge sheaves and heaps of long savannah grass. What a blessing the scythe was. With green poles upright and woven, under and over, over under and over—until a basket-like lattice formed. Then they mixed mud with water and threw it arms length, handful by handful by handful until the latticed wood frame was thick with mud, solid like a mud wall, pole and dagga, as it was called it became solid and hard when it dried. Tante then did a marvelous hand plastering on both the floor and walls, smoothing it with cow dung. Uloerskont and Tante made themselves a room, a 'randavel,' a round hut, with a small window and the roof was filled like a thatch roof is with bundles of long savanna grass. Packed down, they tapped and banged it into a thick consolidation. This shelter could protect them for now, until they would create a stronger and pretty one made of stones. Stones were the order of the day—loads of stones, sledges of stones, stones of every size, by wagons, passers by, whoever needed a meal or a drink came stones, any available means was accepted from far and wide.

* Tante means teeth.

McCabe was shaping and then designed a large stone house. Kathleen's tool box was the most precious of possessions—and the tools were gazed upon in awe and envy. All the time stones. From everywhere came stones. The foundations were dug and stones built upon the tools were put away safely after use.

When the Christmas bird started to sing Kathleen and her father had a house with calico windows and timbered doors. All the time, the stones kept arriving. McCabe's ambition for a durable house showed promise.

Kathleen and her father Fred designed a large square stone house with 2 stairways to an upper level—private and protective. We will gather stones, we will buy stones, send sledges to collect stones, from every corner of this earth. We will build a stone house not a mud house of strong sticks and mud and cow shit. We will build a house so solid, assegais will bounce right back or bend! That was the house that Kathleen and her father built. Thousands and thousands of stones with mud borrowed and bought labor. Stones that would stand against the fiercest winds, lightning, fire or storms and would stand, regal and stately long after the bones of her creators and builders had returned to dust.

There was no time to waste! No one rested. They shared ploughs, built sledges drawn by oxen, more labor arrived every day—and progress became more rapid. Kraals were rebuilt and strengthened, land was cleared for gardens, nothing was wasted, tree branches and tops were used for enclosures, fences were made, poles used as posts and gates and longdrop latrines were placed in private corners. The gut and entrails of dead animals, always used to place in the holes dug out for latrines—and for the worms who lived and worked down there. It was difficult to protect the new growth of wheat and oats; even flowers began to bloom, they found a way. Weeds must when the devil drives. There were no time schedules, they worked to win, to create protect to build and eat and live. All the time stones arrived, builders built more, Fred shaped them, and a deep foundation held them one atop the other like a Mayan city. Crushed red sand and anthills, cow dung and even sea sand held it together. As the days passed the stone house grew with two kitchens. One kitchen down under, like a cellar. A living room with a large warming fireplace, and a square mantle shelf supported by thick heavy tree beautiful slate-like trunks and flat stones polished with beeswax. High windows and a stairway that led to bedrooms and bathrooms. Kathleen continued to expand on her stone house. Inside this house she and her father would be safe. She befriended a Dutch burgher who came for 2 or 3 days at a time and he did wooden floors and doors and the roof and he knew the secrets of how to do most things. She thought she loved the farmer and felt sad each time he left. She taught him her language and he taught her his. They made a garden. They planted wheat and oats. They made stables and cone sheds—always gathering stones—always building—more stones and Sonnestroom grew into a chapel like house of mixed colored stones, shapes and levels of red earth and anthill crush built in the shape of a square. A large courtyard spread eagled a special roomy shed for her cab and her precious horse and the long stone drinking water trough. One day this house will be standing, upright and proud, when we are ashes and dust! All of us, she laughed out loud.

Two

"**S**ome people win and some people lose," Kathleen thought. She found Mr. Font planting wheat with a middle-sized shovel. He was concerned that as one sows, so shall one reap. It took her quite a time to convince him how wrong he was. Mr. Font seemed to her to be a loser. He had gone with his son to the kloof* between the hills to get timber. Great magnificent trees grew in the deeper Kloof where water was perennial and massive beams were cut from their trunks and used as roof supports and rafters.

The oxen were dragging these beams lengthwise on their crude sledges all through the new bush like new game trails. The hansom and the horse were used to collect rations from Bathurst and indeed was the envy of all the settlers who had to walk many miles to get a meal and live sheep. Even worse was driving the live rations home. Font left his young soon looking after his flock of sheep while he returned to fetch something he had forgotten.

The sheep were tied to prevent them from running away and placed in the shade of some trees. But the vultures spied these

---

* kloof = cliff.

immobilized creatures and in a huge ghostly swoop came down and devoured them right before the eyes of the terrified child.

Fred McCabe was born a powerful man. He now awoke with the calls of Africa. He loved the haunting cry of the fish eagle and the warble of the weevers. He loved the rich colors of the earth, the red soil that held the stones together and the way the black soil grew everything better than and so incredibly fast. He learned to know the deep snarl and throaty growl of the leopards in the Krantze.* The ominous responsive call of the wild dogs to a fellow friend or mate too often drifting melancholy on the evening breezes.

McCabe came in and flopped onto the handmade leather chair. Kathleen noticed he seemed exhausted. She got a large bowl of hot water and threw into it some simple epsom salts. She sat down at her father's feet, untied his velskoen boots and put his feet into the warm water.

"Kathleen, that is so good. A Bush Valley Spa." "Daddy, let me rub your worthy feet," and she took one foot and placed it on a towel on her lap. She rubbed his feet and turned each toe, she rubbed his ankles.

"Isn't it odd, women get swollen ankles, but it's not like that with you."

"Tell you what, my darling girl, I could doze off here where I'm seated." His own bliss.

"Tell me Daddy, is life all too much like hard work?"

"Yes and no. It was our decision Kathleen. There are moments when I hesitate, but you have to admit it is a fantastic challenge."

"Perhaps challenge is a load of tripe Daddy? Do we need challenge in our lives?"

---

* Krantz = rocky rock cliffs. Dangerous.

"No, I find the adventure and discovery so wonderful some-times; gloriously so."

"Daddy there's magic around every bend. And as for the work, I can't say I do not like it, I love it when we succeed. Look how far we've come. Daddy you are so strong and so clever, I want you to remember that. How you have learned to read the wild, as though it were an open book. Like in the land of footprints, you have learned so much about this maze of criss-crossing tracks. I am so proud of you Daddy."

She dried his other foot, and placed both feet on a footstool.

"How would you like a spot of bramble brandy?"

"Yes please," he said, and surrendered to the enchantment of this beautiful moment.

"Tell me Kathleen, what can your doting father do to make you happier?" She replied, "I could use a little music?"

He looked at her non plussed. Neither of them ever mentioned this before. "My God girl, I will find a way to remedy this. Mean-time, how about some poetry?"

"Yes please Daddy. I'll settle for poetry. A little Wordsworth perhaps?"

He stood up barefooted, smilingly and presented himself in stagelike presence.

> "Then sing ye birds, sing, sing a joyous song,
>> and let the young lambs bound as to the tabors sound,
>> we in thought will join ye throng ye the pipe and ye the play,
>> ye that there your hearts today.
>> Feel the gladness of the May.
>> What though the radiance which once so bright
>> be none forever taken from my sight.

Though nothing can bring back the hour
    of splendor in the grass of glory in the flower!
    we will grieve not rather find
    strength in what remains behind.
    In the primal sympathy which having been
    in the soothing thoughts that spring must ever be
    out of human suffering.
    In the faith that looks thru death.
    In years that bring the philosophic mind.
And Oh, ye fountains, meadows hills and groves.
    Forebode not any severing of, our loves,
    Yet in my heart of hearts I feel you might
    I only have relinquished one delight
    To live beneath ye more habitual way
    I love the brooks which down their channels fret.
    Even more than when I tripped lightly as they
    The innocent brightness of a newborn day, is lovely yet;
The clouds that gather round the setting sun
    Do take a sober coloring from an eye
    That has kept watch o'er mans mortality
    Another race hath been and other palms are won
    Thanks to the human heart by which we live
    Thanks to its tenderness, its joys and fears
    to me the meanest flower that blows can give
    Thoughts that too often be too deep or fears"
"Recollections of Early Childhood" from the earth
    loving mind of William Wordsworth.

Kathleen clapped two pans together. "All Hail to William Wordsworth and to Sir Frederick McCabe!"

He held his daughter in his arms. "I'll get you some music," he whispered. "We have each other remember; always and forever."

That was only the last part of his magnificent poem. They were silent. There was an emotionally laden moment, a flash of time past. It felt of aloneness, yes of lonely, of living life, of yesteryear, of breaking hearts, of now yet, amidst their fears. There is love and laughter—overriding all sadness and fears.

"I used to know more; I'm sorry I cannot oblige, it's sort of gone, like the Bloody wind. At College, we did it in drama as a threesome. I had the last part and my two chums did the first and the middle. Those were such careless youthful days—youthful my darling." "Recollections of early cgildhood" from the earth loving mind of William Wordsworth.

Macabe knew the herds of elephant, never blocked their trails and kept a wary eye on the armies of baboons up in the high ridges where they barked and shouted their defiance of these new intruders. Walking in long strides, broad shouldered and tall. He had a full, thick brown beard that started near his ears, covering cheeks and chin, but through it all one could see his clear, full lips and strong teeth. He was a man used to a good living, having had a cheese factory which he had sold for a goodly sum. He was not afraid of hard work, was a good sailor and athlete. He married a woman of refined birth, and had lost her after 17 years happily together. He had one child and upon this child he doted and he tried very hard to be a proper parent. He often sang an Irish song about Kathleen, and it sounded like a lullaby.

She was his most precious earthly possession. Come what may, he would see his child did not wither in this harsh, ruthless wilderness, where the sun burned by day and the cold pierced at night. He saw a different beauty, ploughed his lands and tilled the soil. He built and plastered red earth and anthill crush, and was thankful for his perennial stream.

Things were not all as was promised, and settlers were not allowed to own or have staff slaves, but he knew exactly what he was doing, damn it all. He had offered to share his land. There was always a way, and he sure new how to manipulate words. Moerskind and Tante Tande˙ were invaluable. No one or anything would make him give them up. Besides, Kathleen found company in her toothy companion, "Auntie Teeth," as she soon discovered, was the meaning of "Tante Tande."

The country abounded with game. Ever exciting and full of wonder. They were constantly aware that they were always fighting for their lives. In some families, children were given the job of herding cattle. Once a child lost its way and was out for three days when they found her. She told them she had seen this huge cat that roared at her and flipped its dark mane. Needless to say, she was not aware of the fact that it was a black-maned lion.

"I say Daddy. There is something I've been thinking about. Take a look at all the children who arrive here, and simply sit and gaze. What if I made a large room and taught them a few things? We could erect a "long-drop"˙˙ nearby and the room. Yes, you know, a school room?"

McCabe rubbed his chin. "Yes, it can be done Kathleen. It's not a bad idea at all. Who do you suppose will teach them?"

---

* Tante Tande = Auntie Teeth
** A long drop is a deep hole in the ground, about 6 to 8 feet deep. A wooden seat is constructed above it enclosed by a small closed room built over it. (It's a lavatory.) A dead chicken or a piece of rotten flesh is thrown into the hole which starts the bacteria. The worms soon appear and become very efficient in the rotten meat through. Everything is devoured and destroyed by worms. It's a very successful process and very continuous. Also known as bush lavatory. The long lasting bush "Klein huis" (little house).

"Daddy, you and I will. There's always a way, it will be most fulfilling. You know how they love learning. We could delegate certain times, say from early morn till before midday?"

"Good thinking Kathleen. Yes, I'll see what I can do. We'll set up something."

"Thanks Daddy."

"Sorry I didn't think of that myself, Kathleen."

Kathleen soon got involved with organizing an outdoor school for the children and she handed over many books which were very much needed. The time, like it always does, sped. The surge of activity was so great no one seemed to notice how time fled. The McCabe's farm, "Sonnestroom," was beginning to look civilized, even rich, with wheat fields and oats. The house had pieces of beautiful furniture and delicate pieces of china, silver and glassware, and each day, they carried stones and more stones. The cows calved and sheep dropped lambs, and in their surprisingly short stay, these people struggled to adapt. Not only to adapt, they created, and the little school grew in a matter of weeks.

It is surprising how quickly people do adapt and learn to solve problems, especially when they are forced to. Others suffered a great deal. One evening, just before sundown, a cart with a stranger holding the reins came past. The driver called out, asking for the direction of Bathurst. McCabe was finishing up his hand plowing. Picking up his plough in his right hand he pointed with the plough in the air as though it was a pointing stick. "Just follow that track," he said, "for as far as the wheel marks take you."

Three

In one foul swoop, just when the wheat fields were fine and upstanding, rust broke out everywhere and hopes of success and income, and much needed money, were dashed to ashes. Farmers were forced to endure fresh hardships and privations. But, where wheat had failed, other crops were successful: turnips, melons, cucumber and pumpkins. Like within the clouds of darkness there was always some spark of silver.

How irksome were the limitations imposed upon them. They were not allowed to employ slaves nor hire the Hottentots, and most humiliating of all was the colonial control measure, to ensure settlers remained where they were placed. They labeled it pass laws, no one was allowed to move without a pass and this pass had to be signed by the Landrost. McCabe was exempt from carrying a pass, because he was a party leader, but on entering another town, on any visit, it had to be produced. It took a long time and a lot of argument, patience, and eloquence from Fred McCabe and Major James Jones, until finally the rule was relaxed.

In the meantime all business transactions were greatly inconvenienced. The situation of the drostdy at Grahamstown and the tangled mass of bureaucratic processes impinged on their affairs. This disquiet was aggravating grave reason. Colonial officials started to withdraw troops from the frontier and news of this didn't take long to reach the Kaffirs, as they were called. They soon started crossing the great Fish River under the pretext of collecting colored clay from the pits on Mahoney's Location, to paint and smear on their bodies and each time they came, cattle disappeared.

Benjamin Anderson was guarding his herd and was brutally killed, his herd driven across the border. There was no thought or mercy; silently in the night, figures appeared from out of the thick bushes near the kraals and brutal murders became quite common, filling the minds of these brave pioneers with horror and fear. This was the frontier and the people were frontiersmen.

In England, one hundred acres of land would seem a fairly wealthy plot, but in Africa it was a very different scene. No markets were close at hand and no transport was available. Harsh sun, frequent droughts dried up rivers, hand dug irrigation and famine. Lack of labor and land, only fit for grazing. Two acres of land was reckoned, able to support one ox. Albany had a capricious climate, with frequent floods and famine. The land was not suitable for crops and the settlers had several crop failures. Then again, torrential rains and prolonged drought, with violent squalls of wind resulted in extensive damage to the new, fragile and frail little farms. Houses, fences and fields were swept away in flash floods and to this desolation was an added plague of locusts, and grubs, which devoured the very last vestige of their uncultivated vegetation. Wild dogs pestered and attacked the cattle, at times cows died for want of fodder. How tyrant-like that added to this was the menace of theft, murder and constant concerted attack.

Courage and human endurance could be taxed no further. The Landrost, Mr. Harry Rivers, appointed by Lord Charles Somerset, the sour, unpopular Landrost, had failed to forward the settlers' requests and complaints to the governor of the Cape, and so they were ignored. But news of the desperation did finally break through via letters to the newspapers and to Lord Bathurst.

The clay pits were where the first conflict between the settlers and the Xosas took place January 1821. It was one of the most dangerous places. This red ochre clay is used by the Africans for their beautification and the anointment of their warriors. The clay was of good quality and essential to the Black People. Therefore it was fated as a source of unending conflict and rage between black and whites—luck prevailed.

$\mathcal{F}our$

ord Bathurst himself and a few of the settlers who were able
to afford a journey, sailed to England and visited the Colonial
Office. The matter was raised in the House of Commons and
a commission of engineering was commissioned to investigate. In
February of 1824 they arrived in Grahamstown to investigate Lord
Charles' subservient British Colony, who determinedly stood up
with urgent and fundamental demands—"the right to exist and to
prevent death from starvation."

These misguided English people who could not use their various
crafts and professions who were forbidden to foregather and were
actually being used as political tools. It changed somewhat. Albany,
because of its crop failures, became a commercial trading town as
opposed to a farming town. Poverty changed to prosperity. James
Hancock started making tiles and bricks from the clay deposits.

Grahamstown became the settlers' capital city and though
there were no very rich merchants, Thomas Phillips' cultural
society was going strongly: artisans, masons, cabinet makers and
bricklayers all began employment and a growing market began with
shoemakers, tailors, bakers and tallow chandlers. The educational

center at Salem where William Shaw lived flourished though no great village developed and Bathurst remained an attempted town with half-built houses and empty land.

It was here that land was offered freely to settlers, but they never took it. Fort Beaufort grew because it was an important military post. Nicer houses were built of hewn stone and slate, paint replaced limewash. The main roads were made wide so as to permit an ox wagon to turn. The ox wagons came to Grahamstown loaded with produce from the countryside. The town was busily trafficked by motley crowds of colonists, Hottentos, soldiers and natives all there to do some business or other. Water came from a huge tank up the top end of the main street where the Drosddy was built. Little furrows carried water down the street to the gardens planted behind the little houses. They built a church as a symbol of faith that dominated the town of Grahamstown, and many more schools were developed by private persons. The fees were 1 shilling per pupil per week, and that was for private schools. Government schools were three pence per week. Often school fees were paid in butter or cheese or in goats or sheep. There was an influx to Grahamstown as it prospered, and even though trade with Kaffirs was forbidden, it took place in a clandestine manner.

The settlers also did a good trade with Boers, bargaining with peddlers' packs of goods spread out on a blanket on the floor. Teapots, spoons, silver plate were traded for cattle or sheep with the Boers. Bartering with the Kaffirs took place exchanging ivory, birds, quagga skins, pelts of deer, and rope which they made from the bark of a sort of wild fig tree, exchanged for beads and cloth.

The barter trade became so large that eventually in order to legalize it all, they had a huge fair. One woman, Margaret Salt, who was a heroine of the Battle of Grahamstown in 1819, used to travel with her wagon to do business with all the farmers inland. Her profits were buried for safety on her daughter's farm somewhere near Tarhastad;* where she buried it is another secret, for she died having never told anyone.

McCabe at this time acquired more land. More land than he ever dreamed he would own. Not to ask, why did these people come to the Cape? People will be people wherever they may be. These English were used as a means of protecting the colony against Xosa raids. They were used to replace the depleted garrisons. They were used to relieve poor rates and army estimates, and to develop the Cape economically.

And in England? The desire to escape the economic problems, the desire to try a new life with better opportunity in a new land of mystery. Hope was overwhelming. The rapid change from a rural to urban life, the population explosion and industrial revolution. The aftermath of war and the human desire to hold at all costs that which the country wants. People, strong, frail, white, black and yellow, young, older, ugly plain and beautiful people, all just people, fundamentally all the same.

---

* stad = city.

Five

The strong south east wind furiously wrapped bits of paper around the base of trees like little used napkins, the trees bent over in full sway arched deformed as if used to the way of the wind. Particles of sand stung against the skin, birds were blown off course and boats washed up onto the sands.

Jules Hora Jacobsen held his hands over his brow, screwing up his eyes and holding back his streaky blond hair. "Damn this bloody wind," he thought, "it even blows one's words away." Was this Africa? Yes, this was Africa, this was the sun drenched beaches, the land of milk and honey, adventure and fear. Here he was to find what he craved throughout his life, adventure, this wanderlust which he had striven throughout his life for. Jan his brother had loaded all the equipment lock, stock and barrel from his small printing business into their Viking Ship, and together with a small paid crew, they had sailed, most of the north and now, following the coast to Africa. Like a migratory bird, looking for a place to nest.

Here where the sun is constant and maybe the land is free, they hoped they would purchase, ride, like the Burghers for 30 minutes or more, as this was the measure of land quantity. When the 30 minutes were up this was to mark the size of the purchased land. For more than 90 days they had dreamed and planned and wondered, as they sailed the churning seas; flying fish landing on the deck and seagulls gliding above them like little squawking gliders.

These two men were handsome: strong, blonde, burned and tanned golden brown, like the burghers, and the skin on their hands was hardened from the ropes and masts. Between Jules' forefingers and thumbs were calluses and a large rope burn had developed a burgundy scab down his left elbow. His brother Jan was a slender man with similar features, certainly a fine figure of a man with streaky blond hair, and a significant nose, full mouth, dark brows and a fall of light brown beard.

They had landed at the mouth of the wide Buffalo River, east of Algoa in the Indian Ocean. They tacked into the mouth of the river towards a very strong overhanging tree, to which they seriously tied their ship. The river was wide and muddy, with a strong current and the water rose and fell with the tides. Masses of game and animals grazed on its steep banks.

They anchored in the muddy river, in deep water by the way the anchor indicated. Wyders sang in the reeds. Proud kingfishers like black and white arrows sleek feathers dived into the waters and flew back into the trees with small fish, where these would be bashed against the tree trunk, sending their scales flying everywhere, before they were eaten.

It was not easy to maneuver their ship into the river mouth though it looked about 30 feet deep. A recent flood was evident and the waters rise and fall was clearly marked by the sway of the trees and leaves and the grasses and sticks, flood aftermath, sieved by Sedge growth, as the swiftly passing water flowed out into the sea.

A dead and dried out carcass of a baboon hung in a bush, where it withered, shrunk and rotted, naked of flesh and bleached. The whitened fangs fierce even in the skeleton. African and forces unknown: Africa here they were, tying their ship up to the left side of this long wide mouthed muddy river. It was safe to stay as near as possible to the inside of the harbor.

It was a windy day and the ship rolled heavily even in this half sheltered port. Hottentots were running alongside, little corn-curled hair styles on some men and a few large robust black kaffirs, as they were called. Some were in a blanket and assegai, and others in a state of complete nudity, wind blew their tossing plumes. If it were not for the grinning faces it might well have been a fearful moment.

Jan looked at the swarthy shoulders of these tribal fingos: fine looking men, trying in sign language to indicate that he did not intend to disembark. Jules, having secured the ship, scrambled up a rope ladder and back on board the ship, drawing in the ladder after him. "I don't fancy a skirmish with those brutes," he muttered, and then just as he turned, suddenly from out of the bush appeared at least 10 of those black men. They rolled into a movement in unison, letting out a strange, discordant melody or chant and keeping in good time. They stamped out with bared feet, arms, breasts and assegais, a barbaric, strange dance.

They advanced towards the portside and all turned inward arms and assegais upraised with looks of seemingly murderous intent, and then with a wild piercing whoop they would all instantaneously wheel off in perfect unison. They did this wild circular movement for several hours and Jan and Jules began to wonder if they would ever set foot off of their ship.

They were still there when darkness came. Their perspiration rolling down their shiny oily skin, grotesque in various degrees of dress, some with hats and some with clothes and others naked as the day they were born. Jules and Jan set about settling for the night and knew a whole new life: an unknown style and new plan of living, in this barbaric sun drenched land. They would think about disembarking in this wharf-less place, tomorrow.

In the early hours of the morning the boat started to creak and roll, then a wicked gale blew up driving everything before it. Despite the anchor, the driving wind was moving the boat from side to side, scraping the riverbank with a most awful sound of cracking and breaking. The ropes were groaning with the strain and the men wondered if all the ropes would hold secure.

The wind raged most of the day, forcing the waves up the river and plunging the vessel forward and back and downward and up. Sleep was impossible and food unthinkable. Water seemed to be everywhere and the fear of being washed loose was strong in their minds. The poor ship was so brutally knocked about, but finally the wind abated. "Hell," Jan thought, "once or twice we might well have come adrift. One hell of a wind that was!" But it was calmer now and tomorrow had come.

S i x

S itting on the bank, a blanket made of skins wrapped around his shoulders, was a lone black man. His face lit up and he grinned as the two men surfaced. He looked like a warrior who might well have flung himself against the 74th Highlanders, and who may have grown to like the manner of these pale-skinned immigrants. Perhaps out of curiosity people sought to know him better, like men who try to understand the dolphins or moods of the kindred of the wild.

Jules' heart warmed to his full, illuminated grin. He had no assegai, and remained seated and grinning. Jules climbed down the rope ladder landing on the muddy bank, the winds had lashed the water way up the embankments. He had his musket just in case, but felt no fear. "Yes, well, man, good morning to Africa," he said with a sort of jaunty, no care attitude, and the fellow simply clapped his hands together but whether in applause or some sort of Xosa language, he never knew.

They had breakfast and shared it with this handsome Black warrior. It seemed as though Xosa wanted to share his all. From that morning onward, Jules and Jan unexpectedly, as fate would have it, began a sojourn with a black man that stayed with them for as long as they lived and learned and taught by repetition and teaching. He had great common sense, he gradually learned to relax and swiftly came to understand. It was obvious he had profound knowledge of the ways of nature in a variety of difficult conditions and to hold his own amongst men who lived face to face with reality. He was intolerant of weakness and lack of manhood. There is understanding between real men. He was keen to learn English which he instantly grasped! Strong and willing, totally sure, brilliant with spoor.

He said he was a Xosa. Xosa is a click that has no comparable equal in the English language. When this X is used the click is made with the tongue and it comes from the back towards the throat. It is vastly used in the Xosa language.

He was an amazing man. His knowledge of the bush incredible. He was of course a hunter, earned his livelihood trying to ranch with cattle on the land. He lived in wild places, which he seemed to have been designed for. He never ever killed for sport, only hunted for food; animals struggle to survive and battle to exist. With bush life, interests and observing nature in all her ways, requires physical endurance, risk and danger. But there's bondage. Experiences create friendship, and loyalty, so that one never takes life wantonly. Discrimination and respect and feeling—it is understandable that nature's greatness is instinctive. So it was. He saw and acted upon signs invisible to ordinary eyes and lived in a dimension alien to ordinary people. He spoke the spoor signs accurately. Eyes ever alert even in distracting serious conversation.

He was a rare naturalist saw nature as a single whole. Had unbelievable power of observation. He lacked education yet understood geology flora fauna and climate. He was part of earth closely concerned with its creatures. A kindly teacher, calm, brave, compassionate. Totally incapable of mean or evil: he possessed purity of heart.

Seven

The two young men, half children really, both filled with memories and wide-eyed innocence, dreams and ideals, neither knew the touch of a woman's body, except the long forgotten comforts of their mother's breast. But great passion dwelt latent in the both of them, expressed only by their intense love and feeling for their land, Africa!

After that was their very life, the veld that held a myriad secrets, and as many threats. For them, death was always hanging in the air like a great circling vulture. The great cleaner who excretes on his own legs and within his own excretion is a certain powerful purification so he carries no bacteria from standing inside the guts of some dead carcass. Nature protects him and he's always there on huge and circling wings, gliding, searching, looking. How often did Willem think of his own death, perhaps from a kaffir spear, or the tusk of an elephant, the deadly fevers, or pierced by the slender horn of buck, or mighty buffalo. At any rate, it's an easy thing, death, he thought; perhaps he would circle with his mother high, high, up in the sky on vulture wings, or roam the veld and bush with his father among the lion and hyenas, or maybe just go rotten into the earth among the worms and ants.

One thing was certain, one way or another the earth always takes you, not only ashes, but flesh and bones. Even in the sea it was flesh and bones to the bottom where there was earth. But now these two young wildly strong men made a decision to begin an entirely new life. They had not let their father down, their father who always wanted sons. The land would be severed from them and placed in the hands of strong men from another land.

Once ashore Jules and Jan came into contact with immigrants and Boer farmers. It was whilst in this harbor town that they met with Willem de Swart; Willem had one desire and that was to sail the seas. He and his boetie* had a farm that was quite near Cradock, but he always found himself wending his way with his team of oxen down to the sea, the call of the sea was stronger than he! He had a powerful effect on his brother, who, partly influenced by Willem, began to dream of the sea as well, and he accompanied Willem to the Buffalo river mouth.

It was not the first time this had happened. This was already his second trip. Both his parents were killed by "kaffirs" and Willem and Pieter were left as orphans when they were just 14 and 12. Unlike the Boers around them, they were not men of God nor were they men! If God was good and kind, especially to little children, then he should have saved their mother and father, especially Ma who needed to be protected. But their pappa had taught them to ride and shoot, they could shoot better than any man already when they were both just small children. Now they were men, they each had their own span, they sewed their own veldskoens, farmed, reaped and cooked.

They grew up, like two discarded chickens without a fussy old mother hen to scratch feed and protect them. They had survived,

* boetie = brother.

though both knew well the cruel fears of threat and insecurity. Children are so lost and vulnerable without the strength of a mother and father. How many times had Ma opened her eyes when Pa said prayers and thanks to the Almighty for the food on the table? Ma would smile, hiding the serving spoon beneath her white cotton apron. She didn't say her prayers, always smiling away. Always sweet.

Ma thought more about love and flowers and lovingly did most things, ja, God had no right to let the kaffirs kill her. She was so good to all things. They always cried together when they talked about Ma. Ma who always put the hot copper pan in their bunks on cold, bitter nights and who made Fet koeks* and gooseberry jam that tasted so good.

Even her death was caused by her goodness. The kaffirs preferred not to kill females, their war was with men. But Ma was trying to shield Pa, she had rushed in front of Pa with a griddle iron, shielding him from the assegais—as if a griddle iron was big enough to shield Pappa. It was Ma who had thrown her two small boys beneath their bunks and then threw water over their bunks in case they set fire to the house. It was so easy and vivid, recalling that evening. Willem rode far off to the Van den Berghs for help. Mevrou** Van den Bergh washed Ma's face—all white and staring— her lips drained of blood and faintly mauve—it was funny how her eyes wouldn't close, perhaps because she had unfinished business. How could she die knowingly leaving her two small boys—Willem and Pieter. Her eyes were still open as they covered her up and took her away, and she and Pa were just never there again.

---

* Fat cookies—bread fried in oil.
** Mrs.

It was Ma who loved the sea, and she who read poems and told them tales of serpents and whales, laughing and using her white hands, as she acted out her stories—Ma who taught them to write and read. They had to read the Bible, and though Pa didn't know, she put the Bible aside, she read and taught them to read many other books. They sang songs and danced little folk dances. Ma had a ripple of life that was always eager and quick and light. They always wished they had loved her more, why had God let them have her for so short a time?

Children grew out of memory but neither Willem or Pieter ever spent one day of life without some faint reminder of that person who was Ma. Now they were men and perhaps the sadness of it stabbed even deeper, for men think more deeply than children. Some English people had helped them also, those English who came with tents and beds, and large coffin-like boxes of platters and plates. Those English who didn't speak to the oxen in the proper way, nor crack their whips. Willem had a buffalo riempie* whip, and he could crack his whip like a clap of lightning. Even now no one could wield a whip and a gun like Willem!

Willem was old now, 20, and Pieter was 18, both big, strong, wide shouldered men, but neither of them looked like Pa. Pa had a black beard and seemed so much bigger than them. It's funny that neither of them could remember exactly the real color of his eyes—perhaps because they never looked into his eyes as they did with Ma's. Ma was braver than he, really, she never seemed so respectful and afraid of God as was Pa.

---

* Riempie = leather made from cow hide.

"Ag Magtig,"* she would say, "sien** my seentjie*** that tree, that river bed, and all its tumbled stones. Millions of years have rolled them smooth, and hollow, trees have been standing forever, and where was God all that time? Someone, let's say, nature, was here long before. And the Bible was written by simple men who lived at the time of Constantine and Moses, who put together folk stories and fairy tales. A man has to think about that," she said, and she would pick a flower and hold it to her nose and chuckle away, as though she had a private life all of her own. Her hands and arms were so soft and gentle.

And Pa, who turned the pages of his Bible with hard, thick fingers, ever trying to instill the fear of Almighty God as though he drew him from the very pages he fervently touched—yes, they grievously missed their parents. Time has passed slowly for them. But their heifers had produced healthy calves and they each had a marvelous span. Each ox knew his name and duty. And if their mother's learning stopped when she was killed, they soon learned to survive. Their land was extensive. Yes, Pa was a strong man, he rode for 40 minutes each direction, through the bush to peg his farm, faster than anyone, he pegged his boundary. He used to tell how he followed a game trail, and made extra haste to get a bigger stretch of land.

Pa was a born farmer. He himself got to be bigger from stumping his lands, and plowing the earth, cutting wood. "It was land for cattle, not for crops," he said, and when other burghers were struggling with rust and crop failures, Pa was building kraals and fences to paddock his stock. Pa could fell a sapling with a single

---

* Ag Magtig = almighty God!
** sien = see
*** seentjie = little boy

chop of his axe and heave it like a javelin throw way over to the wood pile once he slew off the branches at the top.

It was less easy to drive off Pa's cattle for he was known not only for his alert mind, but also for his good shooting and strong enclosures. He made full use of his stock. His Riempie chairs and furniture will surely live forever, even when his sons are long dead. "Wegebleek"* which means bleached away, like old dry bones and forgotten. He built a good farm, planted tall trees that let the grass grow underneath and brought buffalo grass from the river sides to plant it in his pastures, a sweet grass that made the cattle thrive.

Once, when they were gathering grass, a group of Fingo warriors came suddenly out of the bush, screaming out and hurling assegais. Pa, ever ready, mounted, swift as an arrow, blew one's neck and half his head away. He fell to the earth. The others fled, whirring and quivering assegais from glistening bodies through the bushes, towards the plains. The dead body had fallen onto the earth dug out from an anthill, by an aardvark. That's an antbear. His shiny buttocks stuck up in the sunlight. There was a large hole into the anthill. Pa was sitting up there on his big red horse, looking, but they never returned and Pa got down when he was sure they would not return. He pushed with his foot the great wet, red black buttock into the hole made by an anteater, head down first, his shiny buttocks sticking up hard and healthy.

The white soles of his feet, both splayed and hard and tough, sticking out. Tough hard feet that ran across earth. The ants streamed out everywhere, gathered in brown, crawly masses over

---

* Bleached away with time.

the drying blood, into the body crevices, blue bottles,* gleamed on the burgundy skin. Ja, they were used to death—after all they were nine years old when they shot kudu and Duiker & Quagga,** zebra and lions also. Once a body was dead, it didn't matter what happened to it. It was not the living thing it used to be. Death was the same to everything. Even Ma, her soft lifeless hands beside the griddle iron, stilled forever. It was different with Ma, it was so bitter and unfinished. They didn't have her long enough? That was it! Yes, that was it!

And at the farm where she made the butter and fed the fowls, calling, "kip, kip, kip, kip," with laughter in her voice, waving her gentle hands as she sprayed the grain, mixed with oats, outwards, and dipping her hands into the earth, patting her plants, or cutting onions that made her cry. It was no use trying not to think: the farm was too full of thoughts even after six years. Death really meant the end, just up on the Kopje*** behind the house, their remains are bleached dry, rotted remains of Pa and Ma. Perhaps the ants swarmed over her lovely hands and face, for what happened to their flesh buried in the hard dry ground under the stones where the dust and wind blew and the sun burned down mercilessly every day? They made them headstones, but they didn't know when Ma was born.

Willem looked over the heads of his span, over wide black and white tipped horns, the voorlopers holding the riem of the leader's heads. He drove his own team, and Pieter his. He would outspan soon and rest the straining beasts. Decent animals, they would find a place near a spruit**** near the sea where there was graze and

---

* Blue Bottle Flies.
** A brown zebra that was hunted to extinction.
*** Kopje = little hill
**** spruit = small creek or spring.

game and water. Perhaps he could find a group or an outspan lager where they could join up, interlacing their disselbooms* to protect the oxen. It was not safe to be alone. Thoughts of the past must not block his alertness or thoughts of the future, or he could be ended in the time that it takes an assegai to fly from a hand into his breast. There was a range before them, not a tall large range, but it was patterned with black and white patches of shining white sea sands between the bushes. The sound of crashing waves could be heard from the sea. They tested the brake blocks, the wagon stayed on a decline, tightened the reins. The oxen leaned patiently against their yokes, and prepared for the easiest track through the range and beyond, lumbering ox pace down towards the sea.

It took them longer than they had thought to get through these hills, cutting trees, filling up holes and shifting stones and rocks. They had chosen a trail unused and overgrown but easier on the oxen. This was strange terrain. Grotesque plants in places, suffocating parasites and living creepers. Soft sandy soil and some inhospitable scrub, but once passed, this hostility, heralded by the salty breeze of the ocean, lay the whole blue horizon of sea. Sea gulls and terns squawked and swooped in the rumble of the constant crashing waves. The two men started towards the voorlooper and in their excitement they seemed to become boisterous. Willem and Pieter both cracked their whips like pistol shots and the poor oxen unperturbed by their excitement, misunderstood and strained harder, the agter ox almost buckling at the hocks, moving eastwards towards late afternoon.

They finally found a place to outspan, making sure they had their backs towards the setting sun. They found a huge Seringa tree

---

* disselboom = long central beam that draws the wagon.

near a small spruitjie.* Up in the tree, bathed in the last pink rays of sinking sun, were a pair of metal green iridescent starlings with jewel red eyes picking the small fruits of the syringe berries, bunches of berries hung like half full crinkled gray ticks, those large gray ticks ½ an inch long that fill up with blood of animals' bodies.

"Jessis Pieter that agter—Os has more brains in his left hoof than plenty of people I know, I tell you man!" His brother laughed, loud and boyish. "It's the Brawn we need Boet forget about thinking. I heard about an old woman out camping when a lion attacked her and her sister. She took off her shoe and hit the lion on his head with the heel of her shoe. She hit it on the head, and it ran away."

"So much for brawn hey!"

They both laughed out loud.

"Let's camp out here under this tree and Dankie—Hera, we have water!"

"I reckon even among lions there's a coward," they laughed together.

"They have brains, they send their women out to hunt for food. The lazy bastards! The big ole captain guards his manhood, sits on his arse and waits."

They both chuckled like schoolboys. "Wonder if oxen know what the sea is? Would be good to know, hey?"

Then Willem called out—"Nyabanga," as they opened the mealies** from their sheaves—one ox's horn poked his back. "Hey See Kooi*** watch your verdamte horns hey!" But he patted him as though he forgave him his accidental action. See Kooi had very long horns!

---

* spruitjie = little stream or spring.
** mealies = corn
*** See Kooi means seahorse.

The men yelled to the servants and soon the fire was sparkly and crackling. The oxen were watered and resting. The oil lantern from the wagon swayed from the beam now in the large arched tent. Pieter took some bales of mealies out to the span. Frogs began to call and crickets chirped and little bats flitted past the wagon trying to catch the moths attracted by the light of the swaying lantern. They would all rest now.

Eight

Very early in the morning almost at first light, they were awakened by a group of Hottentot fishermen selling fresh sleenbras and crayfish. Pieter flung his legs over the back of the wagon, stood on the footpiece and exchanged a whole mound of fish for a small bag of onions and some mealies. How they longed for a change from game and mutton. Farmers were always awake with the first light, for their days were never long enough, and then from among the little group this voice called out: "Good morning! What a fine, well trained span you have." Pieter was worried for a moment, and put his head into the wagon, "Hey boetie," and then in a tone louder, "Willem, heer is an Engelsman."*

Jules and Jan, seeing their camp, came closer and also chose to make friendly conversation.

Julies extended his hand, "My name is Jules Jacobsen, and this is my brother Jan. We come from Denmark originally. See that ship yonder, in the mouth, that's our ship. She is named 'Helena Maria' named after our mother. Great girl. Done a lot of moving—27,000 tons. She's like your oxen!"

---

* Here is an Englishman.

"You like to have breakfast? We are about to eat."

"Thank you," and they all rearranged their places and they laughingly enjoyed stone bread and braai—fish—steaming hot coffee, dried venison and toasted corn. The fish was divine, crawfish* cooked in its shell, and filets of fresh cod, fresh from the fisherman to the open fire. My God that fish was so good glorious—the company scintillating!

"Jessus** that's wonderful." both young men gazed at the Danes, swallowing every sentence of their seafaring experiences. "Of course this port is not exactly safe. Only one wooden jetty, no anchorage. Table Bays the place! 3 jetties there—for sailing ships. They are planning on great expansion and even steam ships. One has to be a hardy sportsman to brave these winds and waves. Sometimes, the winds are so bad, the boat has to remain in, especially where there is dubious harborage. This here, is very primitive port facilities. You don't want to be blown onto the rocks."

For hours and hours, the conversation was all about ships and farms.

"Look Jules, let's make this straight. You have a 27,000 ton sailing ship and we have a well developed farm. I do have the papers of its size but I don't know it in my head. We will do a deal, like English gentlemen."

"There can always be compensation," said Jules.

"Jessus Pieter, you know what we are doing hey! Pa's land?"

It was not impossible to converse, both Willem and Pieter were fairly well versed in the language. They were out of practice but one soon remembers what one learns in childhood. After all, didn't Ma

* crawfish = lobster
** Jessus is a colloquial way of saying Jesus.

spend many hours teaching them both, first in Dutch and then in English. Washing one's hands and using a serviette, manners were important to Ma. She was strict about fine manners: "manners maketh man," she taught them. In a very short time being together with Jules and Jan Jacobsen, Willem and Pieter were buoyed up with laughter and enthusiasm and fervor. They were besotted with eager interest in the Danish ship, the Helena Maria and her crew, and spent days away from the wagon and their span. The Hottentots were stealing their food, maybe they must be more generous and give them more, perhaps. Neither Willem or Pieter seemed to care. This was fate. There was this silence. They were all thinking: "What, I wonder, is your farm worth?" asked Jan. "What is the value of your ship?" said Willem. Silence prevailed.

"It matters not greatly to me about value or money. I love the sea, I love ships, and all I ever dream of is sailing on the sea, so let's do a deal. Let us exchange our lifestyles and our living conditions—you take our farm, 'Voetstoets,'' it's called 'Moorplaats,' which means 'pretty farm', and it is pretty darn good," Willem said. "Our parents were murdered there, that is where they are both buried." All at once there was great discussion. Willem and Pieter seriously would take to the seas, but not before they knew how.

All the ship's crew and all the out spanned staff had a happy dinner spread out on the lush buffalo grass. Willem had killed a springbok and braaied" it over a fire with thin bread like the Indian naans. They traded onions for fresh fish and everybody readily enjoyed Danish beer. It was a grand evening, two Danes, two

* Voetstoets means "as is".
** Braaied is Afrikaans for barbequed.

Dutch, Xosa and 15 merry men from the ship and the wagons. He was repeating Sight Unseen!

Jules was lying flat, looking up at the stars. "It's so good, this earth, I'd give my loving ship to live here forever," he said. "You hear that, Jan," Willem called out, "what your brother just said," "Yes I agree with him," said Jan, "we have sailed all the way from Denmark. We have sailed to many ports, Jules and I, we have sailed all over our world." "So tell me Jules," said Willem, "why don't you try and join the group of English who have just landed in Algoa Bay? I know they were landless, but not penniless."

Jules seemed to have taken charge—it usually was this way.

"What have we done Jan? Sight unseen! It is rather voetstoets"" "My God, scary—don't you think?" "I'm not even sure we understand all, what these lads have told us? As sure as I live Jan, I feel quite sure. Only thing is, I feel we are getting more—I think too much. I mean, the size of the land, and its written clearly enough, is an hour's ride at trotting speed, from the first signs baring the name de Swart—that is riding from West to East—and then there's another ride from South to North. From the same sign, that's a lot of land Jan? Two spans of trained oxen, a homestead with water supply and an S bend lavatory pan? There are chickens, 2 pigs and several goats. All this for our old 'Helena Maria." I love how he describes the Trek Bokken—storms of locusts and how he speaks of his wilderness."

"How about, how he makes Biltong"? The real thing! The Biltong of Agrica? I will show you. You will be ever thankful, I tell you. See here" he said, "I want to teach you." Willem then drew out

---

* frighteningly.
** Jerky

a strip of cloth and went on: "Wash and dry the meat, then cut it in strips, bend your thumb from the nail to the knuckle, or thicker than that if you wish." He bent his thumb to indicate it was about one inch from the nail to his knuckle. "Smother the meat in sea salt for 30 minutes or so. Use rock or sea salt and add spice. Use all the India spices. Dip the meat into wine vineagar. Take it out. Spice it again. Then hang it up to dry where the wind blows and where it's free of flies. Use Impala, Springbok, Bless Bok, Kuda or Eland. But remember our own cattle. It's always good and better! Hey!"

"You know Jan, this is valuable knowledge I give you!"

"You are bloddy well right" said Jules and they all laughed out loud together.

Nine

It took all of 13 weeks. This odd arrangement that had taken place—they exchanged properties! Willem and Pieter became the owners of a ship, and Jules and Jan Jacobsen had a farm. The farm was a peculiar shape as Johannes de Swart had deliberately included a natural dam between two spruits and a spring. He had always prided himself on his quick deduction and knowledge of the earth, not to mention his speedy and ruthless ride. He had chosen his farm well and with hard work. He and his workers had built and made his homestead, together with his most beloved wife Letticia. Ah yes, Dutchmen love deep my friend.

It was she who filled it with art and delicacy with idea upon idea, all fresh and original. They called it 'Moorplats' and mooi plaats* it became. Here were springs and good grazing and because it was against the foothill it was sheltered in many ways. Johannes believed he was guided to his spot by God, and as soon as he collected his herds he took to his Bible in thanksgiving. Now it was over for them both, forever.

* mooi plaats = pretty farm.

This transaction involved a fairly long trip to Somerset East Magistry. Here they were directed to the Landrost in Graaf Reinet and here were found the documents regarding the allotted land once ridden on by Johannes de Swart on his great red horse, "Kaptein." Willem had a younger horse named "Soldaat"* and so did Pieter. Ma's horse was still quite a young looking mare. It's funny how her horse remained so frisky and sleek. Perhaps that's how Ma was. But the mare was well on, maybe rising 20 soon. Pa's horse died of the fever, a few months after Pa. He was sprightly on Thursday evening, then on Friday the ox pickers bypassed him in the yellow grass meadow. Those egrets knew. The ticks were already detaching their round gray parasitic little bodies. They didn't bury "Kaptein," nee! it would have been an insult to so wondrous a work horse. Wilhelm cut a piece of his forelock and placed it in a little box. Then he let the scavengers eat their fill. That surely is how God would have wanted it. It is sinful to waste for sentiment.

Kaptein's bones were clean and white in less than a week, his great yellow teeth bared and snarling in a skeleton grin. The last blue bottles dotted about silver effervescent green on his lifeless red hairs. When Kaptein died, most of the almost tangible memories of Pa somehow grew more distant.

Presently a magnificent, adventurous plan was unfolding in William's head. "Magtig Piet," he yelled in wonder and enthusiasm. "We can trade, Boetie! We shall sell hides and skins and meat to St. Helena and exchange salt for sugar. We shall laugh at the wind and lick off the brine which will fill our souls full of the elixir of life," he said. "Boetie, we will became the grandest Boer traders on this

* Soldaat means Soldier.

whole fearful coast. We will soon learn it all, Boetie! A burgher is never a loser but sometimes a winner does lose."

They were jumping and springing around in a form of volk-speletyie.* Happy days such young men, merely boys—seamen! Jules and Jan were also excited, but not without a twinge of fear: to be a sailor one day and a burgher the next, that was the exciting part, but the fear was, this was not their business. Sights unseen! Swap! My God! The earth held many secrets, a man had to be attuned to it all; from a landward to a plough. My God, man, that was extreme!

Jules always remembered what his father, a courtier in the court of Denmark Copenhagen, so often repeated: "Nothing is impossible. There is a way to succeed in everything if one is sufficiently determined." These men were fired with the eagerness of youth. Sure, it was adventure they wanted, and if they could not succeed on the land, they still had their printing press. By the time all the legalities were over, it took less time than they thought.

The second team had arrived, for word had been sent to Klaas to bring it. Xosa was delighted to meet old Klaas and their droning voices went on and on and on into the night around the campfire beside the gleaming copper pot.

Xosa understood cattle. Cattle to him were the big thing in his life. Cattle were riches. There was a girl, he said, but her father wanted 7 head of cattle as bridewealth. He opened wide the whites of his eyes, holding up seven fingers and Jules wondered if it would ever happen, and then suddenly Xosa's face fell to the ground. He sat there morose and staring, pondering over his thoughts. They were all men together, yes, well, almost, all men.

* volkspeletyie = folk dance.

He had this magnificent body, but no man without the seeds of man, is a man?

Slowly he stood up, "See here," he said, and he threw off his cat skin loincloth, his legs with shiny, powerful thighs slightly apart, shone in the silver moonlight. "See this man," he said, and put his hand on his crotch. "This is the fine work of the medicine man. This is the thinking of the medicine man." He lifted his penis, showing his dark skinned crotch. He was castrated: The crumpled dimpled empty scrotum of scar tissue and self healing; inside his body is the ash of wood—"This is all the manhood of myself—Xosa's man seed is wood ash," he said. He swung around so that if there was an audience, everyone would see and his little dance the death knell of his hated secret, the secret of his deep sorrow. "See, no man, just a skin." Silence—uncomfortable silence. Loss of words, pain. Jules got up and took the huge body into his arms. "Xosa," he said, "Willem has the best horse, bravest and strongest of us all, but this horse is a gelded stallion! Do you know the meaning of gelded—like you! He has wood ash, but he is the strongest, fastest creature of them all. He is all brave and full of power. What a stallion he may have been." He is true, honest and gentle... like you.

There was another silence. No one spoke, the fire crackled and crickets chirped, and night frogs shrieked their ghostly calls. No one seemed to know what to say to a fellow man without testicles. A hyena's high shrill whoop* pierced the night in a short crescendo of 4 sharp whoops. Xosa jumped to his feet. "The Takalosh,"** he said. "It rides on a hyena in the night, do you hear that? Not too far away—not too far." Jules calmed the man. They sat down side

* hyenas = whoop, an eerie call not a growl.
** Takalosh = eerie belief among Africans. A small male with a large penis, ugly and evil.

by side, Jules holding Xosa's arm, and Xosa told him of the horror and fear of a young warrior whose father robbed him of manhood in the dead of night. The searing fire between his legs as his testicle were taken from his body, held down by men and then thrown full of wood ash and the man left to live or die.

It was his father, he said, his mother had told him so. The medicine man, Nganga, had told his father that if he ate the powdered testicles of his strongest son, he would retain the fertility of his youth forever and would continue to make many fine sons, even when he was an old, old man; Madala, an old Madala!

But it was not to be. Xosa grew up a good specimen. He grew up strong and powerful and bitter and filled with rage. When he was 17, he felt like an outcast. There was no maquetta* for him. He would not paint his body white and dwell alone into manhood. He knew the bush medicines. He waited; the years passed and then one day his rage overcame his heart, he fed his father a massive seedpod of the wild castor oil tree, 'Datura Stromoniam.' He stirred them into his father's Sunday special relish. He remembers the day; sometimes with a splash of remorse, for his father, after his father ate his relish to the finish, within an hour began to lose his mind, yelling and screaming and frothing at the mouth, like a wildcat with rabies, brave and aggressive. His father would never grow old as the Nganga predicted: no, his fathered withered and died. Why he died, that was Xosa's revenge. Xosa cleared his brain of bitterness and rage. No one knew, and he has come through life with two bitter galls to swallow every day, one, because he has no testicles, and the other, because, he had poisoned his father. He firmly believed if he stayed with White Men, the spirits would never find him. He

---

* maqueta = get circumcised, isolated & painted white.

was robbed of his seed. For his manhood, he repaid his father with the seeds of death. The Black Magic of Africa, no not magic, just a spoonful of seeds. It was a divine message: seeds for seeds—"Ja Jules, that's Kaffir business," said Willem, "it's like Pa used to read from the Bible—an eye for an eye and a tooth for a tooth—only nobody wins, do they, Jules?"

And so it happened. Among five brave adventurous men, on daunting illusions strangely exciting—to take root or to rot? From a sailor to a farmer? What a lot to learn. What extreme chance! Not without fear and not without danger. Not without risk! New habitation menaced by fierce marauders, elephants in abundance, rhinoceroses crushing the thickets and in the ravines, lions stalking on the mountain slopes, unseen in the brown savannahs. Hyenas whooping, eerie, laughing, the evenings echoing constantly with shrill tones of jackal serenades.

The sun, the moon, the wind and the rain, no regrets. From a farmer to a sailor, hard work on a dream—it's fate! A long, clumsy ship seems even longer when up upon its deck, tossed in a stormy sea. Fierce winds, creaking and groaning. Heavy, greasy ropes, heavy sails—good cabins the winds—the south East wind? Good God, so much to learn and understand a good helpful crew. A motley crowd of bearded, long haired men with ugly tattoos, would they be safe? Untrained and without knowledge or experience, an unknown quantity, fearsome for two new young skippers. Yes, he could depend on this blue-eyed Danish captain, he felt it in his unerring instinct. New sailors, with sky blue eyes!

Both knew of the dangers of the Cape Coast, but he had grappled with danger before and won. Long ago, his mother read him the stories of how the ships went into inlets and navigable passages for shelter, he had almost boyhood dreams, with dangerous winds, churning the waves and crushing waters breaking all over, rolling, sliding, smashing midst panic and dismay—love the prevailing winds, sailing the ocean—a new life. Is all life chance? Sure, it is strange, a farm for a ship. It will be good. His sky-blue eyes, those of both Willem and Pieter were calm and steady and sure. The sky and the sea, mystery and magic—strange it is, for all—no regrets.

T e n

frica began to instill her spell. After several weeks of moving and trekking together, Jules and Jan soon learned to crack their hippo hide whips and named their own oxen teams, fascinated by the understanding of each beast's knowledge of the wagon. Those near the wheels actually used their weight and feel to push the wheels onto firm ground and away from the cliff edges and dongas. Life in a wagon! It had a variable pattern one soon learned to innovate upon.

Oxen, Jules soon found out, were far more intelligent and stable than horses. They had traveled some weeks now trying to absorb all the earthly know-how of toil and fantasy. Willem and Pieter were wondrously wild. They could track and understand spoor as true as Jules could read a book, or a compass. "Always look for the unusual," Willem had taught him. "It's a language, a broken twig, a heel imprint, a midden, strange shapes. The bush and the veld, Ja, Meneer, like the sea, it is also unpredictable, unless of course, one knows spoor upon spoor," he said. "The wilderness, the stillness, the mystery and the unexpected, the suddenness of life or death. Look up! People don't remember to look up! Ja Meneer, I am teaching you well and when I am finished, you will teach me, in the same manner, to handle and sail my ship. Much as I love the land, I love the sea, I think it's security I will find at sea. He seemed so innocent. I am young; my brother and I, we know the fears and threats of uncertainty and death, but at sea, I have only the water and crew, where the darkness of night is not pierced by assegais, nor cricket chirps, just the endless rumbling and crashing of water upon water. Jules, my friend, I think I would feel comfort," he said. The Captain, Jules suggested, was a superb teacher as well as a wary Captain.

Jan seldom spoke; he was not so sure, and Pieter never thought for a single moment Willem could ever be mistaken. Now they would become sailors, traders on the sea, and Moorplaats would pass from their name into the hands of Jules and Jan Jacobsen. Their father's land, of which their father was so proud, their father's land, where the sweat and strength of their father's body gave birth to everything. To the pastures, the paddocks, the dams, the homestead, the ovens, the kraals, to all the barns and shelters to the oat fields and the gardens, to all beautiful vast Moorplaats, to his head of cattle, goats and sheep and to his two sons. Like all farmers, he had hoped his sons would one day carry it towards better things. His sons would continue the name of Johannes de Swart. Sorry Pa! Sorry.

By the time the de Swart men were ready to man Jules' ship, several weeks had passed. Willem began to worry about the herd left in the care of their resident foreman, servants and slaves. As long as the servants had ample rations, they did their work fairly well. And really, all they had to do was shepherd. Jules had sent Xosa ahead on the one team, fully loaded with ever-faithful Klaas and the Hottentot vooloper.*

---

* voerloper = front walker.

Having loaded his printing press and equipment into the second wagon with Willem's best team, they packed rations and supplies from the ship into the wagon and increased the team to 18. It was a sad day when they parted. Jules watched the ship tack up and down the coast within a few miles of the coast. He had done his best to acquaint the two young burghers with their ship, and his crew. He had no doubt they would succeed. The crew was competent and soon they would be trading salt, hides and frozen meat, and they'd bring back sugar to the colony. Yes, they would make money and maybe one day even return to build a wharf and landyards.

With an eerie feeling of aloneness, Jules and Jan with two Xosa servants, a voorloper and an agteryer* prepared to set off to Moorplaats in their 18 oxen span. Under each side bunk of the wagon, Jules and Jan had a large supply of ammunition, several muskets and musket balls. A hand carved brass bound wagon box caught his eye. Of one thing he was sure, and that was only the white man's musket loader would prevail against the assegai, savage ruthless foes and fierce wild animals.

Jan practiced his now expert whip cracking and Jules yelled out the Dutch words: "Trek—Trek—Loop." He pictured the span all straining on their yokes. The wagon jerking creakily on the rough track towards the north. Jules had a fine linen sheet for the wagon sail and all things promised speed. Around Jules' waist, he carried beneath his tail coat a hide pouch in which was his father's time-piece and his money. Jan had a similar bag that he tucked under the top of his knee breeches. When they got home, they were going to wear the clothes of the burghers that were far more practical on the land. Their beards would grow large and prophet-like, they

---

* agteryer = who rides behind

would ride their land on their smallish veld-reared horses, Boer horses of Arab and Basutu strain.

At first light, they breakfasted of mealie porridge and hot coffee. They each took a piece of biltong.* Resting his back against a tree, Jules pulled his dried meat apart with strong teeth. His brother Jan rested against the wagon wheel while Xosa and the other servants unspanned the oxen. There was much muttering among the men, and lowing of the beasts, though faithful and dutiful, they seemed to resent this early start. Sharp claps of the long whips and staccato cries of the driver hung in the morning air, chilled by the natural din drowning the rustle of the veld.

The great hearts of these two men out in a wilderness, without an interpreter, journied and toiled past scattered farms amidst Bushmen and Beast and on into the almost unknown. Taking his place, the agteryer yelled from the back of the wagon. Jules looked from side to side; there was nowhere else to go except forward, onward through veld and bush. The days were hot and creakingly slow, and after several they outspanned and watered and rested the oxen, always traveling as near as they could to water.

One morning at Burrskill, near the source of the Buffalo river on the way to Fort Cox, the veld came alive with game, all kinds of game, gemsbok, bliskek, wildebeest and zebra. The entire plain was like a patchwork cover of movement dragged over the earth, folding and bending with the undulations of the plain, the fat, rounded silvery hides of the zebra with symmetrical black stripes, and the blue grey wildebeest that dissolved into the morning light.

Long necks and legs of the ostriches loped along on the outskirts and one or two other animals, odd-shaped, picked up in the crowd.

---

* biltong is dried meat.

Zebra foals frolicked at full gallop across the open plain, filled with the energy of their youth and wildebeest calves butted at their mother's udders. "God, man, Jules," said Jan, "what a wondrous sight. Did you know that one kick from that damn ostrich can disembowel an ox, or a lion for that matter, and all that bullshit about them hiding their heads in the sand, my, don't you know, that old fine feathered Black Daddy is a marvelous father," he said. "He takes turns with the hatching of the eggs, God save you if you venture near him when he has chicks. It's not so funny how nature made all the male bird species handsome and the females so nondescript. I mean a female, all colorful, would be mighty easy prey and she'd never get to rearing her young with ostentatious plumage, would she?"

Across the trails came a large herd of "trekbokken." Jules took his gun and, aiming at the springbok on the outer ring of the herd, he fired. The buck leaped up into the air and fell. Then the whole merry veld turned into a churning dust cloud. Like the angry rolling of the sea that got louder and louder until it roared like thunder with the pounding of the galloping herds. Jan, almost hysterical, screamed at his brother, "What a Goddamn foolish thing, for God's sake, Jules, why did you shoot now?" Jules stood, motionless, "I really don't know, Jan," he said, almost perplexed. "I don't really know."

Xosa and the agteryer* ran down to the plain and carried up the springbok. They didn't skin it, it just lay limply over the front of the wagon, its slender, sleek legs dangling down like a young girl. The wagon lumbered on through the dust and locusts. That's how it is in the wilds. The day is fraught with danger from man and his gun or assengai, and the night is full of swift, sudden, roaring death by predators. For them, existence was a never-ending vigilance.

---

* agteryer = one who risde behind.

After a couple of days of constant travel they crossed over a tributary of the Keiskama River and moved on towards their new land "Moorplaats." Old Moerskind˙ who had gone on before was on the track that led to the homestead, he and his wife and sons were like the welcome committee! Long had he served the de Swart family. He never forgave the murder of his baas when he lived and it was agreed that after every rainy season he became the owner of one more beast given to them from the farm. Once he was a slave, but long now, he had his freedom, and he enjoyed the protection and living offered him by the burghers. He already owned 11 cattle that he grazed on the farmland.

He felt he was part of this farm and family, after all, it was he who helped grow the boys up. Some of his own sons were about the same age as Willem and Pieter. His sons who now cared for his 11 cattle. His shiny black sons, they were no different from his Baas' golden white sons. The way he saw them they were all a man's children, his progeny, like the heifers made by the old brown bulls.

A great rock standing five feet high spelled out the name "Mooiplaats—J de Swart." Willem had left his father's name on the rock where he and Letticia had carved and chipped it once. Xosa came forward and great greetings took place between old Klaas and he. Jules and Jan got up on the front of the wagon, and looking out across the acacia trees from left to right over and over again: they now held title for his beautiful stretch of land, where there was very little law except guns and assengai. This wondrous stretch of African veld, dotted with spreading acacia trees, miles and miles of grass lands—this was his land. Here he and Jan were

---

* Moerskind = murder child is a name.

going to carve out a new life. He jumped down from the wagon, stooped down and holding both hands together, scooped up a big handful of earth. "My God, Jan," he said, "this is our land! This is our land! May good fortune fall upon us," and he kissed the black earth and threw it up into the air.

They trundled the ox wagon on towards the homestead. The oxen were tired now, they had to be outspanned and rested. The track to the home seemed to take a long time but actually it was less than an hour. It started with patches of wild geranium. Buffalo grass lawns had been planted, and selected plants, plumbago, wild strawberries, and eyingchees grew everywhere. This was the handiwork of a woman, patches of color blazed here and there. There were stables, well built with wooden doors and inside the stable well cared for were three horses, a tall silo, haystacks and a granary. Long wooden pigsties stretched from south to north so that they got the morning sun. Piglets were snorting everywhere, and a sheep kraal, deep in manure, scented the air with the pleasant smell of farming middens.

Cattle sheds, a milking barn, tack room and plough shed, these were the rewards of years of toil by a man who understood the earth and how to till the soil. A great acacia tree spread over the yard, a leana rope and a small shelf in its jerk, were memoirs of a child's imagination, of happy times and childhood games. Against the side of the Kopje, majestic and quiet was Willem and Pieter's home, once proudly built by their father Johannes and his little isolated family. It was built of hewn stone, wood and a zinc roof. Parts were made a different style, showing different stages of his progress and prosperity.

Willem had said his father had brought Malay craftsmen to build their house, and so they had. The gables combing in their graceful shape something of both east and west. The high roof and wooden ceilings all molded into a home from the many woods that grew in the area as far up to the slopes of the Amatola mountains. Wooden shutters made of slats covered the windows as well as a shutter high up in the roof's loft.

Inside, the rooms were large and airy with shiny bees-waxed floors kept in clean order by old Klaas and his little half-bred Malay wife. Under the wall roof, once occupied by Willem and Pieter's parents had not been used by the boys and consequently smelt of mildew and mould. There were no clothes, but a small wooden naked crib stood against the west wall. A crib, hand made and polished with human love and time. Such was the charm of Moorplaats outside: inside it showed the loves and dreams of man. A white enamel Chester clock stood up on a Syringa wood shelf, a proud possession with an English tie. Riempie interlaced chairs around a square Rietary table hewn from rich slabs of stinkwood and shone with beeswax. Willem's mother had been schooled in England. Copper bed warmers and baking tins hung on the stone walls of the large kitchen, with an enormous fire place taking up the whole wall, one part of which was a Dutch oven, a Criterian iron stove with built in water boiler, a heap of wood for fuel was ready, stacked up in a neat pile, and two large containers were fueled with fresh water. Little brown mossies, or house sparrows, hopped all over as if happy to see people in the place again.

Jules and Jan moved over to the window that commanded the beset view in the living room and looked down over their land. Surely, yes, this stream and dammed up area of their farm, was in the course of the Kriskama River just above black drift. There was no doubt about the farm's incredible beauty. The wondrous, rich green mahogany trees, almost ornamental, seemed to have been sorted out, selected to stay among the pastures and undulating kopjes. There were mauve green hills behind them that seemed unending, gleaming like a mirror was the dammed up area of the stream fringed with trees and spreading like a map into the land. A herd of cattle grazed silhouetted like little statues on the plain.

It was glorious, unbelievable, wonderful. Here, they were on a patch of paradisiacal land, because two young men chose the sea, probably to escape the still real horrors of their childhood tragedy and to forget the dark nights and the assegais. To trade this old farm for a ship—he had to scratch his head—he felt guilty, but one day, he swore, he would meet with those who childlike innocent young men and compensate them. That is how his own father, the king's courtier, would arbitrate it to be: one day when they again will come face to face with Willem and Pieter!

By the time the rains came, Jules and Jan had settled down very well with the help of Klaas and Xosa, and the others' lives took on a faster pace, plowing speeded up, chickens were introduced, Jules built a small, thatched roof rondavel, under the floor through to the other side, he made a tunnel leading from a fire. This was constantly warm, keeping a warm temperature, and in here he raised and reared his chickens. He had a good deal of success and soon began to get callers to trade eggs and chickens. On one occasion a group of British Redcoats rode up on horses. They expressed great interest in Jules and his Boer farm and on their next call, Jules and Jan were invited to Somerset Farm, some 60 miles west. The invitation was delivered to Colonel Fordyce, who had taken time to tell of some of their experiences.

En route he told them how one fine morning, with a train of loaded wagons they were on their way to Kaffirland, traveling Fort

Brown and Leefontein* where they were to branch off to Fort Hare. When the advance guard was descending, at a part towards the right were precipitous crags and just to the left of a steep kloof a large leopard sprang over the heads of a section of men. The horrified men thought the animal was a biped enemy, and as they were marching with arms at the trail, shots were sent whizzing after it. However, when the sergeant told them about the disturber, all eyes were not on Hottentots and Kaffirs but kept peering into the scrubby jungle. Every musket was kept loaded, capped and at half cock.

It was December now, crops were high, there was verdure in the veld, the herons were in the dam and the saddle bill storks fishing the mating frogs two at a time. There was a quiet peace, still hot and wet with bees and birdsong, and the wondrous, wild cry of the distant fish eagle. Great spider webs between the bushes studded with spun silver, and crystal dew drops that sparkled with prisms in the morning sun.

A new room with an S bend lavatory was created for Xosa. Jules and Jan had taken to this land like true earth-loving Boers. The endless beauty of it all was akin to their souls as Africa was to the burghers. Astride his stocky horse with the old mare running behind, Jules was heading for home, the early morning was his best time. Jan milked the cows and made butter with Klaas and Xosa at the homestead. As he breathed in the sweet perfume of wild honeysuckle, like a mirage on the horizon, he saw a hansom cab and for a moment he thought his peace was disturbed by a daydream. Then spurring his horse, he moved on towards it.

He was dumbstruck, holding the reins in gloved hands he saw one of the most beautiful women he had ever seen. She

---

* Leeufontein = Lion Fountain.

was laughing, her long hair blowing behind her and her eyes and cheeks shining like the morning dew. Words failed him. "Goer mere Meneer,"* she called out in an English accent. "Good morning, man," she brought the horse to a halt. She handed the reins to old Moerskind who was sitting beside her. She gathered up her skirts and jumped down. And it was at that moment Jules came to his senses. "You speak English," he said. "Of course I do, I also speak French and a little Dutch. My name is Kathleen McCabe, my mare is lame," she said. She stretched out her hand, having removed her glove, and reached up to Jules on his horse. She said, "Do you know anything about horses?"

Jules had seen many beautiful women but nothing could have prepared him for the kind of breathtaking beauty he found himself facing and she was extending her hand. He took her hand and raised it to his lips. He nearly choked, killed of his usual extroverted charm. Her champagne colored hair was all over like a lion's mane. She had shiny cheekbones high and molded, and her huge amber eyes were slanted just the littlest bit. Beneath her flaring nostrils that flared like a magnificent filly, her mouth. Perhaps, the most attractive feature, full, sweet, upper lip with perfect bow covered her prominent teeth with conscious will, and a full lower lip when she smiled, even nervously, like now, her face lit up into a startling radiance.

Apart from her face, her figure was enough to drive men mad. Jules never was able to describe her body's beauty in words, even to himself. He was totally bowled over for once, and only just managed to bring himself back to reality. "Do you know," he said, "I think you must be the most beautiful creature I have ever seen.

---

* Goer Mere Meneer = Good morning Mr.

I've just had the weirdest feeling, as though from another plane, that you are part of my reason for being here."

"I don't know what you are talking about," she said. "What's your name, anyway, and from where do you come?" "Jules Jacobsen" he said. "Jules Jacobsen. Well that's a fine name, sounds like jewels you see, all bright and sparkling, like the evening star. Tell me, Jules, do you have some means of dealing with my horse?" The horse was standing more or less on three legs with the lame leg slightly bent. "First of all Miss McCabe, let's get her out of harness," he said, and swift and sure he unharnessed the mare, drew her away from the cab and handed the rein to old Moerskint, while he pushed the cab off the track under the shelter of an acacia tree.

"Foot, foot," he called, as he picked up the horse's foot, feeling down her fetlocks and looking under the hooves. He cleaned out some stones jammed right into the side of the frog. "Of course she should be shod, you know, this is no way to treat your animal. I can help you here. We will take her up to the homestead and see what it's all about," he said. Leading the two horses they walked to the house. At the sight of Kathleen, Jan was astonished and as mesmerized as Jules said, "This is Kathleen McCabe, Jan," and all the servants came curiously by. Xosa and Klaas had no doubts at all, all tittering and quite sure, that the spirits had something to do with it all. They wondered, though, to whom it was the spirits had meant this great favor, this beautiful white woman, now for sure, no half-white Hottentot children would be born at Moorplats!

For up until now, there were none and not any were expected. Was it not true that several Hottentot women from afar were planning to use their guile on these two handsome foreigners who had taken the farm from the fatherless and motherless boys, who were forced to do the work of grown men, when they were just small boys, they are always busy working. These white people, it was strange, and kind, how the kaffirs never killed the boys or robbed their cattle or their sheep. But it was different now, these new arrivals, only men, big and strong and it was only with men that the kaffirs made their war. For them life is a man's business, meet it full face, without complaint or self pity, meet it, with bravery and humour.

There were Xosa, a man who lived in limbo, but with unswerving devotion to his white companion, Klaas the keeper, the cattle collector, the compassionate Hottentot beneath his yellow skin, no less a man than any. Ah yes, the wheels of thinking were agog with this appearance of a lovely meisie* and her Hottentot manservant. She had come in her small, smart little wagon, she with her long brown legs and her flashing eyes, like a filly to the stallions! Yes, these stallions, they would have her and then she too would become heavy and swollen and her upright breasts would drag on her body with milk, like the cows.

He suddenly thought of the oxen, ah well, they didn't know the duty and pleasure of being a bull, they were work beasts; witbles,** vaalpens,*** biffel,**** yes biffel would have made a wonderful bull. There's a clever one, shame that he would never pass his brains onto his sons. What a wheeler was Biffel, ya, both he and Bantuman; it was they, who prevented the wagon from going off the road or slipping down the sides of the Krantz. They even helped in braking and that reminded him, he had to make new brake blocks. "Yes," he wondered, "which was it to be? Baas Jules or Baas Jan?"

---

* meisie = a girl
** witbles = whileblessing
*** vaalpens = pale belly
**** Biffel = buffalo

Roused from his immediate shock, Jan purred with his natural charm. He had the advantage! He knew she spoke his language. He passed old Moerskind onto Klaas and taking her with a light touch under her elbow, led her to the riempie chair. He hurried about, getting her some refreshments, honey bush tea, talking all the time, but she bounced up, "Jan," she said, "I have not been in a burgher home, might I just peep at everything? It's just so lovely. Tell me, tell me, Jan, do you belong here, do you own this home, how did you get here and are you one of Charles Sommerset's frontiersmen?" she asked. "You know, his settler people," she bounced about peering and looking and talking and bubbling like an effervescent drink.

Her questions were inexhaustible and her little gasps of wonder and surprise were hard to distinguish from her breathing. Jan followed her from place to place, but she didn't seem thirsty for a drink. She was inquisitive and almost impertinent. "Jan," she asked, "are there no women to meet? This house has the touch of a woman everywhere, a caring, loving woman." They had reached the window that looked out at the kopje. "She's there," he said, pointing toward two heaps of stones upon which an aloe grew. The first heap is the woman and beside her is her husband. They were the people who built this home. Dutch I presume," For a moment she was silent. She looked as though she had entered a room and discovered something forbidden. "They were murdered by the kaffirs," he said, and they both were silent, looking out. At that moment, Jules entered the living room. "I have good news for you, milady," he said. "Your mare is no longer lame. It was merely a sharp stone wedged under her hoof. She seems quite delighted meeting with my horse, 'Soldaat.'* They're

---

* Soldaat = soldier

nuzzling and neighing, and she's safely beside him now in an empty stable."

Kathleen snapped out of her momentary reverie. "For two good reasons, Mr. Jacobsen," she said, "Firstly, she's in season and secondly, she's been so lonely, she must be overjoyed at finding one of her own kind." They all looked at each other. "Do you love solitude, Jules?" she said, "No distraction, no conflict, no reminder of the pain of the world, you hear only yourself, you know?" "Solitude," said Jan, "grants us the dubious grace to be honest, the positive grace, granted, is to discover other imaginations, like other worlds, but you know, there is danger, one can become addicted to solitude."

"Oh dear Jan, alone means alone, except with music, one is not alone," she said, "but doesn't the rustle of the winds, the color of the seasons, or the sounds of unseen animals, send the blood rushing up somewhere, it's like an assault of stimuli?" She turned to Jules and said, "Jules, do you need someone every moment of the day, or do you, alone, enjoy the clear air in your lungs, so that the mind purges itself of the clutter of social and family responsibility?" she said. "Is not freedom intoxicating and the feeling of diminished dependence utterly gratifying, is it not a relief to discover how little one needs other people?"

Jules smiled a wry little smile. "Dear Kathleen," he said, "it's an illusion. Solitude, like any experience, makes impact by comparison. It's good to enjoy solitude, if one knows there is a family, a little herd of one's own, awaiting one's return. The discovery of other parts of one's self is thrilling because you know you are not compelled to bear with one's self forever. Alone can be lived with, we come to terms with limitations, we have to survive," he said. "But sometimes, everything must be sometimes. It's natural sometimes to be alone. In the summer at dusk, when shadows are long, and the day is over, there is a sadness in things, sometimes unbearable. When I'm alone, I remember my mistakes and those who have died, and my spirit is stretched thin by sweet recollection, and often drenched in melancholy. Then I don't like solitude."

There was a silence. "Gracious, gentlemen," she pouted, "I'm sorry I started this all too serious nonsense," she said. "It all just goes to show that there is something about loneliness that has reached deep down in all of us." She dismissed the subject. "By the way, where is Moerskind, you do know that I have about 18 miles to travel back to my father. He would be greatly alarmed if he knew I was this far away," she said. "He's had the most astonishing good luck. He's expecting two brood mares and a young bull from Devon. News has it that they've already landed safe and well in Algoa Bay. And how lucky we are, because during the tropical storms the seas ran as high as the masthead, and huge waves broke all over the decks. The poor animals must have been terrified," she said.

Sonnestrom was just on 20 miles from Moorplats. The McCabes were practically neighbors. Taking two horses, Jules prepared to ride part of the way towards Sonnestrom. He intended to rest one horse and ride it on the return trip, but he would see the hansom home safely with the girl and her manservant. He wondered what part of his destiny this meeting would influence. When he thought about it, he felt some strange excitement, and a crawling, vibrant tangle with his emotions. He was a goodly age, he was 31, and his brother Jan was 28. Marriage and children had not entered his head yet, and both he and Jan enjoyed their freedom: they enjoyed not being hindered by the responsibility of a wife and family. He always told himself he would do all the things young men dream of and he did, having had a strong influence on his brother. But Jan was gentle, more gentle than he, perhaps not quite as strong.

It was to Jules that Jan, as a boy, looked for leadership, for comfort and for guidance, and somehow the big brother image remained. He never thought of Jan as a threat to himself, but he was aware of the great attraction he had for women. They all seemed to want to pamper him and mother him in an irritatingly adoring way. Now that he thought about it, even his mother used to spoil Jan more. He didn't like it, that Jan keenly purred and poured all about this Kathleen McCabe. Somewhere in his mind, he felt that his great desire for new worlds and adventure had something to do with this girl being here on his land.

He looked at the country around him. The veld, now velvety green for the present, rolled all over the hills and huge lumps, mounds of gray dolomite* pushing through the surface like a huge whale back in the sea, trees dotted all over, deep green mahogany, syringa, spreading like canopies and thorny acacias, daintly leaved and huge, snarled trunks from hundreds of years of living. Different shades of yellows and greens, all painted with glints of golden bloom. Yes, he thought, he must remain a leader, here in this incredible land, it was the strong that survived.

How often had he watched the clash of curling horns as kudu bulls fought for leadership or for an ewe in season when the leader of a pack of wild dogs was weak or ill; did the rest of the pack not fight for a new leader? It was the same with all the animals of herding instinct. Surely it was the fittest and strongest and wisest that survived. What was it that happened to men, when a woman was involved? Brotherly love soon became a matter

---

* dolomite = Fire Stone Grey granite like

of lesser importance. Still these were only thoughts. Something strange happened inside of him, he seemed to experience a rush of adrenaline, almost as though it was out of his mind's control.

It was a peculiar rush of blood or something alien to him, each time he visualized the face of Kathleen McCabe. He was even more mesmerized when he faced her. Now with his mighty heart pounding, he prepared to set off beside her, riding one horse and leading another. It seemed the right thing to do for a lady lost in a wilderness. He smiled at her engagingly. "Come on Moerskind," she called, "it's home, you lead the way and I'll spare the horse," she looked up, holding in her gloved hand, the reins, then with both hands. She flicked them. "Come on you frisky mare, home we go," she turned her head. "Goodbye, Jan," she said, "next time perhaps you'll bring a span, maybe yours, and trek over to Sonnestrom? With a span like yours, you only need to tell them and they'd bring you there themselves." She tucked her skirt under her lower thigh and her long brown legs looked soft and tawny in the morning sun.

The sun was high now and its heat had formed a mist which hung over the land like a diaphanous curtain billowing in a soft breeze. A pair of kestrils were circling above, swooping and gliding without a flap. The horse poured the red soil, raising the dust, "I hope I'll see you again soon, Jan," she called, through the little red ribbon of dust trailing beside her. Jules pulled his broad rimmed hat onto his head and took off at a collected canter, Jan watched them go and stood there looking as they got smaller and more distant.

When Jan went inside he loaded his musket and drew the shutters. It was pleasantly cool inside but eerie without Jules. There was a lot of work to be done. A cow had calved near the dam and in her weakened state her legs had sunk into the mud. He rode the old mare, and Xosa ran barefooted to investigate. It was a sorrowful state. The calf was standing on shaky legs, teetering around, but its mother had sunk to above the knees in the mud edges. She was a wild cow and not easy to handle. Breaking down bundles of tree branches, he and Xosa placed them on the mud in front of the animal. They then lifted her leg upward and put it down on the branches. When one leg was free, they lifted the other and then her hind legs. They finally got her out. She was in a greatly weakened state for she must have been there for quite some time.

United with her calf, now she nuzzled as he staggered about on his sapling legs, the umbilical cord still dangling fresh from his underbelly. Old Klaas knew the signs; he saw vultures were circling over the dam. He thought a lion may have made a kill until he heard the distressed lowing. Great pink-necked vultures sat in the trees waiting with eager eyes and huge tearing beaks.

Jan wondered if Xosa would understand. "Xosa," he said, "You know that bird," pointing to the vulture, "that is a wonderful creature." Xosa knew it ate dead bodies. "Yes, Xosa, old man," he said, "I know it's not too much for you to grasp, but it's one of nature's marvels, that! Now if that cow had died which she won't, thank God, he could stand right inside her guts and if he carried the germs of any sickness on his feet and legs, he would then squirt his own excretion down his legs and feet, and the germs of disease might well be destroyed," he said. "And do you know why, Xosa? No you don't, it's because he makes a certain germ destroying property inside of him, and washes his own legs and feet when he excretes, to insure that he himself does neither carry nor contract disease," he smiled to himself. Big spaces and vast lands. One tends to talk out loud to oneself, "Yes old beast of carrion," he said, "old Xosa here didn't know that did he?" He clapped his hand and the huge bird took off with a swish of his tremendous wingspan. As he did so, many more from all over took off with him, shaking the trees as they pushed the branches for take off. And the Kippertjees and moor hens and cranes were all alerted, and a large saddle bill stork went on paddling and fishing and hardly ducks called out in their melancholy way, a strange sound of tears and laughter that echoed across the still silver mirror-like dam!

By the time Jan and Xosa got home the day had fled and the shadows were long. "Tonight, Xosa, you must bring your Kaross and sleep inside, we will find you a room near the big oven where Marta cooks," he said. Marta made fresh bread and had left it on the kitchen mantel stone space above the oven. Jan went to the small cool room used as a larder, pulled down a piece of Impala biltong, and then made some coffee. A small container of wild brambles stood on the table and as he thought, he put them into his mouth one after the other. Suddenly Jules was not there. It was not often that he was alone. So alone. Well, he didn't have only himself. Xosa would soon come in to sleep. Xosa who understood all the sounds of Africa and who knew the signs of danger. He felt comfortable near Xosa.

They had often encountered danger, he and Jules. They really had done so many reckless things. One forgets danger when one is faced with it. It is before that one fears, and sometimes after, but during danger one is not aware of it. Jan opened the door of the living room that faced true North. In the east the horizon was light and showed signs the moon was rising. The last of the day silently as he ate his supper. He thought of Willem's parents. They were dead, miserably dead. He thought of the two small boys left alone to survive, and of those two young men who escaped, now sailing the seas. In a trice a man's life can change. Xosa came in with a goat's skin Karass and Jan shut out the wondrous shadowy beauty of the silvery night. He was tired, maybe he would dream, but he longed to be taken into the arms of sleep.

The journey to Sonnestrom took under four hours and Jules found it increasingly impossible to tear himself from Kathleen. "Jules," she said, when they stopped at a stream to water the horses, "of course you will sleep the night. Rest your horses and yourself, and meet Daddy, what a lovely surprise for Daddy!" She was a happy girl and her voice was eager and bubbly, like wine that sparkled, he thought, like her hair. It reminded him of summer sun. She insisted on hearing his life history, asking hundreds of questions, in an almost interrogatory manner. He hardly had the chance to ask, because she kept talking.

Jules was quite surprised when they finally got to Sonnestrom. It was not like in the Zuurveld, it was below a range. It was watered by two tributaries that flowed into the Keiskama River. Thee were big trees scattered all about it making it quite park-like and spreading shade where cattle stood. The kraals were stout and well put together and a great vlei spread out from the waterbed, filled with birds of brilliant plumage. Wyders and finches and golden oriels. There were flowers everywhere, and the incessant buzz of bees and birdsong. The sun set very late in the Cape! The house was a mixture: first there was the wattle and pole and dagger beginnings. Why was it still there? Windows were put together with solid sawn pieces of mahogany. The newest part of the home was built of hewn stone neatly built with very high ceilings and wooden floors. Shelved corners and a wooden mantel shelf handmade from rugged logs of hand-sawn timbers, filled with ornamental pieces of fine china and items of silver. Bound books were stacked in stately order and two goblets, one silver and one pewter, stood in the center of the table.

Kathleen rushed about looking for her father but he was out in the land preparing a stable for the expected new horses. "Jules, this is our home. We came out of a sailing ship, into a wagon camp, then out of a wagon, and finally after a long journey, we were deposited onto this naked earth," she said. "We were one of the luckier ones. Daddy bought, so to speak, a servant, and his dear old wife from one of the Boers, and that bit of wattle and daub was our home for the first year. 100 acres was given to us free, but the rest Daddy bought, and in fact just being here is because Daddy bought the land. We were all allocated land in the Zuurveld, you know, the area between Bushmen's river and the Fish River," she said. "But we settled for our sun and stream."

"Jules, we have been so lucky. One of the burghers befriended us and we were soon able, with his help, to build a better home," she said. "Do you see my seeds, personally chosen by myself, seeds for all crops, vegetables and flowers? It's all been so much work, so hard. The dirt beneath our feat, so hard; sometimes I think I'm tired, but that's only sometimes. We tried growing wheat, but sadly it got rust and our vegetables were almost certainly all eaten by passing inhabitants, bucks and buffalo, and trekbokken. Now we keep them out," she said, pointing to the poled fences her father had constructed.

A track road led down towards the East. "Where does that go?" asked Jules. "Up until this year, all the English people in Daddy's party had to have their passes signed, before they were allowed to leave their land," Kathleen said. "They used to hire Boer transport and travel up here. Many of them are big game hunters now, and others are doing a very good trade with the Xosa people in ivory, gum and hides. In return the settlers gave these black men tools and material, blankets and beads. It was very hard for the settlers at the start, but now it's easier because they no longer have to pay for rations and implements. Also, they're allowed to use jobless people for labor," she said. "Most of them have bigger farms now. We started with cattle but Daddy had too many disappear. We have sheep now and few cattle." She dashed out and pointed to a huge flock of fat wooly Merino sheep.

"See those," she said, "they are the start of export trade! Their wool is very good, you know, and it is one of the best types. Those are our cattle," she pointed a slim arm, "and one of the boers is transporting two new horses and the young Devon bull. That's where we're putting him," she pointed in the westerly direction, and coming from that direction was her father. She pulled Jules by the arm, it was an electrifying touch. "Daddy," she said, "I'm so sorry if I worried you. This is Jules Hora-Jacobsen, he lives on a lovely farm called Moorplaats where I accidentally got myself lost this morning when I had the crazy urge to ride into the sunrise." The two men shook each other's hands. They were similar in many ways. Big, tall men with fine features, large noses and strong bones, men with big rugged hands and both wearing the clothes of the boers.

The day had fled for Jules, but night comes late at the Cape. Suddenly here was this fine figure of a man, coming in from a day's work. The sun had slid down behind the hill, quietly leaving the aftermath of her journey like a red glow trailing scarf of majestic color, shaded orange, and mauve tinged clouds, silting up above the horizon. A lone stork flapped wearily across the sky, melting into the gray nothingness and an early night jar, was already in full song. Inside the house Tante Tande made herself very busy wrestling with words that Kathleen taught her. She made herself very clearly understood. Fred McCabe had given her two wild ducks and she and Kathleen were preparing a dinner for three. It was a happy dinner full of chatter, serious chatter tinged with English humor. They dined like gentlemen, on the hard rough earth of untamed Africa.

"Jules, my dear man," McCabe said, "you have to stay the night. I see our horses have become inseparable. Ours is a gay old nag, she's prancing about like a filly. I'm afraid to tell her my trusty one Soldaat is a gelding." Under the table, once or twice, Kathleen's foot touched Jules'. There was something about this man. It was as though some plan existed in the big pattern of life. A supernatural power drew them together. The look in the man's eyes sent a wild shiver and rushing of her blood. She seemed to have lost her appetite, her body was over sensitive and turbulent with excitement. There were moments when she seemed to jumble her words, and all the time Jules watched her.

Once or twice, while being addressed by Fred McCabe, he apologized for not listening properly. Soon Fred McCabe was aware of the electrifying atmosphere. The evening's conversation was not normal, and everything seemed odd! After the light faded, hurriedly, the moon had risen, a glorious night was emerging, like the moon always makes it, it seemed to be quicker. The earth transformed to become some silver paradise. Night jars swiftly sped silently past, and an owl hooted somewhere in the distance. All the magical noises of Africa, in a flurry of a million sharps and flats, fractious, calling, restless when the moon is full, a floating seed of gossamer silver, like a miniature silken parachute, drifted gentle on the zephyr through the moonbeams, onward on the dusty road of destiny.

This soft mauve light, this translucent beauty, so beautiful it produced a silence. And then the magic was pierced. "Before

you go out, take your fowling piece," said McCabe, "the both of
you." Disguised by shadows can be sudden death. He took out
his snuffbox and sat down. "That's how it is on this frontier, lad,
you surely must remember that, you never go anywhere without
your musket." They walked out together, Jules and Kathleen. They
walked down towards huge albizia near the horses. They both were
afraid to touch. Like an explosion! "Kathleen," he said. "Do you
want to tell me something, Jules, something new and magical?"
Kathleen said. "No Kathleen, I have nothing new to say, there are
never new things to tell a woman, it's all been said before," he
said, "but what I will tell you is I am burning with desire for you.
I cannot seem to stand the touch of my own fingers upon myself
after having touched you," he said. "I don't understand this feeling.
It has never happened—this is new, Kathleen," he said, as his arms
reached and took her into his arms.

For one moment, she drew her head back then the windows
of heaven opened wide. They kissed with devouring passion.
Their bodies welled and twined like a human flood, hard and
strong and overpowering, unthinking, like a flash flood of moun-
tainous water down an empty riverbed. Once there was an old
peacock, encouped, locked up for several years. It was in a large
aviary. Wild uncontrollable unjudicious Africa! Then one day a
female was put into the same cage and the old cock descended
upon her, almost shrieking, without a love dance of preparation,
his huge mantle of a tail smothering her as he pegged her down
and mated, time and time again, finally falling over exhausted
of everything, as though all his years of solitude had erupted
and overflowed. This is what the peafowl felt, this great lava of
emotion and energy. He had long forgotten old Peeky, he smiled,
at the retching of his memory.

That girl submitted, like the peafowl, with little protest. This is also what people feel, alone in a strange land. They thought of nothing at all, neither kaffir nor lion, hyena or Hottentot. All caution drifted away on the soft breeze that whispered through the ferny leaves of the great albizia. There were no words between them, it was strange, almost an adult embarrassment. It was now the small hours and soon it would be morning. The moon was nearing the horizon and across towards the east. The sky was showing signs of approaching day.

Jules picked up his gun and so did Kathleen, holding hands they walked along the cattle trail downwards to where the two rivers met. It was eerie through the trees. There was always the danger of a leopard. Lions stayed more in the long yellow grass, but not leopard. They lingered in the shadows. The waters shone silver white. A herd of elephants were rolling and drinking, could hear the rumbling of their bellies and the squashy sounds of squelchy mud. Hippo grazed up on the banks lumbering along, grunting. Others stayed in the water with their backs exposed. Black shapes, just curves and nostrils blowing. More elephants came lumbering down, breaking branches of trees so that the cracking sound echoed through the night.

Some buffalo grazed a little distance away, their bodies shining, almost white in the moonlight, their curling horns and great foreheads raised to smell the air. The elephants stayed, huge ears flapping slowing forward and back, huge giants, so gently caressing each other with their trunks. Now they were almost among these huge beasts. The elephants trumpeted and hippo bulls grunted aggressively with huge cavernous jaws. The old saddle bill stork plodded on tirelessly and somewhere a hyena whooped like an eerie laugh. It was a wondrous sight and Jules, his hand upon his gun, drank it in thirstily.

He savored it, the wonders of this wild and wonderful place and this wild and wonderful woman.

They retraced their steps, passing the Albezia tree. "Yes," he said, "Xosa would understand it all, when he passed. He would know, this unmistakable spoor, that told its own story in the African bush." A dove called his mournful song. "Do you hear that bird? Do you know what he's singing? Xosa says, he calls 'my mother is dead, and my father is dead and I am so sad, my heart goes to, too, tooo, tooo, tooo!'" They laughed at his impression. Jules said, "You have seized my heart, my mind. You keep my heart, Kathleen, keep it well, for now I must go back to Moorplaats." "Jules," she said, "yesterday morning, a little later than this I had this urge to ride off into the sunrise, me and Moerskind, old faithful Moerskind. The rest of the happenings you know." "Kathleen," he said, "you must marry me, you must marry me. Will you? Marry me and live with me forever. I have never known anything like this, and I never want to be without you again."

She smoothed her clothes, wiping both hands down each side. My God, what had she done? She chuckled a foolish nervous laugh. She remembered an incident she encountered in London. A small boy in a smart Hosiers had pushed down the nozzle of a fire extinguisher that was strapped to a wall. The fury fire, put-outer, a creamy froth, was spraying across the shop and all its customers. There stood the boy's mother.

"Freddie! What you done!" she screamed, with wide eyes. The scene forever would make her laugh. She wondered why it popped into her mind. Well, what had she done, it was done. She felt the banging of her heart even more. Like a bloody African drum, she said to herself. Putting her hand over her heart she felt no contrition, no compunction or fear. No, it had nothing to do with time. So enigmatic, words and more words came into her mind. She squared her shoulders, and proudly pushed out her breasts. Then brushing herself down one more with her hands. She paused, thinking to herself: just a bloody woman's thing I suppose, we never know what the new day brings do we. I like to think, I've trusted my instincts.

"Julies," she said, "I'll tell Daddy you said goodbye, come, I'll help you saddle Soldaat." She evaded answering. "Go now," she said. She lifted the flap on the side of the saddle and looked at the girth. He loaded his gun and rested it on his thigh. His horse pulled forward, strong and self-willed. They never kissed or held hands, they just looked at each other. The birds were beginning to twitter here and there and the horses neighed and made a lot of noise. The old mare made it clear she resented the parting. Kathleen watched him ride away, his stocky horse rearing to go and the pack horse running on a long rein beside him. She watched till his silhouette disappeared over the kopje. She couldn't see if he looked around or not, but the smell of his body and sweat was all over her. "The answer is yes," she whispered. Looking up, she was sure by the rosy hue in the sky it was almost tomorrow.

$\mathcal{E}\,l\,e\,v\,e\,n$

The sound of chatter among the servants seemed strange to Jan. It seemed as though resentment was expressed in their voices, an intonation of questioning. He pulled on his blue jacket and veld skoens and went out into the morning—a beautiful morning, silver dew drops glistened like crystal balls in the spider webs. The sun's rays stretched way across the sky, straight mauvy pink clouds, like a stairway into the heavens. Early birds hopped and chirruped everywhere and already the fish eagle was high in the sky, white checked sparrows, yellow and black weaver birds, and the hoopoe raising his brown white and black spotted crest. The wonderful hoopoe! Arrogant top knotch.

Except for the birds and the voices of the staff, this world seemed scintillatingly sun struck and drenched with promises of summer, heady with the fragrances of the veld, and the clinging scent of animal dung. Jan took a deep breath and exhaled and then walked down to the staff. A small fire crackled on the ground between some rather flat stones, a three-legged pot stood upon them, over the dancing flames. A red, hand-thrown clay water jar stood on the ground, and beside it sat a colored girl, a pale yellow girl with strange tangled hair, semi-Hottentot, perhaps, a remnant of some primitive hanger-on of the white community.

She had on her lap a child, which she supported in the crook of her left arm. Xosa spoke up first. "Mfasi say she lived here, she says this child belongs to this farm, to this land, she say she is very sore on foot, she says the child is hungry," he said. She opened up the old jacket in which it was covered. Jan went closer and looked at the child. "Well, it's certainly white, a white child," he said. "Who are you woman, and where do you come from?" he asked. "Meneer, I speak very small, Ek* is Maretjie," Xosa interjected, "Mfasi say she went away some seasons ago when she was on the place of her mother's sister. Her mother and father died when she was younger," he said. "She used to have the work to wash the clothes of Wilhelm and Pieter." Then old Klaas came jostling along and waving his right hand half way up to his ear. "Ah," he said, "Marietjie," he remembered. "Baas Jan, this motherless child of nobody," he said. "When she was a younger meisie,** she work here but she go, three or four rains ago."

Jan looked at the child again. It was perhaps three or maybe four years old, and it seemed as though the girl still fed it at her breast. As he gazed at the little bastard, it smiled at him; it was a beautiful child, pale skinned with delicate fingers and brown curls, not the tight curls of the black people, shining curls, soft and round about the thickness of a man's thumb. "God?" It was not easy to tell, but there was something about this child that reminded him of someone he knew.

The child drew sympathy from somewhere inside of him; a strange feeling he had, he felt he wanted to protect this child. He

---

* Ek = I.
** girl

was silent for a few moments, and then he was decisive. "Tell her
it's milking time and she may stay, and have some milk," he said.
He then looked at her. "Dankie Meneer," she said, and looking
at him she smiled. It was not a shy smile. It was a challenging
smile and she looked him in the eye. "Yes," he thought, "unlike
the very young who avoid looking at the opposite sex in the
eye." She was of smallish frame, with paler than chocolate skin,
it was golden brown skin with a satiny-like appearance. Her
cheekbones were high and her eyes were coal black. She had
white teeth, slightly prominent, a long neck and hollow cheeks.
She was almost gypsy-like, unkempt and dirty and her bare feet
were hard with calluses on the heels. She said very little but the
look in her eyes said a lot. Her gaze seemed careless, spent yet
almost proud.

She was obviously tired, thin and she certainly seemed
hungry. She spoke to the child in the Dutch language or a dialect
of a Dutch sort. Klaas gave her a zebra skin and a goat Kaross.
After milking was done and the cattle taken to the field, Klaas
brought the girl to Jan. She looked cleaner and brighter now, and
wore a long boer skirt. "She wants to live in the room and will
work for her food," Klaas said, "and will do the washing, Baas.
She wants to do the washing for you, Baas Jan, like she did for
Wilhelm and Pieter." "Klaas," Jan said, "tell her Baas Wilhelm has
gone away across the sea in a ship, and he has taken his younger
brother with him. This farm is not his home any longer. She may
stay, she and her child, she must help Marta with whatever needs
to be done."

Marta seemed delighted with having a small child in the place
and went about singing and chatting as she busied herself baking
bread in the huge old Dutch oven, and shining the long handled

copper bed warmers and pans that hung above it. She would take little Bosman with her down to paddergang* and gather water Blomme which she stewed with the mutton or lamb, and today because it's "Water Blommetjie Time" and there is lots of sheep meat hung in the Koel** Kamer. She would prepare a different and very tasty dish. Marietje would know the favorite food of Wilhelm and Pieter, and Bosman too must taste of it. And she sang all the time of a red sun and a child, and its father who is gone and lost forever, like a Lady Bird that flew away.

When Jules rode to his home, the sun was already high in the sky. He had found a slip path, a short cut, which led him through dense forest of tall yellowwood trees, tall trees with scanty foliage, with branches entwined with bush vine. He almost panicked once or twice; he noticed that there must have been a skirmish by the tell tale signs. He followed wagon trails which led him back out again into the tracks that led to home. His horse Soldaat seemed tireless, but he changed horses midway. Both horses seemed to have instinctively understood direction, thank goodness, and determinedly pulled their heads, heading for home.

He was tired and dehydrated and hungry. He needed to rest his back. It was so good when Marta busily rushed in with a pail of water for his feet, and the smell of the kitchen was most inviting. He was thankful to be home and out of the saddle. He sat on the riempie stool with his feet in the water, his soft skin trousers pulled up above his knees. His mind was filled with new ideas. His life was thrown into sudden turmoil. He could not think; blocking all other thoughts was Kathleen McCabe.

---

* Paddergang = frogwalk.
** cool

A small object moved near the door and then toddled towards him. He blinked to make sure he wasn't hallucinating—no indeed not, there was a small human being staring at him, standing there and smiling at him, a small white child with little skin trousers and brown curly hair. He was a good looking little boy, with beautiful blue eyes, blue as a cloudless summer sky.

Twelve

J an prepared the tack and got the horses ready. He wanted to leave in the small hours, for Sonnestroom. He felt he would like to meet McCabe and see his daughter again. He waited until Friday and after the evening meal. He casually remarked, "Jules, when Kathleen left, she asked me to call and I think I'd like to go," he said. Jules looked up, almost startled. "Yes, well," he said, "when would you like to go?" "I was thinking about the small hours of Saturday." "That's later tonight," Jules said, "is that why you so diligently cleaned the tack? Of course, Jan, mind you, travel in the very early morning, not at night, the moon is on the same wane and you may come face to face with a screaming Xosa or lion or leopard."

"I have heard lions are partial to horse flesh," Jules said. He thought of the gruesome heap of black bodies crawling with maggots when the flesh was lacerated. "It's safer to take two horses," he said, "though I didn't really need them both myself." He had a searching look in his eye, and his brother was quick to perceive. "Julies," he said, "you are smitten by that lady. Loneliness and the wilderness have powerful effect upon a lusty man. Personally, I'll be guided for once by the Good Book, the second chapter of Genesis, I think. Yes, good brother, the old Hebrews were millions of years ahead of us, they had wisdom." Jan continued, "Yes, they wrote in Genesis, 'It is not good for man to be alone,' that girl would be a lively companion, an able body and a mother of fine sons."

Jules gulped, words failed him. Suddenly he was confronted by his little brother. His little brother, an emotional giant. He felt there was nothing that he could do. Perhaps he should tell Jan of his feelings; should he make known his advancements, should he reveal his emotional load and the thought of despair? "And with thy daring folly conquer all the world." He said. "Did I hear you correctly?" Said Jan, "Yes indeed, you did." A little bravado from the Bard. He could not answer his own questions. But he could answer his brother. He wrestled awhile with his emotions. His private feelings—where were they. Not in his heart, for sure, if it were, his heart would have burst. No this was a mind-matter, he was his own judge, and his own jury.

"Of course I'm smitten man, who on God's green earth would not be? In this naked land or any place, anywhere brother, when it gets you, it's got you." "Keep your musket loaded ready on your thigh," he said, "and come back safely. Good night, Jan."

Jules sought refuge in the quiet of his room. He had a restless, sleepless night and rose before day break to see Jan away. Jan loaded his musket, saddled the old mare, and rode off. The stars were still twinkling but the roosters were crowing. He was angry. He felt like shooting, wanton killing. Maybe he'd shoot something.

Jan had an easy, uneventful ride, he was at Sonnestrom in four hours and the horses were both quite fresh. There was great excitement. People and wagons seemed to be everywhere. But Kathleen, seeing him arrive, went to meet him and helped him dismount. She called the servants to take his horses and ordered them to be fed. A whole wagon of fresh supplies had just arrived, but best of all, two brood mares in foal, and the young Devon bull were now safely inside a stonewalled paddock. The young bull had befriended the two skinny but very good-looking mares. Though a little nervous, they were safely watered and seemed to have settled down.

"Oh, Jan, I am so happy to see you," said Kathleen, and she brought him up under the big mahogany tree where everyone had assembled for tea and breakfast. Moerskind and Tante Tande bustled about with net koeks and bramble jam and cream, cucumber and fresh breads. Already they were eating like the boers. The burghers, Meneer Van Aswgan, and Japie Van den Berg, both brought loaded wagons and the two new horses and young bull walked behind with the other cattle and sheep which had to be delivered from Algoa Bay. The whole exciting day soon fled, dinner came and went, and with it the darkness. Also came thoughts of man and woman.

Fred McCabe kept Jan talking for hours, hungry for company and eager to shorten the night. Finally Kathleen took Jan, both carrying guns, and walked out towards the waning moon. They were speaking of danger, mostly of how people got assegaied in the dark, and then Jan spoke of love and women and she touched his hand. They seemed to be there under the great albizia, the imprint of Jules' body was surely still there, she thought. But Jan's heart was pounding under his coat, he swept her into his arms under the same tree, in the same spot as did Jules. He was timid, yet passion ruled the moment, just him and her in an exchange of bodily functions which lasted until their rapid breathing subsided. She wondered now—if she was on the path of right.

"Kathleen," Jan said, "absurd as it may sound, I must ask you and your father for your hand, it matters not about anything else."

Kathleen was silent for a while, and then she sat up in the thin of the moon. "But it does, Jan dear," she said, "it does matter, and I must ask you not to ask, me or my father." "Why, Kathleen, why ever not, here in this land where one's chances are so few?" he said. "Because, Jan, I want to marry your brother," she said.

She thought, I am also alone, at times I long for my mother, someone to talk with, you know, woman talk, girl talk. We don't lose everything to the land.

Jan was dumbstruck. His perplexed mind was baffled. "Why then Kathleen, why did you give me yourself, Kathleen?" He was suddenly trembling. "Because, Jan, I wanted a comparison. I wanted to know the difference. Don't ask me why, I don't know why, Jan. Perhaps my overwhelming and uncontrolled emotions, have caused me serious trouble. I was irrational. I was thinking that I may have experienced a few moments of insanity. Was it a wild fantasy? Did I lose my senses? Out of control? Had I lost touch with reality? Did my senses desert me? I wanted to know myself, if it could or would happen again. Silly female logic. Maybe it is yes, a comparison of sorts. But I know now that whatever it is, it's about Jules. I believe, regardless of growing and time and all, it simply is, love. I love your brother Jules. Please don't think I don't care. Let's just have shared this night, and each other, let's turn it over like a page in the story of life and put it away. I trust you not to tell Jules. Jan, dear Jan, no finger person could I find to help me than you and I shall always love you, you know, accept my affection. We, will forever be, best friends!"

She stood up, disheveled, she shone like a mythical nymph out of the imagination of the mind and shaking at her bouffant skirt, pulled it on over her slender hips. "Come," she said, "we must get to bed." She picked up his coat and held it for him to get into. The whole incident seemed to have choked away all words in Jan, it was she only who spoke, and she alone, and the soft whispering of the leaves of the Albizia, standing like a great, dark, silent witness.

On Saturday, December 1st, 1823, Jules H. Jacobsen married Kathleen McCabe. It was a long journey, through bush to Grahamstown where a matrimonial court was held once a month. The seat of the Landrost one was fixed at Bathurst for the convenience of the settlers by Sir Rufane Donkin, but had been changed by Charles Somerset in an act of spite, to put Rufane Donkin down, and he, Somerset, returned it to Grahamstown. They were first ordered to return for a license at a cost of 15 shillings. But Jules, being the forceful man he was, was having nothing of it. With McCabe's help, they were married after only a matter of one day. His spirit of affection was not such as to be obstructed by the pressures of colonial bureaucracy.

Kathleen's father was a witness to the marriage and he swallowed nothing, just a welling of emotion as he handed his precious only child, the greatest of his earthly loves, over to the safekeeping of this strong, fair man with a deep commanding voice. It was an extraordinary happening. His daughter and this wandering stranger in the land of burning sun, wild beasts and savage black men, now ready to ride into a future together with muskets at their sides.

He looked at his child. Her beauty was so wasted, unnoticed and rare in a land where only a few scattered people dwelt. And he, what would become of himself, if he were left alone? He looked at them together. There was no denying it. Two more striking humans than they, were not possible to find. Could such a union be good? In some ways it was very good and women's needs are a man to love, a man to desire her, and children. Funny, this thought had not occurred too often, and what of Jules? Who knew if what he told them was the truth? He might well be a murderous pirate. So much was left to chance. Why had she chosen Jules? Jan was a good man.

But, then, he had for as long as he lived always believed in happenstance. Was it so strange? Did Providence provide? Alone in a new wide land. The hand of providence there is no question. Providence is the hand of right and just. That's the way he saw it.

Anthills, what a laugh. How many people understood the intricacies of their castles, the strict order by which they lived and died. Termites, terminus, the end. There was a disciplined perfection, a continuous cycle, hardly, the end: and that's how life is, he thought.

He was older now, and his daughter was young, and she would bear children and she would get old and he wondered what children they would have and what they would become, as he watched the ants busying themselves among his thoughts. With intense interest he was thinking not of the ants, but of the latest events.

Jules watched the great war: great men have great minds, and great minds think alike. He came towards McCabe arm outstretched. "Kathleen says I must call you Pa, same like the Boers! I am honored Pa, I'll be with you to the death." McCabe straightened up straight like a trained soldier. They locked hands and clasped each other. The emotions were clearly visible even to untrained eyes. Words meant more unspoken. Immeasurable loyalty, an indestructible powerful bond. Indestructible powerful close bonding. Tenderness prevailed. Sort of clumsy gentleness. Like a mother elephant who has given new birth. Jules came up to him. He held out his hand, a strong arm with bulging veins. He wore a tailcoat and knee breeches. "Have no thoughts that make you forlorn, McCabe. I shall care for your daughter to the best of my ability." He took hold of the equally strong hand of Frederick McCabe and they each gazed into the other's eyes, like a clash of powerful swords, no promise, no threats. There was a calm understanding and no need for loaded words, just a powerful conveyance, a wordless communication of trust, from the inner inherited instinct of men.

Kathleen came up to her father and flung her arms around his neck, she gripped and locked one hand with the other, and leaned backwards so she could look into her father's face. "My darling father, I now have three men to love and care for and I shall only be really happy if you will come and live with us at the homestead," she said. "We shall freight a lot of our home in two 18 wagon teams, to Moorplaats! Moerskind will remain to care for the home with his family, oh, yes, Daddy, I have asked Jules and he and Jan have both agreed."

In 1826 Moorplaats and Sonnestroom amalgamated and became one huge farm. The merino herd doubled in size, a Devon bull traveled well in peak condition and ready to service cows. The old man belonging to Willem's mother died in her stable, the brood mares safely delivered a colt and a filly, several heifers were born, and old Klaas became the owner of another ox. Kathleen was expecting a baby. Xosa learned to speak the English language, and Fred McCabe was 52 years old.

Thirteen

L ife at Moorplaats/Sonnestroom was tuned to the slow pulse of the African seasons: the smell of dung, the hum of bees on transparent wings, birdsong and wild blossom. When the swallows came it was summer and when the morning mists and cool air made you want to sleep late, winter had come. Cold nights that made one sit beside the fire or lean against the hot stone walls of the great Dutch oven, warm and pleasant. Winter, to some, seemed like a lifetime!

Come spring the joys of first blossoms and spring flowers, spring, that made all life spring forth out of winter, life in tune to nature. These signs signified more than all else, the pace of life and the time to do things, in the peace and freedom of a farm. It was a hard, busy life and to survive, one had to be self-driving and alert. Idle moments were uncommon pleasures.

Towards the end of the summer of 1826, Xosa and Klaas warned Jules of impending Impi attack. He had heard whispered mention, by a large group in the tribal flats, "When the boys lived here, they wished not to kill children, but the cattle here are big and fat and plenty, and you and boss Jan are men." Jules had the uneasy feeling of fear. He sensed impending danger and his fears were greatly increased for the safety of Kathleen. Klaas and Xosa were well informed on the handling of their weapons, Fred McCabe had the wisdom to bring fresh ammunition at every available opportunity. The wagons were always loaded in case of emergency. A large ditch, like an old moat, had been dug in a great circle all around the homestead and it was McCabe who found a way to lead the water into it.

At first thought it was made to keep out the elephants and other wild beasts. A heavy wooden bridge stretched over it and could be lifted with heavy ropes. The horses were taken over it when they were taken out to the pastures. Roofs were stripped of thatch. Because of his unease, Jules replaced it with slates and zinc, and Jan and the laborers lifted the bridge and turned it upside down on the inner side of the ditch. The horses were in the fields, and several more herdsmen were given instructions on where to herd the cattle at sundown, the idea being that each herdsman takes a small group of cattle and spread out into secluded places. The thatch on the outbuildings had been replaced by slate for several months, and what was left was stripped.

Jan was nervous and Kathleen was irritated. She didn't seem to understand. They had not been attacked or pillaged at Soonest-room. The sheep were rounded up by the shepherds and put into a stone kraal and all shutters were closed on the windows. Klaas, Xosa, and all the family were well rehearsed on their strategy and tactics in case of attack.

Months passed without trouble. Then late one afternoon, just when the feeling of fear was beginning to abate and subside, it happened. There was a frightful war whoop which pealed the signal of destruction, and the shout was re-echoed through the adjacent kopjes and valleys. The Kaffirs swept down upon Albany in the thousands, murdering and pillaging as they came. In isolated areas, many were killed and homes burned and destroyed. There was a simultaneous rush and black bodies bearing assegais and great flaming balls of fire descended upon the homestead. There was no time to shout warnings. Shots rang out everywhere, bodies fell everywhere. As fast as the men streamed over the ridge, they fell spread-eagled on the ground. Some had broken their assegais into shorter lengths to enable them to sue their weapons as stabbing assengais at close quarters.

Jan gave a cry of pain. "Christ," he said, "one of those bastards got my left arm," but he continued firing. A Xosa Impi was kneeling and ducking, his left arm holding the bull's hide shield before his eyes. Their leader, a mighty man, stood, hand raised with the assegai. Jules had no option; he aimed and shot him straight into the side of his head, splashing brains and blood around him. The roar of musketry, some almost at point blank range, mowed down the advancing black warriors. The fiery contest raged for what seemed like a long time. It was no more than an hour in fact.

Finally, in the face of overwhelming odds, the white man's musket prevailed against the assegai and what was left of a leader-less, disorganized mob, broke and fled. Fires were raging in the thatch heaps that had been dislodged and removed from off of the roofs, flames danced around the wheels of the wagon. "Kathleen," called Jules, "Kathleen, you are safe and unharmed." Kathleen came slowly forward, her hair falling down to her thickening waist. "Jules," she said, "I've killed and injured several people, I aimed at their heads and faces, and saw them splutter and drop, and I don't feel any remorse. Jules, I feel nothing." Jules held her against his pounding chest. His great pounding heart had now survived a Kaffir war. The warriors were halted by their devastating discharge.

McCabe sank onto the riempie chair. "My God, Jules, Jan's arm is badly mutilated," he said. All the servants had sheltered in the kitchen. "Marta," he called, "bring a pair of hot water." They left Xosa and Klaas on guard in case any more warriors returned. "Here Jan, drink this," and he poured from a potter's jar ¾ glass of old Dutch brandy. "Know where I got this? From Huguenots, in the Cap. I met several of those old French vintners. Knock it back boy."

Kathleen and Marta attended his wound and Fred McCabe conducted himself like a true leader, ammunition at the ready and muskets loaded. It was a horrible wound. The assegai had gone through the top of Jan's arm, bursting the flesh and muscle, leaving a wooden splinter protruding from his flesh. There was a silence. "Be brave, Jan," soothed Kathleen. "I'm thankful it's only an arm. It might have been your throat or head." They leaned Jan against the chopping block and chopped the assegai off, then withdrew the stick from the side that the assegai had traveled through.

The pain was excruciating as the hot water burned the raw flesh. When Jan was bandaged and resting, they did not rest, they all sat up through the night, muskets ready and loaded, and waited for the day.

Fourteen

The morning was crisp and wet with the heavy dew of night. A light mist hung over the land. The horrors of the night were not over. McCabe and Jules, with muskets, finally ventured out, alert to every crackle or creak or outward sign or flicker of movement. A crippled man, or a wounded man can still hurl an assegai. Xosa stealthily followed just behind, his eyes and ears keen and alert, turning swiftly from side to side. Nine warriors were dead and five badly injured, one with a ball that had passed through his breast and out above his right shoulder blade.

He lay patiently on the ground. McCabe looked at Jules. "I think we could save him, old man." "Save him for what, McCabe? To come back and savage and kill?" Jules took his gun and blew out his brains at point blank range, and then like a man gone amuck, he shot the other four as well. No words were spoken. Xosa, with head averted, holding the musket pointing towards the ground, said not a word. They lifted the bodies on the ground and walked down towards the sheep and cattle. Five herds of cattle were safe, but the sixth herd was missing. They had been driven off.

Xosa followed the spoor; the herder was gone. This was Klaas's second born son. He was the herd boy. Xosa trailed the spoor like a hungry hyena to the leftover lion kill and then gave a terrified yell. There, tied to a tree, was Klaas's son. His head was smashed to a pulp, teeth jutting out in broken bits and burgundy skin hanging in mutilated bits. His body had been speared 10 or 12 times and his feet smashed into a pulverized mess of human flesh. "Why?" he wondered.

The pitiful remains hung tied to the tree by the strip of soft leather he wore as a belt. His body was naked and bloody. His penis and testicles were severed and stacked on the tip of a long stake on the ground beside him. Xosa sank down onto the ground. "Leave him, baas," he said. "First I must bring Klaas and then we will track those who have our cattle." With fleet foot he sped back to the homestead, not without the musket, and in a short while he was back. "Klaas is coming," he said. "I have told him of the death of his second born child." Jules and McCabe shuddered at the merciless mutilation they made of a young lad, a living target. They were not sure what to do, drained and bewildered by the night's fears. They sat down on an anthill. At least a clear shot seemed merciful! Vultures were already in the sky.

Xosa pointed towards the homestead. "There, baas, there is Klaas with two horses. We will find these cattle. You will ride the strong Soldaat, who is gelded like myself, and I will run, and we will find the spoor." Klaas brought the horse to Jules and Fred, and handed them over. He then turned slowly to look at his child on the tree. He exploded in a most heart-rending cry. He yelled and yelled and distorted his mouth into a twisted, hideous expression. The noises were wild and animal-like, and filled with horror and grief, chilling and strange and almost insane.

Jules and Fred let him be and rode out of sight. This was a
matter between a father and his dead son. It was at that time a very
private matter: revenge would come later. When his outpouring
ceased, together they followed the spoors with a determined ardor.
When the sun grew too hot they would give up. It was better to
lose cattle and be alive, and no good to tempt fate. God only knew
how many ready assegais were waiting unseen in the dense brush.
But for now it was still cool and the spoors were fresh and visible.
Xosa kept on with incredible speed, fleet footed and tireless.
Soldaat followed on Xosa's heels, and McCabe, musket at the
ready, rode strongly beside Jules. By mid-morning both men felt
the pangs of hunger and thirst. The horses were tiring and Xosa
was beginning to find the spoor was spreading out in all directions,
heading toward Kaffir land.

He climbed up onto a very tall anthill and surveyed the valley
before him. With an excited yelp he came leaping down. "Baas,
the cattle, they're down below this hill," he said. "It's our cattle,
with five Xosa warriors." "Here, Xosa, get up," Jules put Xosa up
behind him on his powerful Soldaat and together they headed for
the herd. Jules was enraged, McCabe was weary. He handed Xosa
a musket and he disappeared into the bush on the right flank of
the herd. Jules rode up and took aim. One man fell. McCabe fired
and another fell. The unsuspecting pillagers were caught off guard,
and fled for the bush, but straight into the face of Xosa who shot
him, sending his body backwards with a burst of blood and fury.

A war-crazed remaining couple were surrounded now and stood
there with raised right arms. An assegai flew past Fred McCabe's
left ear with a fearsome whirring sound, the sound of fear and
destruction. In absolute calm, he raised his musket and blew out
the black fiend's throat. Xosa dropped the last Impi and all five lay

dead. Murder and despoiling lay in every path. Blood and bodies and young men. No one spoke.

There were the cattle. Boesak's herd, poor, brave Boesak, named after a Hottentot hero. No longer would these five wreak devastation! The three men rounded up their cattle, covered with the red dust of death dismounted and drove their cattle homeward. Suddenly, Klaas appeared. He had walked and run until he caught up to them. He was carrying a panga,* a sort of hand-hewn blade with one end made smooth for a handle. His eyes fixed on the shining burgundy warrior on the rack. The corpse's head was in loose sand, and one leg lay over the other in a ¾ prone position.

He seemed to stretch his eyes wide, showing more white than usual, then with a wild, whinnying, crazed shriek of rage and grief and frustration, "Bastard!" he screamed, "bastard, bastard!" And he kicked with his heels into the youthful face, into its eyes and prostate jaws. Pink fluid oozed out onto the sand. He yelled to vent his emotions with incessant beating and kicking. Sickening thuds into the bellies and into the necks. He ripped off the animal skins covering the loins, took hold of the testicles and slashed them with his panga again and again. Then he went at the other bodies, kicking into their eyes and slashing into the relaxed guts spilling the bowels in bile and fluid.

Finally, as he began to ebb and exhaust his anger, grief, and hate, his wrath grew weaker. He finally ripped off the loin cloth from the last dead warrior. He bent down on one knee and just as though he was doing some simple, manual task, he sawed off the testicles with his panga's sharp side. He then slashed a sapling branch, peeled down its foliage, and pegging the bloody testicles

---

*panga = a bladed African tool like a machete.

onto the end of the stick, he stuck the sapling into the earth like hoisting a flag, in a token of victory. "Boesak," he wept, "Boesak, my son, Boesak," and he wiped his tears and twisted his mouth with the back of his blood-stained hand.

The fires were still burning when they came home. Kathleen was overjoyed to see her husband and father and the manservant Xosa and Klaas. "Oh, thank God, you are all safe," she said. "Marietje and I have tried to put the first out. Marta has gone to the bush. She wishes to bury Boesak near the kopje." They did not bury the dead warriors; they made a huge pile of wood and dry branches on the spot and the bodies were burned. Xosa put the remains of their bones into a large hole after the fire had burned out, charred bones still clinging to charcoaled skin.

It was a sad burial. Klaas and Marta dug a hole about four feet deep. They wrapped up Boesak's body in rushes, green and bendable tied in riempie. The bones of his young legs had stiffened in rigor mortis and his arms were rigid at his side. Young chocolate hands with small roughened calluses on his thumbs and forefingers. Marta swayed back and forth, crooning in a futile display of horror and grief. She touched his cold hands an then her breasts, yelling and muttering. Here was the child she had suckled and reared, mercilessly slain. Her fear and grief spread and fell like a light shower of rain, hung sadness, touchable immeasurable imprinting unindurable. She wanted his spirit if only his young spirit could enter her breast. Gently they lowered the rigid corpse down the hole with hand made leather ropes, the mutilated areas wrapped in rushes and wrapped around his head.

The young body thudded to the bottom of the hole and they filled it up with the dry sand. Klaas was wracked with sobbing and trembling and Marta lay moaning. Marietje came up with a small grass basket filled with fruits and a piece of dried meat. She knelt down and placed it on top of the little mound of earth, "so that his spirit will not be hungry before it goes," she said. Kathleen held onto Jules' hand. She had made a stake and tied it onto a piece of flat stone like a slate and in black stain it read: "Boesak. Rest in Peace." Jules pressed it into the mound of earth and leaving the sorrowing parents they turned and walked away towards their home.

He put his arm around Kathleen, and his hand smoothed down her thickening waist. "My God, Kathleen," he almost whispered, "is there where we are to have our child? God damn Somerset, the more he forbids the holding of the trading fairs, the more the Xosas will raid! A far better statesman was Donkin." He noticed each person washing their hands in the middle of the pathway leading towards the house. They had placed a pail filled with water and in the water was a bunch of khaki bush.* Its pungent odorous foliage permeated the area, a strange strong odor and strange it was. It is a Hebrew custom to wash one's hands after a funeral. How did this custom came about? Here it was in this far distant land? He bent down and washed his hands, Kathleen did likewise, and holding each other with wet hands they walked on silently.

Marietjie was extremely attentive to Fred McCabe, who spent a lot of time teaching her English. Hours she spent wrestling with the alphabet, flicking back the long black strands of Malay hair. Looking at her, he thought she may have been Malay. What was she? She looked like a pale Indian or Creole. He often tried to ascertain her lineage and she kept saying her father was a Dutch farmer and her mother was a black slave, but she was very vague about it all, except saying that her mother had died. Repeating

* It has since been proven that the khaki bush is a powerful disinfectant.

she said her mother never woke up again. Her language sounded Dutch. She nervously wrung her yellow-brown fingers.

One morning, while McCabe was wondering alongside the little stream he came upon the girl taking her bath. She was naked. Standing on a large grey rock washing her hair with an oblong tablet of soap, tallow soap, she had found a pool in the rocks filled with clear water, overflowing and moving hurriedly on its way. Her body was slim. Her breasts were darker around the nipples, and they shook sensually, as she rubbed her hair and body. Despite having lost the virginal tautness, she was young, singing an odd song. He thought, how pretty, how lissome was her body and her movements, fluid like pouring golden olive oil? Smooth. He watched the girl for some moments. The stirring of manhood awoke intensely in his loins blocking all thinking. He called softly, her name, then again Maritjie. She turned around, shiny wet and naked, pale golden brown!

About this time Jan's restlessness and agitation distorting his adventurous mind: one minute he felt like looking at his printing press and equipment. Touch, printing, writing, recording life—history the churning provocation. He was not willing to wrestle with agonized affliction—indecision. He the newsman, well aware of the discord between Lord Charles and Sir Rufus Donkin: now there was an affliction! Poor miserable broken soul. Lost his beloved mate to childbirth and cannot get himself together. They referred to him as "a poor sad vascillating creature." Actually he's a good man. And his misery—understandable. Man needs a mate. A very sad loss. He felt hollow. He would rip off the peel of loneliness—chemical, intangible desires.

He slapped his hands on his thighs airily. "Hey Xosa" he called. Xosa who was always busy, came at the double. The rains were

unusually heavy and mud caused damage to wool. "See these sheep
Xosa." He nodded without speaking. "This is a very good grade of
wool. If I could breed the merino with the locals, who are hardy
and tough, we will come up with a perfect wool producer."

In 1841 Sir Rufus Donkin committed suicide.

"And where else in God's green world would lamb ever taste
like ours?" "Why you say that Mr. Jan?" "Because Xosa, this shrub,"
he bent down and plucked the scrubland shrub, "now smell it."
Xosa smelled it long and slowly. He was eager to know, "I smell,
yes it is a funny smell." "Yes Xosa, it's that funny smell, that
flavors our lamb, distinctly. The best goddamned lamb on earth!"
"What about green England's lamb? Mr. Jan that's it man! It's
just not the same! And Xosa, I am born in Denmark hey? Sorry
Sorry Sorry." He held up his hand to apologize. "Mr. Jan about the
crossing sheep? You mean our Hybridised sheep?" "Is it not very
interesting?" "I see London confiscated a printing press because
English policy suppressed free speech and thought." Xosa was
thinking. "We are free here Mr. Jan! Let's write about our wool?
From our crossing sheep?" "I would like to write about you Xosa.
A beautiful story. One day, when we are all dead and gone the
people will smile and read about a great warrior, a brave warrior,
who lived in a stone house in the wild untamed Zuurveld together
with two Danish sailors."

Jan grew restless. He heard of the Cape Gazette and read
its reports. He read of the relocation of the drosty and general
administration of affairs, the discord between Rufane and Somerset,
and the Albany levy. He was agitated, by the menace of theft and
murder and concerted attack, a capricious climate spell and floods
and famine. Moreover, he was alone and it was hard watching Kathleen and Jules. He found great joy and satisfaction from the sheep,

crossing Merino and Saxony with the local variety, and their wool in great demand at 14 ½ per pound. He wanted to start a printing press, but had heard that two London printers, Robert Godlanton and Thomas Springfellow, had had their wooden hand printing press confiscated by Donkin who had to pursue the current policy of suppressing free thought and speech.

Jan hankered after his real profession and began planning to move away. It was not that he had to start from nothing, not at all. He would leave all the farm to Jules, and he would take their printing machinery safely locked away in a small hut-like room with large red roof slates on the roof, which he had brought all the way from Uitenhage. After the kaffirs had fired the thatch roofs, all had been changed to these large red tiles.

During July 1826, the weather changed. Violent squalls of wind did great damage to the farms. Gardens and fences were swept away. To add to the desolation, grubs attacked the vegetation, a huge infestation of grubs and a plague of locusts. Kathleen was heavy with child. Wisdom had taught de Swart, a born farmer, to have built on the side of the kopje facing the rising sun, and they were among the fortunate ones. They had not suffered much damage. Often Kathleen was breathless and bending was difficult, and to make matters worse, Marietje was also pregnant. Her son Bosman ran in and out of the house, if not with Jan, then with McCabe, but never with Jules. He was speaking well and sat at the table when mealtime came. Marta was delighted and almost took over his upbringing from Marietje.

Everybody seemed to take a hand in telling, teaching, and showing, all the while Bosman was learning. He attached himself to the family in such a close way that he now slept inside the house in his own room. He felt like part of the family. Jules had a stone room erected, extending the homestead each time the necessity arose. Here lived Bosman, a quaint little boy with deep olive skin and blue, blue eyes. He was gaining weight and strength. He was stubborn and willful and extremely independent. He had a captivating winning smile. He smiled like an angel and he won the hearts of all those to whom he extended his little brown hands.

In 1828, Shubert died of syphilis at age 31.

The baby was due in October. Jules was planning to wagon down to Grahamstown and collect a Dr. Atherstone. He was pondering whether he should take Kathleen and Marta and the three of them ride together but Kathleen would have nothing of it. "When it comes nearer the time, we will think of it," she insisted. She seemed so healthy and strong. They had built a new room, a baby's room, and Klaas and Xosa had woven a crib of cane and wood. On the floor was a caross of coils of raw wool sewn together with a tree fiber. It had a strong smell of Kraal but was not offensive, "Voerchintz" cloth and tanned sheepskins and little garments and shawls made from Kathleen's clothes. Certainly not the luxury of England, but for a wilderness it was abundant.

A few hours away was a burgher, but it was the burgher's wife who was known to be very conversant with the delivery of babies. Jan moved into Kathleen's stone cottage, Sonnestrom. He wanted to experiment with his printing. Moerskind and Tant Tande now lived there and the place was full of patches of color, a climbing rose, sweet William, hollyhock and Canterbury bells. Under the trees were violets and even the pot plants flourished. Here it was that Jan would begin, here among the doves and yellow weaver birds. He looked over the blue mauve valley, and in the distance saw smoke coming from the chimney of the burgher family, Sannie and Andries Reeder. How often did he mention that this place was overpopulated.

"Ja," he said, "if a Boer sees the smoke of another chimney, he is living in an overpopulated zone." Wonderful, earthy people they were, Sannie and Andries and their sons and daughters, Hendrik Reeder, Piet and Faan and two smaller girls, who both rode together on one Boer horse. Sannie it was, who was coming to be with Kathleen over her confinement. Jan put the oxen into the kraal, put the brakes on the wagon and prepared to settle down. Kathleen's servants were both very busy helping, eyes alert and eagerly looking into all the boxes of provisions. They carefully carried the press inside, a clumsy, ornate, four-footed construction, something like the Columbian Press, but perhaps less decorative. Nostalgia faded from Jan's thoughts and a trickle of excitement rushed through his veins.

September 28 was no ordinary day, though it started as beautiful and in the same pattern as all those that had preceded it. Blossoms still hung hazily in pinks and white and lambs frolicked like little balls of fleece as far as the eye could see. There were planters rains and the pastures were sprung with new green spears through the black stubble of past burning.

Kathleen's day of birth had come and the privacy of Moorplaats was suddenly shattered, broken like the shell of a fresh egg, dropped on hard ground.

This ground was not hard! The noises of the farm, ploughmen and herdsmen echoed everywhere across the farm. Sannie Reeder's span with driver and voerloper busily unyoked the oxen and the fields all furrowed, waited for seed. Kathleen woke up early and knew by a gush of warm water down her legs, as she walked towards her leaded bath, that it had started. It was a short labor and before mid-morning she safely delivered a fine flaxed-haired girl. The head was squeezed to a sort of slight point but Sannie hastily assured her it would right itself in a few hours, as that came often with the first born. Together Jules and Kathleen gazed at their child, a beautiful, perfect little girl. The servants were joyous when they heard it cry. Jules was nervous, uncontrollably nervous. Nothing, he thought, shall hurt his Kathleen. He came to the kitchen where they were all waiting. "Marta, Marietje, it's a girl," he said. McCabe went into Kathleen's room. She lay there, tired and pale and Sannie had washed up all the blood and placed the placenta in a pail, to be planted with a tree in the garden.

She smeared her face with a pinking white cream from the plaenta. "Ach, Meneer," she said, "Placenta, it's the pure miracle of life. It renews the skin. Meneer, now this is it, you see," offering some on her hands to Jules, and she smeared more up into her ample throat. "What a pretty little girl," she said. "Look here Meneer," McCabe smiled at Kathleen. "How do you feel, my love," he said, and he picked up her hand as he sat down and held it against his heart. A gentle spring breeze was blowing, and the crisp air came through the window. She breathed in and out in a sort of little sigh. "Bring her to me Sannie," she said, and Jules came in with some warm milk and placed it beside her bed. The baby simpered as Sannie placed it to her breast. They were all looking at this miracle of life. "Moya," said Kathleen. "That's the word Xosa uses for a wind. We shall call her Moya, the gentle wind."

Three months later Marietje gave birth to another son. She had worked steadfastly up until the day it was born. She was speaking well now and tried hard to emulate Kathleen and all she did. She enjoyed speaking English and proudly spoke her words as Fred McCabe did. It all started in the afternoon. Marietje's water broke and slid down her legs onto the hardened floor. She made not a murmur but kept strong as the water snaked its path across the earth. Her eyes narrowed and she caught hold of her long hair and twisted it round restlessly and nervously. She had been through this before, and, as if remembering her pain and fears, she clutched at her protruding belly and let out a weird animal-like yell.

It was this that attracted Kathleen. She did not know what to do with her. They brought her onto the stone stoep,* the verandah of the house and placed her on the riempie bed. Marta rolled up something, a cushion of sort, into a form of a pillow and put it under her head, reassuring her that all would be well, and life is precious and she gave forth a lengthy jumble of Hottentot words that only she seemed to understand. Within the hour Marietje had her first contraction. Kathleen tied a riempie from one side of the iron and leather bedstead to the other and placed the riempie in her hands. "Press down Marietje, press down with each pain," she said. Marta tied some blankets with fibrous twine from the beams of the roof. Kathleen several times thought she should take her inside into a bedroom, if for privacy, at least, but she didn't. They remained on the open stoep.

Maritjie became increasingly hysterical with each contraction, her deafening screams echoing across the whole endless veld. The shadows were lengthening and Kathleen wondered whether someone should ride for Sannie. Sannie, who didn't care for Hottentots and who hated the kaffirs, "Never trust them, no Katrina, they are not to be trusted. They will all stab you in the back, mark my words, you will one day remember my words," she said. No, Sannie would not care or wish to bring another kaffir bastard into this world, and Marietje snarled and shrieked and

---

* patio

squirmed at the mention of Sannie's name, Sannie who knew all about these things. Marietje looked so slim and small, her pretty face wet with perspiration, tears falling from her eyes and mucus running down from her flaring nostrils.

She bit into the riempie with her teeth, gasping and rasping out guttural and animal-like sounds, clenching her hardened little brown hands until the knuckles shone white and pointed small bones, bloodless under her taut skin. She howled and cursed and grappled with pain until the sun went down. The atmosphere was tense—even fearful. Then twilight came, with Marta holding one leg and Kathleen the other, they pushed her legs upwards, ending the knees up against her belly and chest, trying to give her the strength to bear down. Marietje was heaving and gasping and groaning. Suddenly the skin tore around her genitals, blood spurted out on the left side, as her body struggled to reject its burden. The child's head could be clearly seen, bridged behind her small dilated bones. Suddenly, almost as if the bones parted, the child slid onto the towels, its head squeezed and squashed and swathed in a creamy substance. A large child, covered all over, its naked little body in fluid, placenta and blood. Marta wrapped it in a towel.

Marta handed it to Kathleen, who held it while Marta hastily tied the umbilical cord. Marta handed to her, standing. She then severed it with a kitchen knife from the kitchen. Xosa and Klaas brought pails of water and they cleared up the bloody mess. Kathleen looked at the child, a large boy with creamy olive skin, a twilight child. She took it to Marietje. "You have a big perfect child Marietje," she said, "you have a big lovely boy." Marietje closed her eyes and turned her head away. She had no desire to see this child that caused her so much pain. She was too tired to care.

Two days later Maritje developed milk fever. Her small breasts swelled up and her body was in great heat and fever. Marta went into the veld, returning with the leaves of a huge succulent aloe. She slit and opened them up and removed the shiny transparent jelly like flesh from inside the aloe leaf. She then heated the green flesh to a hardly bearable heat and placed them over each of Marietje's breasts, laying them there with a length of Indian cotton. This poultice was done every few hours for several days. In between this, the child was trying to suckle the yellowish milk. It was a strong child with a strong cry, "strong like an elephant," said Marta. "He roars and he has the color of a lion. He tore from my body, so I shall call him Lion." And they named him Lion.

Marta put her hand into her apron pocket tied another thread, a thin black thread with which she had tied the umbilical cord, a piece of hair from an elephant's tail.* "Ja," she said, "he will grow to be strong, like a bull elephant." It is a big baby, big limbs with soft brown curls. No one would say who the father was. "No," Marietje said. "the father must say for himself." Bosman was six now, but he didn't seem to understand what a brother was. To him, everyone was his brother. He scrambled through each day with the family. He was lucky in many ways, a fatherless little bastard, gregarious and energetic, with a winning smile that captured the hearts of all who met him. When he was six he was given the task of guarding the cattle, cattle which were the life blood of the settlers, as they were the life blood of their black neighbors not far away across the Fish River.

---

* The hair of an elephant tail is considered extremely lucky and a symbol of strength.

Fifteen

All children, girls and boys, were given the task of herding, driving their charges out into the hills, in fear and trembling. Often they were attacked by wild dogs who tore the living flesh from off the bones of the cattle. Amidst wild animals, elephant herds and even lion, children guarded the herds. One child died of exposure to heavy rains and another girl lost for three days came face to face with a black-maned lion. It did not harm the child. Little Bosman was used to hardship and seemed a fearless little boy, greatly interested in all the insects. His greatest pleasures were when he was allowed to accompany Jan or McCabe. Now Jan had moved away and McCabe was often with his mother and their new child, it just seemed like a small nuisance in his life.

1825 saw changes at Moorplaats. A certain Mrs. Mathews and her husband, who was once held prisoner at the Siege of Paris during the Napoleonic Wars, opened a boarding school in Grahamstown. The Landrost of Grahamstown had appointed him to this Salem Academy, to this school. Fred McCabe sent Marietje's son Boesman. Mr. Matthews became the revered and respected schoolmaster for 42 years at this school and Bosman his only colored pupil. 1827 also saw the birth of Kathleen's son, Julius. Moya was walking by the time Julius II was born, a beautiful blonde child, full of laughter and love. They were so happy to have a son.

Marietje helped care for them all. She nursed Kathleen over her confinement, loyal and caring, and took over several of Marta's chores. Marta still grieved over the death of her son Boesak, who was so young and strong when he died. She had five others, all working with the sheep and plowing. Klaas had quite a herd and often said he now felt like a rich man. He had failed to get a daughter but was well pleased with his five sons.

One day when McCabe came in from his horses he was carrying the boy and he placed him on a riempie* chair. "Kathleen," he said, "Lion is your half brother. Of course I'm sure you already knew." Kathleen was silent for a while. "I suspected Jan, Daddy," she said. "I thought it was Jan's, but as the days passed, I began to see for myself." She stopped. "It feels so odd, Kathleen," he said. "There he is, a fine little fellow, my son. I have a son at 52 years of age. My son, suckled by a sweet half-caste servant girl who drifted into our lives and our home." "And into your bed, Daddy," said Kathleen caustically. She then stood erect, almost resentful. "Sometimes, Kathleen," McCabe said, "we are not strong, sometimes we are just frail, weak human beings. I see no crime, my darling girl. It happens, but I do feel a great sense of responsibility."

Her father seemed happy as he fondled the little boy. She stood there looking at him, this powerful man who was her father, a gentle giant of a man who denied his daughter nothing. It was hard for her not to feel, yes, sort of degraded, that was the feeling she had, the feeling of degradation. She had no right to judge her

---

* Riempie is strips of cow hide.

father or dare to deny him anything, and she could not understand why she felt this resentment within herself. She looked outside and beside the horse trough she saw Marietje washing the laundry with tallow soap. She had removed her dress, the one Kathleen had given her, and a cloth was tied around her breast. She was naked above the breast and below the thighs. She seemed yellow gold and young of flesh and her black hair was braided in a single braid, which fell down beside her head as she rubbed at the washing with a homemade washing board. Kathleen raised her hand and pressed the four fingers of her right hand upon the spot between her eyes and her forehead. For a moment she closed her eyes. Then suddenly, as though she had dispelled her thoughts, she said, "What is, is, Daddy. We will have no skeletons. Africa is so full of skeletons. Just think! Lion will be Moya's uncle, I suppose!"

She picked up her son. He was so beautiful. White, white blonde, blue eyed, cherub like. "Now, then, Jules, Julesy-boy, see this little Lion. This is your uncle, Julesy." Then slowly she said, "But you can call him Lion." She laid her child down on its tummy on the woolen karass. "Marta," she called, "we shall have tea." "Marta?" Then louder, "Marta?" Out here in the veld, she thought, it mattered little. Nature would never be quelled. Nature always rose triumphant. Those who survived beneath the blows of life were the lucky ones, the strong ones. Man needed to be especially strong in this land. Now she needed to be wise and strong, and she wondered now, what to do with Marietje? What was a bastard anyway? And what really was a marriage? It was all no tragedy compared to the tragic things that had already happened on the farms at this place.

These odd women, so unlike in breeding, but similar in courage, were brought together by the needs and desires of man's natures and drives. It is not hard to make a child, yet it is so hard to think

20 years hence, it is hard to answer questions. It is hard to know what's coming tomorrow. It is better not to think, to live for now. Our lives, so very uncertain; and, how very brief. She thought of Bosman, another strange mongrel child. Would her father be saddled with him? Her father for reasons of his own had sent him to a school in Grahamstown.* It was true Bosman was the only non-white child in the school, and besides no one really knew what was once a white skin in this land of harsh sunshine. The English all florid and pink and the Boers so tanned and brown.

Both Bosman and Lion were olive skinned, but Bosman had clear blue eyes, the undeniable mark of a white man. Lion had sparkling brown eyes that flashed green. They had curly hair, but they were fortunate it was not the tight little spring curls of the Hottentot or the Negro. As time passed, Marietje mingled and blended into the home. No one noticed it happening and no one cared. She did for Fred McCabe what she did in her girlhood with Willem. Only she received more caring and goodness from this mature older man. He was a strong man despite the white in his beard. She felt more safe and secure, perhaps for the first time in her nomadic life.

Older men do care for women more than raging youth. For Fred McCabe, she was a smooth, soft woman, warm, obedient and giving. She laughed and sang and bathed naked in the stream. She had all the tantalizing wiles of all women, a bushveld Pygmalion to whom receiving of care was more precious than life itself. Yet there was something strange within her. He had long thought of taking a new companion. He had thought of riding away to Grahamstown or Albany to see if there were any eligible women, new widows

---
* Grahamstown.

perhaps? No, to him, life was here on this farm. Here where these marvelous sheep produced marvelous wool, sought after, and of superior quality, cleaner washed it was said.

Now Kathleen was engrossed with her own life, he envisioned his life alone and lonely in these distant outposts. He needed a woman to share this veld. Perhaps he should marry Marietje. He had spent hard and lonely years. He and Kathleen had stood almost alone in the bush, surrounded by land in which neither spade or plough had touched, and with the keen knowledge by both man and beast. Here they took root, amidst the menace of marauders, of elephants in their hundreds that roamed slowly all across the Kowie and then to the Ado. Rhinoceros crushed the ravine thickets and lions stalked and roared in undisputed sovereignty on the winterberg slopes and far out, across the savannah, wild dogs howled and attacked the cattle and ever, there was the regular nightly serenade with the eerie whoop of the hyena.

He was accustomed and conditioned to fear. He was a survivor, and by God, he would not care. He had long ago learned to grasp with both hands the gifts that nature bestowed; and among these included a chance of pleasurable moments with Marietje. He found some new, exciting pleasures with her instinctive gentility. One night he announced to Kathleen and Jules that he felt he should marry the girl Marietje. Both stood there in stunned silence. "I want to marry her, Kathleen," he said. "I would like Lion to be part of this family." Both Jules and Kathleen looked up. "And not only Lion, I want to include Bosman." Jules said not a word. Kathleen shrugged her shoulders. They had all grown quite used to Marietje and fond of her. Lion is a darling child, thought Kathleen, and a child is a child. I too would want that he be cared for, since you are his father. There was a strange new acceptance and so it was decided that McCabe and Marietje would live in Sonnestroom with Lion. Jan was planning to move to Grahamstown and there would start his paper.

Jan was filled with eager intent. He had packed his wagon and prepared his team and servants to move towards the village. Grahamstown offered the most opportunity and Port Elizabeth was fast growing in importance. The newly formed Albany Shipping Company had proposed to build a harbor and Col. Scot erected a blockhouse, an important military post housing a lot of soldiers on the Kat River. It was called Fort Beaufort, named after the ancestral name of Lord C. Somerset. Jan arrived in Grahamstown, an interesting and almost cultural little society. There were 800 houses and 4,000 people of all races and vocations. Here was Jan's present dream. He wanted nothing but to print his paper. He had dreams of influencing thought and stimulating action until one day his journal would become as their Bible. He would strive for these pioneer peoples, urging their claims and progressive measures. He would be both founder and proprietor and editor of this exacting occupation, and he bought some land and set about to build his home, set here in the forbidding hills away from the rows of neat white houses, an architect of his own fortune.

His builder Piet Retief, a grand, rough, good-hearted Boer, was a staunch and wonderful friend who carried tiles and bricks and James Hancock's earthenware right from the clay pits in the valley. So time passed! In only a few years Jamestown Journal was a great success. He was supported by all the merchants. He was a beautiful man. He advertised town doctors: "Genuine patent medicines, chemicals and drugs, sold wholesale and retail by Dr. Bell, surgeon apothecary and chemist from the Royal Exhibition of London." He became a freemason, friend and news writer of burgher farmers and traders and gave a lively record of the day-to-day happenings of all the town's affairs for sixpence* a copy.

In brilliant red coats, the 72nd Regiment and the Cape Mounted Rifles who were stationed on the outskirts of the town provided gaiety and entertainment with balls and quadrilles and fun-filled parties. Great excitement for all was the horse racing on the flats just outside the town and all its peoples turned out in full force and color to share in the fun. On one occasion a certain lady arriving on a horse she bought from the military was astonished when at the sound of the starting gun, her horse took off into the race at full gallop, with bonnet off and hair flowing behind her. She came in hanging on gamely among the three winners. Jamestown Journal made Jan a significant personality. He went into partnership with Piet Retief who started a thriving butcher shop and for another sixpence they would sell you four pounds of pretty good meat.

These brave people, now part of the swirls and eddies of humanity in Africa, continued inexorably. Jamestown Journal, edited by this handsome single man, befriended by all the affectionate and hospitable folk, found peace and the sweet taste of success and contentment in recognition lulled by a false security driven by easy achievement. He was totally unaware of the dangers that lurked near the borders of their territory.

How difficult it was for old Tante Tande and Moerskind to accept that Baas McCabe had brought this yellow woman who was known among the Hottentots as a fatherless half-caste Hottentot, who drifted across the veld looking for a home. She was a lost women, first attached to the de Swarts' home Moorplaats, It was there she spent most of her childhood and it was she who helped the boys when

---

* six pennies.

their parents were buried. She was about the same age as de Swart's boys, they got a young surrogate mother? He was not surprised, she was not a black man's woman, nor a Hottentot's woman. Marietje! Ja, those, they said the mother of their God was Maria, and she, also Maria also had a son without a father. Now the Baas McCabe has taken her and made her the woman of Sonnestrom.

Tante resented this with jealousy and yet, she felt pleased. Perhaps it was a form of uplifting. It made them feel less like servants and somehow more acceptable: this white man had taken this yellow woman into his bed and they have a child? And it is named after the king of the animals! Oh, yes, she was jealous again. Marietje had inflated ideas, she had learned too much about the white man's God and Maria. Even when she lived with Willem, Maria was also the mother of Jesus Christ, who was born to be king. Perhaps her hard young life had affected her. Perhaps she wanted to be like the white man's Maria, 'mother of God.'

She calmed down, and good thinking overcame her. As it was now, she was the newish mother of Sonnestrom and the mother of the boy Lion. So if Marietje was good to them, they wouldn't mind. She must have deserved and earned some good, to have become so lucky! Ja, it was a very confusing situation. This wandering Hottentot girl was new in the home of Mizz Kathleen, and they, were house servants to one of their own? Whatever would they call her. Should it be by her name or by the name the burghers use, Mevrou. They settled for M and whenever Marietje called or wanted anything, from then on, it was "Mevron." And as it happened, soon it became quite an order to call her Mevron. One Saturday, when life was good. A strange man passed by asking if he could water his team of oxen at the stream. He was an uncommon sight in this part of the country as McCabe was soon to find out.

Richard Gust he said his name was, and "praised be the Lord; I thank you for watering my oxen. I am a Quaker, a trader, and a man of peace," he claimed. He traveled unarmed, despising a gun, never carried a gun as he guarded his cattle, nor reported any losses, lest blood be shed when soldiers recovered them. He went unarmed into the bush filled with hostile kaffirs to fetch supplies, with only his faith in God as protection. Once at Salem, when a horde of kaffirs arrived to burn the settlers' houses down, he rode fearlessly out to meet them, opening his coat to show them he was unarmed. He called out in an aggressive way, asking if anyone spoke Dutch. One kaffir came forward and he asked the black man why they wanted to burn the houses of these white people. Nonplussed, the kaffirs replied with foolish answers, some saying they were hungry, but Gust confounded them, as he pointed to all the stolen cattle. They then asked for bread and Gust promised them bread. He turned his back on hundreds of armed warriors, rode to his house and returned with all the bread he had, and several pounds of tobacco, and he instructed them to give it to their chief. The kaffirs kept their word, and returned in quiet, and all through the wars, the Gust's house was never touched or damaged.

McCabe was delighted to meet this man and invited him to stay and eat and rest. He told him of his life and experiences and his fears and loves, and finally about Marietje and Lion. And so it was, Gust took out his leather bound Bible with a gold ribbon place marker, and reverently he called McCabe and Marietje together, and he read from the New Testament all the teachings of Jesus and St. Paul, and then he searched the Old Testament just like the boers did for guidance, and finally he got to the sermon.

"Join together this man and this woman in holy matrimony," and he went on reading about love and comfort and sickness and health, which all didn't seem so important. "In the eyes of God you are man and wife," he said, and he handed McCabe a written sheet he tore from a book in his coat pocket.

Married under the heavens by a man of God, Fred McCabe to Marietje McCabe. No other names were mentioned for no other names were known. Fred McCabe felt a certain satisfaction, an expression of honor as he looked at the bit of paper signed by Richard Gust; pathetically primitive though it was, it was meaningful to him, in this raw, unlawful land. To Marietje it was nothing. She knew little of what this rough old man was saying. It seemed only important to him that this other old man hold her hand. They seemed happy, these two old men together. They had something in common. And whatever he was reading was something of a ritual they understood better than she did.

Peace and plenty was reigning and without famine or floods the lands prospered, the settlers at last appeared to be reaping the results of their toils and travails, big game hunters came and vigorously traded in ivory. Hottentots were treated like colored folk though they continued to be vagrants, thieves and completely non-law abiding. Fugitive tribes were held back by Col. Somerset and his army of colonists and loyal natives. Mzilikazi fell to his master Chaka and with his followers fled, to become the Matabele. Slaves were liberated. Chaka had now put his warriors with ox hide shields and broad stabbing assegais, dangerously near the borders of their territory.

In September 1828 Chaka was brutally murdered by his brothers, and the one named Dingaan became the Zulu chief. Summer 1833 was stricken with a severe drought, a subsequent crop failure, and the consequent trigger off of tempers among the frontiersmen. In December 1834 while friends were full of good will towards men and assembling for the Christmas season, the whole colony was terrified by a sudden burst of barbarians who wrapped the whole frontier line in the fire and smoke of their burning homesteads. Astonished, unsuspecting people, utterly unprepared and utterly defenseless, were met with death instead of cheer. Brothers, sons, husbands and fathers fell, and wives, mothers and sisters looked on in horror.

Farmers in more isolated areas could offer little or no resistance. Jules and Kathleen and their children were saved by their devoted servant Xosa high in the boughs of a tree, alert and forewarned. McCabe was warned in time and sent to the hills. Tante and Marietje, who held Lion in her arms as Moerskind drove the horses, remained at Sonnestroom. McCabe set his brood mares loose and loading his muskets. His own construction barred the doors and from the left with ammunition at his side and Bosman loading his gun, they brought down and injured hordes of war-crazed warriors. They saw the frenzied natives ripping up the pillows and mattresses and hurling handfuls of feathers into the flames. They stabbed the pigs and slaughtered the cackling hens and murder and despoiling met all in their path.

Bosman was 15. He was well-spoken and a keen shot and like most men or boys of his age death was just a part of life. The Kaffirs, finally having caught sight of McCabe's place, hurled flaming torches up towards the left as they came nearer. They fell to the shots of the muskets. Bosman showed no signs of fear and with deft and nimble fingers kept loading and shooting. It was comparatively quiet at last, the kaffirs had moved on, taking clothes, furniture and household goods, all they could lay their hands on. One had taken a turtle shell and placing it on his head, marched off triumphantly, wearing it like a Chinese water carrier.

Streams of warriors swept past the undefended posts, jeering and boasting of their triumphs. Wherever they had gone, they wreaked death and devastation.

McCabe and Bosman, when all was quiet, came down from the left. The house was burning and the smell of blood was everywhere. McCabe dusted the straw from his leather breeches and was about to address Bosman, when there was an icy, ear-piercing whoop—he looked up in that instant, and in the blink of an eye, too late, the assegai crashed straight into his chest, and with a bone cracking, sickening thud, came out at his shoulder. Instantaneously a shot rang out. Bosman had got him, a kaffir wounded in the hip, which left his powerful black arms free. Bosman had fired straight into his face. The kaffir reeled over with arched back and fell to the ground.

McCabe sank to the ground. There was a strange guttural sound in his throat and his blood was pouring out of his chest and mouth. "Dear God, boy," he called to Bosman, "I think I'm dying." He was sucking in the air through bubbles of blood and pink fluid which he spat out of his mouth. "Bosman," he said, "there's no time boy. I shall die if you ride to Moorplaats. Stay with me, boy. This time the bastards have got me." He caught hold of Bosman, trying to suck enough air to fill the one lung that could be filled. The shiny black assegai protruded from his back and the stick from his chest. Blood oozed through all his clothes, making black maroon patches, like the clouds that shadow the earth.

"Pa McCabe," said Bosman, "I cannot draw the assegai out, and your pain is too great for me to chop it off. I know not what to do, Pa McCabe," and he held McCabe's hand, and he cried out, turning his mouth into an alien shape. "Mama," he called, then he remembered the missionaries, and their Gods, and he called out, "Maria, Jesus, God," and he remembered what they teach at school, and he screamed, "Our father who art in heaven," and he fell down beside McCabe, whose face was deathly pale, and whose life was ebbing away as his blood ran through his clothes onto the red soil. Suddenly McCabe heard Bosman's words. He felt the doubt of life eternal, but maybe, maybe, he would have to face some God when he died. For death was coming, he was sure. His eyes fixed on Bosman, and he lifted his large left hand, his right hand was limp from pain. "Bosman," he said from the bubbling guttural throat, "Bosman, I heard you pray, 'Our Father who art in heaven, forgive me my trespasses.'"

Then Bosman, in his sobbing voice, joined him, and wrenched with hysterical sobs, he held McCabe's hand and in hopeless, helpless dejection, he stumbled and sobbed the words. Tears ran salty into his nose and mouth, as he kept crying out, desperately, "give us this day our daily bread and forgive us our trespasses, our father who art in heaven, hallowed by thy name, thy kingdom come, thy will be done, on earth as it is in heaven. Give us this day our daily bread and forgive us our trespasses as we forgive them that trespass against us, lead us not into temptation, but deliver us from evil," and he repeated, "deliver him from evil, God, and take him to heaven, for he is my father, God."

And he kept wrenching the words from his young body, "he is as my father, God," on and on, until the sounds in McCabe's throat ceased and his body became still and his face was calm and all went still.

Sixteen

With the abolition of slavery, the situation had become so explosive that it would have taken only a minor incident to detonate it. This came sooner than expected, when one day a military patrol out on a foray, retrieving stolen cattle, managed to shoot and wound a Kaffir chief. His bloodshed was so inflammatory among the natives the battle only spread like wildfire from Winterberg to the sea. 20,000 of Gaikas warriors surged upon the unsuspecting peoples and totally unprepared soldiers.

The settlers were murdered where they stood and others took refuge in churches. The vestry was occupied by the Lt. Col. England. Women and children were up in the gallery and men were searching and struggling to get in to use rusted weapons. All business came to a total standstill. Hottentots, loyal kaffirs, farmers and families came into the town for protection. Cattle, sheep and goats were crowded into the streets at night, by day they were taken to the nearby slopes and hills by men unfit to fight. The entrances of the streets were blocked by wagons and the central areas protected by the military cannons. All who reached

Grahamstown were given shelter. People were huddled together, shuddering and horrified at each fresh report of a murder or pillage, one woman gave birth after her husband was murdered, on the floor in the sanctuary of the church.

On the 4th of January, 400 armed burghers arrived from Uten-hage and patrols began to be more properly organized. But what devastation they found: incinerated homesteads and slaughtered stock. What had not been stolen had been destroyed. Gone were 15 years of grinding toil. It was in one of these patrols that Jan found himself. He and his friend and partner Piet Ritief. Retief had taught Jan even more about the veld and bush and though the country was in the wildest state of alarm they valiantly volunteered to help man the defenses. In the colony with widespread distress and confusion, all possible resources were mobilized. All boys over 16 were sent to the front. It was such a pitiful state of confusion and despair. Losses were appalling, 456 houses, mainly farmhouses, had been totally destroyed. Another 350 were partially destroyed but pillaged and severely gutted.

Thousands and thousands of horned cattle, almost 200,000 sheep, almost 6,000 horses were driven off by the natives and 60 wagons were captured and destroyed. So back went the settlers to their smoking ruins and devastated lands. There seemed once again little future and the horrible threat of starvation.

Jan slumped into his chair. Piet Retief tied up their horses. "My God Piet," he said, "for six hours today I listened to the tragic testimonies and horrors these people have suffered. Relief funds have come from Ceylon, India and Mauritius, but none from

England. Do you hear me Piet, none from their own people." Piet shuffled his veldskoen. "Ja, Jan, that verdammed London missionary society had sent to England their misguided and misleading reports. Gott,˙ how I hate these fanatics!" he said. "Religion, Jan, is nothing but a trouble maker. Now where then is God, that no help came to these people, especially the trusting ones? Those in England, those English believe we brought the war upon ourselves because of our bad treatment to the kaffirs—impoverishment to them!"

Jan was busy writing. No credence was given to this fact that never before had the kaffirs been so rich—in cattle and horses. Jan wrote and printed in his new busy press of the settlers losses, in property and stock—but there was no way he could measure their losses in human lives, broken families and ruined livelihoods. He and Piet soon got to work and the journal began to print the whole truth, the lamentations of the widows and the fatherless and the horrors of an eruption of savages.

In England, the situation was viewed quiet differently. Theirs was a picture of the wronged and abused blacks and colonial aggressors upon the helpless, uncivilized and ignorant victims. This was the picture in the public mind, especially for the Hottentots and shiftless, homeless lot of thieves, they seemed to be given special favor—"The Noble Savage" who was supposedly put upon by their bad and corrupted white exploiters. All the time Jan printed and published but resources were crippled and it was a cry in the wilderness and a painful attempt to make the settlers' outraged feelings public. He had no success in trying to change the policy of the tiresome English government.

Finally he joined Piet Ritief who formed a deputation and confronted the Lt. Governor who told them he would not budget one hair's breath. He, the governor, wanted equal rights for all

---

* Gott = Dutch slang word for God (guttural scraping throat sound).

classes. However, Jan's big success was at hand—it happened that an unarmed Kaffir was shot by the Lt. Governor Stockenstrom. The case aroused enormous interest and it was Jamestown Journal that exposed it all. It was proved that the shooting had been done, but was justified and condoned in time of war. However, the Lt. Governor, not satisfied, then charged the magistrate for maliciously a false charge. Long legal issues followed and the Court gave judgment for the magistrate on the grounds that it was his duty to investigate charges of injustice. Stockenstrom later resigned as Lt. Governor and was given a title of Baron and a pension of £700 a year. He returned and became a burgher.

Jan's persistent reporting and coverage made him part of the whole town's rejoicing when they won their case. He was acclaimed by all, he constantly wrote to encourage the people to apply themselves with verve and diligence and was involved with the publication of papers which aided the people on how to survive and defend themselves against being attacked by the barbarous enemy. Plans were offered for new houses with defense aids. They were double storied with ladders that could be effectively withdrawn, or narrow stairs that were easily barricaded. No longer were roofs thatched and covered in mud. All roofs were made of fireproof materials. It was about at this time that Jan's friend Braam Piet Retief persuaded him to trek north. From the hills of Refuge back home to Sonnestroom.

When Tante Tande, Moerskind, Lion and Marietjie returned home, smoke was smoldering everywhere—but they passed the horses on the way, which was a sign. Horses stayed together in a herd, it was strange that they were running free across the vast and wild area of the farm. Moerskind knew at once. He warned them all of impending disaster. Stopping the carriage a fair distance back from Sonnestroom he unbridled the horse and turned her loose. They then walked cautiously back. Lion let go of Marietje's hand and ran beside old Moerskind. Gradually they approached the homestead. It was early morning and the fires had been partially put out by the dewfall in the night.

It was strangely silent at Sonnestroom. Jan heard no roosters or the squealing of the pigs. He gave a little whistle, a whistle Boesman understood, and crouching behind the brush wall of the goat kraal he waited. He whistled again, and then he saw Boesman. The boy came out from somewhere in the home and stood staring, waiting for the sound of the whistle. "Boesman," he called and the boy came towards him. His hair was stuck together with dried blood, his lips were dry and he seemed drained and lifeless. Marietje and Tande ran up. They became hysterical, "Wat is dit Boesman!" they yelled in Dutch, "Wat is dit?" And Boesman just stood lifelessly. Moerskind took the boy, who answered in English. "Mama," he said, "Pa McCabe is dead. The Impis came, and we fought them, Pa McCabe and I, but there was one who had not died, and it was he who killed Pa McCabe. The Impi was injured, and hiding behind the barn," he burst into uncontrollable wrenching sobs, great, deep, dry, hopeless sobs.

Moerskind took his elbow and they walked into the death house. Tante was babbling in an up and down crescendo of sound, but Marietje said not one word. Boesman picked up the cloth that covered McCabe and he lay there staring at them. His eyes seemed fresh and blue, even in death. His beard was thick with black blood and beneath him pools of burgundy stain. His legs were rigid and from his lips a wet, pinkish fluid had oozed. "Boesman," he called, because he appeared that the women were quite useless. "It is you and I, Boesman, we are the men. You must take a horse and ride to Moorplaats." Tante took Lion by the hand and Marietje stood motionless, her lips were moving but she did not utter one word.

Death was everywhere. Pigs, chicken feathers and men, many black men, legs and arms everywhere, crumbled bodies that died where they fell. Boesman took Lion and ran for the reins. They were going to get a horse. They took a pail of wheat and barley and maize husks. It was not easy to catch a horse out in the veld and it was hours before they returned, but they finally came in with Soldaat and a mare. Boesman saddled the horse and taking the mare of a lead reign, he set off for Moorplaats. Lion ran behind him. "No, Boesman," he yelled, "let me ride with you." Boesman dismounted and returned for a saddle and almost with relief he let Lion ride beside him. "Mama," he shouted, "I will ride with Lion." Moerskind ran out with the musket. "Take it, Boesman," he said. "You know well how to use it. You are men, you are children, but you are men."

The boy reached out for the weapon and pushed it into the hold against the stockman's saddle. He was afraid. He was hungry and sickened by a feeling he did not understand. It seemed hard to make himself think, and now here was his smaller half-brother who wanted to ride with him. He felt better not to be alone. The horses, driven on by the smell of blood, sensed danger and raced on towards Moorplaats at great speed. They were not carrying heavy weights and only slowed down when they came to a drift. Both boys squeezed hard their legs and stayed on, holding the reins with wet hands. They knew the track to Moorplaats and so did the horses. They had been well trained by Pa McCabe. They rested at the drift and watered the horses and all the while both kept scanning the bushes.

Xosa brought Jules and Kathleen and the two children cautiously back. He had returned on foot first to see if all was safe. Marta and Klaasie never left. Klassie was clothed in the skins of a warrior beneath his trousers and he had many assegai in his rooms. Of course they were a collection of Impi assegais, but they were his now. He was certainly not going to allow his cattle to be driven off, so he had stayed, and in Impi dress he guarded his cattle. The Impis came in small numbers and though they fired a few outbuildings, they left taking only a small flock of sheep. When Jules asked why their losses were not so great, Xosa pointed to a weird blood-smeared totem pole around which was the jawbone of a hyena and tied at the top of the pole was a dead chicken with a small miniature assegai through its eyes.

All around the area in a crescent shape were feathers, all kinds of feathers, elephant hair, springbok tails and masses of bush pigs teeth. A fire's embers underneath a smoky clay pot stood outside the front of the homestead. Jules looked east towards his great Merino flock. There they were, all safe inside their stone-walled kraal. "Thank God Kathleen," he said. "I'd thank Xosa," said Kathleen, "Xosa's magic." A small flock of sheep was a small price to pay when all across the colony were death, destruction and devastation. Kathleen looked toward the strange concoction of Xosa's witchcraft. Against the Impis magic, it was mightier than the sword. As she gazed at the blood stained pole, far back in the blue distance her eye caught sight of two moving objects. "Jules, Xosa," she called in an agitated tone, "look Jules, I thought they were buffalo, but they are not moving this way."

She stretched out her arm and indexed towards the two moving shapes in the distance. Xosa scaled up a tree to get a better view, but the objects had disappeared down a little valley, appearing and disappearing. Suddenly there they were again, clear as day. They were moving horses, going at a desperate pace. She thought of Sannie. "Oh God, not Sannie, not the Rheeders. Or Daddy, no, Daddy would never ride a horse at such a pace," she said. Jules stood waiting. They were all waiting for the horses to come into view. Boesman shrieked, "Xosa, it's Boesman! Baas Jules!" The horses galloped up the track dripping wet with froth at the bit and white foam in between the hind quarters.

They were steaming hot, and Boesman slid from the saddle. "Miss Kathleen," he called, "Pa McCabe is dead. Mr. Jules, you must come! Pa McCabe caught an assegai in the chest, it went right through and out of his shoulder. And he's dead, I know he's dead. I covered him up and Moerskind said I should go to you, and Lion rode with me all the way, and Mr. Jules, you must come." He slumped down beside them, utterly exhausted. Lion came up. He looked like Fred McCabe, a tall, strong boy, 10 years old. He was flushed and red and his wet curls stuck to his forehead. "Boesman stayed with Pa McCabe while Mama took me in the carriage to the hills, and Tante and Moerskind came with us," he said. "We all went, and then when we came back the Impi killed the pigs and fowls and drove off the cows. But Pa McCabe had let the horses free and they had run and run. Boesman got the Impi, but he had first got Pa with the assegai."

They took the two boys in and sat them down. Kathleen brought them milk and bread with Konfyt made from a pig melon. She felt a wave of nausea. She knew not from what. "What now Jules?" she said, and she wept and wept. This was no time to leave his family. Jules needed all the men at Moorplaats and was loathe to leave his wife and children. The children were happily occupied with a little lion cub, "Tombi" that Kathleen found stranded near the hills and she saved it for Lion. The little cub was weak and hungry, probably too weak to have kept up with the pride, or its mother. Kathleen would never have left it. "Does it not remind you of Lion?" she asked. "See they look like each other. I would like to give this little cub to Lion. It suits him, don't you think?" No one gave a ready answer but she had already decided this was her gift to Lion.

Until they had word that all was peaceful, he could not risk leaving his family. He closed his eyes. He felt as though a great weight was upon him and it made him sullen. He felt a sensation of almost brutal hate. My God, if the Impis were near, he'd take pleasure in blowing off their heads, their merciless thick skulls. What was it that kept them from his home? It could only have been Xosa's weird magic, for nothing is left when the Impis pass. No beasts, no homes, no food, no white people, not even a dog. They're all destructive, like a ranging fire, nothing is left.

He thought of Fred McCabe. McCabe, there was a man! Yes, it was hard to think of him dead at the hands of the Impi. He seemed almost beyond destruction by assegai, so powerful and determined. Kathleen's shock was still to come. Oh, yes, he knew Kathleen. Hers would be a private shock, somewhere in her dreams or among her flowers, aloof, proud Kathleen. There she would wrestle the void that is her beloved father. He thought of his brother Jan, how he needed Jan. My God, he thought; he felt stricken with apprehension. Perhaps he was developing this unbalanced attitude of fear, or what was called "frontier mentality."

After several days of scouting and careful spoor tracking, Xosa came to tell Jules he thought that all was clear, so he prepared Boesman with his snaphaan and Klassie and Kathleen and Lion all with muskets and everybody slept inside the long large room with yellowwood floors. He and Xosa loaded lots of ammunition, then rode over to Sonnestroom. They rode straight in at full gallop and were met by the stench of rotting flesh. Vultures were perched everywhere. Moerskind was digging a hole. It was to be the grave of Baas McCabe, and there beneath the roughly woven sisal cloth protruded the veldskoen and leather knee breeches of Kathleen's father. It was so strange, he also wore his English tail coat. He had been dead days now.

It was clear to Moerskind that some of the slaughtered pigs could be salted and put in the cool stone room, so he had cleaned and gutted and heavily salted them. They hung decapitated from the rafters. He had not moved McCabe for each day he had hoped to see Miss Kathleen come to take her father. Dead Impis lay everywhere, flies buzzed like swarms of bees. There were feathers and burned out fires and vultures sat in the hundreds up in the trees. Jackals and hyenas had taken pieces of flesh from the remaining pigs, and even in the trees were bundles of feathers. Parasitic life preyed on the putrid flesh and hyena spoor marked the softer parts of the sand. Moerskind came running towards them, "Ach Meneer," he said, "Baas Jules, all is dead!" He had lost his front teeth now and he held up his two gnarled hands before his mouth, either to cover his emotion or his missing teeth. He was spent and tired. "Where is Tante and Marietje?" they asked. "Marietje, Mevrou Marietje is sick, Baas, and Tante is beside her." Both Xosa and Jules went inside.

The room where Fred McCabe slept was built into a fine large room now, with tall windows and long yellowwood beams. The house was only gutted where the old thatch roof remained, which was only the veranda. Marietje lay on the bed, her eyes were vacant and staring. She had torn all the clothes from her body and ripped them into pieces. She had curled her body into a fetal position, her arms clasped tightly about her knees. She had tied a cloth around

her stomach in a bandage-like way. At the sight of Jules there was
a flicker of recognition, and as though memory had returned to her
she uncoiled. "Miss Kathleen," she said haltingly. With trembling
fingers, she untied the bandage from her abdomen, and from
within it, she took an envelope. It was addressed to Kathleen. "To
Be Opened In The Event Of My Death," was written across it.
She handed it to Jules. Marietje was guarding it with her life, her
promise to McCabe to deliver safely this letter, Kathleen's letter.
Even in her shocked demented state, that one thought was quite
intact: a long melancholic reflection of the uncertainty of life.

They made a rough casket from the wood stock in the stable.
They made it where his body lay. Xosa was careful not to hurt him
as they rolled his body over onto the wooden bottom before they
put the sides on. It was the most, and all they could do. The hole
was just a little deeper than 4 feet. They slid the casket across the
earth until they got to the hole, then they let it down, scraping it
against the rough sides with plaited riempie ropes. They threw
in the ropes as well. It was easier to make new ones than retrieve
those that tied the casket. It was an ugly sound, the sound of dry
gravel, hard, rough and cruel, on the casket. They shoveled it on
in silence. No one said any words. Jules and Xosa and Moerskind.
It was a job that had to be done.

200 meters from the homestead was a deep hole Kathleen
had once wanted as a well. Weeds had grown all over it and thick
criss-cross poles were laid over the top to prevent accidents. One
by one they dragged the Impis and dropped them head first down
the well hole. There were 9 in all, and as Jules looked in, there were
arms and legs and plumes sticking up everywhere. All over the yard
were drag marks like one sees in the bush when a lion kills. On
top of the dead Impis were piled the pigs, all those that had been

mutilated, as well as the guts of those that Moerskind salted. And they then all filled it up with earth, whatever mounds they found, until a mound of earth rose above the old well hole.

They went in to rest. Tante had a large pork roast and a pot of new pumpkin leaves. Marietje did not speak and Jules struggled to get her to say something. "Come home to Lion," he said. "Lion needs his Mama. And Boesman." At the sound of Boesman's name, she looked up with sad eyes. "Boesman," she said. "Boesman," and repeated, "Boesman," over and over with a sort of pleasing smile as though she were remembering him. Jules too was too restless to stay. It was urgent to him and all he wanted was to go back to his family. He was greatly distressed about Marietje and he wondered what he should do. The first thing was to get back to Kathleen. He put her letter safely away and intended to set off in the morning. "Moreskind," he said, "if you are afraid, go into the house and look after Marietje. Very soon I shall return." He and Xosa, Xosa so strong and wise, rode back warily, watching every tree, anthill and movement.

Kathleen was waiting for them. She did not feel safe without Jules, alone with three children, a 15 year old boy and the servants. She breathed with relief when they rode in. Jules took her in his arms and held her. "I have a letter for you," he said, and he took it out from his saddlebag and handed it to her. They went inside and the children ran gladly to meet him, but not Lion or Boesman. They stood there waiting, they knew not what for. They felt like strangers in this house. They were not at ease. "Boesman," said Jules, "your mother has had a great shock." Lion stood waiting to be addressed. No one addressed him. "Your mother has had a terrible fright and she is now ill. You will both stay here with Miss Kathleen for a while. You can sleep in the yellow room and help with the farm," he said. "Morning time is lesson time," said Lion. "Pa McCabe gave me my lessons in the morning before the middle of the day." Jules thought for a while. "Boesman," he said, "perhaps you can help Lion." Boesman said, "No, Mr. Jules, I would prefer to work on the farm."

Kathleen had slid away to her bedroom. She sat at the bottom of the bed and opened her letter. It was dated "Feb 4, 1836." It said, "Kathleen my darling child, this is my last will and testament. All that I have, we have shared and most of what I own is yours. I would like it, Kathleen, if you and Jules would take care of my son Lion. It is my wish also that the boy Boesman be given a chance to make a life of his own. I would like him to have some of my horses. He may have one mare, perhaps and two others. He has a great love for one of them, he will be able to tell which one it is, and I would like to leave him £50. He has a longing to go to the sea. Marietje, of course, may live in Sonnestroom for as long as she so desires and from my shares of the stock she may and should have sufficient funds. The carriage and horse is also for her, a dream she harbours come true. For somewhere in her obscure past, a carriage was always a symbol of social standing. I ask you, Jules, my dear son in law to see to this.

"What, you may ask, has become of your mother's jewels? Kathleen, it was her wish that you should have them and if you remember, together, we once planned to each plant a tree near the entrance of our Sonnestroom. You planted an orange tree, and I an aloe. Kathleen, at the root of that aloe, sealed in a watertight jar with beeswax, are your mother's jewels. Beautiful they are, some of which belonged to your grandmother. I intended to give them to you on the day that you had a son and gave him my name. I regret that my union with Marietje offended you; my life with her was more pleasant than it was without her. I was too old for wooing and looking and courting. One day, this land will reward you richly. It is ideal for sheep farming, Merino sheep. I care not where you bury me, but I had hoped to lie somewhere beneath the sods of Sonnestroom, somewhere among the lilies. I want no hollow show. Because of the uncertainty of life at present, I'm sending this letter with my devoted Mari and my son Lion into the hills. I ask that generosity is bestowed on all staff and that you see that they are treated fairly. Wherever you are, or wherever you may be, with you will be always the caring wishes of your devoted father, Frederick Heath McCabe."

Kathleen curled up into a heap. Her hair fell down over her shoulders. She gathered up the skirt of her crinoline and burying her face in the folds of the skirt, she exploded into heart-rending, uncontrollable weeping. Jules let her cry. Kathleen was not a woman who shared her tears. Her tears were private and for now, her tears were for her beloved father. Jules thought of the rough casket banging heavily on the sides of the shallow grave. It was not a fitting burial for so fine a man. It was raw and rough. No, indeed no, it was a burial for the empty corpse that once harbored a very fine man. It was a spent and useless thing, the breath was gone, and like the Hebrews teach, it is the breath that is the soul: Jules was overwhelmed by a feeling of hopeless bereavement, deep loss, aloneness and devouring finality. His stomach twisted like a purge. My God, this hopeless dejection. This was depression.

Trekking party moving away from the Cape.

S e v e n t e e n

Whether it was political opinion, blood or friendship, Jan was not certain. He knew he wanted to ride beside and together with the strength and determination of Piet Retief. Weary of the ravages of the black warriors, the distance between people and the laws and monetary compensation, Slag-tersnek Hanging, children reared with hatred, British soldiers who shot too easily, and too often, and living in hatred. Piet was merry, mustering all his herds, certain of his capacity to endure, tying crates of hens and chickens slung beneath his wagons. He was weary of constant stress and harass. There was only one way to go, and that was north. Those men, those convoys leaving the Cape Colony, big hearted, space loving, freedom seeking farmers who wanted nothing more than to be left in peace and to till the soil. They were the voortrekkers, and he wanted to follow, to cross the great watersheds to join the hunting and following rivers to their sources.

Into his wagon once again he took his press; someday when he found his Eden he would start again. But for now, he would join the tragic tidal wave of humanity and on his way he would visit his brother Jules and stay a while on his thriving sheep farm. That was how he thought of it. But whether the kaffirs had raided it or not, he knew not. He thought of Kathleen and Moorplaats. And he wondered how his family was. He and Piet spent several days melting pegs of lead and casting bullets.

Piet had selected a few servants, the trusted ones, and lashed his ploughs to his wagons. The dulled shears coated with grease and mud and rust. Seeds, wheat and mealies, corn, oats and vegetables, stones of fruits, peaches, plums and seedlings. God, one had a deep twinge of regret. A human life is so short, time and trees take so long to grow, but so with high hopes and dreams, with their guns over their knees, blankets rolled and bags of dried foods, biltong in bundles and new voelskoen and rush hats.

Piet knew how to pack and tie his wagon and Jan did likewise. Their wagons were different from the others. These were single men, so their bunks of lattice hide were narrow and neat, reaching down to lion and leopard skins on the floor. Well covered in wild pelts left a lot more space in the covered part of the wagon. Small tubs with brass bands stood in the corner of one side and a barrel for gunpowder beside it. A lantern hung suspended on a pewter colored chain, from the center of the crossbeam. Beneath his bunk were smaller tubs, some filled with brandy and some with wines. Outside above the brake blocks hung a bag made from the bladder of an elephant; it too was filled to bursting with water. A great round discolored stiff parchment ball lacquered with the white of an ostrich egg that swung from side to side like a brown, shining, fibrous balloon.

Both Piet and Jan walked their horses beside the wagons, stocky, strong Boer horses with big hooves and flaring nostrils. The wagon drivers cracked their whips like lightning slaps, calling the oxen's names in a strange, wild form of communication. Goats, fowl and bleating sheep, barking dogs and voices; they were going north over impassable mountain ranges, crossing rivers and drifts, and floating their wagons over deep waters, always leaving behind them the track of their wheels, shallow furrows, through the long hard grasses. The spoors of their herds and their horses squashing and flattening trails to become a road for some other wandering followers. On the way they would call at Moorplaats and visit a while.

Eighteen

It was a slow, long journey from Grahamstown to Moorplaats, but full of wonder and breathless moments of awe! Pearly herds of zebra, thousands of wildebeest. Piet told Jan of the language of the veld. "Jan," he'd say at almost every stop or slowing down, "See that herd, those wildebeest are lead by a cow, usually a barren cow. She leads with a strange psyche. When she becomes aware of danger, her alarm is spread throughout the herd, who all become fractious and restive long before the sound signals even penetrate the outskirts. None question her moves or her telepathic communication. She may make mistakes, Jan, we all do, but her moves for the whole damn herd are usually clear and purposeful." He continued, "Ever wonder why zebra seem to be the popular friends of most herds? I don't know that this is true, but the black men tell me, and I'm sure they're correct, they, the zebra, are especially alert and constantly wary. They give the alarm, so all herds enjoy their company."

"Jan, what animals know about procreation?" he said. "We will never compete with, call it instinct, I say it's law. They only permit sex for a short period. Restraint, you see, and then intercourse, is selected only to the most beautiful and powerful of specimens. Most of the males lead a celibate existence. These bloody animals know. They have a code stronger than Moses' Bible, sterner than any religion, yet man interferes, and they're forced to depart from behaving in the pattern of their wild forebears. All animals, without exception, beat man, and Jan my friend, it's not without good reason. Is there some point where instinct is replaced by reason—one day we will understand. Sometimes I'm sure that the unlovely baboon—he knows—study them my friend, it amazes the mind."

Piet went on, "Watch their sentries, relieved and posted, their defense lines and social order. They can count to three, you know. The Hottentots will tell you better than I. If there hunters go into the busy and two return, those baboons know one is still there and you'll never out trick them. If you do, it will be only once." Jan listened for hours to the unending truths of the veld. Piet, his friend, his strong kind Boer friend, who read the flight of the birds and the spoor of the beasts, who knew the moods of the wild kindred like Moses read the Torah; so passed the ox pace days and timeless camp fire nights, glowing logs, weather beaten faces in the firelight, delicate tracery of leaves and branches above, and a closeness of comradeship scarcely paralleled in human affairs. Silence never hung over them; Africa is not a silent land. There is always sinister and watching eyes. Warnings, cries and threats, all part of the just love of the bush, expressed in a million varied voices of the veld.

There was great excitement for everyone the day the wagons arrived. Warm greetings and thankful feelings for their survival. Jan and Xosa clasped each other. Klaas, Marta and their sons were older now and the children were so tall. Kathleen's children! Kathleen was still a beautiful woman, her daughter showed promise of being a beauty. Jules was deeply tanned and careworn. Julius, their son, was thin and surly and Marietje, who had aged, was pale and vacant. They drank wine and ate, feasting on lamb. Sannie rode down to join them and to be sure, she was not left out of the news and excitement as they later drank their honey bush tea.

Braam Piet was as large and as imposing a man as Jules, with graying hair, a black beard that reached to his chest. His eyes fixed on the lion cub chewing on the sheep head. "Some day," he said, "he must go back to the bush." He bent down and touched it, and the cub growled in a fearsome way, protecting his sheep head. Piet had met Jules' children, Moya, who was 11, and Julius who was 10, and then he saw the two boys, Boesman and Lion. Kathy called out, "Boesman," who came forward, a tall gangly youth, standing on the brink of manhood, a Braam meneer. "Piet Retief, this is Boesman, the son of Marietje," she said. "Go on, Boesman, shake hands," and timidly Boesman extended his hand. Piet Retief shook his hand. Kathleen then said, "And this is Lion. He wishes to be called Lion McCabe, the younger son of Marietje."

Piet looked from boy to boy. One had clear blue eyes and the other hand laughing hazel-brown eyes. They bore signs of a similar cut, and Braam Piet, the wily Piet, humourously remarked later, that both had "only a small touch of the bar brush, however good looking." Piet and Jan took shelter at Moorplaats and remained a long time, enjoying a family life they had never known before. They helped to build, for part of Piet's life earnings came as a result of building and contracting, they extended the homesteads, going up a second story, making a modern defense plan, a stairway that could be barricaded and used to protect all that was above it. They carried stone from all over the land, using the oxen and wagons.

It was marvelous how Piet's team was trained and the intelligence of the cattle was way in advance of the horses. Whenever they were called, the oxen would line up and walk forward to his place at the trek chain at the very call of his name, loaded with stones. The team would pull as one beast, their huge horns shining at the tips, in the sun, with their yokes on thin necks, fastened by straps of rawhide to the yuk skey. When one was out of line, the driver would call his name, and he would correct his position. The wheelers who kept the wagon from leaving the road, helping with the braking and easing in an almost human way were especially chosen for their high intelligence.

At evening time, when the oxen came home to the shelter of their kraal, Piet would stand near the entrance as they passed single file. He'd run his hand down their spines, "Goodnight, Vaalpence," "Goodnight, Sox," "Goodnight, Pietsboy," each one till 23 oxen were safely inside the kraal and night food aplenty filled the contraptions on the sides that Piet called the mangers. Piet loved his span, his "boys" as he called them, and it was a heartwarming sight to see.

Life at Moorplaats with Jan and Piet was unusually pleasant, progressing at great speed and with much more security. Wherever this unusual Boer went were learning and laughter. He was so able in every way, and from his ever-alert brain they all gleaned. The longer he stayed, the taller grew Moya, and kindling within her girlish soul that flashed in her amber eyes were the rumblings of a woman.

Horses foaled and cattle gave calves. It was joyous when heifers were born. Fillies and heifers and ewes were good; a farmer was lucky when heifers were born, but for himself, a farmer wanted sons. Jules had only one son, and Kathleen had not conceived again. This son worried him. He was quiet, surly and thin and showed great signs from his lugubrious expressions, resentment, and even jealousy. Not a happy child. Maybe it was because he was not as robust as Moya.

He had trouble with his breathing. His nostrils were always blocked and his breath was not pleasant. Kathleen was greatly pained by this and tried numerous herbal cures. They sent orders to Dr. Atherstone in Grahamstown, which were returned with a wagon that passed near the area. Often now, the wagons left taking wool to Algoa Bay, and many were coming in fast and furious. Ships were bringing out plows and tools, silver, china, seeds, wheat and cloth. Wagons regularly brought the goods to Moorplaats and always medicine for Julius. The farm had several wagons, trek wagons and half tilts and merryweathers Pieter Maritzburg had made a custom built four seater carriage which was always drawn by four horses.

In 1841 Lion turned 15. One night he was walking down towards the stream and found Marietje sitting on a stone beside the footpath. She was crying and choking and wet with perspiration. "I'm sick my son," she said. "I'm dying. I have such pain. It was a puff adder; on the way to the river, the river I love so much." Lion looked down at her yellow legs and the flesh was blackening and swelling. He was a strong boy, and picking her up in his arms, he ran to the homestead. "Miss Kathleen," he called, "Miss Kathleen!" And they all came out as they laid Merietje on the latticed bed. Xosa disappeared out of the door. Jules slashed the wound with his hunter's knife. Lion sucked at the wound, spitting out the blood into a cloth. Xosa returned with a dead chicken and put the bloody flesh upon her wound. Braam Piet tied a tourniquet above her knee and Kathleen bathed her face.

Poor Marietje looked too terrible; her eyes bulged in fear and her heart throbbed visibly in her neck, an irregular, faulty pulsation. "Call Boesman," she said, "Lion my beloved son, your nameless brother." When Boesman was found, he hastened to her bed. He smelt of horses and his hands were dirty. "Mama," he said, "I'm here, Mama. I was working on the carriage, Mama, the carriage you love, your carriage." He looked at his mother, a frail yellow woman with large doe-like eyes and long black hair. She was swelling up, becoming bluish purple. "You will have a good life, Boesman," she said, "your life must be good. Help your brother and stay together. My father was a burgher, a Dutch burgher, my mother a slave. It was hard to be a slave. She was so pretty, I sometimes see her face!" She lifted her hand to wipe the beads of perspiration from her nose and brow, but the effort seemed too much and her long brown fingers slumped across her chin and mouth.

Boesman lifted her arm gently and placed it at her side. 'Mama," he said, "who was my father?" He repeated in a voice breaking with emotion and desperation. "Mama, tell me, tell me please, mama, you would never tell me, who is my father, tell me now." Her eyes opened wide, her breath was short. Her mind wandered into the past, she spoke of other places and her mother, and she chuckled now and then, trying to focus her eyes, "Ladybird, ladybird, fly away! My children" she muttered with light brown hair and blue eyes. The muscles and limbs were visibly enlarging collapsing into swollen masses. She was gasping as if in pain as though her heart no longer wanted to pump. Her neck started to swell and words no longer came easy. She was struggling for breath and nothing or anyone could help. Death was taking her—like a crawling canopy of locusts over a wheat field.

Braam Piet came panting in. He had gathered herbs, which he had searched for out in the veld. He crushed it up, mixed it with water, put his hand behind her head and lifted her head to get her to swallow, but the muscles of her throat seemed to paralyze. She seemed unable to swallow and the fluid ran down her mouth onto her chest. Slowly she spoke. She squeezed the words out now. "My seun,* my sleintjie, my kinder, liefde, kinders my seintje, Boesman, 'ons was kinde,** Boesman," she muttered on incoherently, "net kinde,***" hy is jou Pa Boesman, onse seuntjie, jou pa is a ladybird," she gave a sort of chuckle. "He is your father and he flew and flew and flew away," and a rattle seemed to move down instead of her breath, and they all stood watching, and Braam Piet said, "Bring me the Bible," but nobody moved.

Boesman and Lion stood transfixed and they watched and watched and their tears ran down and splashed onto the floor and they stood muffling sounds and helpless until the phlegm-like rattle in their mother's chest became silent and she breathed in, and never breathed out.

Once again on the kopje, another mound, and another stone. Boesman and Lion found a huge flat tall stone and they asked Piet Retief if he would get the oxen to drag it to the kopje. Two oxen pulled it sledge-like across the field and finally to the grave of Marietje. "Thank you, Mr. Retief," they said, and looking him in the eye they asked, "Mr. Retief, what was it our mother said? It was Dutch and it's been so long since we spoke Dutch. It was difficult to understand." Lion understood nothing. He was a fine looking boy was Boesman, he gave one a feeling of goodness, healthy, like a fresh baked wheat loaf. He had beautiful white teeth and his hair had grown curly, as dark as his young beard. "Your mother spoke of being a child," Piet said, "'a childhood love,' she had said, 'we were children,' she said. I take it she meant she and her childhood love, and she spoke of her little boy, her little Boesman, and a ladybird who flew away, who was the father of her little Boesman." Boesman

---

* my seun = my son
** ons was kinde = we were children
*** net kinde = we were just children

asked, "Do you know who the ladybird was? I understand he was my father? One of the first persons who owned this farm?"

"He was," replied Piet, "he was the elder son, Willem. He had a brother Pieter, who would rightly be your uncle. They, your father and uncle, bought Mr. Jules' ship, well, they exchanged Moorplaats for a ship, and they now trade across the seas. I am told they have become very wealthy now, trading, and have helped build a wharf near the mouth of the Buffalo river. Their ship often calls. I heard when I left with Mr. Jan that they were negotiating the purchase of another ship," he said. "You do know that the graves of the de Swarts are those very near to your mother's grave, the resting places of, I think your father's parents, who were murdered."

Lion was suddenly there beside him, a lovely hazel-eyed boy of 15. He spoke up. "What shall we do now, Mr. Retief?" he asked. "You said you were going north one day. Please take me with you Sir. I am growing up now. I want to go with you. Often I have this desire to kill, sometimes when I lie on my bed and think of my father, I want to get up and go out and kill. The Impis. I would just like to kill them all, or as many as I can. They steal and rob and kill. They burn down houses and plunder cattle. I see them without mercy. I hate them all, Mr. Piet. My mother said to love my brother," he looked at Boesman, "I do love you, Boesman, though we have different fathers."

"Why should you love me, Lion?" said Boesman, "No reason at all, Boesman," said Lion. "Perhaps because my father taught me how best to live. It is restful to sleep on good feelings. We are odd people, you and I, Boesman. We are of mixed blood, the both of us. We have the mark of the Hottentot. We will always come second."

"Not me, I'm not accepting seconds. And never you Lion, Lion you should be the noble Lion—a strong brave and respected leader.

That's how I see you." "You Boesman, you must do for yourself what you are preaching to me to do." "That is exactly how I'm thinking Brother there will be no 'Second' for me. I plan to live as good as the next man: right up there where my dreams come from."

1840 was a bad year; a prolonged drought wreaked havoc on the colonies. Crops were especially poor because swarms of locusts descended and destroyed. The failure of the seasonal rains as in the past, caused cattle thefts to increase. News was very bad, the Battle of Blood River was on the tongues of everyone and still the burghers moved onwards to cross the Vaal River to go North.

Almost uncannily Moorplaats was flourishing and so was Sonnestroom. Br Piet Retief and Jan lived at Soonestroom, which over the years had grown closer to each other due to expansion. The land was cleared and roads were widened. Buildings were everywhere, sheep paddocks and kraals, cattle pens, pastures and cornfields. New settlements were made for new workers, Hotten-tots mainly, and loyal fingoes, who had moved up when their boundaries were pushed back. Wagons moved to and fro frequently and more swiftly. More horses were being used to carry goods down to the sea to the ships.

Boesman had a way with horses. He always had, so he was given the work of caring for all the horses. He helped stallions mate and helped their mares foal. He rode and trained. He himself was well cared for, earned a good living and lived in an extension of the house at Moorplaats. His brother Lion was in a similar extension built by Piet and Jules. Moya and Julius lived on the wing that faced the north, so Julius got the morning sun but they never grew up as a family and never grew close. Julius was insulting to Lion and often Kathleen witnessed actions worthy of severe reprimand. Once while Thombe, Lion's pet lion, was eating a carcass of a duiker,

Lion was sitting beside her, his legs dangling down near her head. Julius crept up quietly and banged her across the tail with a heavy cane, causing her to spring upon Lion and the deep scars remained upon his legs. Had it not been for the fact that Kathleen was at that very moment looking down from the armory, Thombe might have inflicted a lot more injury. But, trained to run at a gunshot, the lion stopped when Kathleen fired.

There were many incidents of unpleasantness and as they grew older it seemed to Kathleen that Julius was becoming more taciturn, morose and introverted. He wrote "Servants Quarters" across Lion's door and often referred to him as the "half-caste lodger." He was not a good horseman and resented cruelly the horsemanship of Lion and Boesman. But Boesman was proud of Lion's skill and took it upon himself to keep Lion the unbeaten master, the best. Never, as far as he was concerned, would Lion ever be second.

Suddenly one day Piet and Jan decided to trek north. It was not forever they said; they would cross the Dragenberg, explore the north and return to farm sheep. Sheep had got into Piet's blood now, and his interest was mainly in sheep. Wool was moving at a great pace and ships were waiting for more. Jules begged him to stay. Perhaps it was his veld love, knowledge, his ability, his strength, all those things together with his laughter, but the thought of Piet leaving was almost unbearable, they were so happy together. He and Jan brought much pleasure and security to Moorplaats. No one questioned Piet's ideas or suggestions. They were always good. Everyone loved him. Everyone, including Moya. She was 15 now, with long brown legs and a flashing smile. Her breasts shuddered on her taunt young body as she ran and rode and drove the wagons.

"Piet's going north," Julius told her one morning. She swung around. "No Julius, he didn't say that, did he?" "He certainly did, dear sister mine," said Julius, "and don't look so drained. He's much too old for you, Moya." "No, no, no Julius," she said, and gathering up her skirts she ran out down the meadows towards the stables. She called to Boesman, "Saddle my horse, please Boesman, saddle my horse." "You must not ride alone, Moya!" he said. She grabbed the saddle and throwing it across the horse's back, she tightened the girth, leapt on in one neat mount and sped off, the horse snatching at his bit, broke into a gallop as she disappeared over the hills and into the distance towards Sonnestroom.

A Kudu bull sleeping in the shade of a guenya tree sprang up and bounded off, leaving a cloud of dust rising into the air. Boesman ran down to the homestead. "Mr. Jules," he said. "Moya has taken her horse and gone out without her gun. She seems very agitated." "What's unusual about that, Boesman?" Jules said. "Moya often rides alone." "No, Mr. Jules, today was different. There was fire in her eyes, she was wild, Mr. Jules." Jules was slightly disturbed, but he was used to Moya's outbursts. She was almost a woman now and women are supposed to be restless and unpredictable at her age. No, he would wait a while and see if she returns.

Nineteen

nside, Jules told Kathleen. Kathleen listened, wiping her hands on her voerskoot,* as Marta called it. She gave a tired sigh. "I've been noticing, Jules. Moya is soft and ripe as a ripe peach. She looks at Piet in a most inviting manner and drops her head when he looks at her," she said. "Isn't it strange how men pretend to like modesty in a woman, when what they really like is wanton looseness? We all are unfaithful to ourselves, aren't we? We women, it's not that easy to control the desire to be wanted and less easy to control? The want what desires create. She's very headstrong, Jules. We will take a one-half tilt towards Sonnestroom. Tell Boesman to get ready the half tilt."

Moya galloped on for quite a while. She was an impetuous young girl, and ready for a romance. Because she found herself in close proximity with Piet, it was Piet who became the object of her attentions. Boesman was a beautiful young man, ever conscious of himself, not his parentage. He was a most eligible suitor, but he held no attraction for Moya; he was just the young man who tended

---

* voerskoot = apron.

the horses. He lived at her home because her grandfather wanted it that way. In a way she almost resented his presence. No, it was Piet who was wise and did everything well. Once, when he lifted her down from a roof, she trembled when she felt the hardness of his powerful body. She almost wilted when she looked into his eyes. He was her desire, her fantasy, her very existence, for now. No, if Piet went away she would surely die. And Piet; she saw him looking at her. She knew by instinct that he knew so much about—well, if he knew so much, then he knew how she felt.

And as her horse tired and she slowed down, she suddenly realized she was out in the veld alone and unprotected and probably half way to Sonnestroom. The gray Laurie (go away bird) shrieked its go away call and she wondered whether she should proceed to Sonnestroom or return to Moorplaats. She came to a halt, and turning in her saddle, she scanned the road past the trees and anthills. "My God," she thought. If the Impis got her, what would happen? She thought of the heinous things they were known to do, castration, breasts cut off, rape and torture, and her thoughts made her afraid. She was unsure of the distance she had covered, but the horse seemed eager to return. He was pulling at the bit, throwing up his head and swinging his hind quarters round and round in a prancing, restless way, eager to get moving.

Hot and snorting, he was difficult to control. He began to rear, picking up his front feet and taking little leaps into the air. With each jerk of his head, he almost pulled Moya out of the saddle. Then it all went wrong. One of his legs went down into a hole as he reared and threw him completely off balance. The girl came out of the saddle and the reins were ripped from her hands, before she could gain her footing, the horse was up and galloped off, tail and reins dangling, at a full gallop.

Terror seized at the girl's insides. It was late afternoon and she was alone in the veld. The nights were always cold and the unknown, forbidding. She was unarmed and a long ride from the safety of her home. She stood on the track trying to get her thoughts together. Someone would come and look for her, her parents or Xosa, or Boesman, but someone would come. She armed herself with a long stick and then looked for a tree near the road. There she knew she would be able to see whoever was coming and whatever would come. There was a large wild African plum tree with its red and yellow-tinged fruits hanging in bunches. Yes, this was near the road and she could climb it quite easily if she had to. My God, there were wild dogs, hyenas, lions, leopards and elephants. She scanned the tree in case of leopard, no, all was clear. This would be her tree.

She sat down beside it, resting her back against the trunk. Every call or distant echo made her nervous and more afraid, and night seemed to be arriving so quickly. All the birds were heading for home and those in the trees were singing an evensong above the kloof. The light was fading and she looked towards the long dry reeds nearby. She looked through the latticed leaves, soon it would be night, and the nights were more alive than the days, more dangerous, full of growls and barks and watching eyes filled with fears, death ever ready, walked everywhere. Unsubtle, undisguised quick and sudden, and jackals howled and huge-jawed hyenas laughed.

A troop of vervet monkeys ambled along, towards her tree. They were coming for a feed of its fruits before going to bed. But when they saw her, they shrieked and screamed, running up around the tree, long tails held out straight behind them, faces fierce and resentful. Some mothers had babies clinging to their stomachs and they all seemed to make a mock attack. Moya stood with her back to the tree trunk, and started to cry. She cried and cried.

It was almost dark when Jules, Kathleen and Xosa passed the riderless horse. Kathleen had a nauseous spell. "Oh God, Jules," she said, "I couldn't stand to lose a child!" Xosa, ever hopeful, assured them Moya would be safe. He kept repeating that. Her horse was a skelm.* They lit the oil lantern and it swung form side to side as they went along. Jules drove the horses and Xosa scouted, eyes alert to every sign and movement. It was a merciless ride on the horses, traces tightened all the way. They found their weeping Moya on the road. She was hysterical and out of control. So they rested the horses and returned cautiously to Moorplaats. Very little was said. There was not much to say, and it was not the time. But there would be a time to talk.

In the morning, no one broached the subject of Moya's journey, nor the great anxiety she had caused her family. Instead there was great excitement for Thombe had left her straw bed under the wagon in the night and had gone hunting. Now she had made her first kill. There she was, dragging a springbok across the vlei towards the yard. It seemed to have helped solve a problem somehow, because the family often wondered, what would happen with Thombe? Was it to be that she would have to be fed for as long as her sojourn with people lasted? But not at all. Thombe was a girl of great character and independence, not to mention her feline cunning and strength. Thombe, beloved, dear Thombe, had grown up and out, and with sadness they all knew she would gradually return to her wilderness or maybe be shot by a hunter.

_____

* skelm = bad or naughty.

Africa was fast becoming plagued by these goddamned murdering killers. The burghers were all hunters, and now many settlers had started to do the same, trading tusks and skins. Thombe was Lion's great love. He fondled her like a kitten, rolling over and over together in the buffalo grass. She always was careful to retract her claws, often taking his whole buttock or head or foot in her huge jaws in playful bites. It was not so long ago that Thombe was just a snarling, spotted cub hissing and growling, yet dependent upon this family for her life. Now she was free. Thombe could hunt and kill, so she could survive. Their little lion that was reared on goat's milk might well kill the very cows or goats that saved her.

"Lion," called Kathleen, "Once Thombe has got the taste of blood and killing, it will become a very common occurrence," she said. "Perhaps you should give her to Braam Piet. Perhaps he will take her into a safer, wilder land when he goes north with his wagons." At the mention of Piet's name, Moya was triggered into near hysteria. She raced back into the homestead and into her room, flung herself onto her bed, rolling from side to side as if in agony and burst into loud, uncontrolled sobs. The look in Jules' eyes told Kathleen it was her business as a mother and a woman. She started to think how best she could comfort her child.

Julius watched his delicate, white-handed sister writhing on her bed, and with sadistic delight, he burst out laughing. "So, the old man didn't come to your rescue Moya? And you're crying now because you didn't get your own way? He didn't come galloping up upon his steel gray Boereperd?"* He looked down at her with a sneering expression. "Piet's steel gray hair that matches his steel

* Boereperd = Boer horse.

gray boereperd?" he said. "Oh, be damned with you, Julius," she cried tearfully. "It must be horrible to be like you! It's no wonder that no one cares for you. You are so thoroughly unpleasant. That's why Thombe always growls and snarls at you. Animals have a sixth sense we don't have. You know she knows you are nasty and mean and jealous. You may deceive mother, but you don't deceive me, brother. Get out from my room, go on, go away," she said.

She turned over face down. She stopped crying now. There was an uncomfortable silence, so she looked up, he was still standing there. He had narrowed his eyes and the look on his face was full of hate. "God damn it, Julius," she said. "How ugly you look. I wonder what evil thoughts you're brewing? Please go away and let me alone." She looked in the direction of his gaze. Outside the window, Lion had come in from the fields, Thombe had loped over to greet him and they tumbled and played and fondled each other, over and over, two lions who loved each other. Moya looked out of the window where Julius was staring. "You see Julius," she said, "that is love, something you will never know."

During the night when Kathleen and Jules were lying in their bed, talking, waiting for that wondrous feeling of falling into the arms of sleep. They discussed Moya, and decided it was best to let the incident pass without fuss. They talked about Lion, brave, strong Lion, he, who was actually Kathleen's half brother, but he was strong and willing, always there to lend a hand, smiling and happy and full of compassion, an able lad, who rode with verve and had an honest tongue and eye. He was a passionate human, and also knew when to be compassionate. To see him with his lion lady was a rare and wondrous sight. They rolled over and over. The lioness had her jaws around his throat. They made strange sounds—fantastic wondrous bond of love. A huge gentle beast and a strong human being—bonded by an indescribable tenderness, a powerful indestructible love.

And Boesman, this aloof, quiet man who loved his horses and enjoyed being alone. Boesman, devoted to her father who was his anchor and friend, brutally removed from his life, forever removed from his fatherless life. He was a dreamer, and no one seemed interested in knowing his dreams or dared to trespass into his field of thought. Just Marietje's son, a wanderer with a searching soul, a distant boy, part Hottentot, and part white.

And they talked of Julius, their baby! Where had they gone wrong? He was not as robust as any normal boy his age, yet he was also not a dull boy. In fact, if learning was any indication, he was highly intelligent. He learned to read and write and spell much faster than any other child. Yet he was filled with resentment. He hated both Boesman and Lion. He tormented and ridiculed his sister and blamed everyone except himself for his own misdemeanors. He fabricated and lied and insinuated unpleasantries. He was jealous and often showed strong sadistic inclinations, selfish and devious. He was a problem.

And time passed.

Twenty

How the years had sped. Braam Piet Retief and Jan had only come to Moorplaats to visit. They were intending to go North, but Jules had made them a generous offer in sheep farming with him and they had remained on, to man and develop the farm. It grew from strength to strength and now it was a very large estate, with larger flocks, producing Type 5, wonderful wool, which was sought after and bought by every ship that called at all the ports. Their buildings too, became far superior to all others, all with defenses, barricaded stairways. The stream was dammed by a natural clay wall, paddocks were secured. Jules had several small, friendly groups hired by Xosa, stationed and living at selected points and all around the perimeter with runners and lookout posts as a further means of protection.

Andrius Stockenstroom, now a baronet, had retired and the treaty system had broken down. Broken down, Jules often said, because of the great trek and the 6th frontier war. However, cattle thefts were great, triggered off by the drought and to make matters worse, a devastatingly large swarm of locusts. The boys were young adults as it was! So it was Boesman, Lion, Julius, and Moya. New servants came and went, but old Marta, Klassie, Xosa, Moerskind and Tante were still there. Their sons were now some of the best workers and several of them had already taken wives. Jan and Braam Piet often took a wagon to other towns to call upon the widows. Widows were plentiful after the last war, and it was these ladies, together with other soldiers' wives, who set the social standards.

The bad rains, locusts, crop failures increased, cattle thefts and an incident over the theft of an axe triggered off the 7th Frontier War. Just as did Jenkins' ear, the old English sea dog in 1739 which deeply involved both England and Spain, or the Serbian patriot who assassinated the Austrian Archduke in Sarajevo and embroiled practically the whole of Europe in the first world war in 1914.

It seemed doubtful now whether Jan and Braam Piet would trek north after all. Disturbing news of unrest among the natives drew them all together in a front of strength, for survival. Martial law was to be proclaimed right into the horrors of war. No, it would be unfair to trek just now, something in the atmosphere forbade it. In exchange for their help and support, Jules made them partners in the farm. Each had powers of direction and decision. The trusted servants were housed in fireproof upstairs houses, stairways narrow and barricaded. Braam Piet had built superb kraals and stone paddocks unequalled by any other burgher and people came form far to see the modern advances at Sonnestroom and Moorplaats.

As the year grew, so did Kathleen's children. They were able to shoot well, handle double-barrelled guns, muskets and whatever new ammunition Jules had got from England, Holland and Spain. It was always clear to Jules that guns and ammo were of the utmost importance and a top priority.

One evening at twilight, young Julius took his guns and went on a hunt, down over the river and onto the hill slopes on the other side. He had walked for some time, then finding a rock that looked like a seat, he sat down upon it, beside an anthill that had been all hollowed out by an antbear. Birds were everywhere, glorious, singing in evensong. Rollers, weaver birds, egrets, guinea fowl, some preying on the lowly voetgangers* that crawled over the red ground. A curly-horned sheik herd** of impala were bounding in and out of a small open glade. He was just about to aim and shoot when he saw the lion. It looked like Thombe; yes, he was sure it was. Thombe, he recognized her by the white patch on her breast. She was stalking an impala. He stood up and watched her. "Nobody cares about you, not even Thombe," he heard his sister's words, and he saw her romping with Lion McCabe. How Lion loved his Thombe! And what did Thombe mean, yes, it meant "girl."

He didn't like Thombe mainly because Thombe didn't like him. He crept closer, sure it was Thombe. She slowly lifted her heavy paws, getting ready for a sprint and spring. "Thombe," he called, and she looked up and towards him. He took aim, he'd show them. He pulled the trigger full blast into her great yellow unsuspecting eyes. She gave a strange grunt and her forelegs crumpled under her. When Julius came home, he acted a scene he had practiced in the bush. "Oh God," he said, "It was a terrible mistake, I have shot Thombe, I have killed Thombe." He put his hands over his face and rested his elbows on his knees. Moya let out an awful whine, "Lion," she called. "Lion," she screamed, "where are you, come here quickly, Julius says he's shot Thombe."

Swiftly Boesman ran for their horses and in a short time they were beside Thombe. She was still warm. There she lay beside

---

* voetganger = a walking pink red locust.
** sheik herd = a herd of females with one ram.

the open glade. Lion slid off the horse in a clean fluid move and cradled her head in his arms, running his hands all over her great tawny body. "Oh Thombe, Thombe, what did he do to you," and he put his head upon her neck and he wept out loud, hard bitter sobs, deep, sad hurting sobs like a boy, for a beloved pet. Moya stood there silent, her tears fell down her shining cheeks. She remembered the look on Julius' face that day as he stared through the window and she felt sure Julius had killed Thombe. She felt cold and she covered her mouth with her hand to quell a violent purge of nausea.

Braam Piet came in from the fields with Jules. The home was full of weeping and Kathleen was trying to console her daughter and Lion. "There's been an accident, Braam Piet," she said, standing up and wiping both her hands on the front of her apron. Her hair was pinned into a golden bun and her eyes were red and wet. "Julius said he killed Thombe by mistake, Jules," she said. All the while Piet watched the boy. "Julius, have I not told you time and time again that you were not to go out hunting alone?" Jules said. "Yes father," said Julius. "And why then have you gone this time?" Jules said, "I actually went walking father, and only took the gun for protection. I did not mean to kill Thombe. I thought it was a hunting lioness, she was crouching and I could not identify her," he said.

"Give me that gun, Julius," said Jules. Julius handed it to his father. Jules looked at the gun and placed it on the floor. He was not sure what to tell his son. He taught them all to shoot; they had to shoot to survive, after all, was it not the only reason that they were still a family? Braam Piet lowered his eyes. He poured himself a large drink of wine, and he poured Jules an equally large one. He made no comment and they sat down and drank together. The whole incident perhaps made them drink too much. A wind started to blow. What's that they say about an ill wind! And as the wind blew through the gables he drank too much and he talked too much. It was a perplexing atmosphere and he knew something was very wrong. Moya was standing beside her father twisting her hair. She was looking straight at Braam Piet and in his semi-sober state he returned her gaze. She reached out and put her hand over his large roughened hands, and he patted her hand and began to smile a labored slowed down smile.

Jules left the room but Julius remained and he listened to Braam's haltingly semi-drunken words. He spread his legs out one hand on his left knee and he looked up at the beautiful Moya. "Ja, Moya, we all kill things and we feel all mixed up and sad. I shoot a kudu, you see, and it looks at me," he said. "It has no weapons. The beautiful look of innocence, and I pull the trigger and I drop it, and we eat of its flesh. I don't know if it's right or wrong. Men after all are hunters. He needs to eat and he needs to love, and often he has neither. You see, Moya, there may be lots of eat, and plenty to love, but neither may be what makes a man pleased and happy and often one has an ache in the heart and arms." She squeezed his hand, how often she dreamed of him wanting her, of him asking her. He caught the look in her beautiful eyes.

"Nee my lammetjie,* it is not for you my arms ache. Oom** Braam Piet loves you very much, but Oomie loves you as an uncle," he said. He sipped from his wine. "My lifelike miesie,*** you are the nearest thing to my family, but there is a woman, the very sight of whom makes my heart beat so it thunders in my ears, her creamy face and her red gold hair that tumbles down

* No my lamb
** Uncle
*** lovely girl

and blows in the wind. This is what haunts this oomie* of yours, that burns and kindles the ache in my arms, like a fire in the long dry summer grass," he said. Kathleen came into the room at that moment. She had prepared a wooden tray of little snacks. She stood there, as the wind blew through the open door, and her red gold hair fell down on her shoulder and lifted and blew it up around her creamy face.

Lion looked down at his beloved pet. His was deep hurting, somewhere, all over. "Thombe," he said, he sobbed, "you were a noble creature. I loved your powerful temperament. I loved you so deeply, I feel you appreciated growing up with people, in your way. One day, Julius, you will get your rewards, I swear Julius, I swear to all the powers that be, that I will revenge my Thombe's death," he said. "Your day will come, you evil pale face, you evil piece of pus-filled lion shit!" and he sobbed out loud as if he turned on an inner tap and let out a stream of pent up emotions. "Hateful nephew, your day will come!"

The next day brought good news, helping to block out the sorrow of Thombe's demise. Troops arrived that consisted of the 7th Dragoon guards and detachments of infantry, carrying double barrel guns at the advance, a few Bantu soldiers arrived in full Red and Brown array at the entrance to Moorplaats, handsome red clad soldiers. They were headed in command by a splendidly decorated officer wearing an inlaid gold pistol which, it later was disclosed, swas inherited from his father and captured in the Napoleonic Wars. They were reputed to have belonged to the emperor himself.

He saluted smartly, coming to attention. "Mr. Jules Jacobsen?" he said. "Col. Armstrong, sir." He extended his hand and Jules

* uncle

shook it. He requested privacy and was ushered into the living room. Government had decided that the defense of Moorplaats was vital to the economy of Albany and men were to be stationed all along its borders. Entrances and lookouts, all the sheep flocks and Devon herds would be under constant surveillance. Of course the men would set up their camps, but Jules was assured no damage or destruction would occur as the discipline would be fairly rigid. Instructions from government were that this protection would convene right away, and of course there would be considerably more traffic as the wagons carrying ammunition and provisions would arrive daily. Pack horses with spare ammunition and as always a rear guard to protect the supplies.

Col. Armstrong stood up. Jules was delighted at the prospect of military protection. It was agreed and settled and an agreement signed. The lieutenant who accompanied the colonel stood to attention at the side when Moya appeared. She had seen the arrival of the column and looking her radiant best, coquettishly requested permission to enter. The colonel's eyes were totally startled and transfixed. He stared at Moya, a beautiful young woman with long slim limbs, her fair hair gleaming and her wide eyes sparkling. "This is my daughter, Col. Armstrong, my daughter Moya," Jules said. "Her name means 'a gentle breeze.' A pretty name, wouldn't you say?" He took her hand and lifted it to his lips.

"Miss Jacobsen," he repeated, totally mesmerized by this fresh lovely young woman who confronted him. "My God," he thought "what a woman, so fine, to be out in a savage wilderness, where only soldiers fought and died." Armstrong was a dedicated and much decorated officer. His life had been too busy and unsettled for marriage. There were many women in his life and once the idea of marriage had appealed to him, but he was very young then.

Suddenly now the sight of this beautiful, fresh woman roused in him passions and desires that no musket could trigger. He was injured in a fierce skirmish with the Xosas in a place ideal for an ambush. He well remembered it all and he was suddenly weary of it all. It was through a pass, where a narrow track wound through the tangled undergrowth, thick bush interspersed with huge, bald boulders and masses of jagged rock. On either side were towering precipices and an almost perpendicular krantz.[*]

The warriors on top of the heights had allowed them to pass unmolested and then poured a volley onto the infantry. At the first volley he had rushed back to organize the defense, having been in the vanguard. As he tore frantically along, he was struck by a bullet and only got through in the nick of time. How well he remembered the wild confusion, scrambling, screaming packhorses, the pain and the wounded. He remembered pushing his horse down the defile, setting his teeth together, gave the horse the spur. His wound was low down on the outside of his left thigh. The ball passed upwards and out below the right hip. He remembered the shock. His horse had even staggered with the blow.

He had fired his first shot, struck a rock and splinters flew in all directions. It was his second shot that went straight into the breast of the warrior leader. The black leader leaned against a rock, blood pouring from his chest, muttering strange impulsive utterances in his native language. Armstrong had been quite near him then, and a second ball struck the black leader on his head, splattering his brains all over his red jacket and onto his face. He shuddered, and a little revulsion overcame him. Yes, he had managed to sit his horse and reach the cavalry, towards a knot of dismounted fellow officers.

* Krantz = Dutch word for precipices.

The blood was pouring from his wound and he might well have bled to death before a doctor arrived had it not been for John Grant who had a tourniquet around his body, which he at once took off and partially stopped the bleeding. The second medical officer, Dr. Frazer, arrived soon after, but was so exhausted and faint, he needed attention himself. How near to death he came. He thought of the disastrous battle, of the men who died. It was in this unfortunate manner, with pain and delirium he then vaguely remembered it was his 32nd birthday. Day after day he had laid in a high fever almost on the verge of death. His pulse was at 130 and his wound discharging great gushes of pus. Perhaps it was to the dedicated Dr. Frazer working in his wattle and daub hut, that he owed his life.

He felt older than his years. He wanted more from life and longed for the comforts of home He longed for his parents, to be back in England and to the factory with his father, to the little factory that made simple things, pretty things and the only resemblance to war it had were its shiny military muttons. There was safety and security in his father's button factory. Him and Moya—this was what he wanted now. The beautiful Moya, ripe and ready for love, soon found response. Like a match to a haystack, her heart was lost to this handsome colonel. To him, she was the perfect girl whom he could trust with his life and every minute she seemed to get lovelier and harder to leave. It was obvious to everybody. So it was no surprise when the colonel proposed. And when Jules agreed they should marry, he thought his heart would leap out of his body. Captain Hargreaves would be his best man.

The wedding started on a Saturday morning. Sannie and her Dutch seamstress made Moya's wedding gown, a frothy white mass of hand made laces all dancing around her elbows and throat. The wide hoped skirt was filled with lace and as she moved, masses of white lace peeped out from beneath the main skirt, like fleecy clouds beneath a halo. Around her head were orange blossoms all smothered in a mist of voile. She looked unreal, like some painting of another world. She danced about in a girlish frolic and everyone told her how beautiful she looked. Hundreds of wagons formed a laager, all lashed together with chains around the house and garden and in front of the homestead, on the verandas, buffalo grass. Kathleen had fixed a feasting array of foods: whole roasted lambs and smoked hams, guinea fowls and chickens, venison and wines from all the farms.

William Armstrong, the groom, was dressed in full military uniform and his red-coated officer colleagues made a brilliant splash of red. Everyone came in their best clothes. The horses had white ribbons tied on each side of their heads and the vooerloopers* of the wagons all carried bells. Inside the laager on her wedding day was great hilarity, dancing and singing, kissing, rose petals and mixed niceties, merry sounds of "boeremusick,"** concertinas and accordions, harmonica and clappers, and a few old fiddles and ukeleles—who knew what they were. The music was gay and full of country airs, fun and happiness.

Jules wore his top hat and tails and Kathleen looked beautiful, her hair piled up on her head and little ringlets all over her forehead. Piet was the master of ceremonies. Music was lively and even a little melodious. Kathleen, moving from the Dias made for the speeches, headed down towards the front entrance. Piet quickly moved in front of her. He took her hand. "As your MC—I beg, to dance with the mother of the bride." He stopped her from going

---

* leader of the oxen.
** barn music

wherever she was moving. He took her left hand and in a Bone of Courtesy, took her in his arms to dance.

They twirled, and laughed. He was light of foot, for a big man. A strong man. One of those people who give the impression of masterful knowledge and ability. And who knows the answers to all questions. They swayed into a slower moving dance, slow and comfortable. Kathleen had her arms around his shoulders. She was in his arms. His lips touched her head and he held her body over his heart. The pain felt deeper. Here in his arms was the one woman, every bone, sinew and fiber of his being craved and desired. This fantastic woman, unobtainable, untouchable and the obsession unquenchable. God, make the moment last longer. Would be it was forever? A certain poignant beauty oozed into the emotionally charged slow dance, neither he nor Kathleen would ever forget.

Kathleen looked up into Piet's face. She well understood. "Thank you for being part of this family." He looked straight into her eyes and he pressed his lips, softly onto hers. She disentangled her arms and took his face into both her hands. "Thank you Piet, for being part of this family." She kissed him on his soft lips. He pressed his soft lips to hers. His mind drifted out of the world he was in; somewhere, somewhere he could hear closing quite clearly, he could hear closing: the doors of heaven.

Jan was tall and elegant dressed much the same as Braam Piet. All the staff were clothed in special occasion outfits, Lion looking grand and splendid and Boesman equally splendid but slimmer and slight. There were no holds barred or restrictions this day. Jules stood upon a small platform and gave his fatherly speech with Kathleen at his side. Finally he said, "On this day, eat, drink and be merry," and his son Julius chimed out, "For tomorrow you may die."

At that unfortunate moment there was a bit of shouting and frenzied voices came rushing through the opening in the laager. The Hottentot guard group were ushering in two Impis. Both were clad only in a loincloth and blanket and neither wore clothes of war. All the men reached for the guns, single shot carbines at the ready. The atmosphere was tense and irritated. Jules came forward. "Xosa" he called, but Xosa was already there. "What is the story, man," he asked. And a long conversation started. "Who are these men and why are they here?" There was another barrage of click language that most of the burghers understood.

The officers ordered them to be shot. "They're runners, spies," they called. Jules looked at the two men who had dropped their blankets and held their arms out to show they had no weapons. "Mr. Jules," said Xosa, "they say they are not warriors, they are Fingo. They are not warriors and they were only interested in what was happening." Jules looked into their faces. His blue eyes looked into their coal black eyes and he called Braam Piet. "Braam Piet," he said, "they do not have the looks of murderers." "Xosa," he said, "Give them meat and tell them they may stay and see the wedding." He stretched out his hand, reaching for theirs and both men bending their heads and one leg in a form of courtesy, took his hand. "Tell them, Xosa, today is a special day for this father, who is giving away his first born. They may stay in peace, and Xosa, please see that care is taken to observe their every move."

Everyone shouted threats and shouts of mistrust, but Jules turn his back and once again the party soon got into its former happy mood. Finally Moya drove off in the carriage. All sorts of objects were dragging behind and the tinny noise could be heard even as the carriage went far off into the distance. There were hundreds and hundreds of trek oxen, horses and wedding guests. Braam Piet summoned Xosa to inquire where the Impis were. Everyone seemed nonplussed. One minute they were there and then like camouflage, they were gone. Braam Piet pulled his beard downwards with his hand. "I don't trust them, Jules," he said. "We should have shot those lying bastards. They came to see how the land lies." And because Piet was so seldom wrong, Jules had a twinge of fear. "Oh well, it's too late now, Braam Piet," he said. "Somehow they seemed to me to be just simply two curious strangers with no evil intent. Damn it man, surely it's possible they were only fascinated by this full dress occasion?" Xosa shook his head in perplexed inquiry. He too could not understand why they vanished like they did.

It was with great sadness and a feeling of empty loss that Kathleen said "au revoir" to her lovely daughter. A woman needed another woman, and she had found great pleasure in the company of her girl. But this could not be said about her son. He was a perplexing human who was born of her body and of her beloved Jules', yet he was so entirely different. She wondered what her own mother was really like. It was so difficult to remember. She could well remember her governesses and riding in the carriage with her parents. She had childhood memories of comfort and care, but she never really knew her mother. And what of her father's family? She really knew very little about them all, and she wondered how many skeletons lay hidden in their history.

She wondered where Julius could have developed his strange, dark character. She thought perhaps it was a result of the disasters and fears through which they had lived in this wild, warm land where black men fought to keep their land. Well, in a way Moya would be subjected to less danger in England, and her children would be born in less fearful conditions. She thought of her own births; she had been delivered by Sannie and Marta. Perhaps if she had delivered with a doctor in a hospital she might well have borne more sons. Something went wrong, for she well remembered her fever and infection. A lot of women died giving birth, and she didn't, and for that she should feel thankful. Women's minds are always full of questions, questions that are sometimes unanswerable. She felt deep sorrow that Moya would be going away, yet she also felt a pacifying relief.

Twenty-One

As a boy, and as a young man, Lion, who had the minimum formal education, had learnt many things. Not only the ways of nature, the bush, the black mountains, he learnt to handle animals in a variety of difficult conditions. He learned to work the soil and plow, but most of all, he learnt to hold his own against men who lived face to face with life and death. Men who were intolerant of weakness and lack of manhood, men who lived and perished by the assegai. When their turn came, they met death with jest and great admiration for the one who proved to be more skilled and powerful.

Jules and Kathleen were good to him, so was Moya and Braam Piet. He was rather sad that Moya didn't marry Braam Piet. He would have liked Piet at the farm forever. He felt a strength, a sort of powerful protection when Piet was around. He enjoyed Moya's wedding. It was his first big social occasion. He and Boesman were so well treated, and Moya had even kissed him goodbye. He felt Moya's departure very much. He missed the subtle warnings and her quick replies in his or Boesman's defense. He thought about Thombe. Moya as much as told him Julius had deliberately murdered her. How he missed her, his marvelous lion. He constantly thought of her. He still found it hard to accept.

He lapsed into sadness. Lion friend—restrained his thinking! Death was not so bad and so Thombe was dead. "Yes Julius, one day Julius," he thought, "one day you will get your just deserts. I swear half-brother, I swear on the spirit of my life and on Thombe's grave. One day I will get even with you. To have murdered my beloved Thombe was pure hate and it still hurts. It will hurt me forever, you killed my first love, the very essence of my being." He gazed at the sky. "I swear by all that is life, all the stars in the sky, be witness to my aching soul, because I swear, one day, half-brother, your day will come."

In 1846 the Buffalo River at East London was named Fort Rex. The Whigs were again in power in British Parliament and Earl Grey decided to grant the Cape an elective legislative body. The colony was in a good economical state due to the rise in the production and the demand of wool. However, a Xosa walked into an insignificant trading store in Fort Beaufort and stole a hatchet and began the War of the Axe. Col. Hare with 1500 men set out for Sandilies Kraal. They lost 125 wagons in an ambush and the whole colony was invaded. There were many fierce engagements. The Xosa cut off a convoy of wagons some 5 miles long as it forded some drifts on the Keiskama River. Warriors captured and looted all the wagons, which were heavily loaded with stores, provisions and camp equipment. Among the booty was a hospital store wagon and with wild yells of delight they broke up the bottles and drank the white man's magic, killing themselves with poison. One warrior who was shot dead had his mouth stuffed full of blister ointment. Theopolis, Lombards and Port Fairfax were swarming with Xosas and ambuscades and fighting was the order of the day.

At Oliphant Hoek,* in a heavily wooded ravine near the Kawie Forest, the Xosas entrenched themselves in the riverbed, protected on either side by heavy growths of wag-n-bietjie** thorn and rushes. They were in a very impregnable position. But a young man named Besset found a new assault plan and cautiously came up the river's course. They came upon a pool and saw a bundle of assegais float upwards. A moving tuft of grass in rushes under the water was a killer Xosa. They waited, guns at the ready for a black body to appear. Nothing happened then. And then suddenly, a keen-eyed Hottentot soldier, trained to bushcraft, stealthily crept up to a tuft of grass and parting it with his fingers, exposed the huge nostrils of a massive warrior, the only part of him visible. With great force, he plunged his ramrod down into the spot. The water heaved and boiled and the black body rose to the surface and fell upon a heap of assegais.

As his arm drew back to throw, a shot rang out from the almost confused men, and he fell back into the water, stone dead. At Breakfast Vlei, across the Fish River trying to negotiate the steep slopes, some of the cunning warriors had entrenched themselves on a ledge of rock and could not be dislodged. The army had to virtually run the gauntlet and here the brave Besset was wounded. Besset was believed to have had a most fantastically charmed life. Every step in the vast bush was grimly contested. Eventually Peddie was relieved—Fort Peddie. Two powerful chiefs, Umhala and Seyolo, Seyolo with nefarious schemes, joined the gaikas against the white man.

Colonel Someset came upon him and with 2 six pounders, a rocket tube and 2 twelve pound Howitzers fired a volley into the

---

* Elephant's corner
** A thorn bush that catches you called wait-a-bit.

enemy. There was indescribable confusion. Xhosas scrambled in all directions and cooking utensils flew into the air. But it was lucky they made for the bush. Their ammunition had been stored too long. The rocket exploded in the tube and the first shell burst in the cannon's mouth and the shot failed to carry as far as the target. Desultory fighting continued. Besset had been issued with a very wild, uncontrollable horse that took off without him one day, so to try and get some of the fire out of the animal, he raced it up the hill. The horse took the bit and bolted, going up the hill and down the other side. To the utter dismay of Besset he was charging right beside a huge column of Impis rigged out in all the savage panoply of war. A mile long and thirty yards wide.

The Impis were so surprised they gazed at him in amazement, but before they could recover, Besset was off like a bolt of lightning, straight back to Somerset to report on what he accidentally saw. The Cape mounted rifles and the 7th Dragoon guards swept down on the doomed Xhosas flashing sabers, and knocking down the warriors like ninepins. What started as a slaughter became a massacre, and the red soldiers took and killed more than 270 Xhoxas. 100 guns and 1,000 assegais were recovered. The rest, stuffing their wounds with dried grass, fled to the thick bush near the Fish River, only to die a slow and agonizing death.

Organized military operations and superior weapons of war finally drove the kaffirs out of the colony, and orders were given for the regular troops to change their brilliant uniforms for a less conspicuous kit.

Twenty-Two

The war had spread across the whole colony and all boys over the age of 16 were called up to defend the land, including Jules, Jan, Piet, Boesman, Lion and Julius. "Oh dear god, no, Jules," said Kathleen, "Julius is too young to go to war, Julius and Lion, they're just boys and still growing children." But war was war and every able-bodied person was needed. They all joined the Cape Mounted Rifles and were kitted up. Behind them were detachments of the 6th, 45th and 73rd regiments, and dozens of packhorses loaded with ammunition, medical panniers and provisions. The end was a rear guard to protect the supplies.

Jules had difficulty saying goodbye to Kathleen. He called all the workers. "Xosa," he said, "you defend the Missus to the last gasp of air that keeps you breathing. Every day take a horse and check and see that the lookouts are constantly manned. Use Klassie's sons. Every man on the farm must guard and be given guns at night. You must not allow them to carry lighted torches. Remain alert to every sound and movement and guard the stock. If this place remains unharmed you will all be richer men. You will all be well repaid." He continued, "If you need more men, then Klaas and Xosa will engage them. Beware of traitors. This farm is our land."

He rode off, a little troop, his son, his father in law's bastard son, a dreamy half Hottentot child with blue eyes, and the soul of a poet, Braam Piet and Jan. But Piet was in a serious mood. In matters of war he felt no desire to jest. "Maglig˙ Jan," he had often said, "who wants to fall gloriously? I want to fall when I'm too old to run, not by some bloodstained spear or a bloody lead ball! Life is too precious, man! It is so stupid to be brave, when by cunning, we may stay alive." And that was how he led the boys and men, by cool, calculating cunning. For a Boer mastermind, life on the Eastern Frontier was no sinecure. Braam had no admiration for the regular soldiers. He thought they were not able to adapt to the frontier conditions and the soldiers in turn made no secret about informing Piet that the colonists were wild and undisciplined. There was a lot of bickering between them.

In 1847 Sir Harry Smith reached Cape Town and asked for a draft constitution to be prepared. In England the Colonial Secretary proposed the Cape should be made a penal settlement and forthwith 282 long-term convicts were dispatched to the Cape. Under the leadership of John Fairburn, the Dutch joined forces with the English Eastern Province with West. Sir Harry Smith did not allow the convicts to disembark. The Cape's peoples had threatened not to use a single one of these convicts for labor and to generally ostracize any person who aided or abetted their landing or who gave any support to them at all. Even shopkeepers threatened not to give them supplies. Political issues ensued, involving prominent members of the public, one of whom was the owner of Groot Shuur.**

---

* Almighty (in relation to God)
** Groot Shuur is in existence today. Groot Shuur Hospital had the 1ˢᵗ heart transplant!

But the colonists won the battle and finally the convicts were sent to perhaps Tasmania. It was this agitation that showed clearly a showing of unity among the peoples of the Cape. This is one time that the English and the Dutch were joined together.

It was perhaps Boesman's keen sense and understanding of horses that soon got him an assignment by Col. Somerset. He was ordered to carry dispatches. Often he had to make speedy rides of 40 miles or more and the dreamy sensitive Boesman became an indefatigable soldier. He was amiable with most people and was well able to identify various chiefs recognizable by their leopard skin karosses and carrying 7 assegais. He learned to shoot with both barrels and parry with his bridle arm. He was lithe and mounted his horses as though he had springs in his heels. Later he told many thrilling eyewitness accounts of battles and killings, but often grew sickened of the way the warriors engaged in dipping their spears in the white man's blood.

He cared for his horses, and greatly disliked the dangers, shuddering at the disasters into which his ammunition carrying packhorses willingly ventured. Often wounded and screaming with pain they scrambled up and down while dead or dying soldiers were savagely mutilated by their ruthless foes. War was not for Boesman. He longed to escape, to be free of this constant ceaseless fight, senseless killing and bitter, remorseless struggle. Perhaps fate took a hand in Boesman's life for to those who dare, who think big, the Gods are kind!

He was ordered to carry a dispatch containing an account of the battle to the governor who at the time was at the Port; Port Rex, where the ships were comingand going and loading wool and hides and skins and ivory.

The 8th Kaffir War proved the bitterest struggle for supremacy. Disaster followed disaster in quick succession. Many of the Cape

Mounted Rifles deserted, and the Native Police deserted in large numbers to the enemy. In 1852 Sir Harry Smith, a much loved and dogged leader with a distinguished career, suffered his keenest disappointments. He had believed this settlement would have brought peace and tranquility to the ravished frontier but on Christmas Day, 1850, his grandiose settlement collapsed in a welter of blood and fire. Then later, a court dispatcher from the Colonial Secretary, Lord Grey, informed him he had been relieved of his post.

In England the Duke of Wellington made a spirited defense of his conduct in the House of Lords. Despite his humiliation he was treated on his departure from the Cape with great regard, the people all turning out to bid him a fond farewell. The people actually released the horses from his carriage and pulled him through the triumphal arch down to the steam frigate "Gladiator." Lady Smith, his wife, was in tears. In England, likewise, he was treated as a victorious commander rather than a disgraced general.

Well he was remembered as: severe on riders, finicky about men who left a wine glass unfinished or who used a spoon to pudding. He was scrupulously dressed for dinner, he took men into his employ for pure charity or devoted himself always to the prettiest woman present, rigidly punctual and charming with children and above all, on duty at any cost. But most of all he is remembered for his adoration for his Arab charger, "Aliwal." His most devoted, beloved and staunchest servant to whom and for the good of the horse's health, a toast was always made. Often the groom led the magnificent animal around the dinner table, glittering with plate lights, uniforms and brilliant dress while they drank to his health. When Sir Harry returned to England he took his horse home, and so that the noble creature never had an unhappy end, it was known that he personally shot him when he got older. He as well as the faithful groom and almost everyone shed tears. He did not long survive this sad event and the brave old warrior died on October 1860, aged 73.

It was November, and there were threats of early rain. The frontier was aflame and it was fright filled and dangerous. The Hottentots had allied themselves with the Kaffirs. The Hottentots had knowledge of firearms and military tactics making them a formidable element of war. Commandos of Burgher and settler farmers were all summoned to help the military. Piet and Jules were up near a watchtower, a solid construction that resembled a small fort. Jan and the younger boys were somewhere at the bottom. This day there was a depression of spirits. War affects even the bravest and it was worse when a cannon ball or musket shots whizzed over the soldiers' heads.

Bugle sounds and trumpets and incessant musketry replaced excitement with nervousness, then nervousness to anger and anger may be supplanted by barbarism. A soldier, a corporal, standing beside Julius remarked, "If God spares my life, I swear I'll reform my wicked ways." He was a fair, pink-skinned young man, too young for war. "And what do you call wicked, mate?" asked Julius. "Christ, man, all the things in the 10 Commandments teach us not to kill, and here in the army they teach us to kill. Have you done any killing?" Julius looked up towards the sky. It was early morning, and a sea of mist spread way down over the undulating plains, through which the kopjes peeped like little islands in the ocean. "Yes," he said, "I have killed, let me tell you, man, it's nothing to kill, it may even give you a certain pleasure. It just depends on the reasons for it."

The small platoon lit a fire and gathered around to warm their hands. Gradually the sun's rays dispelled the aqueous particles till the surrounding trees were visible; voices were heard and all eyes peered that way. Suddenly there within a pistol shot of them was a band of warriors. They rushed for their firelocks, but when they looked again, their enemy was gone. They had disappeared into the bush before they could draw a trigger. Julius looked at the pale soldier and smiled in a sneery way. "What a pity!" he remarked. There seemed no conclusive means of getting to grips with an enemy creeping through busy, hiding and sneaking, murdering and thievery, but seldom exposed to retribution.

About midday, they dismounted, and in a sheltered wood near a ridge, they pitched a small tent close to a pile of firearms. The whole patrol took out their rations. They engaged in nervous and forced lighthearted chatter, but with no real manifestations of mirth, for they knew that at any moment they could be attacked. The officer in command, Yarborough, said, 'Do make haste men. Silence, keep as quiet as you can, no speaking here." Every word of command enjoining stillness caused the men to be more uneasy than the roar and rattle of canon and musketry.

They were not allowed to remain very long in suspense. Instantly from behind every rock, forest screen and anthill and tree trunk, a whole moving mass of Impis suddenly ambushed them. Screams and shrieks and assegais flew through the air. In one flash of horror stricken realization they all knew they were completely surrounded. Piet yelled out, "Get down!" Lion and Jules stood rigid. The horses neighed and reared and the little pinkish soldier started to cry. Jules stood up and looked at his sons. At least they would die together. "Christ, men, we're done for," yelled Yarborough as he dived for the ammunition. An assegai shirred through the air, finding its mark and he fell holding his hip.

Then, like a whip crack, a yell rang out, a deep, resonant Xosa voice. Silence prevailed. Every Xosa Impi was silent, assegai raised.

A huge man stepped forward. "Yeka, yeka,"* he yelled to his warriors. His eyes fixed on Jules in recognition, coal black and intense. Hesitantly he extended his hand. Jules knew he had seen him before. "The wedding, Jules, Christsake Jules, the wedding guest you didn't shoot, it is he!" cried Piet. Jules was the only one besides Piet who was armed. He let his weapon down to the floor. "Do the same, Braam Piet, or we're dead," he said. Piet lowered his weapon, and put his foot upon it. Jules looked in to the warrior's face and for just a brief moment each stood with the other's hand. He released Jules' hand and then shook the hand of Braam Piet and then Lion and Julius. His face burst into a smile and then he stepped back.

"Izza, Izza,"** he called to this warriors and they backed off. And as suddenly as they appeared, they disappeared into the bush. Yarborough, with a stentorian voice, roared out, "What in Christ's name is going on, somebody help me! I've been hit!" Jan went over to Yarborough. The assegai had gone through the top left muscle on his thigh, clean through and through, the front and out the back. The moments were heavy with shock, fear and the realization they were wet with perspiration, sweat tunneling down the dust on their faces, but no words came. Fatigue and emotional exhaustion drained them.

They looked at each other, and they all understood Jules was silent. "Yes, sir," said Piet, "it's a bloody strange business, that Impi, he saved us all, and had you not dived for your musket, sir, you too would have been uninjured." "Make yourself clear, man," said Yarborough. Piet explained the Impis and the wedding incident. And here they all wanted the Impis shot, except Jules. "Holy

---

* Leave, leave.
** Come here, come here.

Jesus," he murmured, "well, I suppose it is hard to believe," said Yarborough, "hard to believe!" Young Julius looked at the slim pink redcoat, and as he prepared to mount, he pushed his fingers through his hair, grabbing his horse. With one foot in the stirrup, he said, "Reform your wicked ways cringing soldier, either god or my father saw fit to spare your life!"

Perhaps because of the story Piet told and having saved Major Yarborough's life, Jules was sent home for Christmas. Piet, Jan, Julius and Lion, weary of war and skirmishes all came home to Moorplaats—beautiful Mooiplaats. The redcoats had kept guard over the farm. Kathleen was well. Sannie had also kept vigil over her best ffrien and the farm as flourishing. Peace seemed to prevail one again. Xosa had aged. Marta was stricken with the maladies of old age as she hobbled about on tired legs. Old Klassie was overjoyed at his little herd of cattle. He felt like a wealthy man and wanted only that when he died, his sons would always remember he was a rich man and that he left them with all his riches. Sadly, Moerskind had caught the fever and died when Baas Jules was away fighting and Tante Tande was very poorly.

Jules and Xosa were overjoyed to see each other. They were older men now, with graying hair, but each saw in the other's eyes like a window to their minds, and saw the undying love of man for a man and the loyalty that would be broken, only by death. Jules and Piet were soon back into the rhythm of farm work. Hundreds of farm laborers were brought in and taught to shear the sheep since the war slaughtered stock and they were providing greatly increased meat supplies. Lion had become a tall, strong and fine looking men with curling brown hair and hazel eyes. He had broadened greatly and his voice was deep, constantly reminding Kathleen of her beloved father.

Boesman had taken a dispatch to Port Rex, but Sir Harry Smith had been recalled and replaced by Sir George Cathcart. It was at this time after a succession of defeats the Xosa chiefs intimated their submission. Farmers had returned to their deserted properties. The frontier's manpower had shrunk by endless sorties, reprisals, ambush and murders, and at last it seemed that peace may prevail. Boesman, with his great love of the sea that he never quite understood. It reminded him of far away places and now that he found it he never wanted to leave it. He had attached himself to a military camp on the banks of the Buffalo River where he cared for and grazed the horses and watched the ships come in. Soon he would leave the cavalry, and maybe ride back to Moorplaats. He wondered about the people who lived there, about his half-brother Lion, about Kathleen and Jules and the walking world of knowledge Braam Piet. He wondered if they were all still alive and what had become of Moorplaats and the horses, and his mother's carriage.

Kathleen had taken his mother's carriage and one day he was going back to claim it. Mr. McCabe had told him so often, "that carriage is for your mother, Boesman, it makes her feel important," how well he remembered McCabe, the only man who ever cared about him. In fact the only person, really! Who was he, Boesman, anyway? His mother had told him his father was a ladybird who "just flew and flew and flew away." What a hell of an answer? He suddenly felt alone, all of a nothing, but he had felt even more alone when he saw Mr. McCabe lying dead in his own blood all dried up and rigid. He shuddered as he thought of it all. Death was so commonplace in his world.

He looked down and went towards the river mouth a large crowd of people was gathered on the newly built jetty. Some sort of speech was taking place. "Ladies and gentlemen," the

man on a wooden dais was saying, "when I first got this ship I
had only a love of the sea and my physical strength. My brother
and I exchanged our farm for her, and we took an oath that as
soon as we made money we would build a wharf. We have made
enough to have been able to give to our country and to this port,
this jetty and the promised wharf," he said. He was still talking,
but Boesman did not stay and listen. He moved on towards the
ship and there moored beside the new jetty she stood, not one
ship, but two, and written high up on each prow was the name
"Marietje I" and the "Lettie I."

The crew was a mixed bunch: Malays, English and one or two
black men. They wore striped uniforms and all seemed to be a jolly
lot. A cabin boy came jostling along with a satchel of onions. "I say,
boy," said Boesman, "you work on this boat?" "Aye, Sir," said the boy,
"second year now, Sir." "And who is your captain," asked Boesman.
"Over there, Sir," he pointed, "Captain Willem de Swaart, that's
him, Sir, the posh one, opening the new wharf, and the captain of
the Lettie, Sir, that's Captain Pieter de Swart, Sir, them's brothers,
Sir, and theirs very particular about crew." He hurried on up the
ramp, dragging his onions, and Boesman waited at the foot of the
ramp of the Marietje I.

His heart beat and his fingers trembled, for somewhere in his
mind he remembered he had heard McCabe and Jules talking and
he felt, like army officers, who unraveled the soldiers stories and
made them tell the truth. He straightened up, brushed out the
creases in his trousers. A long time passed and no one came towards
the ships. They were drinking wine and pretty women were in the
newly built customs house, government House and government
officials were everywhere. These two captains were very important
for sure. He could see that, so he walked up back towards the new

building. Two sailors stood at the entrance. "Sir," they said when they saw him. Boesman nodded, and they allowed him to enter. A pretty lady came up to him to offer him wine, and then he saw a familiar face, Mr. Joseph Thackwray. He remembered him well, mainly because he was the big game hunter. He hated hunters, especially the way they rode their horses.

No, he also remembered him because he once delivered a dispatch to him and he had ridden at such speed and efficiency he was well acclaimed by his superiors, including Mr. Joseph Thackwray. "Good afternoon, Sir," he said. "Afternoon, soldier," Thackwray said, and then he recognized Boesman. "Ah, yes," he exclaimed. "The dispatch rider who made a phenomenal ride!" He raised his voice. "By God, lad," extending the first syllables, "you could have given Dick King a run for his money, only you were alone, didn't have a black manservant beside you, did you?" "Things have settled down somewhat, hey." He raised his glass and threw the wine into the back of his throat, then, twisting his great moustache. He looked at Boesman searchingly. "The thing is Sir," I would like to work on a ship and if you know the Captain, Sir, perhaps you could help." For one instant, Thackwray almost expressed disdain, and then, in a sort of patronizingly English way, he said, "Very well, then, I mean to say, after all you did ride like a bat out of hell through all those kaffirs and things, yes indeed, I suppose." He leaned towards the Captain, a middle aged man with a fine face, rugged, tanned skin and blue, blue eyes that twinkled like two blue pools in the brown savannahs.

"Willem," he said, "this young fellow rode dispatches for Sir Harary, and for myself. I, what's your name, Lad?" "Boesman, sir," "Boesman who?" "Just Boesman, sir," he said. "His name is, er, Boesman, Willem," said Thackwray. "He wants to work on your ship." The captain looked towards the soldier. "Boesman," he repeated. "And who may your father be?" "I don't know, sir," Boesman said, "I did not know my father, but my mother had the same name as your ship! Her name was Marietjie." Willem looked up at Boesman. "Where do you come from, soldier?" "I am as Mr. Thackwray says, sir, I am a good rider and I rode dispatches for the governor, any day as good as Dick King," he said. "But where do you come from, man?" said Willem. His eyebrows screwed up. He looked at Boesman impatiently. There was no doubt about it. The Boers could detect it. This boy was of mixed blood. "Then where did your mother live?" "She lived on the farm, Mooiplaats, sir," he said. "And your father?" "I never knew him, sir, my mother would never tell me, sir. She said he was a ladybird that flew away. I grew up with a Mr. McCabe, sir." Sir was silent, looking at his glass, pondering, he poured himself another drink. His mind flew back, like a ladybird; back to his boyhood. He remembered Marietje!

Just then, his brother Pieter came up and joined him. "Pieter," he said. "This fellow was born on the farm Mooiplaats, says his mother's name was Marietje." Willem swung around and looked at Boesman. "Magtig Willem," he mumbled, "Magtig Broer!" Pieter and he were stunned into a deafening silence. They lapsed into thought. Pieter knew that Marietje was the woman with whom he had lost his virginity. Just boys, and boys will be boys. Willem looked up at the young soldier. "Do you mean to tell me you never knew your father?" he said. "No, sir, I asked my mother many times, but all she ever told me was my daddy was a ladybird, you know, those little beetles that eat aphids on roses," Boesman said. "and she would look to the sky and smile, and she would say, 'he just flew and flew away.'"

Both men looked at Boesman.* One thing was undeniable, he had the piercing blue eyes of the line of the de Swart family. He raised his hand and felt behind his neck. Both he and Pieter had a strange ridge of bone that ran behind each ear. He remembered his papa saying once, "it was the mark of the de Swarts." "Were you injured in any of the skirmishes," Willem asked. "No sir, but I have had a few hefty falls from my horse," he said. "Turn around" said Captain de Swart. He walked up towards the soldier who seemed quite nervous now. "Don't worry, lad," he said, as he placed his hand behind his neck, "These ridges?" "Born like that, sir," Boesman said. "Tell me what can I do for you?" "I love the sea, sir," he said. "You want to be a sailor?" "Yes, sir!" His mind swept backwards. The wide-eyed virgin boy whose hands had touched no woman's flesh except the long forgotten fountains of his mother's breast. A teenage boy, brim full with the stirrings of manhood and driven by the passionate urge of youth, eager clumsy careless youth. He thought of the lovely yellow girl, and her soft skin well he remembered her—Marietje! His sins exposed, sins of innocence perhaps? He lost track of the present momentarily. "Yes sir," repeated Boesman. "Yes sir I do love the sea." "And so it shall be young man. What did you say your name was?" "Boesman Sir, my name is Boesman." "Well Boesman, your ladybird father is a thinking man. Goed my soldaat Seuntjie."** (You will be a sailor Lad. Your ladybird father will see to that.)

Christmas was wonderful. Kathleen, overjoyed to have her family home, prepared a great feast that lasted several days. It was the celebration of homecoming and thankfulness, Christmas and

* Boesman = Bushman
** Goed my soldaat seuntjie = "Good my soldier boy"

New Year all rolled into days. Lambs were roasted and great loaves baked, cakes and pies, poultry and pork, guinea fowls, chickens and summer fruits. The latest treat was home grown strawberries and Devonshire cream. And Kathleen loved Jules and Jules loved Kathleen, and their love was never stronger. Jules built a new wing onto the house for Lion and Julius, who was to go to London to study law. Moya wrote about all the wonders in England, filling him with enthusiasm and eager intentions. After long deliberation, his parents agreed that he should depart to England so that he could study law.

The day soon came. The ship was due at Delagoa Bay. The carriage set off with Kathleen and Jules and Julius one beautiful morning in the new year. On the long ride to the harbor Jules was using four great black horses and his new carriage. They rode down the drive from the entrance with a feeling of pride and opulence. He and Kathleen and their son plus a newly acquired footman. All the staff turned out to bid Julius farewell, sheep shearers, planters, herders, and those who sowed the French wheat seed, dairymen and harvesters, watchmen and laborers, kind of standing beside the stony driveways. And there behind the plough was the half-naked, bronzed figure of Lion. His brown hair tumbled in the breeze and the muscles in his youthful body rippled like the waters on a disturbed pond. Aloof and proud, he held onto his plough. He had just completed his furrows and unleashed the oxen. He turned to see the carriage as it passed. He stood there in the sun, his rush hat was in his left hand. He wanted to wish him well, but words would not come. "Go Mr. Lawyer, farewell," and he lifted his right hand in exuberance. Then he lifted the plough angrily like a toy. He lifted it up towards the sky staring after the carriage, then pushed the plough hard into the soil. "Farewell grandson of my beloved father; lily white skin and evil dark soul. Good bloody riddance," he muttered to himself.

And as the years passed and the grisly wars ended, new laws were made, farms expanded, the children grew into adults, and older adults got older. Four years passed.

Twenty-Three

K oosie Odendaal had brought the mail. His horses were hot and steamy, for it was midsummer. Their sweat frothed white between their hindquarters, about where their testicles once had grown. These were geldings, though one of them had the thick neck muscles of a stallion; perhaps he was gelded too late. Koosie wiped the animals, rubbed them dry. God how he hated the gelding operation: the way they would hold the poor colt down, tie his legs to a heavy post, double up the forelegs and dozens of men all held the cold down while the old burgher would bring out his sharpened knife, and then feeling for both testicles, without mercy, would open up the scrotum and sever both oval glands and throw them on the red earth. A handful of wood ash was powdered onto the wound and the bleeding colt was released, dripping blood all down his hocks as he galloped off with only the aid of nature to heal him.

How often had he seen Mr. Putzier slice off the testicles of the boars. In fact the old Putzier used to visit most farms on special different days where he did his foul operation. He acted like an exhibition of superior knowledge, and always with an all-knowing smile. He was German, thin and gaunt, and the pigs all looked so fat in comparison. How often, Koosie used to hope perhaps some day, the kaffirs would get his balls and hang them on the thorns of a droggie bush. And he wondered how Mr. Putzier would feel with blood dripping down his leather trousers and wood ash in his scrotum.

But today Koosie must not think. He brought letters for Mrs. Kathleen and it was important news, he was sure. He tethered the horses to the steel hinge and throwing the wet towel with which he had just rubbed the horses into the trap, he straightened his jacket and trousers, stamped both feet to rid the dust from his tired voelskoens and sauntered into the homestead. A long bodied red hound stood barking at him; he didn't remember seeing this dog before. In fact, he'd never seen a dog at Moorplaats, and it didn't seem too friendly with its hair all raised and bristling on its neck. He hesitated, but within seconds the laborers were all there and Kathleen and Jules came out calling greetings to Koosie. When the greetings ended, Kathleen carefully opened their letter and Jules ordered some honeybush tea. Kathleen stood there reading, "Jules," she said, "it's from Julius. He's coming home, our son, the lawyer. He's sailing on the 'Eastern Star'" she said. "Oh Julius, if only he could bring Moya with him." "Not with two small children, Kathleen," he said, "but someday soon if you long to see our grandchildren we shall certainly go visit them. But for now we must prepare for Julius. Let me read the rest of his letter."

He reached over and took the letter from Kathleen's hand. Kathleen, all excited and eager, suddenly seemed at a loss, as though she didn't quite know what to do with her hands. "Five years, Julius," she said, "five years have passed and now our son is coming home." She sat down beside the window and looked at Jules. She said, "Call Lion and tell him the news that Koosie just brought us." She scanned the fields, beautiful, undulating summer fields. It looked rich and well cultivated and as far as the eye could see on the north side were flocks of merino sheep. These were Lion's lands. He and Piet, it was they who tilled the soil, it was they who taught, labored and turned the wilderness into the largest and most successful farm in all the land, about them Jules' brains, together with Lion and Piet's strength and power.

Kathleen had resented being half sister to a Mulatto but somehow it melted away. She remembered when she found Thombe. She knew instantly the cub was for Lion. He was such a warm and considerate boy. Her feelings were harsh in the beginning. She was even a little jealous the way her father fondled and loved his boy. It was then that she shed her prejudice and resentment. If her father loved so deep a love, so could she. After all, it is not difficult to love. She had always lived every new day to the limit. Of course it was a battle—like overcoming an addiction, she imagined. She felt in her inner self. She had to accept, to reason. She conquered her intolerance. She walked up to the heavy wood mantelshelf. An animal tail was beautifully attached to a wooden handle. She could not quite recall exactly why and where it came from. She waved it about while she went over her thinking. Perhaps Marietje made it. She replaced it. She thought, my father grew to love that girl, that slim yellow forgiving Hottentot woman. I am so sorry I was not more accepting. I am so sad and sorry. He was just human. I had no right to be hostile, she spoke out loud as though she had an invisible interrogator. She desperately wanted someone.

She had a conscience—why should she thank "the giver of all things"? There was this sort of animal tail neatly sewn onto a handle. She again caught hold of it from the heavy wooden mantle shelf. She spoke out loud; admonishing herself. I knew my father loved his son. I could see and feel it all the time. Woman know that look. I used to think my father loved him more, because he thought I didn't love him enough. "Why should I have loved him?" Then she realized what she said. "My father grew to love that Hottentot woman and it is not difficult to understand: I was behaving like a really snotty cruel child. Did I actually learn from my father? Guard against evil? He was lonely, and time was passing. I was not kind and warm and compassionate like Marietje. I should be thankful to her for giving to the family, Lion!—his beloved son. I am having this biblical feeling. Damn! That's not it. I have been intolerant and even unkind but I have dispelled it, I really have. Somebody say I'm forgiven, and she sobbed. Somebody say…"

She did not finish the sentence. Lion was standing there, his face was serious. "To whom were you speaking Kathleen?"

"Oh Lion," she said, "It was not a soliloquy, it was me and my own conscience."

"I heard you Kathleen. I heard it all. I did not intervene because it was good for you to let it all out like we all do at times. And we all need to do that at times."

She looked up at him. He was so tall, six foot two, and so wide—a beautiful man—her half brother. The tears were running down her cheeks. He took a clean vadoek* and wiped her cheeks. "I will forgive you as a representative from God. How will that do?" he asked. She put her arms around his neck and he held her close.

"You know something Lion. Louise was right. All she said about you, was right."

Moorplaats was like the Mecca of the settlers, the success story of all the Eastern Cape. Jules and Kathleen were guests at all

---

* dishtowel

government dinners an ships' captain's parties with regular social visits and calls from the Landrost to the secretary to the governor. Jules was invited to serve on the Legislative Council, and often traveled by ship to Cape Town to attend meetings. Life was different now, there were homes. Gone were tents and mud ovens, the mud floors and walls. Things had changed a lot from their unspeakably difficult beginnings: Yellow wood floors shined with beeswax. It did not seem so long ago that Julius had left to go to study law. The years had fled so swiftly and in that time how close she had grown to this bronzed son of her father, Lion. Her half-brother! He actually reminded her of a lion, tawny golden, wild and full of power, ever watchful and alert. She felt safe with Lion. She had battled with her earlier inner resentments, perhaps she pushed them to the back of her mind. People were all just people in this insecure land. And she silently gave grateful thanks to the giver of all things. No she had shed her burdening resentments—wrongs can be put right.

Her father dearly loved his son, as he had loved his son's mother. He was a lonely man. He wasted no thoughts on skin color. People were people. His yellow woman was warm and gentle and very willing and happy to please her father. Kathleen regretted having been intolerant. There were times she was so filled with remorse, she wept silently into her feather pillow. Always when she thought of her beloved father a surge of sadness filled her body like a heat wave. In Lion she found comfort and strength. For Lion in his maturity was her father, she became good to Lion, for it gave her peace. Perhaps this feeling was love, a great and deep love, had grown between Kathleen and Lion and she never missed her son, even half as much as she thought she would. She wondered if and when Julius returned, if he would spoil it?

Yes, she was not kind to the girl. For God's sake, she was filled with regret even now, for having been harsh and intolerant—till the day she dies she felt she would be haunted with remorse for the way she dealt with Marietje giving birth to her father's son—on the outside bench on the patio. For Christ sake, what was she thinking? Yes of course she had regrets—of course, she is choked with remorse. She cries too often with sorrow and no one knows, except the telltale tear-wet pillows.

Twenty-Four

When the ship in which Julius was traveling back to Algoa Bay was only several weeks away, Jules and Kathleen set off with the best horses for Algoa Bay. They intended to take the journey in slow stages. Kathleen took her best gowns, crinolines of Indian silks with precious handmade laces and satin ties. She wondered now, after five years, what her son looked like and what she would feel when she saw him again. The carriage arrived at Fort Brown. Jules and Kathleen stayed in the home of a settler friend, Mr. George Wood, and his family. Mr. Wood was a legislative member, who had made a large fortune trading with the natives in ivory and skins. He was a thin taciturn gentleman who had two sons. He served as mayor, being a generous benefactor to the town. He donated a vast stretch of hilly land above the town, near the mountain drive, which gave an extensive view of that land. A stretch of cheerless, strange land where settlers were once expected to try and farm the arid soil. One hundred acre, desolate, waterless naked plots which had been delegated to them and upon which they were to exist.

Kathleen looked at herself now in a narrow glass. She was 50 and Jules, her beloved Jules, was almost 60. Jan had moved north and found a sweet Boer girl and was happily married now. He had started his own newspaper which was going from strength to strength, but news was rather slow and very infrequent. Their lives had also been hard. They all knew what suffering was. They lived a life full of fear, and adventure, draining, depressing, exhilarating and exciting. It was a distant memory from the day the women were carried through the surf on the backs of strong soldiers and big black men to the yellow sands. There they sat upon their baggage on the sands of Algoa Bay and bewailed the chance of being eaten by lions there where they were, stuck midway between what was to become Port Elizabeth and East London, with the pink blooms of the spekboom* and the exotic yellow reds of the aloe. What a lot of life she'd lived and what a lot of death she'd seen. Never was she without the constant lurking threat of death, as a survivor in the wilds of savage Africa. The wild and striking grandeur of the mountains and valleys which caused extreme conditions of the mind, often alternately, exalted and depressed. Now she was in a curious state of mind. She had such mixed feelings for suddenly her son was returning to his home in the wilderness. Suddenly she felt old. She had always been so careful with her hands, yet they were still rather careworn, though not too badly so. They were the hands of a woman who had used them, a woman who was half a century old.

She looked out of the windows, pushing wide the shutters. A little church and steeple silhouetted against the sky. Within its walls, how many women had endured such privation trying to feed and care for their families, even cooking within its sacred precincts? God, how they had suffered at the hands of the marauding and

---

* Well known tree in the Cape.

bloodthirsty kaffirs. God, did God ever help? She thought of the endless plains of wildlife, herds of buffalo, zebra, wildebeest, kudu, warthog, elephant and lion, how the great creatures wandered away north up towards the great Limpopo. So strange it was to her, what a paradise, a bushman's paradise. Among the many birds, the storks, egrets, that kill ticks, those that kill snakes and rats, the storks that eat the egrets, the lilac breasted rollers, oranges, guinea fowl, all warring on insects and locusts, marabou storks ever darting among the brown-winged destroyers and the quaint weaver birds, twittering and bustling, always busy fluttering across the clearings. The mind is so crammed with what was, what is, what will be?

She thought about the forest and the hills, vivid streaks of powerful sun, dim aisles, hung heavy with monkey ropes and fronded fern, the lovely sound of running water. A sense of age and mutterable remoteness, the subdued song of the bush, and the prolonged murmur of the winds. A pioneer had to bear the brunt of all things, pioneer people who clear and toil and change the hills and bush into acres of smiling farms and a promise of greater blessings to come. She gave silent thanks for survival. Yes, her little family had survived, but not her daddy. Unpredictable guerilla warfare, the war of an unprecedented kind, where settlers were marauded and murdered and their black-skinned murderers melted into the bush, into the euphorbias, spined cactus, aloes, and became invisible. Listen to the song of life—Her father always told her.

A blue and gold flash of the maeterlincken bird passed into the silence of the past. She turned back slowly; there outside, the groom was busy rubbing down her horses. Their life, hers and Jules, despite adversity, was heavily loaded with good fortune, with love and passion, and she smiled a smile of comfort. "Poor Dick King," she said, "for his heroic ten day ride, muddy and utterly exhausted, his official reward was £12 and the next day his horse was stone dead. That poor willing horse. It was his horse who was the real hero, the dumb honest willing creature!"

By afternoon of the following day Jules and Kathleen's carriage was nearing the Kowie River. Great clouds darkened the sky and the birds, thinking night had come, were heading for home. Thunder rumbled all over the gloomy sky and the horses were fractious and wild. They had to cross a tributary that led into the Kowie River over a manmade drift made of many stones that had been carried to the drift by past travelers who had crossed before them. The water was shallow, perhaps not more than half a wheel deep, but the horses refused, rearing up, bulging white eyed, whinnying and neighing. Jules jumped down to see what was wrong, and as he did so, heard a terrible roaring sound and snapping of branches and other strange sounds. And then he saw it, and he was mesmerized, for coming down the stream was a wall of frothy brown water, snarling and tumbling and hurling all before it unto the sides, over the bush and rocks.

It was a weird and frightening sight and it was as though the horses had sensed it coming. Instinctively the horses reared and turned away from the river edge, the driver shrieking his commands and the footman/voerloper running behind. Kathleen was inside the carriage shouting hysterically to Jules, who was transfixed by this strange and eerie sight. A young Kudu cow, wide-eyed with terror, was being swept and tumbled before it on the outer edge. Jules reached out toward the animal, whose body hit him hard, broadside, against his ribs. The animal staggered free to safety but Jules was thrown into the swirling waters. Miraculously, he only managed to save himself from being swept away by clinging to a tree limb, which fortunately was stout enough not to break. When the driver had got the horses to a halt and tethered, he left them with the footman and hastened to help Jules.

Kathleen was almost beside herself and quite hysterical. She had never encountered a flash flood, and neither had Jules. She didn't care about her dress and rushed wildly towards Jules. He was visibly pale, muddy and dripping wet, scratched and bleeding. "My God, Jules," she said, "you let it get you. Why didn't you move out of its way? Jules, for the love of God, what made you linger so long?" "Perhaps it was the terror of the kudu," he whispered, "I thought I'd catch the poor thing, get hold of it and save it. I think I did, Kathleen." He gave a deep groan and wiped a bloody hand across his body. "Somebody out there loves me, Kathleen, why else am I here?" he said. Kathleen was steering him towards the carriage. The horses were still wild and restless, though quieter. She bundled Jules inside, trying to rub him dry. She wrapped her shawl around his shoulders and took out his hip flask to give him a drink. She held it up to his lips and then took a sip herself. They were both in a state of shock. "We must now get to Grahamstown, Jules," she said, Jules held his ribs. The pain was excruciating and he tried not to grimace. Kathleen stayed at his side tucking him up and settling him, and then hitching up her skirt, she tied on her bonnet, wrapped a shawl around her and went up front beside the driver.

She knew she must get to Grahamstown, Jules needed immediate medical care. She looked back at the river, full and flowing as if it had been there for always. A fierce wall of water came, and spread into a smooth river, which it left behind, all the way. Dr. Frazer, she had to get him, he was the famous old army doctor and well known for his devoted services. Dr. Frazer would help her, she just knew it. She called out loudly to the horses, jerking on their long reins and then surged forward on towards the narrow wheel marked tracks.

The road seemed endless; sometimes the track sank under the wheels, delaying them even further as they rattled through and onward, and it became frighteningly swiftly dark. It became increasingly hard to see the track and their oil lamps offered little or no light. There was nothing else to do but stop and God, how they knew the perils of the night. They had never hardened to the fears of the unknown and the unexpected. They had learned by indomitable determination to accept and overcome misfortune and disaster, even at times when nature itself seemed to have conspired against the doughty pioneers. Misfortune had for so long been a companion. They were almost reconciled to each other. Suffering had become part of being and life. Maybe the day would come sooner than they thought.

But the night was without peril, not without sounds, and morning came. The horses had been hobbled, and had not gone far. Each person knew his duties and each one had set about them. Jules had had a long, painful night, and had developed a strange, dry cough, which troubled him all the way. It worried Kathleen; she had listened to it through the night. How endless time was, sometimes that short distance between dark and light dragged slowly on, but the light had come at last.

She patted Jules' face. "Come now, my darling," she whispered, "we must get you to the doctor." Jules looked up at her. "Kathleen, my dearest love, you have never let me down, and I shall never let you down." He reached for the leather strap to pull himself up. "You get up front and we shall ride on together," he said, but as he stood on his feet, his face paled, and perspiration glistened on his nose and forehead. His breathing seemed odd, almost delayed. The sky seemed to spin all around him, and he sunk slowly down onto the carriage seat. "Oh my God, Kathleen," he said, "something is really wrong." Kathleen raised his silver hip flask to his lips. "Drink this Jules, here take a sip of this," and she forced the brandy into his mouth. He seemed not to see her for a while. He closed his eyes. She threw a cover around Jules and sped swiftly up towards the reins, stepping lithely over the footbag up beside their assistant driver.

The young boy who was used as a voorloper was now standing behind the carriage. He was being trained as the new footman. "Come up here, duivalag* and hold vas** you hear," and she yelled at the horses to "walk on." The pull at the reins sent them into a canter, as fast as the carriage would go. They arrived at Graha-mstown, dust-covered and weary, the horses heaving their wet, sweaty bodies as they breathed in and out. They raced past the Drost grounds. Soldiers were parading. Slowing down she yelled, "Dr. Frazer, please direct me to Dr. Frazer." "Dr. Frazer is at Fort Peddie," called out one of the frontier officers. He then swung around and said, "No Madam, he is at the place of punishment down at the old Provost." Kathleen frowned. The officer looked at Kathleen in a quizzical way. "My dear sir, this is a matter of grave importance," she said. She moved her carriage impatiently. "High Street, straight down High Street," called the officer.

She wheeled her team and sped down towards the provost. An open wagon was moving in the opposite direction and seated in front beside a bandaged ensign, accompanied by an officer in full dress and some of his staff, sat the slightly bent doctor. Kathleen

---

* duivalag = devil laugh
** fast

did not know this until she enquired about the whereabouts of
Dr. Frazer. With this, the smallish man straightened up. "I, Madam,
am Dr. Frazer," he said. Immediately the street was thrown into
turmoil. Men were standing at attention and officers were giving
commands. Dr. Frazer climbed into his wagon and then directed
them to his surgery. He saw down beside Jules, who looked pale,
yellow, and wan. She hastily introduced the doctor and he almost
dismissed the courtesy in a bid to get on with his business of
helping the ailing man.

"I am acquainted with who you are," he said, "but I have not
been informed of the nature of this man's illness." Jules' head was
wet with perspiration and on closer observation, the whites of his
eyes seemed to be yellow rather than white. He started to heave in
nausea and gazed ashamedly towards Kathleen as he spewed on the
floor. She slipped forward with a bowl, and wiping his brow with
one hand, she held the bowl before him. The doctor busied himself
looking down Jules' throat and into his eyes, tapping his chest and
spleen, pressing and listening. Finally, he asked for a specimen of
Jules' urine. He took it from Kathleen and poured it into a glass
container. Kathleen was horrified. His urine seemed to be black, a
kind of dark, purplish black.

Dr. Frazer, up until now, had said very little. He held the
urine up towards the light. "Madam," he said, "I will need your
assistance." He took her to the side of the surgery room and told
her that Jules had black water fever. "It is not caused form the river,
or any water," he told her. "It is caused from a mosquito." He tried
to explain to her how the bacteria got to be in the urine, and that
the only way they could save her husband would be to make him
drink so much fluid he would be drenched. He was worried that
the disease was already well advanced. Kathleen walked over to

Jules. He was visibly curious despite the spectre of his illness. The paleness erupted and sweat burst out on his brow. She wiped the wet sweat with the back of her hand. "My God Jules, my dearest," she said, "you have black water fever and you must drink and drink and drink as this is the only treatment that can cure it." The doctor was looking through his bottles and vials, and, muttering to himself, kept reading, moving and replacing vials. "Quinine," he said. "Not quinine, we must drench him with fluid, Madam. We will have to drench the poor man." And drench him they did. Together they nursed him, pouring liquid down his tired throat all through the night, until a few bird sounds heralded the burst of dawn. Kathleen sat hunched up on the wooden bed under which was a large porcelain chamber pot and the chamber was half full of burgundy fluid. She was too tired to move any more. Her emotions were spent and her energies diminished by pure physical and mental exhaustion.

She dozed into a state of limbo of rambling thoughts and fears. Where was Lion—she was nervous to show him warmth and love? My God she so wanted to! To show her mulatto brother. He knew she was an honest woman. He would believe her. She has suffered already for her reservation. It was gone; now she wrestled with her feelings, her sorrow, and she wept constantly with remorse into her pillow. Can't she be forgiven—how much more should she suffer? It was all different now, her concept of family had changed as she changed her entire lifestyle. It's not an instant thing—it grows and gathers until the old feelings are smothered and become non-existent—and the here and now reigns and goodness prevails.

She dozed semi-awake, between sleep and a twilight world of dreaming, where voices seemed distant and sounds unreal. But she heard voices, yes, it sounded like Lion. She thought of Lion constantly. His strength and his calm. She had learned to depend upon it, yet over in the back of her mind she held back something towards this young man, her half-brother. She had never showed warmth towards him even when he cried, something he always fought against. Lion never cried. He was born a man, and a bushman didn't cry. There was neither time to cry, nor a shoulder to cry on for these men of the veld. Even as a small boy, Lion thought of himself as a man. He was so much like her father. This son of that yellow girl. And here too, she felt a pang of sadness. His mother, that poor woman. Her only great desire was to ride in the horse-drawn carriage, and how often had Kathleen denied her that?

She felt remorse. Why oh why had she vented that cruelty? It was so small a gesture and perhaps so great a pleasure denied to a human who gave only kindness, who gave all she had to give, who gave only devotion to herself, to her lonely father. In her semi-sleep, tears pushed through her rapidly moving eyelids and the voices now were loud and clear. That was her family outside, and she stirred, pushed her feet into her leather skoen and opened the door that led onto the low veranda. Clear as the morning mists, the voice was Lion's; Lion and Braam Piet had come! Oh God, how thankful to hear them! A wave of comfort enfolded her whole being. There was the wagon; the whole loaded span had arrived. Lion sprang from the front, knocking a lantern with his hip. He landed on the ground, and bounded towards Kathleen, followed by Braam Piet.

"We had news Miss Kathleen," he said, "we had news of the flood and Mr. Jules. It came with a runner and some of the passing wagons." Braam Piet put his arms around her, tenderly around her shoulder. She clung to his broad solid body full of strength. She felt his heart beat against the side of her head and she felt the vibes and the mood. She was wrapped in an aura, undeniably and unmistakably. His body trembled right to his fingertips, and Braam

Piet was transfixed. How long had he dreamed of holding her in his arms. He found it hard to breathe. His body seemed to switch off inside him somewhere and he just held her, pressing her body against him. Lion stood by. Even to the innocence of youth, it was obvious. He knew, instinct, the overt passion tell-tales, that told of the essence of emotion, the depth and source of feelings that came from deep inside a man. He knew he must say something. "Where is Jules, Miss Kathleen?" he asked, "Take us to Jules," and the spell was broken. Braam Piet jerked himself into reality of words and Kathleen looked now for her kerchief. There was none so she picked up her skirt and wiped her nose and she looked into Lion's face staring at her, and all the resentment for that moment was flung on the winds and she put her arms around Lion. "Thank you, Lion," she said, "thank you." For she knew it was Lion who braved the ride and brought themselves here to help her. He lightly touched her shoulders, afraid to really touch her. "We will take you home, Miss Kathleen," he said. "Oh damn the Miss Kathleen, Lion, please call me Kathleen, and I'll be so happy to get home," she said. "Lion, Julius' ship is not yet here in the Bay. We will all meet the ship first and we will then all go home together." She remembered once the parting at "assegai bush," when she and her father, full of youth and enthusiasm, separated form the other settlers' wagons to take the route with their Boer guide into the Albany district, devoid of communication.

Elephants in hundreds roamed leisurely from Kooms. Rhinoceros crushed the thickets of the ravines of the Fish River. Lions stalked on the slopes of the Winterberg, their roars echoing down into the lower districts. Hyena laughed and jackals howled and through these nights and sights, of shrill yells and insect bites, settlers trembled and children listened, and they grew up, those who survived, in these hazardous of vicissitudes, even under constant threat of armed marauders.

Jules survived the days and the next week, and thirteen days had passed when news came of the ship's arrival, bringing their son Julius. It was a strange mixture of sadness and excitement. Kathleen, the ever-adoring mother, was dressed in her best laces, and Jules, still quite unwell, pale and perspiring profusely, stood beside her. It was a fully rigged steel ship of 1,740 tons, "Eastern Star." How it had all changed since 1821, when the ships' captains had to marshal their passengers into small groups, and then into flat bottomed boats drawn up alongside, the men, women and children clambering down rope ladders helped by the sailors who manned the ships. Then the boats were warped towards the shore by means of strong ropes fastened on the beach. Of course this could only happen when the surf was least violent and even then the operation was fraught with great dangers. When the boats reached shallow waters, men leapt out and waded ashore, and women and children were carried by soldiers of the 72nd Scots Regiment stationed at Fort Frederick or others carried on the shoulders and in the arms of powerful black men towards the steep ascent of hillocks and sand hills.

At the settlers' camp, local farmers carried all their goods on their wagons and those farmers had traveled long distances to come and help, those great farmers with their long stemmed pipes and their naked Hottentot servants. Soon the settlers too were all wearing the blue coats and soft skin trousers the farmers wore, with rush hats and home tanned leather "velskoens." How often she'd heard them mutter, those farmers, "allemagtig," and she remembered the children's pleasure when they traded raisins and nuts and ran about gathering shells and teasing the soldiers who guarded the piles of stocks brought by the supply ships that were stacked near those sheds on the beach. So, swept like a tragic tidal wave, the settlers had all moved out to establish their homes.

It was so different now, a few constructions in Regency Gothic style, stone and brick buildings, and tiled roofs, with Welsh slates. This Port Elizabeth, named after Sir Rufane Donkin's wife, who had died so very young, was dotted with white houses now a full magistery, since 1825, lifted and vanished was the pall of misery that once hung over Albany. Time had passed like the turning of the watermill wheel that combed their Merino wool, that made their blankets and coarse cloth. Now these were homes and there was hardly any homes of consequence that did not have among its furniture pedestal dining tables, leather upholstered chairs, mahogany sideboards, chiffoniers (some in walnut), davenport desks, bun feet mahogany chests of drawers, Victorian dressing tables so cherished and loved by people who survived the storms and stresses of unbelievable hardships, struggling to achieve a little graciousness to their lives. Here they were, part of it all. Jules had worked so hard for it, and her heart sank as she looked at her beloved husband. He seemed unusually quiet. Braam Piet and Lion were also beside him. It was hard for Jules to be robbed of his power. He did not understand the meaning of debilitation.

Suddenly Kathleen let out an excited yell. "Look, it's Julius," she called, "Julies, my dear son," and Julius had crossed the short wooden construction from the ship to the side of the stone built wharf. He stood at the wharf and behind him was a petite girl, blonde hair blowing wildly in the south wind. Kathleen ran forward down the cobbled path and onto the stone wharf where sea gulls and ropes obstructed her way. "Julius," she called, and her son came forward and they clasped each other swaying in the wind. "Let me look at you," she said, and holding both his hands at arm's length, she leaned back and looked him up and down, then suddenly Jules was there and Braam Piet, and standing back at least 20 paces stood Lion.

Jules was very pleased to see his elegant lawyer son, and Braam Piet was joyously congratulating Julius in a jumble of words and in both languages. All the while, the girl stood, as the carriers brought box after box of luggage. Then Julius spoke and turned towards the girl. "Mother, Father," said Julius, "this is Louise Brumley," and with that the girl came forward and curtsied in a timid way. She was a pretty woman with large blue eyes and a clear pink complexion. She was very windblown by now and kept her small hands above her brow, holding her thick, fair hair out of her eyes. "I am so happy to meet you both, Mrs. Jacobsen, Mr. Jacobsen," she said. "She has come out to teach, Mother," Julius said. "She is the niece of Mr. Barnabas Show." When everyone was formally introduced, Louise saw Lion. He just stood there alone and reticent, like a large silent figure of leonine beauty. Their eyes locked.

"Someone introduce me to this handsome man," she laughed in a girlish way. And Julius said, "This young man is Mrs. Jacobsen's half-brother, Lion. This is Miss Louise Brumley," and Lion took her hand and raising her fingertips to his lips, gave a half-bow. Kathleen was dumbstruck by the action, for there in one flashing moment she saw her father again. It was as though Lion was born to the manor. A carriage arrived and Louise was met by her own relatives. The journey home was gentle. The team lumbered on with uneven tempo, together with the luggage and Braam Piet, and Lion took the horses and Jules and Julius took turns sometimes with the oxen and the wagon and at other times in the carriage. He had become more eloquent and spoke of setting up a legal practice as soon as possible. He wore his tailcoat and knee breeches and found the clothes of the farmers "coarse and undignified" and spoke disparagingly of the verdure of England versus the yellow veld.

He was very surprised on his arrival home. Everything had changed tremendously. The house was now white, with black gables, long and spacious and very large. The waxed shutters shone clean and bright and the stoep supported by stone columns. The stone floors were wax polished and one could just remember the original house beneath the new innovations. Roads were well constructed and the water supply came from a reservoir. There was an extraordinary development in his absence, and living in his home now gave him a feeling of grandeur. Ever more interesting was the storeroom which was filled with ostrich feathers, skins of wild animals, lots of ivory and weapons of the Bechuanas. Crude but deadly is how Jules described them. "There's a good business, Julius," he said, as he closed the doors. "We trade this with the kaffirs, we give them mutton! We exchange it for rich fur dresses and cloaks of the natives of distant regions, leopard and lion skins and buckskins. The market is closed on Sundays, but wagons come from all over with produce, bandy, wine, maize, barley, oats and wheat, salt, raisins and bedfeathers," he said.

And that's how Julius found his bed a soft warm haven of feathers in large duvet covers. There was a certain luxury about his bed, and he thought about Louisa. He thought about Louisa Brumley more and more, until it was almost an obsession. Awakened by the call of a hoeope* one morning, he got up and entered his mother's study. She had acquired a piano and a beautiful Davenport Desk. He slid his hands over the wood and opened the drawer. She had in it a document tied up with a white satin ribbon.

---

* A beautiful well-known bird.

It looked so important. He untied it and opened it up, unrolling the scroll and scanned his mother's handwriting.

This was his mother's last will and testament. He scanned it swiftly with a trained eye. My God, his father had left everything he owned to his mother. His father must have thought he was dying when at Dr. Frazer's. He became a little wary. Cautiously he closed the door. He felt he was trespassing. His eye caught the name, "Lion McCabe." He read on, "To my father's son," and as he read, his blood boiled in uncontrollable wrath. "Bloody half breed bastard," he muttered, and his lips curled and his face paled. And then calmly he rolled up the scroll and carefully replaced the ribbon. A smirking smile replaced the expression of wrath and hate and his whole mind was thrown into a plotting, scheming turmoil. There was no hurry, but he would think about it, tonight, not tomorrow.

At breakfast he noticed his father seemed quite odd. His eyes were dull, and the whites of his eyes were strangely yellow. Kathleen made the coffee and smell of hot bread in the oven cheered Jules a little. Kathleen was bothered. "Jules," she said, "you must drink boiled water all day. Please don't drink coffee." She withdrew the coffee and placed large earthenware jug of boiled water and a long tumbler before him, but he had no appetite at all. "Kathleen," he said, "get the horse and carriage. I'd like only you and Xosa, and we will take a ride across the farm out into the fresh air, out into the day." Xosa, who was fast going gray, was a gentleman now. Sometimes he wore tails and knee breeches, and a hat. This was what his family wore and this was his family. He knew he was precious to Jules and to all, but Xosa worshipped Jules. Jules was his savior, his father and mother. Jules was his life, for Jules he would give his life unhesitatingly. Jules was the happiness life had given to Xosa, and Xosa was now uneasy.

"Take me old friend," said Jules, "take me over this soil we have tilled and toiled and shared together. We have grown old together. We two have hunted and fought and laughed and feared. We have shared many seasons, yet it seems so mercilessly short." They set out together with two horses. The day turned up so beautiful. Birds were singing everywhere and high, very high up in the distance circled a tiny speck, of fish eagle called, and its echo settled over the hills. What stories they could tell. Xosa took the horses walking and trotting all over, through open spaces and under trees where the leaves crackled and sticks snapped under the wheels. He crossed the little stream where once Marietje danced and played half naked in the moonlight, and finally they came past the kopje where the graves all nestled.

"Xosa," Jules said, "you take your friend up here today." Xosa and a silent Kathleen went with him and he climbed out and pointed to a level space. "Kathleen," he said, "we will be together when we die, won't we? You see this place is for us. This is where our joys began and this spot is where they will end." He pulled her towards his chest and circled his arm around her. "My beautiful Kathleen, we have known the joy of loving, and I thank you." He then said, "See here Xosa, this is the place where I will go to rest." "And me, Mr. Jules, where is the place for your Xosa to rest?" Jules suddenly looked him in his eyes. They were desperate eyes, already wracked with the painful fear of grief. "You, my very special man, will lie beside me on the other side." Xosa's face lit up and he bent over slightly and clapped his hands together gently, a sort of gentle salaam of gratitude. Kathleen was silent, as always in life, one must talk of things when the moment presents itself, and this seemed like the moment Jules had chosen. She looked at him. He didn't seem at death's door, not by a large margin. Men were morbid sometimes. She remembered one of those English officers who had a simple cold once, and he wrote his will, and told all his comrades, "If I come out of this alive," he had said, whereupon most of them had to run and hide their laughter. Maybe Jules was unnecessarily fearful. He had seen so much death, and escaped it, up until now. Perhaps he found it difficult to handle physical debilitation. On the other hand, he may well know. Perhaps he hid more from his family then they already knew, and the threat of parting took a grip on her mind, and she started to weep. This was her moment, this was now her time for weeping, and she cried and held onto Jules and covered her mouth so Jules would not see the plain, ugly expression of grief.

"Let me cry Jules, just let me cry," she said. "This whole scene has wrenched momentarily every atom of happiness from my soul. Know that I love you and if we should part, how I shall be smothered in the horror of total grief," and she folded up in a soft female way, holding her cheeks, and she almost fell down on the earth between the little stones that stood above the graves of the people she once knew, and others who had lived before her. She wept out loud. This was a place of sadness, and she let out her emotions from the deep rivers of her soul, this place where there is so much beauty, it was their place, where these wild flowers and lilies freely grow.

It was strange how Kathleen had not noticed before just how much Lion gave to the household. Xosa looked to Lion as the next man, no, not Braam Piet, it was Lion, Lion, Xosa always said, was the clever one. He mended and invented. He made things well, and made things grow. He rode out and helped the sheep and understood the moods and feelings of everything and everyone. No one seemed to talk about either, perhaps because they all knew how Kathleen once resented her father's bastard boy, her half-brother. But now as she matured, that meant nothing to her. It seemed to fade as she got her priorities right. She now saw in Lion the beauty of his soul, his ready smile and cheerful manner, and from his calm, she began to draw strength. He was always there when she needed him, and quite frequently now, she felt again deep recurring remorse for not previously, showing him more love, more kindness, simple sibling care!

She went out of her way to include him now, and was often startled at his manners, his unusually, handsome good looks. Jules leaned on him more and more and consulted and accepted all Lion said as read. Braam Piet had always done the same. Julius made no effort to disguise his obvious jealousy and often took to belittling Lion. The atmosphere always altered uncomfortably when Julius and Lion came together. Julius was planning his new legal practice. He rode away frequently to Salem and had obtained premises that had been rebuilt from the remains of an early fort. The stone floors, arches and stone columns indicated that Julius had quite a flair for art and decoration. He was also looking for Louise Brumley. When he found Louise, they had become friendly. He made it his business.

Kathleen went to her desk one morning, she found several things altered, not the usual way she had left them. Her visual memory was accurate. Her diary, a large volume of years of writing, was left open and it was clear to her someone had opened her will and had most probably read it. This had not happened before. Her desk was very private and there was never any need to close or lock anything away. She didn't like what she felt. So she carefully put her diary in the drawer and retied her private papers and placed them in an obscure part of the desk. Her diary was a record of almost all the years, all the events, gory, sad, happy and otherwise. Someday her children would be able to read it all, a complete record. It might even be history. That's what a person told her once, as she witnessed a public flogging of a soldier in front of the Drostdy Gate, she recorded it all. There were also hangings that took place in front of the old gaol. How she had hated that, but it was well recorded "for posterity," she had claimed. My God, she thought, as if there wasn't enough death and dying without ordinary citizens having added to it.

She closed the drawers; they seemed a long way off already, those days. She was one of the lucky ones, she was not listed in the 1843 Directory among those widows who were bonnet makers or seamstresses, or even innkeepers, nor had she lost any of her children. Why then had she this feeling of impending doom? Jules' illness seemed to be easing off now. She knew he was not quite well; not many people survived Black Water fever, after all. She felt, with careful eating and medical attention, Jules would soon be his usual strong, good-natured self. She was always positive, and this was no time for depression and despondency, or fear.

Julius came home on the weekend, and with him was Louisa. Yes, Louise grew prettier and better looking on acquaintance. Really, she was very beautiful. Julius seemed obviously enchanted by her, awkward and unconscious of his rather clumsy impressions. When Lion entered the living room, the whole scene changed. Louise glanced up at him from under her eyelashes. She looked at him from his shoes upwards. Her eyes lingered on the powerful thighs and the bulging calf muscles that seemed to want to burst from the legs of his leather trousers. He had a flat belly and a wide leather belt made from the skin of a hippo. He was so big and so attractive, Louisa shuffled onto either side of her buttock. The call of youth was strong, but the call of womanhood was stronger. She wriggled uncomfortably now, until she could contain herself no longer. "Lion," she said, "I'm told you are a marvelous horseman." She completely disregarded Julius, her eyes now on Lion's face.

She stood up and moved towards him, her whole being charged with forces of human electricity. Her heart beat like a captured bird. She was trembling. This was a strange new experience and as she timidly reached one hand out towards him, her eyes met his and she felt his gaze. All of hell's fury would hardly compare with the hate that shone from Julius Jacobsen's eyes, the wrath that was reflected in his strangely twisted face, as he stood there, just staring.

Xosa was constantly with Jules. Unbelievably close, they spent hours out in the hills, shared wine and food and time, or walking up the trickling streams and along the sloots where baboon played and monkeys scrambled up trees. They watched the mealies grow and helped the ewes when they dropped their lambs, then returned home when the day was done, to watch the sun set behind the kopje. The great banks of clouds dissolved into muted shades of orange and mauve and deepest gray, that turned the shapes of the moving sheep into drifting black shapes that moved across the fields, and stilled the day and rested everywhere.

Jules' days seemed more precious to him now; they all came and ended too soon and seemed shorter than the nights, for his nights were plagued by restless tossing and turning, his body with vague pains and twitches he'd never known before, his shallow sleep taunted by dreams and distorted imagery and often mind disturbing nightmares.

Twenty-Five

The rains lasted longer than most rainy seasons, which made the land green and verdant again. Little rivers were still rushing over the stones, trickling like a summer melody, but up in the kopje it was getting dry already. The baboons displaced rocks, looking for scorpions and juicy morsels, sending the stones rolling down, bouncing and hitting the sides, absailing to the bottom. Far across the fields were flocks of merino sheep, sprinkled with oxen and horses and wild game that wandered into the fields to graze. There was harmony with the beasts of the earth. They were satisfied to share their food.

Up on the kopje Jules sat on a rock under a tree, always an escape place, turning his hat in his hand. He was troubled in his mind. Julius, his son, was the reason for this perplexity. Jules had taken to rising early these last few years and every morning for a week now he had watched Julius snooping in Kathleen's desk and among her private papers. He had not made his presence and observation known to his son, for he was curious to discover the reasons of his distasteful search. As he twisted his hat, he was in low spirits, he was pondering; perhaps, because he was a lawyer, the boy was only curious. Kathleen had always made it known absolutely and clearly from their early childhood that her writings and her place of writings were strictly her own domain. No, it was his manner more than anything that disturbed Jules. There was something rather unwholesome about it, almost sinister.

For fighting in three frontier wars Jules became Sir Jules Jacobsen, a knighthood from the British no less, and he was also granted a large stretch of crown land. Kathleen was now a "Lady" and celebrations, gossip and chatter were rampant throughout Albany. Kathleen remembered her own mother, her grandmother and grandfather were the Viscount and Viscountess of Troubridge and she remembered her childhood among people of wealth and titles, the feudal nobles of Canute! Those memories were quite vague now, though in her mind rang the thought that history did make a habit of repeating itself and her dear father, though never saddened or troubled by her marriage, may have been thrilled in a way to see his beloved daughter, a titled lady in her own right, a station in life not unknown to her forebears!

Her own mother had been the daughter of the Viscount and her husband's father, a noted cheese baron in Denmark. The honor was unexpected. The knighthood of his father greatly pleased Julius, even though England handed out frequently such rewards, well groomed and always looking the perfect elegant gentleman. Jules, irritated by his son, regarded him with suspicion and wondered what new problems confronted him. Yes, it was a problem within his private family, generally unused to domestic discord.

Already the whole year had passed, but not without disaster. Most horribly the wreck of the Birkenhead where 437 lives were lost. A troopship from which only 150 people could get into the lifeboats, all soldiers went down with the ship with discipline and great courage, to their deaths. Sir Harry Smith, a well-loved and popular man and personal friend, had left and was superceded by Sir George Cathcart, aide de camp of the Duke of Wellington. The long 8th Frontier War, the longest and most expensive war, ended. The land river convention recognized the independence of the Transvaal, and Cathcart adopted a policy of indirect rule, as did Mr. Shepstone in Natal, a separate form of control, a policy of segregation. He re-created tribal systems in reserves administered their own customary laws, which were not to conflict with the white man's ideas of justice. It was a separation of black and white persons, Pretorius and Potieter both are succeeded by their sons. The young Pretorius, together with Paul Kruger, were not taking steps to draft constitutional reforms via their committee of the Volksraad.

The news came of Julius coming home, and the strange flash flood and his illness. He could not understand why it was he associated his illness with that crushing wall of pale brown water. He was tired of wars and soldiers and was far more interested in new ways of shearing his sheep and finding equipment to plow his lands faster, always ever haunted by the odd feeling that his life was running out. He had so much to do still, and so much to tell Kathleen. He had many plans: move across the seas and land. He wanted to take Kathleen back to England, her home of birth, where their daughter lived among the daffodils and constant damp and green, and then he wanted to return to this home he had carved out of the rocky kopjes among woodland streams, deep krantzes and yellow grasslands.

This land where the sun had no mercy and water soon dried up. Had he forgotten how swiftly time had fled? He looked over the landscape and he saw some tented oxwagons, stragglers, late deciders, perhaps, yes some boers were still trekking, having taken years to decide to leave the earth they dearly loved, almost alone and treacherous sometimes going up north gathering and forming little groups who then followed the tracks and inroads left by those who had gone before them.

Potgieter, who had crossed the Orange River in floods, having swum his horses and cattle across and then constructed a huge raft to take the wagons and baggage and people and pets across the tall lanky. Potgieter was a great leader with great energy and determination, a fearless and courageous fighter. He had moved north, further to the east towards the true high veld. He had searched in vain after riding north with 10 men to find a route across the Dragensberg to the sea. It was on the banks of the Vaal. He had first learned the Matabele were on the warpath. He attacked the Matabele. He'd had a 9 day battle in the Marico Valley and defeated them. Potgieter claimed all the land from the Vaal to Zant Zoutspanberg by right of conquest. He founded Potchestroom. He had also attacked the Zulus with Piet Uys and his son Dirkie, among his commandos of 350 but they were defeated and Uys and his gallant son of 15 were murdered leaving only a sad, useless story. A legend throughout South African history was of how brave Dirkie, died trying to save his father.

Then Pretorius wanted to punish Dingaan.* More than punish, it was a battle, a revengeful battle! He'd had a force of 500 that included some of the English settlers. They camped on the banks of the river. On a Sunday, 16th December of 1838, they were surrounded by Zulus attacking again and again but each time the Zulus were driven back with cruel losses. Pretorius was one of the few wounded, leaving more than 3,000 dead Zulus. He had victoriously moved on to the high veld and some of his people founded Pietermaritzberg not more than a laager in a hot hollow of the hills. His victory had

---

*Dingaan: Famous Zulu leader

stood his prestige high and was the turning point of the great trek. He renewed the confidence of the trekkers and helped to set them free to organize the first Boer Republics' provinces that became permanent European settlements of the Union of S.A. and at the same time leaving the Eastern frontier insecure against the Xhosas. They had formed too many separate states, and always there was friction, and with friction, came war instead of peace and war between British and Dutch. The Boers; their education was the veld and the farm, neither literary or industrial, their children were thus robbed of being more educated and civilized. They formed a civilization based on poor whites and a landless black man separated by a rigid color bar. Nevertheless the trek certainly speeded up exploration and economic development due honor must go down in posterity to those pioneers who will have bequeathed a legacy to the future.

This was the land in which Jules lived, and now both Potgeiter and Pretorius were dead and those tented wagons moved from out of his sight, into history perhaps, or oblivion. They had moved on like time out of sight, while he reminisced with his thoughts of yesteryear. The twigs snapped behind him and Jules swung his head around, there stood Xosa. He was a gray man but he still had the body of a warrior. Jules noticed the hairs on his chest, snow white and sparse against his burgundy skin. "Hello, my friend," he said, and Xosa replied, saying, "Hello Sir, my father." "I'll never know why I'm the father. The way you cared for me Nkosie, it should be the other way around," Jules said. "I am losing my power, friend, see here," and he squeezed up his fisted arm to the elbow, forming a muscle. "My power is shrinking like the rain clouds on a summer day." He wiped his chin and brow. Xosa took him under the elbow and they came down the kopje. "No Sir, Mr. Jules," he said, "the power of the eagle is only finished when the eagle flies no more."

Twenty~Six

ulius moved out of his home to his new practice in Graham-stown. Jules and Kathleen gave him a pair of horses and the trap that once belonged to her and her father, the one Marietje so dearly loved. In a way, Kathleen was pleased not to have it in the sheds. She always imagined the corrugated iron squeaked and cracked far more, above that trap, then at any other place in the Traps Sheds. Women always filled their minds with guilt and foolish things they should forget about. Why did the blasted corrugated zinc always make odd sounds? It was the expansion and contraction of metal under the African sun and in Africa it had to be worse. Julius had built a shelter for this trap and had acquired land and stables for his horses. There was no doubt about it, Julius was a determined man destined to become a very great lawyer.

What Kathleen did not like was that he had bought a slave. Yes, he had bought a young man, left behind by one of the boers; that was a frequent happening. His acquisition was a mindless soul with great physical strength, though obedient and willing and grateful for kindness. Slavery had been abolished but this man was lost without a keeper, once beaten into submission probably. No one knew the truth, it just seemed that way. He was physically healthy but seemed to have the mind of a child. This suited Julius, who felt quite certain that from this black person, he would mould a good manservant. Julius was obsessed with Louisa, his mind was filled with the dreams of all men, filled with ecstasy and fantasies. He thought the feeling was love, yes, this to him was love, and he now thought of marriage.

In this land, the best thing a man could have was a good home loving wife. He worked very hard on his new premises and up above his offices of practice was his dwelling. His bedroom was furnished with an iron bed and paddcas, a flop, bolster dressing table and matching toilet glass and a chest of drawers. Large father pillows and carpets made of animal skins. It was a pleasant room. The living room, dining room, and kitchen were well furnished. Julius had bought saucepans from England and polished chairs and a handsome set of firearms were still to arrive. He was very pleased with his new home, the contents of which had cost £9,18s. 1 pence already and he had paid 8/6 for a handsome two leafed kitchen table, from a local wood carver.

He liked his independence. He enjoyed being alone; he was a loner, he didn't care for people at all. He looked down from his window and watched the people and carts and wagons that passed. He looked at the soldiers and boers on their boer horses, the traders and hunters. He pulled down the blinds. He was a superior being, he thought. When he had established himself firmly in Graham-stown, he would open up chambers in Port Elizabeth and soon he would be the most respected and most superior lawyer in all the land. Julius also spent considerable energy on preparing his home. He had completed his home upstairs, with kitchen, lavatory and bathing room downstairs.

He prepared a place at the back of the house behind his offices of law practice for his obedient manservant. He made a separate lavatory and toilet area, adjoining the quarters that were to be used only by his servant, "Swarthaas." He believed Swarthaas was once a normal boy, beaten and bruised by his former owners until his brain, unable to mend itself from constant bruises and bumps within the shelter of a cranium, still, unhardened by age, became permanently partially crippled. "He can run like a deer, this slave," his former owner told Julius, but Julius could tell by the look in his eye and his manner that not only his running ability had been spoiled by his owner, the Portuguese nomad with eyes like burning stones. It was odd to own a fellow human being, and Julius experienced an odd pleasure, the thrill, touch of megalomania perhaps.

He had learned of the treatment the slaves had received, far back in his own early childhood. His father helped to abolish slavery. He thought of black men only as a threat, never mind Xosa, they were all not to be trusted, murderous and full of hate. How often had he heard it said, "Never trust a kaffir." He was born in the wind of flying assegais all around him, the very sight of an assegai made his blood curdle and boil. He remembered his sister Moya crying out in her sleep and waking up in terror saying, "assegais." Those ugly, terrible assegais, and she would cling to Julius, her brother and protector and they slept in the same room through childhood.

It was comforting. He enjoyed the memory. His sister was so easy to be with, so loved by everyone, but not him, they never loved him as they loved Moya. That was yesteryear, now those years were over and done. He was back in the wilderness and it was different now. His father was a very successful person of great and good repute. His father was to be Sir Jules and his mother was a Lady. Their farm was making a lot of money selling wool, trading with the ivory floor in London, selling ostrich feathers from Uitenhuge. There was a lot to be said for this trading. Yes, well, he too would be recognized. He would be the superior academic, to whom all people would look up.

Julius was correct. He soon became a very successful legal man and an equally successful businessman. He made many trips to the bay and had dealings with ships and shipping. Ever a loner, he employed no one except Swart haas and did all his transactions alone. He was a curious character, elegant in black clothes, and fought a hard-winning legal battle.

Now again came a prosperous time for Sonnestroom. The disasters of the previous year did not deter the purchase of wool. More and more ships were arriving and leaving. Sir George Grey, a dashing man of 42 years, became Governor of the Cape Colony, perhaps because of his popularity dealing with the Maori peoples where he had previously been most successful. There were now three British colonies, Cape, British Keffaria and Natal, these were free republics, and only one the Orange Free State, had a stable government. The others were wresting both with each other as well as innumerable African tribes surrounding them. Sir George set about to resolve the frontier problems, but there never was peace.

Jules felt the time had come for him to take Kathleen and travel by ship to England, back to her homeland before she was any older. She took out her trunk, and one for Jules, and they talked excitedly of how they were going to do it. The trunks stood on the floor in an empty room so they would not take up space. "Do you remember Sannie, Jules, my dear friend Sannie?" she said, "she always told me, 'Kathleen,' she said, 'one day will come when you will take your trunk and sail away to England.' And I said to her, why should I want to do that, Sannie? And she said, 'because they say, the English want to die on English soil,'" she said. Jules said, "Ah look Kathleen, this African earth is thirsty earth, it's hard, like the life we live upon it. Your soul is soft, Kathleen, soft like the meadows of England, like the petals of the English rose," he said. "That's what he said, Jules," Kathleen said. "I wonder where in the Bible she found that knowledge," Jules said. "I only ever saw her read the Bible." "You are wrong, you know, Jules," Kathleen said. "We spent much time, Sannie and I! I used to read her Wordsworth and writings and poems. She used to love them so much and often I had to read them over and over again. I wonder where dear Sannie is now?" "Perhaps she's living happily in her husband's free republic," he said, "or on the other hand she might well have been murdered in one of those large laagers the trek boers built enroute to lands away from us British. She may be dead, Kathleen." "Oh God Jules, I so hope she's alive and happy," Kathleen said. "Perhaps one day we'll also trek inland and meet her, but for now it's England," Jules said.

"There is so much to do, Jules, I'm so excited," she said. "Feel my heart." And she took his hand and held it to her breast, and gazed excitedly into his eyes. Then she looked at his face. It was pale and wet. His wonderful clear blue eyes were tired. "Kathleen," he said, "feel my heart." And he took her hand and held it to his chest and his heart was pulsing in his neck slowly and irregularly. His hands were clammy and for the first time, she wondered why she hadn't noticed it before, his flesh was soft and puffy and where she took his wrist, her fingers left indentations. "Oh God, Jules," she said. "Don't you let me down, you have to fight, Jules. You have cheated death before, and you will do it again."

"Xosa," she yelled, "Xosa come quickly, call Lion!" In an instant Lion was there, towering above this man to whom he owed nothing but love and gratitude. He picked Jules up as though he was a lightweight, and lowered him onto the blue leather chaise settee that stood under the window in the living room. "Bring him a drink of brandy, Kathleen," he said. Xosa came in and knelt down on the floor beside Jules. "Jules, Sir," he said, "I can go for the doctor or I can take you to him, but it will be too long to fetch him. Miss Kathleen, shall we go?" Kathleen held the brandy to Jules' mouth, and he sipped it, mincing his mouth as if he were tasting or just finishing something he had eaten. "No, Xosa, I will rest. Take me to my bed, friend. I need to rest my tired body," he said. Lion picked him up and carried him to his bed. "Mr. Jules," he said, "one of the cows has calved today and her udder is full of colostrum. Is it not true that bees* will help an ailing heart?" "It's not the heart, Lion," he said, "it is this," and he moved the feather duvet downwards exposing the upper part of his abdomen. It was round and distended. "That is the liver, boy, do you know where the sheep got bloat, with a great distension of the bowels, you know how we pierced it once or twice, saying, 'kill or cure?' Well, Lion, this is how I feel. I feel a failure in my bodily works. This is bloat! And frequently of late I felt like saying kill or cure, Lion," he said. "I want to speak to you and Xosa, and I'd like you, my darling Kathleen to leave us, this is man's business for just awhile. I am not dying."

Kathleen moved out of the room. Taking Lion's large hand, Jules said, "Lion, I think I AM dying, and what grieves me most is leaving Kathleen," he said. "It is my wish that you and Xosa will guard her until the end of her life. You are strong like your father,

---

* bees = colostrum.

Lion, and as much a gentleman as he. I have watched you grow, and I understand the man you are. You are truly the son he always wanted. I trust you, Lion. I trust you like my very own son, and I love you like my son," he said. "Between you, my precious old friend, give me your hand" and he clasped the hand of Xosa, and he held in his other hand the hand of Lion. "Send Braam Piet to call Julius and the doctor if you so wish. But I would prefer it if both of you would remain with me. I never wanted to be alone when I die. I hoped to leave the world an older man than I am but it is not to be. My Kathleen will well reward you both. You are my family," he said. "Now pass me my brandy." "Kathleen," he called, and she was beside him in an instant. "Kathleen, my darling, Kathleen," and she lay beside him and they both were silent. They were all silent, She held his brandy so he could sip.

Julius had sent word for Louisa. He wanted her to come to his home and dine with him. He had just obtained a fresh supply of Cape wines and Peach brandy, and was so thrilled with his new abode. He'd like her to visit and see for herself. He would fetch her from her uncle's house on Friday afternoon before sunset. Louise was ready and waiting. She looked very beautiful. She had on a powder blue frock gathered in at the waist, and cut in a heart shaped yoke at the throat. The sleeves were out to widen her shoulders and she wore a matching bonnet. Her blues eyes were sparkly. The wind blew her crisp little ringlets that escaped from under the bonnet.

Julius felt his heart miss a beat. If only she knew the thoughts he'd had of her. She seemed so fresh and innocent, so fair and white in a land where women darkened with the African sun. "Louisa," he said, syllable by syllable, and taking both her hands, her fingers protruding from fingerless gloves. He lifted them to his lips. "Louise, you are so lovely," he said. At that moment, her uncle made his appearance. "Uncle," said Louisa, "this is Julius Jacobsen, Julius, my uncle Mr. Barnabas Show." Julius shook his hand. "Preacher and school master," said Barnabas. "Lawyer," said Julius. They passed a few words of friendly chatter, Julius refusing the hospitality of a cool drink. "No sir," he said, "perhaps later, when I will safely return your lovely niece," he said. He climbed up into his carriage holding the reins. He secured them to the back of the footboard, and helped Louisa into the carriage. She lithely stepped on the footplate and alighted beside him. He unfastened the reins, and lifting his hat to her uncle, pulled the reins to move the horses.

They moved off without straining and walked off unbriskly for Julius had not asked more of them. He was enchanted with Louisa. It did not take long before they arrived at his home along the Track Cradock Road only slightly outside of the town. It was exciting for Louisa. First she looked at his offices, and then at the kitchen with its large oven. She ran about asking questions in a curious manner, and then she saw "Swart Haas."* "Hello," she said, as she peered into his coal black eyes and she reached out her hand to him. But Julius stepped between them. "No, Louisa," he said, "this is just my manservant, and not a very eloquent one either." She felt like a child who had its fingers smacked and withdrew in a timid way. "With tuition he will be an excellent servant," Julius said. "Perhaps even become a majordomo in time." She looked through his tidy house and they dined on roast lamb with potatoes and melon and a fresh wheat loaf. They had coffee and peach brandy.

It was after Louisa had perused several of Julius' books and the conversation had begun to be about themselves that Louisa

---

* Swart haas = Black hare.

dreaded the time had come to go home. He was reluctant to take her so soon, but obeyed, saying her wish was his command. He was quite silent on the way home and only when she arrived did he ask her if she would come again on Sunday.

On Saturday evening Braam Piet came racing to Julius. "Julius," he said, "you must come home. Your father is dying, I think. I never spoke to him myself, but I left him with Lion and Lion said he might be dying." "To hell with Lion," Julius said, "is he some kind of physician?" He was busying himself with his toiletry. "I think you must come right away, Julius," he said. "I am going for the doctor now and hope to take you home to tend your father." Julius turned around slowly. He was slim and tall, sallow, pale of complexion. Not by any means an ordinary man. He had the cold, elegant looks of a sallow count and often seemed as though he was short of breath.

Pollen made him sneeze so he never had flowers anywhere near him, and mostly covered his nose and mouth whenever he was near a flowery tree, especially a mimosa. Braam had with him a bunch of wild vlei lilies and as he looked at the blooms he yelled at Braam. "Take those goddam flowers out of here, you blasted, damned fool! Get out and go find your doctor. My father has been dying for over a year now, so I think I might well complete my business tomorrow and ride out to mother and father on Monday. I have some important business on Sunday," he said. "Is any business more important than your father, Julius?" Braam said, and he closed the door leaving only the smell of the lilies and the sound of the swiftly moving horses' hooves on the cobblestone streets behind him.

Julius was overexcited on Sunday. He sent Swaart Haas to the church and told him to remain there until after the final sermon, and Swaart Haas was only too happy to go. Julius then collected

Louisa before the sun set, telling her all the way how he had to leave as his father was not well. She was most concerned, being an orphan herself and was most sympathetically attention to Julius. She had been alone at her own home when Julius collected her, as her Uncle preached all day Sunday, and then also took a service after supper. "I've brought you this," she said, and offered him a small porcelain bowl of egg cakes she had baked, together with the daily bread, in her uncle's large oven.

Julius had made a cold supper of cooked chicken, a new goats milk cheese, and wine, and they dined. Rather, Louisa dined, and Julius watched her. He was not hungry and kept looking at her, to a point of discomfort. He drew the blind closed. "Louisa," he said, saying one syllable at a time, "Loo-wis-a, I want to marry you, will you marry me?" For several moments she kept her eyes averted, then having thought about her reply, she looked up into his face. "Julius, I am very honored," she said. "Thank you for asking me, only I am not ready for marriage on so short an acquaintance. Why Julius, I have never loved and know not yet what it really means." She reached out her hands and cupping her hand under his chin, partly caressed one side of his face.

Like a trigger of a musket, Julius caught hold of her, twisted her backwards, his mouth covering hers. He fell down upon her. She was unable to scream. He kept his mouth over hers in a smothering slobbery kiss. He tore off her skirt, under which she was in her knee lace pantaloons and white stockings. He pinned down her arms, he was on the floor now, and she was hysterical. "Oh God, help me!" she cried, but Julius again smothered the words with his own mouth. He held down one of her legs with his foot and held both hands in his one hand with the other. He ripped off her pantaloons, exposing her white little body. He bit the flesh of her throat with his white teeth and she screamed and screamed. He threw off his own clothes and fell upon her sucking for air and perspiring profusely. He was grappling for her breasts, licking and sucking all over her forlorn body, as she cried pitifully. And he forced her legs apart, heaving to and fro and finally fell upon, into her body.

She screamed in a heartrending call and fell silent. She went limp and lay still. Then it was all over. In a sickly, deathly silence he drew away from her body. His own body was smeared with her blood and her groin and thighs were wet and with his semen and blood. He seemed surprised at his own actions and stood there naked except for his stockings and vest. He looked at Louisa. She had spurned him, turned him down in her silly feminine way. She was groaning softly, her eyes were wide open, constantly whimpering, like a bitch puppy mauled by a big dog in a fight, bewildered and terrified, defiled and beaten into submission. She crawled towards her skirt, covering her body with her small hands. The hands were fumbling and trembling. She moved as if in a coma, she crawled on her knees towards her clothes, stumbling and pulling her skirt onto her body from the feet up, laving her underwear, she clumsily stumbled toward the steps. She never looked up nor saw anything. He moved towards her and as he did so, she urinated, like a terrified puppy. He stopped, and she stumbled down and onto the street.

It was dark. She stumbled along the cobblestone road. She did not know her way about. She felt ill. She wanted to vomit. She did not know where but she had pain. She was trembling. She wiped her mouth. Where was she going? She had to think of the tracks. Oh God, she called out crying aloud. She was trying to remember her uncle's mission. She had on only one stocking and it had dropped to her ankles. Her shoelaces were loose and her shoes were coming off. She crouched down to try to fasten her shoes, and then a dog brushed against her body. She was terrified. Then she relaxed. Oh Rex, she spewed out, thank God. She said Help me home Rex. But Rex seemed interested in every smell around her. She followed him waiting when he lifted his leg to urinate. So many many times. She felt God had sent him to help her home. Where are you Rex, she watched in the darkness. She watched his moving body. She had no idea she had to cross this velt. She followed, after what seemed like hours. Lantern lights became visible. Yes, sure enough the lights were her uncle's mission lights. Where was the dog? It seemed he entered on a different side, confusing her but she followed. Finally she found her room. The door was unlocked. She opened and entered. She stood inside a second. She was thankful. She moved to her iron bed. It was neatly covered with a white quilt. She pulled off the quilt, flung it to the bottom of her bedstead and sat down. The lantern was still burning and moths were flying around it.

She closed her eyes and held her head in her hands, struggling to get her thoughts right.

A washstand stood on one side of her room with a stone top and a sort of soap dish on the side. A large white porcelain bowl and a jug with red roses all over it stood in its middle, half filled with water. She took the jug out and poured water into the bowl, bend down to wash her mouth, over and over, then taking a small towel set about cleaning her body—neck, arms, everywhere. There was a bathroom of sorts, but it adjoined her uncle's quarters. She felt she must be quiet. She was not sure what she suffered; pain, fear, shame. She stayed with the washstand—squeezed out the towel. My God, where was her strength? She started to cry again. She whimpered. She squirmed. She wept. She fell upon her bed, it squeaked as she moved. It's only my bed, what is heavy is a man's body. Oh God, let me die, she wailed, and buried her head on her small square pillow. Heaving. She shuddered—where was she? What was happening. She called, "Uncle where are you?" Her head swirled and then there was the sea. Yes, yes I'm going on that ship with my uncle. I'm going to teach in Africa. Excuse me, she called, someone help me to the ship. The ship to Africa. In her delirium she called out. The big wooden ship to Africa.

Twenty-Seven

Julius wiped his body clean and put on his nightshirt. He too was silent. He poured himself a brandy and another and another, throwing it back into his throat with one gulp. He moved over to the window, opened the blind and peered out. When he last saw her she was a disappearing shape, stumbling and falling on the cobblestones and he watched her disappear into the dark. He put down the goblet and then dressed himself carefully. He lit the oil lamp, and went out toward the stables. He brought the horses in, one at a time, struck a flint, lighting the other lamp that hung beside the stable entrance. He then took down the harness that hung on a large hook. The horses were snorting, both of them. The smell of blood, he muttered to himself.

She was a goddam virgin! He gave a nervous chuckle, but the way she looked at that bastard, Lion, no one would have guessed. He filled up his water cask and hitched it to the side of the trap and quietly closing the stable doors, returned to his bedroom. He placed the light on the table beside his bed, took off the shirt and dressed himself in preparation for a journey, taking his cutthroat* and musket and many rounds of ammunition, placed them in a coarse satchel and carried it into the living room. Her white lace pantaloons lay on the floor near a dark stain patch. He took them up and threw them down. The dark patch on his floor, My God, the blood was still wet. He tread the underwear onto the dark patch with his foot, soaking up the little patch of blood and left it there. He then tread on them again and again as though angrily mopping up a mess.

The door clicked open and as he looked up, there Swaart Haas stood, silent. "Clean up the room, Swaart Haas," he said. "You clean up everything and wash Missy's clothes. And you stay, do not leave the house, do you hear?" He gesticulated with his index finger. "Do not go out, you understand?" The black man looked at the clothes on the floor. He had seen enough in his slave days to understand. He looked at Julius, staring at him with his coal black eyes. Julius took his horsewhip, put on his hat, struck another flint and lit the oil lamp and then moved out. It was still dark, but now he'd ride to Sonnestroom. He wanted to go away. Swaart Haas gathered up the bloodstained clothes and neatly folded them into a small parcel.

When Braam Piet found the doctor he'd raced home. The horses were exhausted. Lion had given orders to bathe their feet and feed them well, lest they succumb from over-exhaustion. There was a constant movement of traffic at Sonnestroom, people were fearful, distraught, talking in whispers. They all knew of Jules. Old Klassie had died the previous summer and Moerskind lived like a recluse, doddering and senile. He no longer remembered anything, withered and crinkled, he just sat in his house and smoked a big

---

* kind of razor for shaving.

Dutch pipe. Marta was always there, old and thin, but always there, nursing her beloved Kathleen. There were so many persons, all children born of Jules' workplace people, plus many others who worked as farm hands.

A small school had been erected for workers in the area, and was well attended and full of children, all eager to learn. The missionaries had begun to teach them their religion and the small Wesleyan chapel was generally filled to capacity. This Sunday the service was held on the green grass of Sonnestroom and a choir of voices were singing hymns. Something they must have felt would be of help or perhaps as some mark of respect. Wailing sort of hymns that drifted over the valley. Someone played a concertina. Dogs were barking all the while, trying to tell them this was not their territory.

Inside the doctor pummeled Jules' distention, tapping the hollow abdomen like an African tomtom, blue veins spreading over it like an ill-defined map. As he pressed his wrists and ankles the indentations remained, and now to make matters worse Jules felt nauseous. The doctor took out some ether and opening and closing his nostrils, forced Jules to deeply inhale, "to induce a perfect insensibility," he said, and it certainly did. It made Jules quite cheery. He became quite humorous and a little later stupefied from the effects of the ether. But he knew his life was ending, ebbing away somewhere. "Doctor," he had said, "I know I am done for. I would like to spend these last sane moments with my beloved wife. It is sad that life should end so soon, my friend, but death has no great fears for me. Look how yellow are my hands! I shall be safely planted, nearby on this farm, in the soil that I love. Things grow so easy in this soil. Yes doctor!" The doctor left his little bottle of ether. "If you have great pain, he said, "inhale yourself to insensibility." He

also took Kathleen into the room and told her there was nothing
he could do for Jules. He had renal failure and a non-functional
liver. All one could do was to make him comfortable.

Julius arrived on Monday evening, and he went straight into
his father's room. Jules was lucid, greeting him with a smile and
extending his hand to touch him. "I'm sad I will not be alive
to see your sons, Julius," he said, "and I only just missed seeing
Moya's children in England. We work too hard and don't do
enough time off, you know, with our short lives. "You live more,
my boy. See and do everything you can while life is yours." Please
pass me the vapor," he said. Julius passed him the little bottle
and he inhaled with one nostril and then with the other, a deep
inhalation. "It's almost instant you know," he said. "See my yellow
hands. This stuff makes me rather insensible to this pain," and he
touched his abdomen just below where the ribs end. His chest
looked strong and still quite youthful, with only a sprinkling of
gray hairs among the thick pad of golden blonde. His forehead
hair was only slightly receded and his now yellow skin was clear,
though very tanned and rugged. He was still a handsome man.
His hands were strong with only a callous or two, and on his little
finger he wore a gold ring with a crest, a Viking shield, the head
of an eagle and a scroll.

Julius looked at his hands and the ring. He called for Kathleen,
but Kathleen was beside him on his bed. She had not moved all
day. She was looking at him, filled with emotion and resentment.
Jules did not even resemble a man ready to die. His body was
strong and his legs robust and his arms well muscled and full of
power. Life had cheated him. After all, if one is given a life, then
surely allow the full three score years and ten, especially Jules, a
man who had worked assiduously for all mankind, wild and full of

ardor! A man of creation and goodness, preservation and compassion. A wonderful man who bequeathed so much, to tomorrow. Defeatedly she shook her head, bowed in denial, in disbelief. We need humans like Jules. Earth needs him. Why dear God does Jules have to go? She was devastated. She was drenched in sorrow. She was not brave like Jules.

Two days later it was the 1ˢᵗ of March. Jules was still alive, but around him hung the aura of death. His eyelids were swollen and his eyes yellow, heavy, but he had not lost his vision. Great drums rolled and beat inside his head, but it did not impair his hearing. His throat was dry and his tongue felt thick and leaden, yet he still spoke, and he spoke incessantly of his joys and memories, rambling on about the new seasons, the wells of life, the ever-present fears of death, about his sadnesses and his joys, and then he said quite clearly how thankful he was to his beautiful woman. Pointing to Julius, "and you my dear son, you mend your ways. Might your mother know of your misdemeanors and dishonor?" and he gave a husky half cough-like chuckle, "aye, son, your own father, hated that you killed our Lioness. I have no doubt, my darling Kathleen, Julius will return" but he failed to finish his sentence.

All that talking was an effort. He'd been talking all day through, for already it was darkening. The twilight seemed upon them, that depressing hour when the day dies and is lost in the embrace of the night. He called out for Kathleen. He was holding her hand all along, she had not moved once and she clung to his hands and her lips started to tremble and her tears fell upon his once so protective hands. Then his voice flew to the forests and the veld, and she heard for a fleeting moment his boyish call echo in the hills. As she did always, long ago. "I love you Kathleen," he said, "I love you." That echo grew further and further away, the echo she shared with the wild winds. She sobbed suddenly, bitterly, deep heavy sobs, her whole body heaving and drowning in the hot midday air. Grief is agony. She kissed his fingers. She covered Jules, leaving his face exposed. She pressed his eyelids down and placed her fingers upon each eye, and tied a scarf under his chin and around his head to close his mouth.

At Sonnestroom, the gloom spread like a heavy blue gray storm cloud. The staff spoke in whispers and often the sound of weeping escaped from the lips of all the women. In the palm of the kopje, the bare-backed kaffirs were digging, rhythmic beats, first one and then the other, it sounded like the distant sound of a turkey buzzard. They were not in unison, lifting their picks and bringing them down with a thud. The earth was not so hard and when enough soil was loosened they picked up their shovels and threw it onto a mound at the side of the grave. Sitting on a stone just above was a lone black man. A proud powerful man. Around his head he wore the feathers and plumes of the blue crane. He was graying now, and he was also stripped to the waist. He was dressed in his war clothes with bands of hair around his ankles and bands of empty seedpods rattling like the crackles of a great veld fire. His eyes were staring as he held his assegai high and he lowered it as if he were throwing it. He stamped his feet softly, singing and whining like a hungry caged dog, chanting strange chanting!

His body was unmistakably strong and still showed signs of the fire that raged within him. Here was a Xosa warrior, a true single warrior, magnificently lithe and almost graceful in his movements. Now and then a strange guttural growl emanated from his throat, animal like, like an inhuman expulsion of the very air that made him breathe. The diggers kept on spitting on the hands before they lifted their rough pick heads. They were digging two graves one beside the other, the graves of black men were not usually beside the white men. But that Xosa warrior, he was the shadow of the great Baas, and it was he who ordered two graves to be dug. As the mounds grew higher, overhead the vultures seemed to glide in great arches. They knew the sound of graves being dug, and as they flew their shadows moved across the earth up into the koptje, like drifting spirits.

Kathleen had not come to terms with Jules' death. She was emotionally drained. She had been through several deaths, starting at an early age with her mother's death. She had seen so many bodies lying dead. This was something else. This was half of her own life and soul. She felt she was bleeding to death: Jules, Lion, Braam Piet, Jan they had all fought on the frontier. In fear indescribable! They were all used to the faces of death. She remembered her father, his feet sticking out the bottom of the old blanket, and the bodies that lay about him, flies in swarms buzzed about them with thousands of their eggs, clustered in neat rows in their nostrils and ears, upon their eyelids and lashes, like tiny little creamy oval pearls, to become maggots that eat clear away dead human flesh. They always started around the edges of gaping wounds. She was no longer afraid of death. Once the spirit, the breath had gone, what was left was finished with. Lion was making a casket for Jules. She could hear them banging and cutting and chopping wood. Jules, what was left of him, would be buried in a coffin, Lion would create. She felt comfort and certainty.

And then, as she pondered with her perplexed thoughts, horses arrived on the lawn. Pandemonium broke, created by voices and horses and shouts and orders of command, whips and carriage wheels, commandments and field cornets. Kathleen and Julius were stunned. Here were the highest-ranking officials, redcoats and silver sabre and polished buttons shone in the sun. It was a lovely sunny day. Kathleen was informed that the Voksraad had requested a state funeral be held in Grahamstown, but Kathleen had promised Jules his resting place be in the kopje, so arrangements were made for the funeral to take place on March 4th. Lion was instructed to place Jules' body in his coffin and it was mounted on the wheeled gun carriage and placed in a hay shelter outside of the house. The lid was left open and all persons were allowed to pay their last respects.

It was an amazing day. A bewildered Kathleen did not realize—when it had all subsided and happened. He had never told her fully of his recognition, though she had known of his accomplishments. It was an odd strange feeling. Today, her husband was to be buried. He looked marble like, lying in his natural wood casket. The servants passed by, swooning and weeping in strange mournful sounds, and all the time working at speed a grief-stricken Lion was carving the wood at the head of his coffin, cutting and chipping in a race against time, his face severe, driven, distraught, determined and deadly serious. He chiseled and chipped, disregarding anyone who passed by Jules' casket. His face was strangely twisted by grief. Yet he was totally distracted in his determination.

Jules was to be buried at 3 p.m. Governor had arranged for a Wesleyan minister to conduct a service because Jules had not learned to speak Dutch, although the Dutch reformed church was the state church. The minister was on his way and was expected midday. The Lt. Governor of the Eastern Districts, the Landrost, the British garrison frontier armed mounted police, loyal fungoes and Hottentot Levies and standing in a solitary line, their black bodies gleaming in the light. Their plumes blowing in the breeze, a straight row of black warriors, a humble and respectful contingent of Moshesh the Chief.

The officials handled the arrangements with expert military precision. Groups were placed in position 30 minutes before 3 p.m. Horses and guns were drawn up and then along the dusty road trotting at an easy pace, a trap and two passengers came into view. It was the preacher and beside him in a white bonnet was a lady. As the small carriage drew nearer one of the voerloper youths went forward to take the horses, and the commanding officer went towards the preacher. He had stopped along the road and changed into a black robe. "Mr. Barnabas Show," said the officer, they shook hands, "this is my niece, Louisa Brumley." Officers and soldiers tipped their hats and saluted and the preacher came forward. Louisa took his arm and they walked towards the gun carriage. Lion was still chipping and scraping, but as he looked up he said, "Yes Sir, I have finished," and his eyes caught Louisa's. He stood erect, holding his chisel half behind his right buttock. "Miss Louisa," he repeated, and she reached out her hand and he took her left hand in his left hand and kissed it, still holding the chisels at his side.

The preacher looked at the casket, then reached out and removed a small piece of wood from off the carving on the casket. Lion had been carving night and day, and now it was complete. Lion had carved the head of a lion and the wings of an eagle. The pracher looked at it. "Sad," he said, "so beautiful, a carving must go to dust like the incumbent of his earthly box," and then Kathleen was there and she leaned on the arms of Braam Piet, and when she saw the procession getting ready she moved up towards Lion and slid her arm there to his arm. A bugle played and commands were yelled to a deathly single beat of a huge booming drum and the entire mass of red uniforms, with plumed hats, blue crane plumes, upon shining black warriers, Hottentots and guns all

Moshesh the Chief

moved towards the kopje led by the preacher, his black robes blowing in the breeze.

Mr. Barnabas read his sermon, quoting all the virtues of the unique Jules—the deceased. The son in law of the Master General of the Eastern Frontier Party, Lieutenant of HM 25th Regiment Agriculturalist Supreme, Captain and sailor, husband, father, knighted by HM the Queen for successful effort and perseverance and promoting the welfare of his fellow settlers, for further improving the country of his adoption. A tablet will be erected by the government as a tribute to those talents and that worth by which he was distinguished, alike in social and in public life. The preacher was still going on with his sermon as the bugler played

the last post, and then before the eyes of everyone came a large
Xosa warrior. The black warrior stumbled forth, from behind the
stones on the kopje, his eyes were black as stone, and opened wide
and staring. White froth bubbled in the corners of his mouth. "My
master, my teacher, Jules, my friend, my father, our spirits will
depart together!"

He held high his spear, as he stood beside the mound of earth.
"This is Xosa's resting place," he said, "we, Jules and myself, we
together lived life, and together we die. Will be together now in
death." Before another move was made, holding his spear high
above his head, he threw it high up into the kopje with great
power. "We will both be gone!" And with a piercing yell, he then
raced back towards the rocks from where he had come, and fell
upon a deadly spear he had arranged for his demise, the head of
which went straight into his heart. Braam Piet stepped towards
him. The bright red blood was oozing from his chest. He lifted
him up and Lion held on to Kathleen. The officers came forward.
It was an awe-inspiring, jaw dropping moment, halted in time.
Unbelievable, open mouth shock.

Braam Piet was unsuccessfully pulling at the sharpened
spearhead. He lifted Xosa's limp chin. His face was smiling, a
frothy, happy smile. His eyes were wide open. Kathleen gave
a scream and sank into Lion's arms. The officers did not quite
know what to do. Louisa stood by, horror stricken. "Hold her,
Louisa," said Lion, and he put Kathleen onto Louisa's arm. He
then went toward the officer. "That grave, Sir, is where that man
will rest." He turned to the preacher. "Give him a gentleman's
service, sir, for no two men ever loved more than they, true
respectful love." He was now unable to control himself. And in
a trembling broken voice, his tears falling on his golden face, he

wept. He just looked at the officers and then to the governor. The governor immediately triggered into action, summoned a carriage and pulling off the British flag, they rolled Xosa's body into it. The governor took off his hat and placing it on the black man's chest, he saluted. "That's the best I can do for you, Sir," he said, and several soldiers silently amd solemn lowered Xosa's body into the grave beside Jules.

A spine-chilling shriek went up from the black men who, up back, had stood motionless. Then, as one man, they together all crouched and with another shrill, ear piercing screech, they hurled their shining spears, whirring up into the hills with unbelievably great power: and only the echoes of their screeches returned. They all stood in silence after the second gun salute. Lion sprang forward. "There is nothing good enough. Sir, nothing is good enough Sir for this man. Then all the Xosa warriors faced the grave, staring at the burial spot. They were silent, simultaneously they all started to walk backwards, as though they were witnessing some strange apparition. Backwards, backwards. And suddenly they were all gone. They were all gone. The air did not smell of gunpowder or smoke. It was filled with the sweet smell of wild flowers, and the birds sang like they always did.

Kathleen looked for Julius, but he was not there. She held on to Louisa and they clung to each other. The bugle kept playing the eerie last post and guns fired in salute at last. She was exhausted. Finally the last of the mounted and walking troops had marched and ridden out into the dusty distance. Reverend Barnabas Show remained and they sat down in the living room. They were going to have tea. Lion was strong and attentive. "Lion," said Kathleen, "thank you, that was the most beautiful wood cut I have ever seen," and she cried softly, raising her kerchief to her lips and eyes. "His soul was as high as the eagles fly, and his body as strong as the lion," Lion murmured. "He was like you, Lion," said Louisa, and she got up to take Kathleen her tea. The door opened and Julius came in. As he did so, Louisa gave a terrible scream. She dropped the precious teacup and cowered against the wall, she went pale and limp, then slid down in a small heap onto the floor, like a dead fearful fainting. Julius served himself tea and sat down quietly, while everyone about him fussed over Louisa. Kathleen had her taken to the bedroom and laid Louisa down. She was too exhausted by her own ordeal to notice the terror on Louisa's face. "You rest awhile Louisa," she told her.

Braam Piet arranged for one of the coachmen to accompany the preacher back home and he promised Mr. Show they would arrange to bring his niece home when she would be strong enough to travel. Lion could not quite understand. The whole funeral ceremony was grueling. He felt quite weakened himself, now this wonderful girl whom he knew to be quite strong, had suddenly collapsed. He drank his tea. After the preacher left, only he and Julius were in the living room. Julius looked at Lion. "I suppose you feel like some sort of hero, carving your bloody Lion on my father's coffin. No one asked you to do that, did they?" He stared at Lion and kept looking at him intensely. Lion stared back at him. "No, Julius, it was just me, and I don't give a damn about what you say. Two great men were buried today. Two men that I shall never forget, and the likes of whom, you will never be." He finished his tea and left the room, closing the door softly behind him.

Louisa was up early. She was ill, vomiting into a porcelain chamber pot when Kathleen found her. Kathleen brought her some honey bush tea, black it was, sweetened only by nature. "Drink this, Louisa," she said. "It really does make one feel a little better." Louisa looked up at Kathleen. "You really are so kind," she said, and they started to talk a little about themselves. Kathleen told her about Jules and Louisa about herself. She was an orphan and had never really known the joy of having a mother. She had been brought up by a maiden aunt, and it was her own choice to come to Africa and teach in the mission school with her Uncle Barnabas. She was a gentle creature, and Kathleen took to the girl. She insisted on her staying at Sonnestroom until she was very strong and a journey could be made to Grahamstown.

Something rather puzzled Kathleen. The girl would not come out of the room, not even at mealtimes. She had a small gold-edged Bible, and though Kathleen never saw her rading it, she seemed to clasp it in her hands all the time. Trembly, pale, little hands, help-less and small. Her eyes were searching and full of fear, but when she was curious they were clear and full of innocence and one felt driven to protect this girl. Julius returned to Grahamstown. He insisted that the legal aspects of their family's disruption should be attended to. But Kathleen waved him off, saying that there was time later to see to these things. When Julius was gone, long disappeared into the distant dust, out of sight and the day had grown a little older, Louisa came out of the room. She took Kathleen by the hand and walked all over the meadowy gardens, down through the aloes, where once Kathleen's jewels were hidden, everywhere except near the koptje. She sang and seemed as if she'd been reborn. Kathleen insisted that she stay awhile.

Twnty - Eight

A fter Louisa had been at Sonnestroom for nearly a month, Kathy felt she would be a lovely companion. So she wrote to Rev. Barnabas Show, asking him to allow Louisa to remain on at Sonnestroom. Kathy offered to be her guardian, saying her sojourn on the farm would be indefinite. She explained that Louisa was a frail girl in need of a woman's company and that she could continue her teaching at the little mixed farm school. Kathy hoped Louisa would outgrow her seclusion, her secret weeping, nightmares and fears, and perhaps open up and disclose her feelings with another woman. So the household with Louisa at Sonnestroom was much more pleasant.

She'd gather flowers and fill up little vases and containers in all the rooms and corners. She could cook and bake and soon learned to use the big oven. At times she was nauseous, in fact quite frequently so, but of course it was not uncommon with young girls. She wrote a lot, she liked poetry and made charcoal sketches of birds and ducks she visited down at the dam. All the while, Kathy could see Lion was laughing too eagerly at her puns and jokes. He forgot to eat when she spoke and often forgot to eat anything himself, quite unlike Lion who always had a robust and healthy appetite. Lion had lost his heart to this light little lady, and light she was, her golden hair and clear blue eyes, and her delicious musical laughter. Let them live, thought Kathy, life is so short and even shorter out in a wilderness where one is soon bent beneath the blows of life.

Tomorrow, she'd take them up into the hills, where the waters of many little streams ran down into the river, all together and all those big yellow trees that were still standing gave shade to the beasts that sought it, and cattle stood belly deep in sedge grass. There, near the vlei, marvelous smelling vlei lilies permeated the air and a small spring above a tiny waterfall, replenished pools, the flowers were everywhere, and sounds of frogs hung heavy in the air, with bees busy gathering pollen from flower to flower and where colored dragonflies joined together in procreation. This was paradise for her and Jules, and how often did they flatten the grass and the ground cover, making love, desperate, passionate, breathtaking love, while all around them the wild game and birds of brilliant plumage sang melodious songs, there their passions cooled down to calm, on that ever damp and wondrous sedge.

She would take them to share her place, her heaven. "This is my heaven, Jules," she had told him, "I don't care about the Bible and promises of some unseen hereafter, this is our heaven, Jules. We are so lucky to just feel this almost perfect peace and joy, you can be happy with promises, but this, here and now, this is for me," and she too would frolic and dance and sing and love. She was young then, though now she still feels the joy she no longer will lie on the sedge and roll in absolute surrender and let her body dissolve into another.

Always looking forward to tomorrow, and new tomorrows came. Louisa was sick, again she sat with the porcelain chamber pot** on her lap. She had odd glimpses of fear and Kathy frowned as she watched her wash the pot and replace it under the bed or run to the lavatory pan. She waited until Lion returned from the veld. He'd been out since dawn. "Remember, yesterday I said I'd take you to my place?" she said. "Well as soon as we've eaten we shall go there. It's not a long walk, but it's not a short one either, so bring a wrap Louisa, and we will take our guns to be safe." "Oh Kathy," Louisa said, "I'm so happy," and after lunch didn't come soon enough. She had her bonnet on and was ready to go.

It was a glorious day. March was coming near to April and the sun was no longer burning hot. As they walked, the country seemed to change. Everything changed. She held on to Kathy and then ran on ahead and Lion went after her, and he took her hand. They looked at each other, and their eyes joined like the dragonflies. "Oh dear God Lion, I think I love you," and he took her in his arms and lifted her like a feather and kissed her on the lips and kissed her on her face and arms and neck, and Kathy stopped. She well knew the ramp and road of uninhibited love, but she was here and they were not free. Louisa then drew away and suddenly frolicked on towards the vlei, which nestled at the bottom of the hills. Lion, with powerful strides, bounded up the sides of a rock ledge. Rocks stuck up, rough and rugged and mighty. They played like children.

"Hello, Louisa," he called again and again, "hello Louisa, I love you Louisa," and the echo repeated it way into the distance. "Hello Louisa, I love you Louisa." "Oh Kathy," Louisa said, "darling Kathy, it's so beautiful, if I were to choose where to be buried when I die, I'd like it to be there, where Lion just called, somewhere there

---

** The container kept under the bed was called a 'Poe'.

under those rocks," she pointed, "wouldn't that be heaven, Kathy?" "That is heaven, my lovely Louisa, God's sake girl, you're alive, you are very young, take all life has to offer you, take it with both hands and live."

Louisa caught hold of Kathy's hand and squeezed it to her cheek. "Kathy, I do so love you." Lion climbed down from the ledge and they lingered awhile before they made for home. Like happy children they sang and romped, climbed up and down and gathered flowers and talked and laughed, and no day was ever more happy, no heart more giving. "When one is so ecstatically happy, we tend to wish it would never end, but I tell you this, Lion McCabe, if I die before you, I shall be there waiting for you when you breathe your last breath, or if you have deathly fear, a near death fear, I will rescue you and take you away." And no love would ever be more wonderful or more perfect, or more soul stirring.

On Sunday, when all the workers were in their homebuilt chapel and Kathy was writing in her study, Louisa and Lion again went out towards Kathy's place. They were so excited, they now were alone and they were electrified with love. They chose the afternoon, the same hour as Kathy had taken them previously. They ran childishly, feeling and touching and kissing and talking, so Lion was alive and joyful, always filled with honorable manly intentions. Louisa was so soft and gentle, he felt he should carry her sometimes, but she would have none of that; she was lithe and light of foot, and she tried to do everything that he did. Beside the vlei, she gathered flowers and filled her arms full of lilies; she looked like a delicate painting done by a master that had come alive from out of some precious frame.

"Hello Lion," she called, "I love you," and they heard the echo call softly in the distance. "Hello Lion, I love you, hello Lion, I love you." And Lion caught her in his arms and the flowers fell on the sedge, and he kissed her and kissed her, her face and neck and head and hands. They tore off their clothes and they rolled on the sedge over and over, and their bodies dissolved into each other's, and they groaned into an unconscious limbo of ecstasy, the heights of which soared with the eagles, higher than the hills and the sounds of life disappeared like the echoes.

They lay on the sedge, the ground cover was flattened, their bodies wet with sweat and the salty tastes of passion. "My darling Louisa, I want to marry you," Lion said, "I so love you Louisa," she smothered him with kisses and burst into a flood of hysterical sobs. She wept bitter sobs of anguish. "Lion, Lion, my precious, most precious Lion," she cried, "I love you, I love you, but I cannot marry you." And she told him haltingly as she clawed the earth with her hands. She told him of her rape, as she sobbed and halted for breath. "It was on a Sunday, Lion," she said, "Julius wanted me to dine with him. My uncle was preaching and was taking the late sermon. Julius had sent his manservant Swart Haas to church. We were to dine together at his home. I had gone one other time already, and he was quite pleasant so I had no reason to mistrust him. On that Sunday he raped me, Lion," she said. "He brutally injured me." She sobbed and sobbed, hiding her face in her hands.

"I have no knowledge of men, and I had to run through the streets at night with my clothes torn and my legs all soiled. In my terror I came home without underwear, half naked through the streets. I crept into my room, my uncle was not back from his sermon, so I drank some milk with a few spoons of sugar and went to bed. It was horrible, it was so terrible Lion. I was ill and took to my bed for weeks. My uncle wanted to call the physician but I was so afraid and ashamed, I thought he should not." She sobbed incessantly and her lips and hands were trembling. Lion put his arms around her, and he could feel the trembling of her body as she sobbed. "My uncle never knew. I preferred that he did not know, for he is an important person in the colony and I would die rather than bring disgrace upon him. Julius never came again, but his servant Swaart Haas did. He told me he had found my clothes on the floor and had wondered if I was alright. I had no idea Uncle was coming to bury your dear Jules, he said it was a state funeral. But when Julius came into your living room, something too awful happened, it was as if I had no vision, no head, and I just fell down. I was so afraid of him."

Lion listened to her, his head bowed. He was speechless. He had no idea how to handle so delicate a situation. He was silent, voiceless.

"Should we not tell Kathy?" he inquired.

"No, no, no Lion," she cried, "never tell any person. I trust this only with you, Lion. I don't want you to marry me, I cannot, not after this, but I cannot help loving you. Please Lion, promise me now, you will never tell any living person. Do you promise, Lion?" And she put her hands on his lips with a wet face, looked up at his pleading.

Lion simply said, "I promise you, my love." He would talk to Swaart Haas. That was not bound by any promise.

And they clung to each other. She was whimpering softly like an orphan puppy. "Don't think about it Louisa," he said. "I will always love you and I will always protect you. See how strong I am?" And he scooped her up with one arm and swung her around and around and held her to him. His whole being was crowded with mixed emotions, and at that moment he knew he could

kill Julius as easily as he squashed a horse fly. But though he was
bruised and pummeled within, in a maze of tortured grief, hate
and love and depression, his great tenderness and caring emerged.
He knew Louisa would not marry him. So much work, there
was always work. A farm is work from morning to night. They
returned home less boisterous. They had a silent supper and but
for the barking of the dog and a distant whoop of a lone hyena,
Sonnestroom rested until the new day came again.

As the month passed, the days were growing cooler and the
winds were starting to blow through the timbers and the roof.
Braam Piet began to assume the duties of family head, and Kathy
was thankful. She needed someone to lean on. He knew the earth,
Braam Piet, he read the seasons and understood the language of
the wilderness. He was a Boer with an inborn love of the earth,
a love for which he was prepared to die and a love that was
surpassed only by his love for a woman. All through the years of
struggling, war, famine, locusts and marauding kaffirs, they had
stuck together. He and Jules, but Jan was his first friend. Jules'
brother was living well with his newspaper in the Transvaal. They
had all loved Kathy, but it was Jules who won her. Braam Piet had
stayed on at the farm.

It had worked out well. He never had coveted his neighbor's
wife, though God knew he wanted to. There was a stronger security
when people stayed together and it was true that two hearts were
better than one. They had grown and grown and worked harder and
harder. They were the lucky ones. They had found Canaan without
having to trek north, Voorwaarts with heavy wagons and oxen that
patiently leaned against their yokes, where white men shouted
and cracked their whips. Here he had found a trusting partner and
friend. Now that friend was dead. He felt guilty. He had part of the

farm. What more could he ask? He had all, all that he could, with justice, ask of God. But Kathy was a widow now, a lady of rank and beauty. She was older, yes, but half a loaf is better than none. She was alone without a man in Canaan. "Ja," he thought now, "while there is life in a man, it is never too late." He had to think of the best way to handle this lady and to make himself acceptable to her as a man, and not just another man who helped to manage the farm. He wondered if he would ever cross the threshold of her bedroom, and he wondered whether that dream he always dreamed was any nearer than it was when he first saw her.

Time passed. Louisa was changing, and it was obvious to Kathy that she was pregnant. She found Louisa silently looking into space, as though trying to stare forward into the future. She seemed hesitant, and troubled by bodily discomfort. Kathy remembered Louisa's horror and how she collapsed when her son Julius came home for his father's funeral. Julius was once besotted with love for Louisa. What had happened there? Now there was this tremendous deep love that Lion and Louisa shared, but something was wrong. There was something odd about Louisa, but that she was pregnant, Kathy was sure! She did not ask questions; she knew Louisa well, and she felt sure Louisa would tell her all in her own time. But already time itself was telling, so her own time of telling was near. That very week one of the heifers had a difficult birth down near the dam. The calf was a breach birth, and the cow was in distress. Lion was experienced and used to these things, to him it was no real problem. He took a bucket of hot water, a knife and a bundle of cloths, and hurried down to help her. Kathy, hearing of this, called Louisa. "Come, Lu, we must go down towards the dam, we may be able to help Lion. There's a young cow in distress."

Louisa looked a little nervous. "Of course, Kathy," she said, and she handed Kathy her musket. Kathy never went anywhere without out; it had become a way of life, Julius had taught her that. They followed behind Lion until they reached the cow. She was a young heifer, and as nature intended she knew instinctively what she had to do. Her back was arched as though she was urinating and she was bearing down on her womb, her tail held up in the air. Her eyes were bulging and the blood and water ran down her hindquarters onto the top of her swollen udder and then soaked into the ground, leaving a damp, wet spot in the trampled yellow grass. Lion stood for a moment. "It's a bad birth," he said, "the little bugger has come feet first," he handed the cloth to Louisa, rolled his sleeves very high, washed his arm and hands with tallow and beeswax soap and then, patting and calming the young cow, he gently got her to lie down.

He pushed the calf's feet back into her vagina, straightened out its forelegs, put them together, put his arm into the cow's vagina and pulled. "Press down, girlie," he said to the cow. "Come now, press and we will do it together." The cow was looking backwards, eyes bulging and bloodshot. She half rose, then she had a great contraction, and Lion, putting his arm down into her vagina, pulled the calf by its front legs, as she bore down on this little life that burdened her body. She bore down again, with less strength, the smell of blood aggravating her fear. Lion, with great strength, pulled mightily at the little calf. He did not let go. All covered in placenta it slid into view, the umbilical cord still tied to the mother. The young cow swung around and rose to her feet and began licking the caul of the skin that covered it, and then methodically chewed it all up and swallowed it. She licked the calf over and over as it stood on wobbly legs, already feeling with its head for her udder. No one spoke; suddenly it had all come right.

Lion wiped his hands on the grass, took some water from the bucket and wiped the calf's eyes. "The umbilical cord was broken but she passed the afterbirth quite well," he said. "She'll be alright now." He washed the blood off of the cow's teats, and some from off her body. The little calf put its head under her belly, feeling with his head for her udder. It was over now, and the cow was beginning to nuzzle her calf. "Lion, you are just wonderful, no doctor could have done better." Kathy looked at Louisa. They stared at each other and never said a word. Louisa knew that Kathy knew, and her lips started to tremble. She picked up her skirt and wiped her face, then smoothed her dress and as she did so, Kathy could see the distinct swelling of her belly and the thickening of her waist. "It's the same with a woman, Lu," she said, "we are the essence of life. We carry life, we create it, make it, and then deliver it to the world."

"Sometimes we have mishaps, or have mistakes, but that's not so uncommon. You are vital. It's easy for a strong, healthy woman with the bloom of youth and your bones are still soft with girlish immaturity. Young girls bend like a slender sapling, and once having delivered, spring swiftly back and mend again." She took Louisa in her arms, an unusual gesture for her, and she held the shivering girl. She asked no questions and neither Lion nor Louisa spoke. This was theirs, and if they wanted to tell her, they would. Still, Kathy was glad now that it was all out in the open. She was glad it was no longer a secret, and for Louisa it was a great relief. To her, it was as if a great weight had been lifted from her shoulders.

She loved Kathy, she wanted Kathy as her mother, and never would she have ever wanted to hurt Kathy, yet she found no words to tell her that the child growing inside her was the seed of her son. So her secret was almost an obsession, no one would know, only Lion, and she was certain that Lion would not ever let her down. What she really feared most was that Kathy might not want her at the farm; nothing else really made her afraid. "I have been alone, almost all my life, but now I have a family, Lion," she told him one happy evening and he also knew the agony of rejection, of not being wanted. Together they were blissfully happy, for them it was the first time they were truly happy, and the w inter came, and passed, and faded into spring.

Through these months Kathy was concerned for Louisa. The girl's breasts were swollen and tender and her body was taut and distended, with blue veins showing through her flesh. Her arms were think and the bones on her breast stuck out quite prominently. It was not that she did not eat; she ate quite well, too much lamb and mutton, maybe. It was tiresome, they also had a fowl, and Louisa liked the white flesh of fowl. Kathy very busily had helped her prepare the baby's new clothes and Lion had carved a crib quite unique from the trunk of a yellow wood tree. Kathy even experienced a certain excitement. There was always something wonderful about a birth of a child. But Louisa was pale and looked frightened. "Are you afraid, Louisa?" she asked her outright.

"Yes, Kathy," she said, "I am, I am very afraid."

She wondered what to say. "You know, Louisa, when I had Maya, I had a Boer midwife and it was during one of those dreadful wars. Jules was on guard and fighting among spears and war cries and red coats. My fears were for life, not just for the life I was about to bring into this world. I had a double fear. But you, my dear child," she said, "are lucky. It is calm here now, and Mrs. Visser is all ready and waiting. She is the best midwife in the colony. She says a woman should have a baby every other year, so that the nation grows and grows. You need not be afraid. I will stay with you and it will be all over in a couple of hours."

But Louisa seemed restless and unhappy. "You will be very proud when you see your baby," Kathy said, "it's like a miracle, from out of your body comes this new life. Meuvou Visser will bring the baby safely into the world and I will wrap him up and give him into your arms." Lion was with them and he too seemed restless and worried. It seemed generally understood that Lion was this child's father. The child must be his and Louisa's. But when Louisa's pains came, it was different. Louisa gave a frantic scream, water fell from her body uncontrollably and she was filled with fear, wide-eyed and hysterical. The midwife was quite prepared for it all, though. She was a large woman with an extraordinarily large bosom. She had firm, fat fingers with a solid grip. Her face was small, and her chin sank into another layer of flesh that formed more than a double chin. Her arms above the elbow were very large, taut with hard flesh like an overfilled sausage made from the entrails of a sheep, she wore flat veld skoens and despite her size busied herself; swift of movement. She was very cheery, humming and passing little platitudes and pieces from the Bible.

"No, yes, Mrs.," she said, taking it for granted that Louisa was Lion's wife, "we people are strong mense (people), we are here to multiply, and it's not too difficult, it's the duty of woman to bear the children, that is how the Lord decided it," she said. "Your water has broken now and soon it will be all over." Louisa gave another scream and her fingers went white as she clutched the side of the stinkwood bed. "Maytig (Almighty), Mevron, breathe in, you breathe in deeply and hold onto something," the midwife said, "my mother used to say bite onto the bedclothes with all your might." The room was now ready with pails of hot water and tallow soap, and swaths and cloths all over. She walked over to Louisa. "Do not be afraid, Mevron," she said. "Here I am with you and everyone knows things do not go wrong when I am delivering."

Louisa was writhing on the kaross, and she reached for her Bible, the perspiration on her face. "Mrs. Visser," she said, "read me the part about the sins of the parents. Let me hear why God deserted me." She screamed again. "Oh God," she said, "you took my parents away from me, you left me, God," she screamed again and again and bit her lip, and the blood, pale blood, stuck in the corner of her mouth. Lion, who was outside of the room, was beside himself. "Meuvou Visser," he said, "can I come in?" Instantly she answered, "This is woman's business, Meneer, get on your horse and go out into the fields, or go and kill a beast, so this girl can have some red meat that is full of blood." Kathy moved over to Louisa's side and took her hand. "Oh Louisa, Louisa dear girl," she said, "do not cry, I will be as a mother to you." Louise held onto Kathy's hand and they were both crying and each time Louisa cried out, Kathy felt her pain. "Bear down, Mevron," said the midwife, "when the pain comes press down, press it out like you do when you go to the lavatory, press now." And she pressed on Louisa's stomach, kneading it downwards, down towards Louisa's delicate white knees. She put her ear to Louisa's abdomen.

"Do no fear, Mevron," she said, "I would say this is a boy. It is always the boys who do not want to break away from their mother's womb. Girls are different, you know, they come quicker. That is what I have found. I cannot say that this is a fact you know," she went on, muttering. Then she asked, "What would you prefer it to be, then?" But Louisa was beyond caring, she knew only pain. She always knew only pain. She felt it when her parents died, first her father and then her mother. She felt it when her aunt made her pray instead of play, she felt it in her loneliness, and in her fears.

She felt it when she was assaulted, instead of loved, by the first man in her life, then in the terror of her shame. She felt pain in her secrecy, and not being able to tell of it. All her life was pain. Here was a child, not of her choice, and it was a bitter pain, and the pain was more than she could bear. And where was this God of mercy her uncle preached about? He had not noticed her, pretty, fragile Louisa! That was how her governess had described her once. She was writhing and crying and screaming.

The midwife was becoming agitated. Three hours had now passed and still her bones had not opened enough. Kathy could see she was distressed and somewhat puzzled. She squeezed out a damp cloth and splashed it with rosewater, then wiped Louisa's face. The girl's eyes were swollen, her lips were bitten raw, and she closed her eyes and moaned softly. Again, she cried out, "Even now you have deserted me, oh God! Oh God, what did I ever do so wrong? I was a virgin like Mary, and I was torn like a savage and I was…" and she never completed the sentence. She screamed again in agony and she pressed as Mevrou Visser said, and this thing was not coming out. She was pressing until she had no more strength.

Mevrou Visser was in a state now. "Send the husband to the mission. There is a kaffir there who knows how to get the bones to open," she said.

"I will send Lion," Kathy said, and Louisa just caught the sentence.

"No, no, no, do not send Lion away, no, no, Lion, stay with me, you are better than God, stay with me Lion," and she cried out in helplessness. "Lion, oh Lion, my beautiful, strong Lion, please, please, don't go away, I beg, I beg," she said.

And then Lion crashed into the room. "My God, Mevron," he said, "what in the name of God is wrong? Can you not help her,

Kathy? Help her please, help her," and he fell down beside the wooden bed as Mrs. Visser was struggling to knead the child from her womb. And the hours passed, and Louisa lost much of her precious blood, as Merrow Visser tried to move her bones with her fingers and tried to move the child within in her.

And when the night came, an owl hooted outside of the house. Mevron Visser looked up. "Meneer, would you please go and chase that creature away."

She was afraid now, and she took the Bible and put it into the pocket of her apron, then continued her work. She didn't want to say what she was thinking, but Kathy had long since known of the superstitions and mores of these Bush peoples. The owl that hoots upon the roof; yes, she knew it well.

But Lion ignored her request, he stayed on his knees beside Louisa. "Louisa, keep trying, it is hard, the first baby," he said. "Please keep trying Weezie," and he put his leonine head down beside her golden hair, wet and darkened by her sweat and tears. She screamed and clasped onto Lion's head, and then as though she would burst, she squeezed with all the breath and strength of her body, and the midwife grew excited. "Ja, Mevrou, press liefie, it is coming at last, press my liefie, press," and she pulled at the head with her fingers, covered in blood. Louisa heaved and heaved, and then the head came through, misshapen and elongated, but alive, and the blood-covered body slid suddenly from her body. Mevrou Visser caught hold of the baby, and swiftly bound the cord, bent it over and tied it up with a black string. "Magtig," she called, "here, my Lady, take the child and breathe very lightly into his mouth. Give it a smack and then rub it and then wrap it. I must attend to this girl, she is bleeding so badly, we must get the afterbirth."

Kathy smacked the child and then breathed softly into its mouth, it was covered in placenta and mucus, but she breathed softly, very softly until the walls of its tiny chest seemed to swell and it gave a soft cry, the cry of a newborn child, and she wrapped it in a blanket and held it to her body to keep it warm, rocking automatically. Louisa was whimpering as the midwife kneaded her tired and spent body. She was losing too much blood and Mevrou Visser was perspiring and praying and working and washing. Louisa looked dazed. She didn't seem to care anymore. Her eyes seemed yellowish, she was so tired. "Lion," she whispered, "Lion, are you here? It's so dark, I cannot see you," and he brought a candle stuck in a bottle near to her and he was weeping. "Louisa my precious, Weezie, it's over now, it's over Weezie, you have a son, a big, long boy."

Louisa felt no more pain. She was drifting now, drifting peacefully at last. "Take him, Lion," she said, "keep him for me. The time will come when you can tell him who he is. You will know what to do. I have spent such happy months in this Eden. In this garden of Eden." "Kathy, my darling Kathy," and her voice went soft into a whisper. "Oh Lion," she said, "you are better than God. Tell God I said so. Tell him, Lion. I love you Lion," and her voice went weak. "Call him Eden, Lion, call him…" and then she spoke no more. Mrs. Visser picked up her hands, and they were limp. "Magtige Gott," (Almighty God" she said, "help me. Oh God in heaven, I think she's dying," and she put her head on Louisa's chest. "Magtige (God), here," she said, "I am so sorry Meneer, I am so sorry," and she turned away, and she burst into great heaving sobs. Lion knew Louisa was dead. He just stayed on his knees and his head lay beside her face, a forlorn, innocent face. And Kathy held the baby, she was crying and rocking and sobbing. And then she stood erect and took command.

"Mevrou Visser," she said, "will you clean up this beautiful child? I will come back in a moment." And she gazed down on the wooden bed, at the tragic couple. "Come with me," she said. "Please excuse me Mevrou, I will not be long, we must take great care of this baby, you must take great care, Mevrou Visser." and in total desperate despondency she haltingly called again to Lion. Her mind seemed to fail her. Lion remained on the wooden bed, his body heaving. She fumbled for words, for strength. "That child is my grandchild. My grandson, Mevrou Visser."

Kathy and Braam Piet rode to Barnabas Shaw. It was a nonstop ride through to Grahamstown. They told him of the tragedy and how well Louisa had held her secret. They told him of the child and that the child was that of an unknown father. At first he was unconvinced—no, it could not have been so—and then he thought it over and he recollected Louisa's ailments, her stays in bed. He could see no way he could be burdened with an illegitimate child. He was quite thankful that Kathy and Lion were prepared to take on the responsibility of bringing it up. It was the will of God, he said. "The Lord giveth and the Lord taketh away," he muttered to himself. And Kathy narrowed her eyes and listened. "So be it, Mrs. Shaw," she said, and bidding farewell to the venerable reverend gentleman she and Piet drove silently back home in the coach. The horses were exhausted.

Louisa was buried beneath her echo. There on the ridge where she would hear Lion call, and she would hear the echo reply forever. Lion carved a casket for her, until the skin of his hands were red raw. All through the night Lion chipped and carved, and between them they made her a beautiful casket. And when it was all ready, she was laid to rest inside on ostrich feathers, and wild deerskins. She looked pale and white and waxen, like a beautiful still painting. They closed the lid. There were no words, there were no other people, just the servants and gravediggers, Braam Piet, Lion and Kathy. Solemnly they let down the casket on strong riempie ropes made of hippo hide. It made a thud at the bottom of the hole, then they closed it up, with stones on top so that the hyenas and jackals would not dig it up.

Twenty-Nine

In February 1857 a strange thing happened with the Xosa tribes. Kreli, who was the paramount chief of the Xosas and who lived beyond the Kei, had a mouthpiece in the form of a witch doctor, Mllakaza. This witch doctor had a niece named Nongygawuse who told all the superstitious tribesmen that the dead warriors of the past would all return to life, a dreadful hurricane would drive all the white people into the sea, the sun would set in the East and new grain crops would appear … But before this could happen, crops and cattle had to be totally destroyed before the date. On February 18, the poor tribes, low in spirit from the aftermath of two wars and in addition aggravated by the loss of their cattle from Rindepest, turned in desperation to magic to make good their losses and to punish the white people. Missionaries and officials tried to dissuade them, but nothing deterred them, and so it was the Xosa nation almost destroyed themselves in a national suicide. They destroyed all their crops and cattle, and famine swept through the land; the Xosa people entered the colony as supplicants rather than conquerors. Out of 105,000, only 37,000 Xosas survived. Black labor was very cheap and plentiful. Hungry and seeking help, they swarmed into the towns and villages.

Julius summoned Swart Haas and sat there bending his Sjambok and letting it spring back into shape. "Now look here Swaarthaas," he said, "gather these men, only the young and strong. If the women are very healthy and have no children you may also gather them. Tell them I have been able to get people in another land and over the sea to give them work. Some will be needed to work in sugarcane fields, some in cotton fields, and others will work in houses doing the work that you do for me. There is much food in this other land, plenty of cattle and many goats, and never will they be hungry again." Swaarthaas looked at his sleek, pale, quick-talking master, playing with his toy. He knew his master was bad with women, and he was afraid of his fearsome sjambok. So far he had escaped it. There it hung on the wall, and well he knew the meaning of its sting. It hung here like a huge sting of some phantom monster, thick on one end with a hole through it, so that the riem that made a loop to hang it up with, went through, forming a small loop tied in a knot as a handle and it hung on a hook, tapering down to a slim narrow point, oiled and shining and free of mould.

He shivered as he recalled the bite of the Sjambok and he wondered and dreamed of how it felt to be on the glory end of it, instead of receiving its stinging cuts. He slid into his childhood and momentarily drifted, dreaming of the little cell beneath the large stone house where he knew his mother, and the nearness and warmth of her soft flesh. Julius lashed out with his sjambok. "I'm speaking to you, God damn you," he said, as Swaarthaas cringed against the wall. His mind was still in his childhood days and he cried out in a childish voice, like a child in pain. The childish voice surprised Julius, as he swished the hyde sjambok through the air, avoiding the man. "Did you understand what I told you?" he said, as he wagged his finger. "You bring them here, and I will find them work. If you bring me 24 good strong men and women you can go to church on Sunday and rest all day, no work at all." And then he dismissed the conversation with a bored sigh. Swaarthaas quietly regarded the lull in his aggression.

Within a few days Swaarthaas had gathered a group of 21 very strong men and three well-built young women. He lured them with the promise of a golden land, where people worked and were rewarded and there were no empty stomachs. Julius was well pleased, appraising them with the eye of a cattle dealer. Julius gave them food and put them on a wagon, for now they were all going down to the sea. Julius would go on ahead in the horse and trap. He summoned the ox wagon driver, and voerloper, telling them to cut hay for the oxen and to fill the water containers and oil lamps. The journey was simple, he said, follow the sand tracks to assegai then to seven fountains, graze the oxen, and rest, and then cross the Bushmen's River at Rautenbach's Drift, on towards the Sunday's River to Zwartkops and then to Port Elizabeth. There he had arranged for them to leave the wagon and go on a ship to this land where the crops were rich and food was plentiful. They were not unduly suspicious. Almost happily they set off, some with high hopes and dreams of paradise. The tired oxen would be plodding towards the harbor with a singing cargo of men and a few women. Their next stop was Zanzibar or Tanganyika.

Swaarthaas, alone in his cell-like room, was fired with excitement. If they could go to a land and work, why not him? He plotted his escape, he knew how he would do it, despite the fact that he was ordered to remain in his master's dwelling. He was also going to go to this land, across the sea, and he would never be the property of Julius again. If he was in another land, how could they find him? And he feverishly tied his small bag of belongings together and put them in a blanket. Small items of sentiment, a carved wooden giraffe, several warthogs teeth, beads, his old blue boer shirt and veldskoens. He looked around, and from under his kaross he took a small bundle. It was white pantaloons with dark stains, blood-stained pantaloons. These he would hide somewhere.

The white lady's underwear was stained brown with bloodstains that had faded; he carefully rolled them into a neat roll and stuffed them into a pouch made from the skin of a cerval cat and then tucked them all into his blanket and tightly secured it so that what he carried seemed like a large ball. "Swaarthaas," he repeated to himself, of course, the Black Hare. Why was he so named? It was simple, no one could run or ever was as nimble-footed as he, nor anywhere near as fast as he. He, Swaarthaas, would run to the sea, he would follow their tracks and he too would be free and take a part in the food and riches of that promised land. Here he was a slave. He was a young mand and could only ask for his freedom when he was 40 years old. Yes, he would also get a payment of £868 if he had a good character. He didn't think his master would say his Swaarthaas was good. His mind was made up. He would run behind that wagon all the way to the sea, then stealthily steal his way onto the ship. He would be sure that no one knew he was even on the ship, and he wondered where on a ship he would hide, and what a ship looked like.

He followed at a distance during the day and hid near the wagons at night, snatching a few hours of sleep and once even got bold enough to steal food, a change from his veldkos. When the wagons reached Swartkops, Swaarthaas was stunned to see a naked black man in the stocks. He had been caught stealing cattle and had been put into stocks outside of a small military barracks. He was a Xosa warrior and when night came, Swaarthaas whispered with him. He asked for water and Swaarthaas took his sheepskin water bag and held it to his mouth. It was hard for him to understand what it was all about. The man's head seemed to come through a hole in the wood and on either side were his hands coming through other holes and then his feet came through at the bottom.

It was a strange, puzzling sight, and Swaarthaas was not sure whether to tackle this brain-teasing puzzle. Suddenly a soldier came out from the barracks and he dived into the nearest bush taking shelter with night. Had it been daylight, he would most certainly have been shot. He watched the soldier pace up and down, then walk around the prisoner in the stocks. Another soldier joined him, but the night was dark, there was no moon, just the flicker of lights from his lantern and the rays from the barracks doors. Swaarthaas made not a sound nor a movement.

The man in the stocks moaned. "Manze," (water) he croaked.

"Give the fellow a drop of water, Fynn," the soldier said, "I suppose its water he's asking for," and Fynn moved a few paces and returned with a mug of liquid. "Of course," he said, "if he'll take us to the stolen herd we'll release him. I can't say I approve these inefficient measures of frontier control, it's extremely injudicious." He undid the top board that came over the man's head, freeing his head temporarily. "Here then, you foolish kaffir," he said, and allowed the man to drink from the tin mug. "You nomads are all damn robbers, and favour the damn doctrine 'might is right,' don't you?" he said as he let him drink again. "Damn imperfect moral perceptions, engage in war for the purpose of stealing cattle, ill-gotten deep-rooted habits."

"I say, Fynn, isn't it strange how one always feels one is being watched at night out here," said the other soldier. "It's quite unnerving. Replace the stocks," he ordered, but it was not easy to put the top back. The man's hair was thick, so he took out a sort of cut throat and sliced off some of the prisoner's coarse, curly hair and dropped it near his protruding feet. "Do you feel we're being watched?" he asked of Fynn.

"No sir," replied Fynn, "haven't had time to meditate yet, sir."

"Fire a shot into the air," he ordered, "just in case there are any prowlers ready to chew off this fellow's feet."

"He couldn't run very far without feet, Sir," Fynn said.

"Fire a shot Fynn," he ordered, dismissing the idiotic remark. Fynn fired a shot into the air. Swaarthaas made not a movement. He had been watching how they had placed the stocks. He waited until they returned to the barracks, then while they laughed and played cards, Swaarthaas crept on his hands and knees toward the prisoner. As he reached the stocks his hand came upon the short cut off hair. He lifted it to his eyes for closer scrutiny. Then he gathered it up and tucked it into his shirt pocket. He then set about to release the black prisoner. They fled together to the bush. Like brothers they clasped each other and as a parting gift, Swaarthaas begged a little more of his hair.

The following day the wagons arrived at the bay. Julius was there, very elegant in his dark coat and hat. He carried a square satchel in which he bore his paperwork, and walked stiffly towards the wagons. He speedily got the men together, sending the wagons home with rapid instructions and fresh food supplies. Julius spent some time with the ship's captain, and once his business was done, the emigrating men were taken to the small boats to be taken to the ship lying short way out to sea. By twos and threes they climbed onto the boats, 121 men, 2 women, a large older man with a dirty, matted beard, and a small bag over his shoulder.

"Mr. Jacobsen, all 125 seem healthy and sound," said the captain. "I trust they will remain that way in New Orleans. This is my last trip in these seas until we reach Zanzibar. Those Arabs have a lot more in their dungeons." Then he ordered his crew to accompany them to the ship; taking Julius by the elbow, they walked off towards the building at the end of the half-built wharf, the one with the tin roof that was beginning to rust. Julius was puzzled. He was not sure, yet he felt the Captain must have erred. By his reckoning there were 124 in all. Still, he had no intention of disputing an error in his own favor. So taking up a quicker step he walked down to the shed.

Julius was very pleased with his business. He felt master of the situation and a great deal wealthier. Maybe he could take advantage of this situation again. He whipped his horses and made for home. It was a journey filled with scheming and planning. So filled with thoughts was he that he passed his wagons outspanned and never even noticed they were there. At any rate, they were not his own span. He had hired them for the trip, but he intended to purchase more land, build a larger and more stylish home; he would use both stone and bricks, but stone was what most appealed to him.

Perhaps he would move to Graaf Reinet or Craddock where the climate was dry and free of disease, much suited for raising fine-wooled sheep. Why, some of the boers had sold their farms for the price of a good wagon, so they could emigrate to the colony and the 'verdomde (damned) Engelsman.' Already the wool exports from Albany exceeded the western Cape and even surpassed the wine industry as a source of external revenue. Braam Piet lived very well on his father's land, HIS land, and when his mother died, surely it would all be his. Still, he would become a landowner by his own efforts as well. Julius Jacobsen, lawyer, landowner, successful farmer, gentleman and statesman. He would be a power to be reckoned with. A gentleman from an independent judiciary, articulate, educated and instrumental in the approach of representational government in the colony, perhaps like his father who had set up a mill in Bathurst and started to make blankets and hats and helped the whole frontier community to weather those frontier wars. His father found time for so much and did so much in his short life. He admitted to himself that his father was quite a man, a pioneer in wool.

With pleasure he remembered the lambs frolicking about the hills. He remembered the flock growing as his father bought more and more sheep and the sheep shearing and the young ram sales grew. His father and Braam Piet and that Godammed Lion—always Lion, Lion with his fit thick neck, thick like the fat tails of the sheep. Well, to hell with Lion, to hell with them all, he was a man now in his own right; and a successful and wealthy young man. He patted his pouch reassuringly, and whipped the horses, even though they were breathing heavily and needed to halt. He continued his trip, totally lost in his thoughts and schemes and plots and plans. He arrived in Grahamstown and headed for his home and office.

He wanted to become a vast landowner, a landrost, maybe even the governor. Perhaps he would feature in the long dark corridors of history like Major Abercrombie, who once, by dint of hard riding, made an incredible ride to Cape Town in six days, an epic feat. Or like the ride by Richard King, who would surely become an imperishable name in the annals of that fickle jade called history. Or would he, with wealth and wisdom, be bypassed and fade into oblivion.

The horses were exhausted, it was the end of the day. He had almost forgotten what day it was. "Swaarthaas, he called, "Swaarthaas, you blithering idiot, where are you?" He tethered the horses to the tie up pole in front of his home, another in his ample back yard. The horses were restless and sweating and tired, they were not the best of horses and had not the strength of a good English horse. He was angry now, and unlocking the door, he entered, calling for Swaarthaas incessantly, but Swaarthaas was nowhere to be found. Cursing, Julius then went outside and brought the horses and carriage into the back yard. He took off his gauntlets and untied the harness, freeing the animals. He threw a measure of wheat into the stone manger together with some other grains while the horses rolled in the sand. He pulled up the long pole that kept the entrance closed and shut the horses inside the yard. They came immediately into their manger to eat.

He was greatly irritated at having to do these chores himself. He filled up a drinking trough with water from a well filled metal tank, rainwater that drained from the roofs. He then entered his house from the back door and went straight to Swaarthaas' dark quarters. He kicked violently at the door, then pushed it open. His eyes scanned the empty, cell-like room. "How dare you, you black bastard," he said. "I have paid for you! Just wait til I find you!" He kindled a fire, and was so filled with anger it was difficult to start his flint. Finally he set his oil lamps alight; for the moment his thoughts and dreams of tomorrow were lost in a frenzy of violence. "You blasted unreliable black dog," he muttered. He had some soot on his hands, and he looked around for the 'vadoek,' a grubby cloth used for wiping most things. It was damp and squashed into a small heap at the outer surface, "stinking kaffirs, never learn the art of cleanliness." He wiped the soot from the base of his thumb and threw it down onto a slab shelf above the big oven.

He would think about what he would do tomorrow. He sliced some dried meat from the strips of venison that hung from a line of meat in the larder. He suddenly felt alone with his wrath.

Tomorrow it would be different. He was tired and smiled at the thought of his bed. He looked for his bed warmer; it hung on the wall, its shining copper bowl shining in the lamplight. His mother used to warm his bed when he was small, and deep within him he longed for the comfort and care of his mother. Her warm feather beds and her reassuring, able and caring hands. Yes, perhaps he would go home to Sonnestroom Moorplaats. It had been a long time since his father's funeral and he had been so busy with legal affairs, courts and making money. He had been on this strong lucky streak all these years; he had worked it well, and made himself a respected and wealthy man.

It was strange how this childish yearning for his home and erstwhile boyhood bed kept returning. "Blast that bloody mulatto Lion," he said. And soon as he completed his legal commitments he would return to that valley whre he and his sister grew, and where the veld and hills also grew, from a dwelling into the finest farm in all the colony, surviving the successive frontier wars, and the onslaught of nature's vicissitudes. Well, this colony would all remember his parents, his father's fortified farms and the architecture that came from both his father's innermost and original buildings. They turned a wilderness into Canaan. She tended the farm and all its appurtenances while he led and fought the frontiers through all the wars, always in discourse and asseveration for peace and justice to all men, often a go-between sent almost alone to assuage and pacify the resentful enemy. It takes a lot of growing up and life experience to understand the man that dwelt within his father. He had avoided going home, but now perhaps the time had come, and he nurtured the lingering thought. He would go down to his beloved Sonnestroom a month before Christmas. He would summon his clerks for instruction during his absence and find a nice Hottentot maid to replace the perfidious Swaarthaas.

November came and in the first week Julius, in his comfortable carriage, led the horses at a trotting pace through the morning mists kicking up the yellow dust, to the north of Albany towards his home. He had now acquired two farms from disgruntled trekkers who had taken their families and wagons across the Dragensberg, ending their symbiotic relationship with the goddamed English forever, they had hoped. On one of the farms he had placed an agricultural family that had come out with a Scotch contingent. Now they were to run and manage the farm that had several rams and a flock of merino ewes. They had already successfully lambed with surprisingly good results. The other farm was under reconstruction, "Riversend Park." This was his special place and he had already bought a flock of crossbred sheep together with a flock of Saxon Merinos. He had embarked on a partnership with an ex-army major.

The major's family was already on a steamship bound for Algoa Bay. Hundreds of Hottentots were cutting stones and a lone German who understood building trades was redesigning a spacious home. It was unlike the pleasing simplicity of style other settlers had adhered to, for Julius had dreams of a gentleman's residence in a grand Georgian manor style. He had so much to tell his mother. Proud of his successes and his mounting financial reserves, he trotted his horses onward. He hadn't realized that three years had passed.

His mother was three years older and his father's body was rotted away into the yellow dust in which he was buried. He remembered Tombe, the Lioness, that he once cunningly shot. He thought of his sister. Somehow he had lost touch with her, though she had sent several letters from England that he had failed to reply to. He was a busy man. If she wrote now, he would find time to reply. He had no dislike for Braam Piet either, but he hated Lion, his mother's half-caste, half-brother. He hated his blood tie with a mulatto, and resented his part-uncle's tremendous body strength. He wondered what he looked like now and what his position was on the farm.

He did not have to ponder long as he finally rounded the last bend, and all the valley came into sight. There at the base of the foothills lay Sonnestroom, and to the north, Moorplaats. The stony ridges of long, solid buildings stood out sharp in the sunshine. Clouds hung suspended in the sky, huge, fleecy bundles of white against the blue, blue sky. The hills were velvety green and the big old trees looked a darker shade, almost black against the hills. There beside the kopje, filled with lilies, were the whitish tombstones. The vegetation thickened as it grew down towards the rivers like dark fissures of black-green beside a rocky ribbon of water. The krantz (steep cliffs) seemed smaller than he remembered them, standing up and falling towards the creek. The rivers, small trickles in the ravine bed, were running freely. Patches of scrub changed to thicket and taller trees, flaming red aloes, marched up the hillsides and in the Krantz: Vivid vermillion Cape honeysuckle blazed out among the thickets.

Rich wine red Boerbourn, masses of wild and beautiful flowers grew in the grass along the tracks. The tracks were far better now, one could almost call them roads, but parts of the bush were still heavily armed with parasitic growths and twining creepers. Foot-paths and game trails were now hardened and smooth, and where the grass was burned black, the foothills seemed baked and white. Where did they lead to, these footpaths of Africa? And then there was an opening and a widening of the path and a dam shone like an oil patch in the veld. A horse was galloping up the path towards his carriage. He slowed down to a halt and the sound of the horses' hooves was hard and clear on the hardened path.

Within minutes the horse came galloping and breathless up to the carriage. It was Lion and before him on the front of his saddle was a small, fair boy. They both had the windswept hair and faces full of joy. Lion halted. "Good heavens, man, it's Julius," he said. The little boy was most excited. "Lion, Lion," he said, "Can I ride in the wagon?" "That wagon is not a wagon," he said. "Good day, Lion," said Julius, but he did not extend his hand and nor did Lion extend his. He was blonde and bronzed and a little red on his nose and neck. He looked more like an English soldier than his grandfather's half-caste son with his long, tanned fingers and his broad chest, his huge defined muscles and golden hair on his chest that shone in the sun below his thick neck. He was riding a huge horse.

Thirty

With a flashing smile he replied, "Good day, Julius. Your mother will be very happy to see you."

"Eden, boy, say good day like a gentleman should."

The little boy smilingly called out, "Good afternoon uncle, may I ride with you?"

"Yes boy, why not?" said Julius, and his eyes were searching. There was something in this child's face that gave him a strange emotion.

Lion jumped, dismounted, and lifting the child placed him beside Julius. "Mind that you don't fall out, Eden," he said, "you stay close and sit tight." He half saluted, "I'll see you at the house."

"Bye, Lion," called the child as Lion rode off on his large horse. He called back "Bye, my boy."

Julius remembered his father had a stallion, a large chestnut, similar to that horse, and what a weight it carried; 20 stones—with saddlery carbine saber, extra ammunition in a bandolier on its neck, nose bag, heel rope, spare shoes, blanket, saddle cloth, and cavalry cloak. My God, the English horses were powerful creatures. Here the Boer horses were small, tough, but not the one his father had. Perhaps he was still going strong. Well, he'd check on that. He watched Lion until the horse was gone out of sight and only the faint dust clouds lingered in the air. He looked at the little boy. It was a beautiful child with fair fine golden hair. The little boy laid his small hand on Julius' thigh.

"Shall we gallop faster sir?" the little chap said.

"In a while," said Julius, "We will walk the horses, so that you and me can become friends first." The little child smiled up to him happily.

"Lion will teach me to gallop on Drostdy King when I'm four."

"Which horse is Drostdy King?" asked Julius.

"That one, the one that we rided on. I like him better than the others."

"Would you like to ride then?"

"Yes I would, I will ride all horses."

He held onto Julius as the horses moved the carriage over a small donga (ditch). Julius felt a warming emotion to this child. His intelligent replies and his happy laughter—it was like an instant affection. He had never bothered with children before, and black children with their pot bellies, bulgy navels, flies on their faces and running snot noses that left caked white mucous cracked dry around their wide nostrils, actually nauseated him. He reached out his hand.

"Here," he said, trying to be gentle, "you come sit between my legs, and you can hold the reins and we will gallop, together."

The child moved over and climbed onto the seat, his little hands holding onto Julius for support. He was filled with joy at the idea, and Julius wondered as he looked at the hands. Hands that small could grow into man's hands who carved and ploughed and played a harp, or wrote fine lines with a quill, sailed ships, and beat other men, even flog them to their death. He once heard his father tell about the horrible parade ground between Drostdy Arch and the Drostdy House, where soldiers were tied up and flogged on an equilateral triangle grating which was especially erected for that purpose. Other soldiers formed a line four feet wide leading up to it, and stood with fixed bayonets, and the one to be punished was striped to his waist, fastened by his hands and feet to the grating and whipped with a cat o' nine tails dipped in salt water. The army doctor was the only person allowed to stop the beating and only if he thought the victim would die. Thirty-nine lashes, but many times there were more. Yes, it was the Duke of Wellington who opposed the abolition of floggery. "Discipline." He had said it was to maintain discipline. They are cruel, the English, they have always engaged in barbaric punishment. It must take strong hands to administer thirty-nine lashes to some naked, broken body, strong large man's hands. He looked at his own hands.

The child was shrieking with joy as the horses cantered over the anthills and dongas jolting the carriage so that the carriage almost jumped off the ground at times. He found himself smiling. God knew, it was a long time since he participated in childish fun, and he held onto the child protectively, slowing the horses down to a trot when the track was a little too rough.

It was in this happy mood that he rode into the gates of Sonnestroom Moorplats and found his mother waiting. She ran towards Julius.

"Hello, my son, oh dear Julius, how lovely to see you again." She put her arms around him and hugged him, then as suddenly as she clasped him she let him go. "Eden," she called, "Eden, where are you?"

Braam Piet came forward.

"Kathy," Eden said in his baby voice, "It was nice on the wagon, we galloped and galloped and this uncle let me drive." He looked up at Julius, "Thank you, uncle, it was a nice drive." Everything Eden did seemed to be at a trot or gallop. He ran to Kathy.

"Come along, my darling, we must have some tea. Uncle Julius must be both tired and hungry."

But the child rushed out of the room. He ran out to Lion who took his hand, and they led the horses to stable; large stables that held several horses.

"Now Eden, pal, these horses will all be fighting if we put them together."

So the carriage horses were put into a double stable in a paddock where they were able to freely come and go and graze, and water. Together they returned back towards the homestead, Lion having instructed two of the farm labourers to attend to the animals. They put the carriage outside in an open shelter which was usually used for visitors who only stayed a day or two. Kathy was already serving tea and Braam Piet was engaged in passing cakes and sandwiches and wonderful hot scones with bramble jam and dairy cream. It was a jolly occasion and Julius had brought a little excitement. He opened his trunk and took an exquisite Eastern rug from it. Kathy was delighted.

"Julius, this is so beautiful! I shall put it in the living room in front of your father's chair."

"It's a pity about Eden," said Julius, "Had I known about him I would have certainly found him some startling Xosa toy on the market. I once saw a wonderful toy made from the striped tails of civet cats. Tell me, mother, where does this child come from?"

Kathy looked up with a curious expression. "That's Louisa's child, Julius," and before he could say another word she hurriedly added, "And Lion is his guardian."

"And Louisa, where is she?"

Kathy was both shocked and startled, but it was only then she remembered that Julius was in Cape Town when Louisa died and when she and Braam Piet rode to the mission to tell her uncle Barnabas of her death and to make her burial arrangements.

"Julius, Louisa died when Eden was born. It was a difficult birth." The words dried up in her throat.

He slowly rose from the Riempie chair in which he was rocking. He replaced his teacup on the small yellow wood table. He never looked up.

"And why did you not send word, mother, when I returned from Cape Town? Every month the wagons came to the Fair."

"Julius, I don't know why I didn't tell you. Perhaps because I felt it was a very sad tragedy and a parting that belonged to Lion and Louisa—and not to you."

He had turned lugubrious, tall, and elegant; he looked like a man of the law. He was almost thin, and his epiglottis seemed to protrude more as she saw him swallow, and the lump in his throat moved up and then down. He looked like neither herself nor his father, though when he walked she thought he reminded her of his uncle Jan. He twisted the gold buttons on his jacket, a nervous gesture, first one then the others.

"Please don't admonish me, Julius, I might just as well ask you why in years this is your first visit to see me."

He dismissed her answer. He remained standing.

"Am I correct in assuming the child's father is Lion?"

"Julius, I do not know who Eden's father is."

Braam Piet, who had removed himself with Kathy was about to pour tea, returned now, with Eden running like a herald in front of Lion and Braam Piet. They all came in together from outside into

Julius and Kathy's interrogation, and broke it up. Kathy caught the little boy up and sat down with him on her lap.

"I feel like a true grandmother, I do so love this child." She held him close, "Isn't there something about a child that seems like spring? When blossoms burst and green shoots sprout and seed pods explode everywhere like voices of spring?" She laughed and laid large pats of fresh cream upon the hot scones and passed the tray on and kept one on the plate for Eden. "Here, my darling," she said holding him lovingly, "I shall place you at the table." Her hands lingered on the child like that of a caring mother.

The child looked toward Julius.

"What about uncle? What about some scones with jam for uncle?" he said in his small voice.

Again Julius felt this strange odd feeling, a feeling of caring, even love that emanated from this tiny person. It was a feeling alien to his emotions and it drew a strange love or something, from deep within him. He felt again the old jealousy for Lion. Why was it he was to be forever bothered by this mulatto uncle younger than himself, who always seemed to win, and upon whom this Africa had lain her spell? He could feel his jealousy riding, he could feel strange mixtures of feelings.

In December 1858 the Volksraad in the OFS passed a resolution in favor of federation with the Cape Colony. Marteunis Pretorius was made president until the popular Sir George Grey returned for another short stay. At this time Julius met a lovely woman. They were married in August and went to live in his magnificent home Riversend Farm.

Her name was Elizabeth Wodehouse, she had been a student of architecture and immediately set about building a castellated tower, esenellated battlements, and windows on a style similar to

Queen Victoria's Scottish residence Balmoral Castle. She used selected kysna yellow wood, created a huge banquet hall, and imported exquisite Eastern carpets. Here she and Julius presided benignly over many lavish parties and guests. In the Grontwet of 1858 the policyof the Trekkers was summed up to the effect that "No equality was permitted between the white inhabitants and the black peoples either in Church or State." In the Transvaal they had no recognized constitution. Marthinus Pretorius and Piet Potgieter had succeeded their father who had been killed, but the younger Potgieter also died and his widow married Stephanus Schoeman who became general of Zoutpansberg and heir to the feud with Pretorius. Aided by the young Paul Kruger from Rustenberg, together they had started a constitution and in 1858 it was revised by a special committee. This was a time the Basutu men threatened Moshesh. There was much marching and counter-marching which lasted for some time. All white males between 16 and 60 were liable for military service. Roman Dutch law was the common law. A judicial power was exercised by the Landrosts assisted by the Leemraden and the High Court of Justice.

During Grey's tenure of governship more newcomers came to the colony. Trade flourished and wool did extremely well. Banking faculties expanded and a railway line was constructed from Cape Town to Wellington and the Grey institute at Port Elizabeth and Grey College in the O.F.S. But despite the educational advancement there was little peace among the disunited European races in South Africa.

Julius was never involved with wars, though his father had commanded and emerged unscathed through three wars. He was sheltered beneath his wheezing chest, for in a state of nerves he was stricken with asthmatic spasms. Julius became a wealthy landowner and a High Court official, a speaker for the people and a critic of the constitution and policy, but never would he enter a church. He was looked upon as a supreme critic and advisor, the Honorable Julius Hora Jacobson, and legislative member.

Sugar cane was introduced to Natal from Mauritus but was hampered by transport and labour. Grey approved the import of Indians from the government of India. Labourers were paid 10 shillings to 12 shillings a month plus their keep. They were under contract, and after five years they received a free passage or its equivalent in crown land. In five years Natal had 6,500 Indians. It was hoped they would add to the country's prosperity, but because of their standard of living they became unwelcomed strangers instead.

Kathy had renewed vigor because of Eden. She watched him growing and each day he seemed to grow more lovable, gentle, and charismatic. Everyone loved this child. It was strange, as there seemed to be nothing but goodness about the child, everyone wanted to care for him.

He was now six years old. Kathy had a good tutor and he was learning very fast. This little boy, born in such sad and miserable circumstances, and so well nourished and cared for now, had come from a fragile and fearful mother, smothered in a life fraught with loneliness and pain. She thought of the Bible all Boers lived by, the "sins of the fathers." Damned be that, she thought. Whatever pains the child's mother had were obliterated in wonder and purity by the child her womb produced. She was not sure, but she had an instinctive feeling that somehow Julius was Eden's father. So she never for an instant had any doubt that Eden was her bloodline, her own precious grandchild in whom she found such infinite joy, a fresh found joy in her shortening years. For indeed her years to enjoy him were only brief; and the years fled and then came 1864.

One day Lion, now a broad, full blown mature man, announced he was taking Eden, the tutor, his horses, and his wagon and was going to trek up towards the Orange River.

His life, he said, was pointless. He wanted a wife and land of his own. He had lived too long in one spot. He was in wars as a boy and had loved and lost his woman. He found great joy in learning from Eden's tutor whom he had befriended, and now he had this unquenchable urge to move to reach out somewhere.

He stood in the bay of the window, the curtains billowing up behind him, as though he was a drifting cloud looking at Kathy. His green brown eyes were earnest.

"This time has come for me to go, Kathy."

"And what about Eden,? Lion, how can you take him with you, away from me?"

"Give me a child until he is seven and I'll give you the man. It says, Kathy; it says so in your own Bibl: So you have made the man. He must learn more and more, he's like a little waxing moon, Kathy, he grows by the minute."

Kathy was no longer the strong woman of before. Her tears fell down her cheeks.

"Lion, I know I've been cruel to you when you were a child, but if you give me that boy you can have all that's mine except very few things. You may have this farm when I die. For you and for Eden and I'm sure you will find a lovely wife, better if you travel alone."

He looked at Kathy and was distressed at having caused her this agony.

"I love this farm, Kathy, and I love all that's in it, including you and Eden, but life is passing me also. I know when I must change. Come with us, Kathy, if you love the boy so deeply."

She looked at Lion, but she felt void of strength. She knew she could not change this fascinating man. She just looked at him and staring back at her were her father's eyes: the strong proud eyes of her beloved father. It was strange that she had not noticed it before.

"I am too old to chance my life in an ox wagon on the move, Lion. Though I must say I am tempted to say yes. What about Braam Piet?"

"I don't know, Kath, I've not yet told him I am going. Braam Piet will never leave while you are here, Kathy, surely you know that. Braam is like the male swan…Poor old Braam."

Lion clapped his hands together in a gesture indicating the end of his talk. He locked his fingers together. Swans are monogamous. They only mate once—for life! Even death does not change the swan's ways.

"William says that people who hold their fingers in this position are inwardly thinking they are masters of the situation. Body language: like when one's angry, the knuckles go white, in a fist-like clench. But it's not like that with me, Kath. I will never hurt you or try to, my feelings are not like that. In fact, I hate to leave this home. I just know I have to go. And I want to take Eden with me."

"Tell me, Lion, tell me once and for all. Is Eden my Julius' son? Do you know who his father is?"

"Kathy, I am not free to tell you, I made a promise to Louisa and I swore on the child's life. I would not tell anyone until the boy was old enough to want to know himself. I think he'd be old enough when he's seventeen. William says that's about when a boy blossoms into manhood.

"It is cruel to make them fight at sixteen; I know, I was younger than sixteen. I know the terrors of war. I didn't really fear death so much, I just didn't want to lose my strength, you know, or a

leg or an arm or an eye. I had great fear of being maimed and
disabled. It's a hard thing not to have a mother you know, and
I'm not robbing Eden of a mother. I shall bring him back to you,
I promise. Pretorius wants all the servants to carry a pass despite
the fact that he resigned last year. Jan H. Brand is now president of
OFS. It's quite a stable government for the moment, never mind
what Braam Piet says.

When the rains are over we'll go, Kathy. Please don't make it
hard for me."

The months passed and Kathy seemed lifeless and depressed—
so much so that Eden noticed.

"Are you not well, Kathy?" Eden asked one day.

She nearly told him. She was crying out inside to say: no, no,
Eden. I can't bear the thought of you going north like the Trek
Boers and that I may never see you again.

"No, Eden, my darling boy, I am just getting older and I get sad
at the thought of leaving this beautiful world. I suppose death is
dull black like a black night and when one gets older we think of
death more often."

"Kathy, I cannot think of you and death, you're so special that
even after you're long gone you will always be alive for me."

She moved over to the boy. He was tall for a ten year old—a
tall, fair, handsome child with clear blue eyes. He was so mature
in many ways, and William Maxwell his tutor had matured his
thinking far beyond his years.

He put his arms around her and she held him to her body,
looking over his blonde head. He was so tranquil and unspoiled.

"Yes, well," she said softly, "you will take care to eat well and be
wise when you travel. Do you think you will love it?"

"Oh yes, Kathy, I will love it. I will be with Lion and nothing will harm me and we'll have campfires and I'll never stop learning because William Maxwell will be with us. But I will miss you, Kathy. And maybe my soft bed."

And they stood there swaying, the older Kathy and the young boy, and there was a sadness that hung in the air almost tangible like billowing bales of drifting smoke.

The rains lasted longer than usual, and everyday seemed to be wet and gray. In September Pretorius and Paul Kruger joined the Free State Commanders, Fick, with a force of 1200 men from the Transvaal. Brand refused to promise the men farms in the conquered land so they withdrew to the SA Republic. After having routed a Basutu Force, at this time Moshesh was 81.

Christmas came and went and just before the new year Julius came to visit Kathy. In great splendour he came, bringing his wife Elizabeth with a splendid carriage and six horses.

Kathy liked Elizabeth, a spirited woman, vivacious and full of fun. Elizabeth took an immediate liking to Eden, and together they explored the whole of wonderful Moorplaats, sometimes on horseback and sometimes just walking. They would set off early in the morning and return for breakfast.

After a day or two Elizabeth asked Julius, "Tell me, Julius, who is Eden's father?"

Julius looked at his wife, "His mother died in childbirth when he was born and my mother has brought him up."

"But he's so devoted to Lion. Is Lion his father?"

"I don't know; he certainly doesn't look like him, does he?"

"Then for goodness sake, Julius. He didn't come from a stork, did he? Sometimes he resembles you, do you know that? He seems like you!"

"No, I don't Liz, but I'll tell you when I came to see my mother several years ago he was here, and he has always been the most lovable child. And now he is a very fine lad. But I have never been able to discover from anyone who his father is. Lion is so goddamned protective of him, I suppose it's his son. You do know Lion is part coloured, don't you?"

She laughed. "Well he's certainly one of the most handsome men, Julius, coloured or not. He's fair," she paused, "which is unusual…"

"Lion is my grandfather's bastard son. There now, he is my mulatto uncle," said Julius, and he looked at his wife as though he had just disclosed a skeleton from his family cupboard.

"Julius, my dear, a man's colour is not what makes the man. I don't give a damn about the colour of a man's skin." She dismissed the subject with a sort of disdain. "Some of these chocolate babies are just so pretty, I'd be happy to adopt one."

Julius swung around.

"If you were born here in Africa you would not make so silly a statement. My God, Elizabeth, look out there," and he pointed to three children playing in the sand, "Those little chocolate babies grow into that, and that, and that," and he pointed to each of the children. "And then when they're adult they look like that," and again he pointed to a middle-aged black man, naked to the waist, chopping wood on a large tree trunk which was used as a chopping block. Just at that moment another servant wearing a white apron came up to the chopping block with two fat fowls. He bent down, put their heads on the block, and chopped their heads off. They dropped the chickens whose bodies bounced once or twice on the ground, blood squirting from their necks, hopping lifelessly without their heads. The black children thought it was hilarious and they all joined in merry laughter. Finally the cook gathered the two birds by the legs, their bloody necks dangling downwards, and went towards the kitchen.

"That, I presume, is dinner," said Elizabeth.

"I imagine so," said Julius, "but you see how they enjoy decapitation. That is all those black people think of you. Only they would add fierce imprecations and blood curdling yells as they slash you to pieces."

She shuddered a little.

"I don't understand Assegais and Pangas and axes and spears, perish the thought, Julius darling, nothing can make me see their children as anything other than just beautiful children. Tell me, Julius, can we take Eden home with us? He would be so happy at Riversend. He is such a lovely boy, he would be good company for me."

"I'm afraid not, Liz. Lion is his guardian and he would not agree to that. Besides, Lion, William Maxwell his tutor, and Eden plan to move as soon as the rains are over."

"What a pity," she replied, "I must have a talk to your mother. Yes," she almost sighed, "I shall talk to our Lady Katherine at the first opportunity."

"I should think the person you must ask is Eden himself, Elizabeth," Kathy was saying several days later on the second to last day of Julius and Elizabeth's visit.

She didn't really ask Eden, she asked him instead if he was eager to go.

"Yes ma'am," said Eden, "I can't wait to go. But I do wish Mama would come with us." He often referred to Kathy as Mama, especially if he was sad or not well. "Perhaps, Aunt Liz," he said, "you would come and see that Mama is alright. She'll be really lonely without Lion and me."

Elizabeth could see the concern in his eyes. "Tell you what," she said, "we will have an arrangement. I will care for your Mama and call upon her every month if when you return you will do the same for me. You will come and call upon me once a month and see that I too am well and not lonely. Is that a bargain?"

The boy stood still looking at his aunt. He was nonplussed but, "Aunt," he said, "I don't know when we shall be back."

"If I know anything at all," said Elizabeth, "I know you and Lion will be back very soon."

"Alright," he said. "It's a bargain," and he extended his firm young hand, but she put her arms about him.

"I'm family, Eden, you may hug me."

And he hugged her torso and felt a warmth he often felt in Kathy. He was very concerned about leaving his Kathy. Well at least Braam Piet was always there and he would also care for his beloved Mama, of that he felt sure and took comfort in the thought that Elizabeth would also do her best.

When the wagons were ready, packed with supplies—brandy and feather blankets, dried meat and bottled yams, cashets of flour and salt, ammunitions and guns, and oil for their lamps—the day came to set off. Lion, usually so sure of himself, felt a little uncertain, and Eden, comforted by his tutor, tried very hard not to cry. But he did cry, and not for a long time after. They said goodbye to Kathy and Sonnestroom. They traveled in silence lest a sound should pierce the balloon of pent-up emotion that so easily could burst.

Lion rode his horse beside the wagon and two other horses followed the span. William Maxwell held the reins, the voorloper (the man the front of the wagon) with worn down veldskoen (leather boots & shoes) held the toe (rope) and beside the span a driver with a large whip called all the oxen by name. It was safer by ox wagon, though he could just as easily have taken horses. The wagons were large, with a bed and a place where one could feel the smell of a home. Wagons had more comforts for traveling than a horse-drawn carriage, especially when one was not sure of where one would be and how long one would be away. Here with a hard-limbed ten year old child, Lion needed some comfort. There was time enough later for Eden to become a man. There was no sound, only the creak of his saddle and the rustling of the long grass. He had brought four horses so if he had trouble he could change the harnesses in a trice.

His was not a boer trek. His was not a trek into the unknown north, with the guns of the Regiment, men and the assegais of the blacks. No, his was a journey into a new world and with him was a child. He watched eagerly for buck that bounded into the bush as they approached and for birds and small game that affrighted as the wagon passed.

He glanced backwards. Eden sat beside William, eagerly looking inside a book—*The Transformation of Insects*, by Duncan. Slowly they passed the farms, it was harvest time and farm workers were plucking the vines. The little towns seemed full of fruit, especially raisin-making vines. Ash pots were boiling to dip some off the branches, afterwards to raisins dried in the sun. Figs were ripe and abundant so in a short time depressions had passed and Sonnestroom was soon days away.

Eden posted letters carefully stamped in the little towns. On the way he would sometimes ride one of the horses alongside of Lion, always full of chatter and curiosity. Each night they would outspan and rest. In the morning when the day was well started they would move on, always resting the animals and seeing them well fed. Lion would shoot a cluiker or a bushbuck or Impala.

Milk and eggs were available from the farms as well as fruit, onions, and vegetables. One day a farmer sold Maxwell a beautiful stinkwood chair with yellowwood inlets where he would sit in the evenings as they listened to the sounds of the night and watched the clouds climb through the air and chase away the remnants of a waning moon.

Traveling had become less difficult than it used to be. Now there were something like roads in the colony, not scrub-covered former tracks—and there was the comfort of the wagon. Often silently they rode, the two men, one in the wagon, one on his horse, and a boy. They rode like hunters ever alert through the thornless Mopani, its large round leaves, and little globules of sugar lumps secreted by the large brown Mopani worm into the butterfly-shaped leaves looked like little erupted warts. Animals loved this sweet secretion, so the Mopani was ever sure to be harbouring brousing game. And so they rode day after day, lost in their dreams, until one day they came upon a few wagons in the open commonage. The smoke of their fire was stealing upwards in a great trail and a tremendous row of shouting and raised voices. A woman was shrieking hysterically and two Boers were galloping off to the east of the beaten track. Lion told the voerloper to head towards the wagons. There were three wagons, and their spans were grazing, spread out far across the commonage. When Lion reached their camp they had begun to calm down all except one bearded Boer who sat on his horse, across his shoulder hung his snaphaan and in his right hand he held a jambok of immense size.

A large hairy dog sat just behind his horse, and several men on horseback were out among the cattle counting those that bore their brand. Directly in front of his horse lying in the fetal position covering his head was a yellowish light-skinned man. It seemed obvious to the Boer he was about to lay on his sjamboh. He had a nasty lugubrious expression, he was sure his dog would tear the kaffir to pieces, thus he had hung his gun across his shoulder. The native lay on the ground barefooted, his heels grey and cracked, his eyes staring out of his head.

Before Lion could ask a question a young Boer galloped up beside him, and with him on a stocky grey colt was a girl. She wore a hunting shirt and raw hide veldskoen like her mother, her chestnut hair blew wildly in the breeze. Her cheeks were pink and her eyes shone like burning stones, her arms were sunburnt and she held the reins with slender fingers. Her chest heaved and fell and her breasts pressed against her shirt aggressive and youthful and full of challenge.

Lion and Eden stood together and Maxwell jumped down off the wagon and joined them.

"These kaffirs have stolen our oxen and have killed one of our span," said the boy, "and my father is going to make him speak. He must tell us where our missing oxen are." He looked defiantly at Lion and the boy. Maxwell moved over towards the man curled up on the ground. He called their wagon driver to come over as he could interpret.

"My Pa will beat him so he can tell us," said the boy.

"Just a moment," said Lion, "Tell your father there is no need for a beating. Sixpence," he called, "ask this fellow where the cattle are and what exactly is the truth? Tell him if he dares to lie I will tell this farmer to lash him and then put the dog on him."

There was a long exchange of words.

"Master Lion, he said he is not the thief. He is a bushman and those that have driven away the cattle are the Kaffirs. He says the cattle are not far away, across the river, behind the long reeds, not more than a mile from here. He is innocent and was only looking for his goats that are also lost."

Lion looked at the man. He looked like a Hottentot or a bushman and for the very reason that he was terrified of the threat of death Lion knew when they told the truth. Lion looked at the boy and at the girl, and then he looked at the girl again. He felt the stare of her stony eyes and was held by the beauty of her face. He avoided staring at her.

"Now look here," he said, "I will guard this man and you two ride over to where he saw the Kaffirs drive your cattle. He says the culprits are hiding in the hills, but the cattle are grazing one mile across the river, past the rocky kopje (little hill) where there is a small plain hidden by the tall reeds. Go now and I will guard this man till you return."

They swung their horses, about!

"You must tie him up," said the youth and he took a riem (rope) from his saddle bag and threw it at Eden. The old man with the sjambok said nothing. He seemed displeased and mistrustful. To him a fleeing Kaffir was a guilty Kaffir.

"Tie his hands behind his back, Eden," said Lion. Eden dismounted and he looked at Lion disbelievingly. "Go on, tie him up, I said."

Eden moved over to the man, who was now sitting on his haunches.

"Sixpence," he said, "please tell him I am only tying him up to stop him from running away while those two people have gone to find the cattle."

Sixpence had a long coversation again. It seemed a lot of talk for so little to be said.

"The man says it is very hard to find the plain where the cattle are. He will lead us to them."

Lion took another horse and in Dutch he told the old man that he himself would go with his horse and find the opening where his cattle were.

"Eden, you and Maxwell outspan and prepare the camp. I will try not to be too long." He put the man on the horse and loosed the riem on his hands. "Tell him, Sixpence, if he tries to run I will shoot him. So he must lead me to where he saw the cattle."

He tied a lead to the horse and put the man firmly in the saddle. He sat on the horse as though he was quite used to riding. The dust of the young couple was still in the air, and it seemed as though they had headed in the right direction. Within a quarter or an hour the yellow man pointed to an opening beside the rocks. He was vehement,

"Eyole Eyole," (Here Here) he kept saying.

So Lion took his horse towards a bushy undergrowth. The man ducked his head down and his horse obediently went through. It was obviously a place only known to the people of the bush. Lion followed, brushed by the undergrowth. The horse's body parted the reeds with its belly and thorns rasped and tugged at its flanks and suddenly the reeds ended and there was a plain almost green compared to the commonage. And there they were five of the Boer Trek oxen grazing undisturbed.

"What is your name," inquired Lion.

"Gamelo Eyako" and he understood.

"Mchlopo," he answered and he eagerly pointed to his skin. "White," said Lion.

"Alright then Whitey," he said, "we are going to bring these stolen cattle back to where they belong." And taking the lead of Whitey's horse he rounded them up and drove them through the same opening from whence they had entered. It was at this point that the two young Boers met Lion and the captive. Just as they were emerging the trek oxen and into the wild that led to the road, that led to the camp, the two galloped up towards them.

"Ja dis is onse." (Yes, these are ours)

He was looking at the branded oxen but Lion was looking at the girl. She was in her mid 20s, strong and brown from the sun, with slim hands and long legs that dangled beside her horse's belt out of the stirrups. She looked as though she felt foolish having dashed off and failed to find the plain. They seemed so sure they would have found it.

Lion sensed her discomfort.

"Only the bush folk know of places like this," he said, "I had to take your prisoner to guide me. He says his name is 'Mchlopo.' It means white, as a matter of fact, since he is a pale shade of the lighter side of brown. Maybe he is the result of a straying Boer. They seem to have left a lot of their wild oats across the colony, the Boers."

"And what about yourself," the girl said, "as green-brown as your eyes are, you Rooinek (Redneck), so curly is your hair. Like the Engels say, it has a touch of the Tar brush, does it not?" and she roused her face in a defiant and proud manner. "Woodcutters and carriers of water, these people are of no faith, with strength in their arms and speed in their legs. Fast as the cheetahs and as treacherous as vipers. Is that why you pity the thief, Rooinek, is it a kinship you feel?" She was almost teasing, baiting Lion now. "So we have found the cattle, we must let him go, tell him he's been a good boy and he must not do it again? Is that it, Meneer Rooinek?"

"Toe nou (enough now) Petra," said her brother, "Enough now" and she laughed up into the sky and turned her horse and cantered away. Her brother stayed behind with Lion. "I see you have kept him on a rein."

"I promised you I would keep him till your return and now that you have returned, I will hand him over to you."

"Excuse me, Meneer, we should ride together back to the camp and we must talk with my father."

He offered the rein to which Whitey was tethered to the youth, but Whitey made such a fuss Lion took it back and together they rode back onto the common.

Petra's father was waiting near his wagon, he was sitting on a small riepie stool. The sjambok was hanging from the side of the wagon tent and swung as the breeze blew. The girl had brewed hot coffee, having removed her leather trousers and replaced them with a billowing skirt and small white oven skirt in front, rather like an apron.

"Hello Daantje," she said as Lion and her brother rode up towards their wagon. Eden and Maxwell were both eating the breakfast she had prepared.

"Pa," said the youth and he spoke to his father in Dutch. A fairly long conversation ensued and then the youth said, "My father thanks you, Meneer."

He dismounted and sent his horses back with the wagon driver and voorlooper. He extended his hand to the old Boer.

"My name is Lion McCabe."

"Neels Potgieter," said the old man, and then the youth, having started speaking repeated,

"My father thanks you for your help and is pleased to have his oxen returned. He says we must take the skelm to the landrost so the court can punish him."

"Tell your father this man is not guilty," and he repeated the story as Whitey had told it to him. "I tell you man, this Whitey is not guilty. I know these tribespeople very well, I know them

better than you Boers think, as did my Pa before me. My brother
was Sir Jules Jacobsen, knighted by Queen Victoria for fighting
in three wars, and for helping to bring about peace. But mainly
because, Meneer, he understood how to bring out the good in
man. Perhaps I have gleaned from him, but I do know that this
yellow man is not guilty."

The girl was staring at Lion. Her eyes watched every word as it
passed his lips and her brother interpreted it to his father. All the
servants from Lion's group were listening and finally the old Boer
said, through his son, that it was upon Lion's head if anything else
was stolen. Lion released the captive.

"Sixpence," he called. Sixpence was there in a trice. "Tell him,
Sixpence, tell him he is free, but if I should ever find that he is
either a thief or a liar then his spirits should be there to save
him from my wrath."

Sixpence told him all he was told and more and Whitey just
sat there.

"Feed him, Sixpence, and let him go. Tell him I believe him,
until I find out otherwise."

The girl had become quiet, then she appeared.

"I have made you some breakfast," she said, and she laid out a
table and riempie stool. Then wiping her hands on her white apron
she moved off to bring more.

Lion felt much pleasure in being cared for by a woman.
Daantjie told Lion they were going to the Orange Free State. Most
of their stock had gone on before, and had taken two months to get
there from Natal. His mother was in the Free State now among the
Dutch. She was of Huguenot descent and did not like the English.
She had taken many of her Hottentat servants with her as well
as his eldest brother. He told of how his mother and brother had

formed a laager of wagons. A whole circle of wagons came together and all the sheep and cattle were encircled in the center. He told of the boundary line that had been made by the governor at the Cape and how Moshesh had been given a month to get out of the Free State by the President. Many English had brought sheep and horses and were leaving for Natal in case a war broke out; martial law would have stopped them leaving.

"So why do you go to the Free State?" asked Lion.

"Because that's where Mother is and that is where our cattle, sheep, and goats have gone. There could be a war if Moshesh refuses to leave, but we have heard that Moshesh's ambassador came with a white flag flying at his saddle and had asked for another month. The President refused!"

"Anyhow Meneer, they don't want Rooineds, only the Burghers of the Free State have to go. So you and your son will have no need to fear!"

"Men!" chipped in Petra, "Men must fight. Sometimes I think women would be just as good. We women would make very good soldiers. We are more decisive than men, we women, we would simply decide. And maybe we would decide life is more important than death and we would decide 'no war' and we would give the Kaffirs their land and move onto other land, and that would be that." And she wiped her hands downwards on her white apron again. And Eden laughed,

"That, I think, Petra, would be a good idea."

And they laughed together and Petra put her slim hands on Eden's shoulder and she said,

"My brothers are all so big now, Eden, it's as if I had a nice English brother. I don't like to say goodbye, you know," and she flicked her hair backwards with maternal softness. "Ya, you will grow up too, full of fire and burn yourself up like all men do. Sometimes life makes me want to cry. I don't like to think too much. We women, we may be tough, but we have the tender hearts," and she sat down, her knees drawn together beneath her skirt and she hugged her thighs and exposed the lower part of her long slim calves.

Lion felt a strange curdle deep within his groin. She was not a scatty fool, this Petronella. No, she was all woman, ripe like a rich burgundy plum, tired of the rugged insecure life of the wagon perhaps. He could see by the look in her luminous brown eyes that as strong as she was, she was soft. She was soft and warm and lovable.

"Tell me, Meneere Rooinek, may we travel together, all our wagons together and the journey will be safer and better for us all. When the time comes to part, we all go our own ways, that's the time to say goodbye." She was full of fun and laughter, keeping her eye on her Pa and her brown eyes flashing green when she played with Eden and Maxwell, ever near to Lion.

At Nilsonskop they out spanned near to a huge flock of sheep, some 2000 of them, several horses and a few Hottentots. In the wagons behind the sheep were some Englishmen: Ms. Elgie and a Mr. Sydney Turner.

Sydney Turner was a killer. He loved to hunt, had no mercy and was very proud of his list of slaughtered game. He kept tally of how many wildebeest, blisboks, springboks, lion, leopards, and hartebeest and then he told of how they had run down guagga and shot them for his dogs. Petra flew into a rage and Eden joined her.

"Ja," she said, "You goddamned bloody Engels. I just wish the next time you load your gun it explodes right into your god damned face."

Eden and Maxwell half wished to have her courage. How they would have loved to have said the same. Lion was listening to their account of the burghers.

"The Dutch have mustered up a rough lot," he told them. "4000 horses and 300 wagons drawn up in the towns square with more wagons arriving. They said another 208 which would cover three miles and they were to start for the boundary. The Dutch wore no uniforms, just their own homemade buckskin."

Lion was interested to hear this news, but as Petra had caused hostility there was no way they would become friends. These two were heading for Natal away from the war with all their sheep, wagons, and wagon homes.

Lion decided then that he would go towards Kimberly, no further than the Orange River. Eden had to post his letter and he rushed it off before the post wagon left. He too was glad to see the last of the greedy, bearded English who turned his stomach with their hunting tales. But to go behind the Drakensberg? No, the thought did not appeal to him. Perhaps it would be at this place that he would say goodbye to Petra and Daantjie and he felt a little wistful. His newfound young friends would go. He found the new yellow man of great interest. When he was released, and Lion guaranteed his innocence, he asked if he could stay with the wagon train. Lion had reluctantly agreed to this, but now they were all very pleased.

Whitey, as he was called, had a wonderful knowledge of stones, rivers, and trees. He soon learned to lash the trek chains and cook and even sew, and he knew how to find a Tuma.* He loved the wilderness and he loved Eden. And William Maxwell, ever the

---

* Tuma = a wild potato.

teacher, taught them all, even old Neels Potgieter, a cousin to the younger Potgieter (son of the voortrekker leader) who died in1854 a year after his famous father. Once when Lion was discussing Whitey, he quoted, "To those who think big, the gods are kind."

And Eden remembered well those words.

When they reached the Orange River, Petra was in a state of nerves. To her father's wagon she went, and she told him, "Pa, you have educated me well, you have guided me well. I am a good god-fearing daughter. But Pa, love his driven away all my desires of virtue. I love this man, Pa, I am weakened by the very look of his eyes upon me. There's a storm in my heart, Pa, and I think I'm going to die. I knew when I first set eyes upon him, that I would never let him go. I will go wherever he goes. I have been a good girl, and God arranged that he came to us and helped us. He solved our problems and saved an innocent man, never mind whether he was a Kaffir or not. That is a sign, Pa."

Her father did not reply. He was searching for time to think up a suitable reply to his daughter.

"Magtag (Godalmighty)," he said, "I am not quick to make up my mind about people. It is true I like the man, but he is Engels, and he does not read the Bible."

That night she got her chance. She flung herself upon Lion, flaunting her beauty, her desirability; she took his hand and placed it upon her firm breast, she lured him to the bush. In a flood of inhibited passion and partial moonlight, she forced him to feast upon her young womanhood, burning and piercing into the very depth of all that was herself.

"I love you, Lion, but not with the love of ordinary woman. No, Lion. It is the love that you need my lovely Liflik Rooinek." And the blood of her virginity was splashed upon his loins.

She said goodbye to her Pa and to her brother, and went to bed in Lion's wagon. There were no tears of sorrow; she was a woman now, a burgher woman of Huguenot blood she was proud, brave, and strong. And of course, she was a clever woman. Perhaps a little too far away from the usual Boer vrou, with their black flannel dresses and wide collars, and long sleeves buttoned at the wrist, with all those flounces on the skirts and kappies (Boer caps) that completely covered the head down to the shoulders. Magtig, this was a hot land, a hot and thirsty land, and she had long shed her skirts in favor of a buckskin shirt and narrow trousers. That sent all the men who saw her into a state of masculine readiness. For what? For nothing, because it was she who was waiting. And she was not goingto be like those well-fleshed tantes (aunties). She knew what she wanted.

Now she had found a man she could love. A man who had strong arms and a wide hard chest. A man who reminded her of a magnificent lion, and when she heard his name she felt sure that God had something to do with the design of things: his name was Lion. So safe with the consent of God, she felt she must have this Lion to be the father of her children. They were married the same week in Burgherdorp. He was her man now and she didn't care a jot about his life before he met her, or what he had done. He said he was unmarried and that was all that mattered. Eden was a witness and William Maxwell the best man. Christmas came and went.

Eden got his letters posted, his letters to Kathy and Elizabeth and hoped they would get all the news.

In 1867 the Orange Free State defeated the Basutus. It was wet and miserable traveling now, and far more intereseting. Petra made life full of fun. She would take Eden when they outspanned and often Whitey also came, and with her shotgun, using only one barrel, she would shoot a Karhaan (guinea fowl) with one shot.

"You know, Eden, we Boers have had to survive. My Pa could shoot through a crowd of people and get his target in one shot. So sure was he. Daantjie can also do that, but I have not had that courage. But we would never be hungry, and a Korhaan makes a very good meal." And she took Whitey by the arm, and placing a piece of anthill at 100 yards, she taught him how to shoot. "One day, Whitey," she said, "When your people do not hate us Dutch people, I will give this gun to you."

Lion seemed a contented man, whistling and singing as he filed the horses' hooves and rubbed their feet with an arsenic mixture to drive away the ticks. It was a constant job to keep them free of ticks, and now there was another horse: Petra's stocky grey. Maxwell was now onto advanced learning for Eden, collecting textbooks at various post stations. The wagon train was full of learning. The servants actually started work earlier to try and fit in time for a first rate free lesson. They were all able to write and their reading was even more advanced. Whitey was a star pupil, grasping all that was taught him swiftly.

They moved early, so that when the hard ground was hot it did not burn the animals' feet. They rested midday and traveled again in the late afternoon. It was not difficult to find good grazing grass in these parts. News was about that a diamond had been found in April by a bushman on the banks of the Orange River during the midst of an economic depression in South Africa.

In October, Lion had found a spot to outspan on a farm that belonged to a Boer named Van Niekerk, very near the banks of the Orange River. Whitey was wildly excited, unusually excited, by the water in the drift and this drift was exposed. Never is the river so exposed, sort of shallower, the stones beneath become visible.

One day, just before midday, Eden and Lion were seated on a stone near a drift. It was hot so they decided to bathe. While Lion was splashing and dipping, Eden saw this stone as the sun caught it; it shone brilliant fire inside its tumbled surface. He turned the stone about and found three of these stones. One was as large as his hand could cover, and the other two of lesser size. He was looking into his stone when Lion got up and came over.

"Look Lion," he said, "I think this is a diamond. See how it glints inside when the sun hits it."

Lion did not have the same enthusiasm, but nevertheless they collected as many of these stones as they could. Whitey found one with a chip on the side, and it shone like the morning star. Soon they spent all their free time gathering and searching for stones. Eden was sure they were diamonds, and William Maxwell assured Lion these might well be. Everyone had some, and everyday they spent time up and down the riverside into the water from the drift, even entering deep water and bringing out stones to be examined. They had a good collection each one of them and Lion filled a bucket; crystal quarts and agates among them, but it was the clear blue white ones, that shone blue, that excited them most. Eden had a glass that magnified.

"Look here, Lion," said Eden, "See this stone, I think it is the same as the one Kathy has, which she says is her best diamond. It's dull outside but look in. I am going to collect as many as I can find, we might well be very rich if we find they are real diamonds."

It is very rare to find a drift in the Orange River. A drift is like a stone strainer, and when water is very low sometimes the drift can be a little exposed—a stone ridge beneath the water.

One day, after several weeks, they moved toward Colesburg. They all had stones but Eden had an exceptionally large one.

In Colesburg Lion noticed for the first time that Petra was swollen.

"My God, Pet," he said, "where is your waist? Have I been blinded by this bush happy existence?"

"I wondered," she said, "Perhaps, Lion, you don't notice me so much. I have been pregnant five months, and only now you notice." She started to cry, "Could you not see I failed to eat breakfast and how often I went into the bush to vomit? How many times have I wanted to tell you. Lion, I am with child and you will be a father again. Eden will have a beautiful brother. God, Lion, five months and only now you notice it." She put her hands over her face and he noticed her fingers were fatter.

He had just taken his great luck for granted. The strong are respected not pitied. The weeping woman, the fainting female, they are the ones men pander to. Not the strong capable help mates, strong healthy lovers. He felt ashamed and he took her in his strong, gentle arms. "Forgive me Petra, you are such a wonderful, capable companion, you never give me cause to worry or wonder. You are a wonderful woman, and I love you very much. This very day you will see a doctor." He changed harness and put on the four horses, leaving Petra's gray neighing and galloping wildly, not wanting to be left alone. "Eden," he called, "saddle up and ride him or he'll break a leg carrying on like that. Horses are sociable creatures and he can't be left alone." So while William took the lessons, Eden rode up beside the wagon and hey went to Colesburg to find the doctor. Lion held the horses and Petra sat up beside him. He was quiet and ashamed that he had neglected her, chasing stones along the riverbanks and sleeping under the stars.

One or two wagons stood outside of a corrugated iron building with windows that slid up and down, one large square pane above and one below. Beside the building was a small stone Methodist church, with a large, round stained glass window and a weather vane stuck at the point of the gable roof. On the door of the flat building was a sign: "General Merchant." Lion called Eden to go in and inquire where one would find the doctor. They were directed down the same street to a dwelling of similar style but the front roof of this house was the Doctor's Surgery. There were no wagons outside; here, only a single horse was tied to the crosspole built for that purpose. Eden tied his horse to the other end and walked over to Lion's wagon. Lion then went towards the doctor's residence, and lifting a pewter knocker, gave it a knock. A plump lady came to the door, her hair pinned down behind her head in a folded plait. She wore a wide crinoline skirt with frilled sleeves with a small white neat collar and a brooch pinned directly in the middle.

"I'd like to see the doctor," said Lion, "well, rather, I would like the doctor to see my wife," he said. The lady smiled. "Do come inside," she said, "the doctor will be with you in a short while." Lion brought Petra inside and they sat down in the small room with a lamp on the desk. "Doctor Merriman, M.D. (Heidleberg)," it read, on a diploma hanging on the wall. Within a few moments, Dr. Merriman entered, a pink-cheeked man aged between 45 and 50. Lion told him of Petra's pregnancy and that he noticed her fingers were a little swollen; he wanted assurance that she was well. The doctor gave Petra a good examination, but found that in his opinion, she was a fine, healthy young woman and should have no difficulty with childbirth. Lion paid his fee, and as he took his money from his pocket, a couple of his stones fell onto the doctor's desk.

"Are you a geologist, then?" the doctor inquired of Lion, and Lion told him about his stones.

"My son thinks they might be worth examining," he said, "and my son would like to be a geologist."

"My dear Sir," he said, "if you are interested, I have a William G. Atherstone coming to see me later today. He is a colleague of mine. We trained together, but he has a very good reputation as an amateur geologist. Good gracious, man, call in later and show him your stones." And so they waited in their wagon while the horses ate from feedbags and drank water from the doctor's buckets. Dr. Atherstone arrived earlier than expected, and they were invited inside by Dr. Merriman.

Dr. Atherstone was greatly interested in the stones and grew wildly excited. He tested them first with water; water does not stick to a diamond, he said. He examined them closely, found they could cut glass, and eventually took off his glasses and looked up. "I believe they are diamonds," he declared. Eden took out one of his stones. "This is for you, Doctor," he said, "it will make a pretty brooch for your wife." He laid down the uncut stone, about the size of a pea, and they moved off, leaving the doctor looking at his stone through his Polariscope. Out in the street, jubilant Eden and Lion hugged each other. "Petra will be able to do many things now."

Thus, it happened all of their stones were diamonds. The Colonel Secretary Richard Southey informed Sir Phillip Wodehouse and soon Lion's stones—and they had many of them—were on a sailing ship to jewelers in London. The results were unbelievable, and Lion was in shock. He was a wealthy man, Eden was a wealthy young lad. Petra was very happy, William Maxwell was beside himself, Whitey wanted to buy a farm, and the servants from the wagon train relied on Lion to see them right. The diamond rush followed with incalculable results for South Africa and many more diamonds were wrestled from the veld.

Eden, despite his exuberance, grew quiet; he was in adolescence now, and Lion thought that was natural. Only Petra seemed to please him, soon Petra would have her own child. "Lion," she said one evening, "you must take that boy back to his home. The responsibilities of a man have been placed upon him and it's too much. He is just a youth, a boy. We must all go, I need a good home for my son to be born in." They returned back now south towards Cradock and homewards back to their beloved Sonnestroom. No joy was greater. Three years had passed, and Kathy, Lady Kathy, Mama, was so much older. Eden clung to her, his eyes wet with tears, and she told him, "My darling child," she whispered, "Oh thank God you are back." But it was different now, they were back with much more money and they related their whole story to Braam and Kathy. "Oh Eden, I want this farm for you," but Eden did not answer. Eden wanted to go to America to study geology, and sometime, when the moment was right, he would tell them all. For now, this was a land where one could be young and rich, yet he wanted to go.

Petra was well accepted by Kathy, who was well pleased by Lion's choice of woman. Kathy was ever the Lady, who so graciously always seemed to say the right thing. Once again life at Sonnestroom returned to the happy family they all knew. Elizabeth, true to her word, had cared for Kathy, calling upon her whenever she was able. Eden and Elizabeth renewed their friendship as though he had gone away only yesterday. He was tall now, gangly, neither boy nor man, but through the metamorphosis always shone the gentle charismatic Eden, so young, and already a gentleman of means. He was an embryo of great manhood, self-motivated and spurred on by determination. Kathy saw in him her blood, something of hers, and her pride for him was beyond all words or description.

Petra's labor started very early one morning. "Lion," she called, "I think my time has come." She held her hand under her abdomen and Lion could see the great round shape she always covered so well. She seemed shy of her distention, like it was a private thing only she should see, but Kathy had arranged for the doctor to be installed in a guesthouse. Never again would she know, though she well remembered, the terrors of childbirth in a barren wilderness with the nearest doctor two days ride away. A fine young doctor, a second-generation settler's son, was in attendance, together with a Scotch midwife from the Mission, and together they delivered Petra's baby.

She had a beautiful 7 ½ lb. girl. When first Petra heard the baby cry, she asked, "how is it?" "Mrs. McCabe, yes, it is a beautiful girl, and she's well and perfect." Within moments she was washed and swathed and they placed her in Petra's arms. Petra stared at the baby in her arms, a new person made only by herself, and Lion, of course, but really it was hers. It smelled strange, a sweet, human smell, and when the doctor and nurse had cleaned everything up and fixed up her bed, they sent in the anxious father. "It's a girl, Mr. McCabe, a beautiful golden girl." Lion kissed Petra tenderly and took the tiny bundle from her arms. "My child," he said, "my beautiful child." "Our child, Lion," she said. "Sorry, Petra," he said, "our beautiful child," and placed it back against Petra's breast. Petra looked tired but had lost none of her beauty. They were so beautiful, mother and child.

There were people everywhere. They all came in, Kathy first, and Eden, and Whitey, and Braam. There they all looked at this miracle that was hers. "Kathy," said Petra, "thank you, I want to say thank you, and now I think I'll rest." "What are you going to name her, Lion?" asked Eden, who found it hard to think humans were ever so small. "I can remember you that small, Eden dear," said Kathy. "Did you bear me, then, Mama?" he asked, and she looked at Lion. She did not know how to reply. "No Eden, your mother died when you were born." Petra closed her eyes. She had never questioned Lion about Eden. She had waited, she had always waited, but he never told her. Lion spoke, "When you mother died, Kathy took you and brought you up, and she is the only mother you know." "But I have your name, I am Eden McCabe. And this baby will be?" Lion quickly leaned over and picked up the tiny hand. "This baby I will name. Petra, all our others you may choose their names, but this one, allow me, this baby is to be Kathleen McCabe," he looked at Kathy and she moved up to Lion. She hesitated, then she clung to Lion. "And I am deeply honored." Petra fell asleep. She was too tired to think.

When Eden was 16, he wanted to go to America. William Maxwell, who now ran a public school near Sonnestroom in Cradock, wanted very much to go with him, which pleased Lion, as he was just a little dubious about Eden's youth and going so far away. The journey was also long and hazardous, so they booked the best ship they could find. By reputation, a certain ship called the Marie Star was the only ship one could take to America. Kathy insisted that Eden take only this ship. She felt very protective towards Eden, and so did Elizabeth. Elizabeth so far was barren; she and Julius had tried unsuccessfully to have children for several years, but no matter what they tried, there was no success. Elizabeth began to feel unfulfilled. She came frequently to see Kathy and never left Petra's children alone. Petra, in the meantime, had two daughters, Kathleen and Kimberly, beautiful girls that romped and played and brought the song of spring like blossoms to bees. When Eden left, Kathy knew she would enjoy these girls, especially her beloved Kathleen. She did not mind Elizabeth's interest. The poor woman; it was sad when a woman longed for motherhood. Once she had a dog who was barren and when another young bitch produced a litter of puppies, the barren bitch went through fire to try and nurse them. The longing was so intense that the barren bitch actually developed milk in her teats and happily and blissfully suckled the puppies, together with the younger bitch. Perhaps it was something like that, the surrogate mother. But regardless, Kathy felt only sympathy, and Petra, busy sewing and riding, was only too happy to oblige.

So the days passed, and the time came that Eden was due to sail. That morning, Kathy had a headache, and Eden hung about her bedroom. "Mama," he called, "may I come in?" "Enter, Eden," she answered and he went in and sat beside her bed. "Eden, I cannot go to see you sail, I feel you are the very core of my self, and I'm too old to wave goodbye. I think I may just not be strong enough," she said. "That's how life is, my precious boy, there is a time for everything. You must go because you have a calling, and I would like you to have this wonderful farm. Braam Piet, who has no children, you know, he never married, he has given me all he owns. I really don't know why, he just felt that if he died it would not be settled. He is also old now, but has always been a more integral constant and loyal friend. He was my brother in law's friend, of course; you do not know Jan, he also is old, but was a very successful newspaperman, devoted to Braam Piet Retief. No relation, except a long way down the family line to the leader Piet. Then he worked with my beloved husband.

"He never was a trek Boer, he stayed with Jules, to defend us against the black warriors and their plundering way of life. Then Jules left me; they made him Sir Jules, you know. He was such a brave, wonderful person. Such a short life he had," she said. "Sometimes, Eden, I see a lot of Jules in you. Perhaps that makes me love you all the more. This farm must be yours, and perhaps a part of you will give to my daughter Moya in England. She married an English officer and has three children I've never seen, in England. It's funny that I don't often think of them, though I would love to, you understand, but what one has never had one never misses very much. If she should ever return, take care of her, Eden. I only ask you this because I also want you to have this place. No heaven is better than Sonnestroom, and what a story it could tell—so much death and disaster, rot and rust and bloodied mud. But I don't want to depress you, I intend to stay well until you return. That very thought alone will keep me alive, so just kiss me, Eden and send me lots of mail, and go quietly away now through the door. Go now to Mr. Maxwell, it will be a long day until you come back."

Eden kissed her. He held onto her and he felt her body shudder with a deep sob. "I love you more than any woman on earth, Mama," he said, "I feel you with me all the time. I told you in my letters," he whispered. "Yes," she said, "and I too felt the bond. Go, my darling, you must care for yourself, guard your life as you go, take the horses past my window on the narrow drive." He went through the door, a beautiful broad, strong young man. A plough blocked the narrow passage. "Whitey," he called, "bring the carriage through here," and with one hand he picked up the plough, pointing it in the air, circled it round, indicating with it, "here down past Mama's window," he said. Then he replaced it on the other side of the road, jumped into the carriage. He waved his hands. He knew Kathy was watching him. Kathy's heart almost missed its beats, melting into memory of Jules and his plough and there before her it repeated family history.

Lion was devastated by Eden's departure, as he felt also as though a part of him was gone away. But it was right, Eden was inexhaustibly engrossed in the study of geology, and America was rich and young like himself, full of interest, gold, mines and stones. When Eden returned, he would be a master in his field. Lion was sure of that. He remembered Louisa's dying words: "The time will come one day, when you will tell him who he is," and he wondered whether he should tell Petra that Eden was not his son. Yet there was no doubt, it was better to be silent. My God, he thought, there is a void without the boy. He dearly loved his girls, they were so beautiful, and gave him so much pleasure. Now Petra was pregnant again. He wondered if perhaps it would be a son. Farmers always want sons, cows must have heifers, but farmers like their sons. He dashed the thought. "Girls are so lovable," and surely more so to him, he was rather a ladies' man.

He loved Petra, she was a wonderful woman, but it was so different with Louisa, delicate, frail, blithe spirit. He thought about her, his first love, (Thombe flashed into his mind) what a painful life she had had until they met, and God, how they loved. "Bastard, bastard, Julius. It was he who killed her," he thought. He, the father of his own precious Eden, strong and fair and handsome, full of wisdom, alert and full of life, a kind person, so kind, not even a trace of malice or evil. "Ja," he thought, if God really made men, then he shouldn't have made them all modeled on Eden. Why were some black, and others yellow, and some bad, killers like the English hunters? No, God didn't make men or why would he have made Julius inside of Kathy? "That is a lot of bullshit," he said out loud. He would take the carriage and would buy those six black stallions that the Irish Catholic priest had brought out on the ship. He could afford them now, those Catholics knowing the scarcity of horses, had a good eye for business. Bringing horses, yes, he loved the horses, this would take his mind off things, and he would make them the best team in the country. He would handle them himself.

He took his money and one day he and Whitey climbed into the carriage and drove towards the city to the Catholic mission 17 miles the other side of Cradock. Lion bought the stallions. He didn't care about the cost, when he looked at them, he just knew. "I'll take them," he said. And within that week, one month before Petra had her third child, he had delivered to Sonnestroom the wonderful team of six black stallions and an American-type carriage, all shined up with brass fittings and well-oiled harness. He built a large square meadow and set about training them. He wanted to handle this team, train and teach them for short turns, sudden stops and pacing, gallop, canters and trots. "My God," he thought, "this country will know all about Lion McCabe's black stallions!"

Every day Elizabeth grew more disinterested in her architecture. She had created a splendid home, styled like a Georgian manor, the first of its kind in the colony, and wagons and carriages often drove past just to look at it. There were acres of undulating veld pastures, flocks of merinos in the thousands, spread across the hills like snow, yellowwood trees and flowering peaches, walnuts and orange blossoms, far more elegant and expensive than anything at Sonnestroom. Of course Sonnestroom had two streams that met, a chosen spot, Kathy called it, but not as beautiful a home as Elizabeth's "Riversend." Julius had several traps, Cape carts and carriages, and walked about his land like the opulent high court official that he was. He had made Riversend a showpiece, with a horse training field, breeding pens, shelters against the weather and beautiful barns. It had stone buildings and slate roof, and wonderful timber. Elizabeth was brilliant with ideas and innovative creations, but she was not a happy woman.

The giver of all things had denied her the joys of motherhood, and even the Dutchman's Bible looked upon barren women as accused. She so loved children, it was so unfair. There were times when she was intolerant and neurotic, and Julius had no sympathy for her either. She even considered that perhaps it was Julius' curse. Why should it be her? There she was, a handsome woman, who was not a woman. Women are producers of people, and she was a non-producer. God, she'd give almost anything to have a child. She thought, yes, a child like Eden. Now there was a mystery. There was something strange about Eden's birth, and no one seemed to want to talk or say about it. There, for certain, is a person she could love exactly as her own, but so far, she'd never know because she'd never had her own. So, filled with longing to see Petra's children, she ordered her carriage. "Come on, Julius, let's spend the weekend at your mother's," she said.

Kathy was subdued, but greeted Elizabeth in her usual gracious way. She was feeling her age these days, and often she found herself thinking of death. She wondered what the end of life meant? Did one feel pain, or did one just slip into blackness—oblivion? Braam Piet had a terrible Asian flu, and the doctor was treating him. She had a fear of catching it and refused to enter Braam's room until the nurse made her a mask. "You can all jeer if you will," she said, "but nature has her little tricks. She is bent on getting rid of the old, and efficiently, on with the young. I intend to be here when Eden comes home. I would hate to die before seeing him as a successful young man." She gazed into the air, smiling suddenly. She tied the mask across her mouth, then behind her head. "Yes, well," she said, "the blasted bacteria will struggle to get through this," and she went to visit Braam.

He was faring very poorly. "Kathy," he said, "this thing has got me, I can feel it in the bottom of my lungs. I cough like a horse with tuberculosis, and sometimes I have to struggle to breathe."

Kathy listened. "Braam," she said, "I have always depended on you, don't you let me down, don't you dare die on me. Braam, I am not strong enough to take it."

"Listen, Kath," he said, "I've never told you this before, but when I go, lay me near Jules and Xosa. I liked that kaffir, we owed him so much. Me a Boer, alongside of a kaffir; they hate us Dutch people, the kaffirs. But I believe Xosa never hated me. A good man, Xosa, a hell of a good man. I so miss his whit leethy grin yes I loved tha man."

"What does the doctor think, Braam?" she said. "He says I must remain in the bed, until he tells me not to," he said. "Christ, he has strapped my chest with this hot cotton stuff to keep it warm. Smells like the camphor tree. I'm so tired, Kathy. Perhaps that's how we go, we get tired and go to sleep."

He held out his hand, and she took it. Unlike Braam's usual hard grip, it was clammy and damp. "You heard me Braam," she said, "I will never, never replace you, you are a one-time man." She said her words slowly. Special very very special!

He smiled. That was a big compliment from Kathy. "You, my Kathy," he said, "are still lovely. Stamped in my mind, brain and head, I always see your red-gold hair and amber eyes. You made a fire in my heart, and it will only be put out ,when I go."

"Braam, men get a cold, and they all think it's the end," she said. "It's we women who know how to bear pain and sickness better than you. So, just let me make you a good, strong, chicken broth that's easy to swallow and full of goodness. Keep yourself warm till I come back."

He did not seem to see her mask, and she felt glad about that. In the morning when she came to see him, the broth was untouched and cold. My God, Braam never lost his appetite, she thought. She asked the nurse why he had not eaten and why she had not removed the soup cup. "Lady Kathy," she said, "he said you had brought it, and I was to leave it, he would find time to eat it in the night." It took a long time before Braam got up, and even then, he was weak and perspiring. He no longer was the strong, indestructible Boer.

Elizabeth was happy with Petra's girls. She adored them, and they played for long periods on the carpets, on the grass, in the fields, everywhere. Julius was fascinated by Lion's stallions. He watched Lion training them hour after hour. "Where did he get them?" he asked Whitey.

"Near Cradock, Master."

"And what is he going to do with them?"

"Master, he's going to ride them in a show, against a Huguenot farmer from Paavh and an English also, I think," he said. "The English is not sure, but the Huguenot, he is sure. People from all over come to see the team in harness, the way they handle in the brass carriage. In America, people spend much money on this showing. Baas Lion will win, you'll see, Baas." "Lion always wins all things." Julius muttered under his breath, but Whitey did not hear it.

By the end of the month, Julius was also preparing and planning to buy a team. He had heard that an Englishman on Somerset Farm had brought out a team of grays which were quite unbeatable, and he had sent word that he would like to look at them. Fortunately, the gray team's handler had gone to England to investigate some stones he thought were diamonds, and had failed to return. So the owner of this farm who belonged to the British High Commissioner decided to sell the whole team, carriage and all. Spurred on by Lion's interest and envy for his uncle, Julius was eager to also try his hand at team handling. For a while he was wildly enthusiastic and did very well. He now had a marvelous team, harness-trained to perfection, obedient to the touch of a rein. He also started to build a training square and soon he started to practice his team handling every day.

Petra's last child arrived without problems. The birth was over in 20 minutes. Lion was thrilled as the baby cried and the nurse yelled, "A boy! A boy!" At last he had a son. He was getting older now, and he was glad. A man needs the satisfaction of having a son and heir to carry on his line. It was a lovely child, tawny, dark-eyed and plump, and larger than the two little girls. He wanted to see the baby's eyes. "Lion," Petra said, "I have given you your son, Lion," and she opened up his napkin and lifted the small uncircumcised penis with her forefinger. "Ah man, there's no doubt about it, there is something special about a boy," she said. "Tell me Lion, is this your first or second son?" She looked up at him. "Petra," he said, "thank you for my son, he looks like my father, and Petra, he is my first and only son." He said the words slowly, looking at her face. "You are a good and wonderful woman, you have never pried into my life, or questioned me about Eden. Give me your hand, for what I tell you now is between you and myself, because now I know I can trust you. Women are gossipers and talkers, but you are not like that, you are different," he said.

"Eden's mother died in childbirth," he said. "Eden only knows Kathy as his mother. I am not his father, but I am his guardian, and I will be there to help him until I die. He is an extraordinary young man, and we have grown together like father and son. He took my name, because he had no other. Someday you will know more and understand. I know, but for now that is all I can tell you. Eden loves you, Petra, you may call him your stepson if you wish. I wish he were my son, but he is not. He is Eden, just Eden." "We have a lovely son, my love," Petra said, and he held her close to his heart, rocking to and fro, the little baby boy between them. "I think he is going to be a quiet boy," she said. "Perhaps I am wrong about his name. The Bible said of the descendants of Ham, 'cursed be Canaan. A servant of servants should he be.' But Canaan is a place of milk and honey."

There was so much space at Sonnestroom it would not have mattered if there were a dozen children. Elizabeth was there more often than not, and she and Petra became very good friends. She cradled Petra's son lovingly whenever she could, rocking and swaying and singing. Petra named the boy Canaan.

"My God Petra, why Canaan?" Lion said.

"Because I like it as much as you liked Kathleen," she said. "To someone once, this was Eden, and to me, it is Canaan, so Canaan it will be. Besides it's a good name, from the Bible." Lion loved his little son, and Petra was right. He was a quiet little boy. He had a good appetite and a quick eye. One felt the child was noticing and recording everything. He seldom cried and he slept through the night like an adult. He had blue eyes and fair hair and Petra said he was very much like Lion. Kathy said Lion was also a quiet child. She could remember that well. And so time passed.

It was a Sunday morning, and it was reasonably quiet on board the ship. Passengers were walking up and down, engaged in conversation and most of them eagerly looking forward to landing in New Orleans. It had been a long journey. The food was fair, the table always neat and set with knife and fork, pannikin and stoneware. Cabin passengers were well treated but steerage was a scene of wretched intoxication and profanity, with almost daily skirmishes mainly caused by the inebriated men and women. The ship, fairly well founded in provisions and riggings, needed to also take better care of the spirits which were on board and which were eventually placed in charge of the ship's chaplain. When crossing the Equator, there was excessive drunkenness and part of the crew became drunk and unfit for duty.

On this occasion, William acted as mate and made notes in the logbook. He was handed a fowling piece that he declined where he sat, most interested in all the ship's papers, charts and quadrants. Blessed with fair weather and light winds though food was running short, they moved on, and for Eden it was all just another adventure. Thankfully they stopped at the Port to take in fresh water, goats, fowls and fresh vegetables; a little late, perhaps, for unfortunately an illness had broken out, and the cabin boy whom Eden had befriended had died, as well as a small child aged about 4 belonging to one of the better class passengers, causing great hysteria.

A few days before, many threats and violent oaths were exchanged in a fierce uproar between the ship's surgeon and the mate. It had seemed as though the argument had ceased, but Eden and Maxwell heard a great scuffle and loud cries that reached all quarters, and looking up the hatchway, there they were, engaged in a scuffle, with the mate, like a madman, hurling challenge of a fight, with fists and sword or pistols. Someone ran to the aid of the surgeon, calling on steerage passengers to come forward to help an officer against the enraged maniac which the mate had become.

The mate was secured and imprisoned, and once again, William Maxwell, who had knowledge of most things, was requested, with Eden at his side, to lend a hand. The surgeon took his station in the Lazarette. Eden's cabin led off a saloon on the upper deck, and on Saturday evening, some people danced on deck to the tune of a slightly flat fiddle and one or two of the sailors played the hornpipe for entertainment.

It was a long journey down the east coast of Africa, around the Cape of Storms, up the west coast of Africa, stopping at the old slave ports, across the ocean to the Caribbean Islands through the Gulf of Mexico and into the port of New Orleans. Finally, amid much confusion and disorder, the ship eventually anchored where almost immediately the ship's mate seized the opportunity and deserted. He would not have been able to be brought to trial on a charge of assault, but it seemed a jolly good riddance. That is what William Maxwell and Eden concluded. New Orleans was a large and lively city, with a large population. It was the biggest cotton and cottonseed oil market in America. It was also starting to be used for the import and shipping of bananas and coffee.

Eden decided he would attend a university called Tulane, which had been founded in 1834, two years before the Boers set off on their wild and rugged trek in Africa. Now Africa seemed a long way away. They had been on the sea for over eight months, eight months of stale water, goat's meat and stale bread, though there were times when he dined on better food like beef and too much rum and not enough vegetables and fruit. How abundant was the fruit back on the burgher farms! Eden and William disembarked, and they were total strangers in a strangely exciting and busy land.

"Student and teacher," said the port official. He spoke with a Spanish accent, and looking down on their traveling boxes, he knew they were not just the ordinary run of the mill emigrants. "I know a very good place where you can stay, Sir," he said. "A very good table and a comfortable sleep." And upon his advice, Eden and William found themselves directed there.

From the depth of depression the diamond finds intensified interest in the whole area. The star of Africa was sold to the Earl of Dudley for £25,000 and Eden, Lion, and William Maxwell had made a large sum; independently: each one of them was a rich man by Boer or frontier standards. There was much dispute, argument and discord regarding the diamond land, boundaries and claims, with annexations and protestations. The complications lasted several years. But with each new find there were stampedes of diggers and new disputes developed. The colonial office in furtherance of its policy of federation in South Africa, believed in the annexation of the diamond area to the Cape, in order to maintain peace in Southern Africa at this time.

Sir Henry Barkly was the governor and high commissioner of the Cape. President Brand wanted to bring in a foreign arbitrator to settle the disputes over land, but the British government regarded itself the paramount power and refused foreign interference. It was also condemned by the colonial secretary, the Earl of Kimberly, who considered the land/boundary dispute local and domestic. Moreover, at this time the European horizon was clouded by the Franco-Prussian war and the establishment of the German Empire. The lands were finally annexed as part of the Cape Colony.

There were far-reaching political, social and economic results. Streams of emigrants from Britain and her colonies, Germany, France and the USA came digging. Most enterprising capitalists were the cosmopolitan Jewish newcomers imbued with new ideas and progressive administration. Urbanization was intensified, competition started between black and white, a new civilization developed and with the detribalization of the Africans.

Vast sums of fresh money were invested, banks were built to cope with increased volume of business, imports and exports rose, and customs receipts and government revenue spurred on the communication systems. The old ox wagon became too slow and expensive, railways got underway: Farmers found new ready markets for their produce, livestock, vegetables, wood, wheat, wine and brandy. Then came the miners, traders and merchants on foot, by mules, on horseback and wagons. People came, some alongside cows, arriving by whatever possible means.

Lion bought a farm of his own and he and Petra moved away from Sonnestroom with their three children. Lion was wild about his team of black horses, and this seemed to be his first consideration, though Kathy demanded that he take his 2,000 sheep, which were his property. He also took his horses, quite old now, 'Drosty King' and Petra's gray, also aging, and Eden's horse, which would never be without Drosty King, they were inseparable. It was a lovely spot, set in the foothills with three wonderful spekboom blooms and white arums beside the little stream that ran at the base of the hills, then dropped to a steep ravine and a cliff that formed a small waterfall.

It was 1873. Kathy was finding walking difficult. "It's not that I can't walk," she said, "it's just that my legs won't hold me." Her once sparkling eyes were ringed with a blue circle around the once amber orbs, and the pupils were still black, the whites of her eyes were often bloodshot, and she struggled to read with a pince nez and a large-handled reading glass. Her hands were not steady, and though she trembled, she still had clear fingernails and was very lucid.

She loved Lion's children, she had a great affection for the barren Elizabeth. Petra was a proud, independent woman, in whom she recognized much of herself. Julius was now chief justice. But it was for Eden she longed. Each time a rider brought the post, it was Eden's letters she sought. When she woke up in the morning her first thoughts were for Eden, and when she lay in her bed at night waiting for sleep, she thought of Eden. "Never in my future, though, always in the past," she thought. She remembered his love and comfort to her, his laughter and caring. The little bunches of wildflowers, his drawings and books, his devoted letters, and she never knew, but wondered, if she would know, only once, before she departed from the world, if he was, or was not, her grandchild. In her mind she felt he was her blood. She had always felt it, but she never knew for sure.

"My God, that Lion," she thought, "how he could keep words." She never really knew what caused the deathless, undisguised enmity between Julius and Lion, or if it would ever cease. Indeed it had intensified in adulthood. Lion was a man of compassion, of honor and honesty, energy and discretion. She felt a stab of sorrow and remorse—how she had resented her father's half-caste mistress and his half-caste son, her half brother. It was bitterness hard to handle then, but when she thought about it now, she felt remorse. She was mystified why she could ever have been so foolish.

Her wonderful father; God how she ached, just to be able to make amends, how many tears she had shed, calling in vain for forgiveness, of Lion also. She was cruel to him as a boy, and yet like her father, he had inherited loyalty and caring, he never hated her. He was a wonderful brother, a tower of strength, and it was to Lion that she leaned for comfort and security. She would make it up to Lion and Eden. Now there were two men, real men, men like Jules, and her father. She remembered when Julies went to war, and she begged him not to be brave: "Take care Jules, for among all the Cape Mounted Rifles, or the Seventh Dragoon Guards, there was no other man like you, never, never!" And Jules used to laugh with pleasant pride and a boosted ego, for he was as sure as she that there would never be another Kathy.

And she thought of Sannie, her Boer friend. Yes, she was a good woman, afraid of God and guided by her old Dutch Bible, and she wondered why she all too often, felt sad. Ever her thoughts were of the saddest moments, and she decided it must be because of Eden; she was afraid she would not see him again, and her years were now so few, and she didn't want to die before she saw him. She thought of his mother, and she was glad, for she really loved Louisa, and she wanted to tell Eden more about his mother, and she would—that was another thing. She should have explained more to Eden about Louisa. She tried not to when he was small, he was such a happy child, she had thought it better not to.

But now she felt differently; he would want to know, now that he was a man. "Oh Eden, come back to Sonnestroom," her very soul cried out inside and she didn't sleep. She was still awake when the roosters crowed, perhaps the light would come soon and she would rise, and watch the sun come up, it was always so beautiful. Something always happened with the sunrise. She lay still, and the big house was very quiet. Old Iya slept inside now because the nurse was in the guest cottage and Iya called her when she was needed. She heard a shuffle in the long yellowwood passage, wide and shined with wild beeswax. Then she heard a bang, as though something had fallen. She wrapped her shawl about her shoulders, and lit her lamp. Then she took a candle, and holding it in one hand and holding her shawl closed with the other, she left her room, and moved out into the passage. It was still dark, and her eyes were not good these days, but in the wide passage she saw a shadow, no, not a shadow, it was Braam Piet.

"My God, Braam Piet," she said, "what is it?" But he did not answer. A strange noise came from within him somewhere. "Ayer, Ayer," she called, "run for the nurse," and Ayer was out in a flash and soon the nurse was back. "Go Ayer, tell the driver or footman to go for the doctor," she said. The nurse was down on her haunches, she was pulling at Braam Piet's nightshirt. "I fear the worse, Mizz Kathy," she said, "he must have been trying to get to you. Before I left him last night he kept saying he wanted to go see you, but I thought he was wandering." Since it was after midnight she was muttering all the time, talking as she patted his cheeks and rubbed his hands and then, taking his left arm, she swung it over her shoulder and hoisted him up. He was groaning and sucking for air. She got him to his room and laid him down and she lit the lamp.

Kathy followed silently. She didn't speak, it was as if her thoughts were continuing from where she had left off in her bedroom. Suddenly she realized it was all real. This must not be another sadness. "Braam Piet," she said, "Braam Piet, don't give up, you are a burgher, a fighter. Piet, fight now, with Kathy on your side," and she put out her hand and he took her hand, softly, without strength he held it. His hands were damp, and his brow was glistening in the lamplight. "My liewe Kathy," he was saying, and then sucked in the air, and his breath was coming shorter now and Kathy said out loud, "Come Braam Piet, we will trek together where there are no hostile kaffirs, and no Engels and we will never see the next man's chimney smoke. Be strong Braam Piet." And in the lamplight, his face grew eager and his eyes opened, they shone, catching the light, and he held onto Kathy's hand.

"Naalpins, and geel bek, Engelsman, en witkop," he tried to shout to his oxen as he drove his wagon. He saw them lying low in the yokes with their knees beneath them, ja it was a fine span of Afrikaner oxen, and with Kathy, they would trek and conquer all the world, and no man would ever be more happy.

Across the veld they would go, in a 20-foot wagon with big wheels over the rocks and anthills, and new spokes and filloes and a strong hand-carved long dusselboom and hard axle. These were his precious beasts, and he loved each one of them, almost as much as Kathy. Kathy and he would also trek. He had trained all these beasts while waiting so long for Kathy. But Kathy was ready now and with Kathy all Africa was his. He was laughing and smiling. Kathy could feel Braam Piet moving his wagon train. He was so happy, he was leaving with the sun and the stars to guide them. "No Kathy," he said, "I am a farmer, not a fighter," he said softly. And she felt him guiding his oxen, as the bamboo whips cracked, bending in the driver's hands, his goods all fixed in rawhide thongs and a kastel from rail to rail for him and Kathy. His oxen were flying now, flying to catch up; he had waited so long. His hand went limp, the saliva leaked from his open mouth, and his chin fell onto his chest. The doctor had not yet arrived. "Lady Kathy, Lady Kathy," the nurse was saying, "Mr. Braam Piet has passed away." Kathy knew. Death was not new to her.

She dropped his hand. Braam Piet had left this world. All these years he had never stopped hating the English, a true Boer, he never forgot a friend or forgave an enemy. He was happy with Kathy. She stood there, in his room. He seemed to be in a pleasant sleep. He had a lovely look on his face. The nurse had wiped him and closed his eyes. He was still warm, but he had gone to his new free land. He was smiling and laughing at that moment, it was most odd: his stallion had broken loose and came galloping and neighing, tearing up all around the house and past Braam's window. It was wild and fractious and out of control, its cries desperate. "Piet," she said, "your stallion has said farewell." But Kathy was tired now, she put her hand to her head. The sun was beginning to rise, the sky was pink and yellow. Perhaps this is how life is, everything gets sad when we get old, perhaps we all die with saddened hearts. She searched for something happy. The birds were twittering already. "Yes," she whispered, "something always happens with the sunrise."

Lion loved his new farm. He and Petra took a ride all around it, he on his stallion and Petra on her gelded gray. It was called "Leeukraal," and it seemed ironic he should fall in love with a farm by that name. "This was meant for you, Lion," Petra said, "I will not say us, because of that I am not sure, but I feel quite sure this farm was meant for you." They stood on the crest of the valley overlooking the cliff that lead to the waterfall. "I had a lion once, you know, Petra," Lion said, "it was a beautiful creature, I really loved her, and I can never, never forget it! When I saw this farm, I was filled with her memory, and I was also stirred with hate."

"Here, here, Lion," she said, "I can't think of you and hate. Eden told me that you were the only person he knew who had no hate, and that was how I figured you—who is it you hate or what is it that stirred up hate inside of you?"

"It was the act I hated most," he said. "Somebody shot my lion, Petra, it was shot because of jealousy. Jealousy is a horrible thing. It's the basis of all evil. If a person is jealous, they hurt, or are envious, they can even kill; not in defense you know, just for extreme hurt. They damage, destroy, steal and lie, and it can all stem from that thing, jealousy. My father taught me to forgive, and this I do, but it is very hard to forget. I would so loved my father to have lived to share my riches, God, Petra, how I would have loved to have shared all this with him. My father was like God to me and my mother was a very small yellow lady. I believe she was the product of a white man and a slave. She was a small woman, I do not remember clearly, but I know she was bitten by a snake, and died. The wars were everywhere, then. My father was killed."

Petra's Boer blood had curdled a little and it was an uncomfortable moment. "So I was right when I said you had a touch of the kaffir in your blood?" she said, wide-eyed. "Thank God our children are as white as the driven snow. I would prefer it, Lion, if you would not tell our children that their father's mother had kaffir blood. I too am a Boer, I do not ask much of you. I am a one man woman, skat, and I will never let you down, but in this small thing, I must ask you to humor me, Lion. I consider it a skeleton in one of those stray boer wagon kists with brass locks, locked away," she repeated, as though there was something not pleasant in the fact. She had a feeling of injustice. "Still, be all as it may," she said, "I love you, Lion, let us ride now," and she spurred her horse forward.

Every day Lion took his team of black stallions. They shone like black satin in the sun, and after a while the white froth of their sweat in the groins turned white, leaving a soapy, white salty mark on their silken bodies. The wagon they drew was long, about 15 feet, but the axle was made in such a way it could sharply turn in almost a swivel. The horses could back, forward, pull pace and trot on one side, then on the other gallop, canter, trot, funeral march and come to a dead halt. People would come and watch him train his beautiful span for hours and hours. Driving this wagon was an absolute art, and his skill was quite unbelievable. He had to be calm and gentle, firm and strong, patient and full of energy. But he loved it and loved his horses like a man loves a woman, almost with a passion, patting each one and talking to it as he fed them green corn mealies or oats when he worked them harder.

He had trained one man to care for each horse, so wherever he went, the six workers went as well. Kimberly was founded now, and there was a great opening up of wealthy which changed the whole of South Africa. Lion was going to show his team on a track in Kimberly. People were coming from far afield as Paarl to compete. Horses were racing, saloons were buzzing. Banks, buildings and traffic everywhere crunching iron tires, cape carts and the jingle of harness rattled up and down the busy streets.

At Riversend, Julius, having constructed a magnificent training square, was also busy training his span of gray stallions. His span was breathtaking, beautiful dappled gray leaders and four uniform stallions behind. Every day they were trained, if not by Julius, then by his equally skillful handler who was once an English coachman for the British High Commissioner. The horses with arched necks, rolling their bulging eyes were powerful, fluid of movement, eager and powerfully obedient. Julius handled them well, but not like his coachman. He held the reins light as a ribbon a double rein calling them by name, urging them, coaxing and grateful to them all. And people came to look and stood at the fence watching as the magnificent creatures stopped, turned, galloped to a halt, swiveled, cantered and trotted; a beautiful sight.

By the end of 1874 and just before Christmas, the great fair was to take place in Kimberly, the diamond town! At this same time there was to be the horse wagon event. A square had been especially erected and the event greatly publicized. There were to be three teams. The chief justice from Riversend, Mr. Lion McCabe of Leeukraal, and Frage DuTort from Paarl, a winemaker with a love of horses. Kimberly was agog. Every inn and hotel was filled to capacity. Thousands of diggers were everywhere. People were packed into the spaces beside the square, which was erected like an

arena, and alongside ran the crude racecourse, not more than two
years old. It was nearing Christmas, and already the farmers were
bringing in turkeys and homemade plum puddings, and bottles of
rich Cape brandy. Bits of tinsel, bunting and decorated cape carts
jingled along the streets.

There was an air of festivity and buzz of activity, horses
neighing and white tented wagons, creaking to an outspan a short
distance from the center. Apart from the diggers, there was a
shrewd Jewish man, Mr. Barney Barnato, who was well established
as a "kopje-walloper" buying stones at the tables. He came down
in a hansom cab, together with what he called his skilled one from
the great diamond merchants of the world. Magistrates, preachers,
doctors, people from all professions and trades had gathered in
Kimberly, many having thrown up their positions with diamond
fever. A whole regiment, officers of the 20th, were said to have dug
£17,000 worth. Farm laborers had deserted their posts, having left
the farmers in the lurch. Bass bottled beer, porter, Barclay's and
Guiness brandy were selling on the fields two & sixpence, three
shillings a bottle. Smoked salmon, smoked fished, and casks of
vinegar, hollands gin and Scotch whiskey.

Lion came in full glory. His horses were fit and well. Six of
his other horses drove another wagon. He moved to the inn
where he had arranged for his accommodations and a barn for
his horses. A large mulberry tree full of black and red fruit grew
beside the barn entrance that attracted his servants, but they
already were loaded with baskets of raisin grapes, purchased for
half penny per pound.

Though rain had threatened, it held off and the day of the big
race, Saturday, came in wondrous splendor. People had gathered
in the thousands, some carrying sun shades and others with simple

straw hats made from the leaves of the mealies, like the Boers. Women wore their Sunday best, and even the children were dressed for special occasions. The whole atmosphere was alive with a myriad of races and different tongues. Lion was calm, and when he called his horses by name, the horse moved up and took its place. He was talking to them as he helped harness them, each man wiping and brushing his charge as he stood beside the animal he looked after.

It was almost competitive; each man wanted his horse to be better than the other. Even now, in an unfamiliar paddock, there was a togetherness, a notable quietness with an entire absence of shouting and scolding. There was complete thoroughness where nothing passed unnoticed, not even the smallest tick buried in the hair above the horse's frog. Now amidst this carnival a small bandstand had been erected and paper balloons soared above the fields. Veterans, cadets and mounted rifles, council in carriages, railway employees, trades wagons, friendly societies of tinsmiths, plumbers, ferriers and harness makers and the most popular hotel proprietor wagons were liberally dispensing liquid refreshment.

Upfront on the judges' stand, which was a wagon strewn with a cover of rich red, beneath an arch of palm branches woven into a sort of canopy, an auctioneer was given the job of speaking with his carrying voice. First to enter the arena was Chief Justice, the Honorable Julius Jacobsen. Beside him sat his horse trainer and handler as the band struck up playing an American song. The horses came in with majestic form: huge grays with arched necks and flaring nostrils, tails held high and hooves lifted. Their bodies moved in unison, and the crowd was awestruck with their beauty. They galloped almost to the end of the field, turned suddenly and returned. They reversed, swiveled, trotted, cantered and halted.

It was a grand, magnificent show, the crowd went wild, and Julius felt exalted. Nothing could have been better received. The Huguenot came next with his team of deep bays. A wonderful performance, spoiled only by the profuse sweating of one of his team. Again, the crowd went wild. And then, before the dust was settled, Lion came into the arena, like a phantom wagon, sleek, black stallions, each one more magnificent than the other. He held the reins lightly, like ribbons in his hands, and no one even saw his movements. The horses moved as one, high stepping, pacing and trotting, cantering and galloping, instant halt. His performance each time was pure perfection, and the band played ecstatically. Never was seen a more wonderful combination. All through the performance the auctioneer gave his comments and just as Lion's performance came to an end, he brought his horses to a halt, and each horse bent its leg simultaneously, making a bow to the audience.

The crowd went uncontrollably wild. Women blew kisses and children shrieked, a group of black people ululated, screaming in high-pitched voices. It was difficult to calm them, but once again all three wagons entered the arena, brass buckles shining, in the hot sun. Unbelievably beautiful, it was as though instinct was replaced by reason; the horses understood and stood there like women in a dance team. It was a hard decision for the seven judges, taking from all parts of the country, and as the wagons circled the arena, notes were passing among very serious faces. Finally there was a decision. The auctioneer stood up and called for silence.

"The winner, ladies and gentlemen," and he unfolded his paper slowly, "The Stormy Black Team, and Mr. Lion McCabe." The crowd went wild. Petra was jumping up and down. "Will the drivers please line up in front of the judges," the auctioneer said. The wagons lined up, Lion, Julius and the Huguenot. Elizabeth sat very near to Petra. Petra leaned over and said, "Leez, I can't say that Lion's team was more wonderful than your Julius'. I don't understand horses that much, it's up to the judges. One of the judges, the German one, is supposed to have trained horses in harness for kings and queens. We must abide by them and be happy for our men. Perhaps on another occasion your husband will be the winner." She looked over towards the wagons and her eyes were on Lion's face, and Lion was looking at Julius. "Leez," she whispered, "I have not seen the look of hate on Lion's face, but I see it there now. Look Leez, that is not the Lion that I know." But when they looked, Lion was smiling, exerting his extraordinary charm, charm that turned his friends into devotees and even further, to love and hero worship.

News reporters and photographers were there. They had a board stating the photographic likenesses, minutes, and attendance, and posters hung all over the trees and walls. It was a long happy journey home for Lion and his family. But for Elizabeth and Julius it was a little different. There was little joy. Julius was lugubriously quiet, saying he was tired. He apologized for not being good company. Once or twice Elizabeth looked at his face. "For God's sake, Julius," she said, "are you not a sporting man? Someone has to lose, so why not you? If I were to have judged that magnificent show, darling, I fear I would have given it to your handsome uncle but not for his turnout and appearance. There was a wondrous togetherness, though not disciplined like yours. It was perfect, Julius. Never have I seen a man and a beast so at one. Not one beast, Julius, but all of them." She continued, "And did you see his manservant, Whitey? My God how they love him. You should see those men that care for his team! They were ecstatic. He deserved the honor, Julius, you should be proud of your uncle."

Honorable Chief Justice Julius was silent. Something was hurting him and it showed. His chest was wheezing, so on the way they stopped at an inn. His chest was tight, but he drank brandy; he overindulged on brandy. There is a reaction in some people with alcohol which seems to unleash the tongue, and after awhile the pent up feelings of Justice Jacobsen came out in an evasive eulogy of imperishable hate. "Someday you mulatto bastard, you will lose," he said. "You will be displaced from your lofty overflowing perch and you will be wasted; you just come to grief." And he sunk his head upon his arms like a loquacious adolescent.

As he did so, Elizabeth heard the name Eden, but not what he had said. It was muffled by his sleeves into biliousness. There was something Petra once said that flashed through her mind. "You must love a man more, when his heart is sore with hate."

Thirty-One

In 1872 the discovery of diamonds and gold changed the whole face of Lion's Africa. Kathy found the news of each day very exciting, and she wrote it all in her letters to Eden. The government of Basutuland was now taken over by the Cape Colony... and Braam Piet had been dead a year. She missed him so. Lion was an important official, a diamond dealer much respected by boer Vitlander. Julius was Chief Justice. Kathleen was eight and Kimberly was six, Canaan only four. Lion was proud of his family, but never stopped talking of Eden, and he spoke of Eden as though he were beloved of his own blood.

In the USA, William Maxwell had opened up a school in New Orleans and was deeply involved with teaching. He often spoke to Eden about returning to Africa to find more diamonds, but those days were already past. Diamonds were a big business now, not just plucked from the riverbeds and cobbled streams and dug up at random. The big boys had moved in now; nevertheless, both huge claims stretched across the lands. The railways greatly benefited the farms and ostrich feathers were now bringing a good contribution to industry.

Disraeli was the leader of the opposition in the British government and many British troops were withdrawn from South Africa.
The Lion of Beaufort, John Malteno, landowner and businessman,
became prime minister of the Cape, and the Cape Colony no
longer was ordered about by the imperial government. Harbor
facilities were improved. The population rose rapidly and railways
ran from the ports to the interior, with their steam engines and
shaking coach bodies. The Cape had absorbed British Kaffaria, and
Basutuland in 1871, and was busy establishing griqualand West,
Natal was threatened by a possible Zulu invasion. There was still
unrest among the Xosa on the eastern borders.

Hardly a year before Eden arrived in America, General Ulysses
S. Grant, a bewildered, radical Republican, became president. The
American people had hoped for an end of war and turmoil. As a
general, Grant had fought a bloody battle at Shiloh and also won
at Vicksburg, which was the key city on the Mississippi. He was an
honest man who kept company with a pair of spectators who had
a scheme to corner the gold market. This had adverse results. He
was campaigning for reelection when Eden decided the gold rush in
Coloroda, the great Comstack, Nevada Tenopah, was too filled with
prospectors, outlaws, hurdy gurdy girls, violent and lawless, promoters
and persons after instant riches to interest him. In Africa Eden had
found riches, playing beside the riverbank! His desire now was to see
his Mama. He knew her life was short and her body frail.

Before he left for home, though, he had a keen interest to make
a trip up the Mississippi in a riverboat. He had graduated well, brim
full with enthusiasm and trembling with the thrill and sweet taste
of success. He had been a popular scholar, never short of female
company. Already he knew the pleasures of love, and was never
to forget how his heart nearly leaped out of his body in the first

encounter. But he was now a handsome man who upon first sight swept people away in admiring bewilderment. His ship was due to sail in five weeks, which only just gave him sufficient time to make a riverboat journey before embarking. He was quite unaware of the slaves who manned the riverboats, and though totally charmed by the river and the picturesque life by the river, he felt pathos and sorrow in the voices of the slaves who sand spirituals and the melancholic songs of Stephen Foster.

On his first morning up the river, the dew was still wet on the hand railings of the boat, and the morning mists hung low across the wide Mississippi. The old steam motor chugged along and the creaks and clangs almost drowned out a knocking on Eden's cabin door. "Enter," he called, and a tall, well-built black man arrived with a tray. "Ah have her tea, Master McCabe," he said. His skin was shiny black, and he wore a black uniform with a white shirt and a large black cravat, bow tie that hung down mid-chest. He gazed at the studded wooden trunk on the cabin floor. "Ma name is Swathard Hooker," he drawled, "and I'm gonna spread yer eating trays." He adjusted his tie. "You'se at West Point, Master McCabe?" he enquired as he folded up Eden's velvet lapelled jacket, brushing off imaginary feathers or dust. "No, Mr. Hooker, I just love your river, and I love the river people."

The man swung around. "This is not mah river," he said. He swung around and looked straight at Eden. "Mastah McCabe, I'sa African person, and came to dis yere land to escape being a slave to a gentleman from a fine family in Africa. Only he was not a gentleman and he was swift to handle the hippo-hide sjambok on old Swarthaas," he said. He looked upwards. "No Massah, the civil war has ended and it has changed only one form of our slavery. I have had my slavery style changed two times already." Eden was quite interested now, but he found it hard to get a word into the conversation. H fund an opening, "What did you say? 'Old Swarthaas?' How come you have a Dutch name?" he said. "Yes sir, dats what I sayed, 'Old Swarthaas.' Mr. Blackbirder could not say it, as it was, so ah got dat name 'Swathass,' and Mr. Hooker, dats the gentleman who paid fer me, well, he jes called me 'Swathard Hooker.' I was a young man then, an ah jes jumped that slave ship together with 124 others. But on a slaverunner like dat, on de high seas, only 63 stayed alive to get to dis here new land, and once again I was a slave. 'Course, I belong to Massah Hooker. He bought me here. It was he who runs the stern paddle wheel riverboats and he was sure glad to find a person who had done work for some other genteel folk. I was a young man then, straight out of Africa."

He stood there gazing at Eden. "But now Massah, gonna get yo breakfast?"

"No, Mr. Swarthard," he said, "tell me more about your journey and what happened to you."

It was a cold morning and as he closed the door of the cabin, he said, "Yes, Massah McCabe, I'll be back," and his breath steamed like smoke in the cold air. Eden was transfixed. Slave runners were illegal since 1808, but here was a man out of Africa who could speak well and seemed to have recorded by memory all his experiences. Eden opened the cabin door, threw on his short coat and looked for the man. He went out on the deck. Very soon old Swarthard came along from behind him. "Massah McCabe, I have brung breakfast," he said. "Will it be in your cabin or in the dining room?"

"I'll take it in my cabin, Mr. Swarthard."

Eden couldn't wait to get him talking again. "Which part of Africa, Swarthard?" he asked before the man had even put the tray down on the cabin table.

"I'm not a man of great learning, Massah McCabe," he said. "I knew some of dem names in Xosa language once, but clean forgot for de moment. It is clear to me tho, dat mah Massah done crossed de rivah he called the Sunday's River. I knew, dats where I was, 600 miles from the port of Cape Town. I remember my father who was a pastoral man. My father was bought by a burgher for $8. He said he was an Angolese slave. He belonged to a Boer family and he sold my father and then me. When I tried to run away to my father I was tied up to a wagon wheel, and I was thrashed and whipped 'sos I would not go again. I was ill for a long time when I was around 12, I fell off a silo onto the sharp blade of a plough and mah head was never the same again, but I can unnerstan why I was a very fast runner, and was given the name 'Swart Haas' and dat name means 'black hare.' My father was driven away. He was not a Xosa man. He was stolen from Guinea and I never saw him again, nor my people no more. I was a slave to a Boer family de first time, den fer a gentleman who was a single man without a woman."

Eden was writing notes. "Do you know who your master was? I mean, do you know his name?" he said.

"Ah only knows he was done called Julyos, and his mother came from across der seas," Swarthaas said.

"And why then my friend, did you jump the slave ship and run away?"

"I was afraid of dat man, Massah McCabe, dat ma could kill people. When he did not want me to witness his sins, he sayed, 'Hey, Swarthaas, you can go to de church,' and I was pleased to be in de stone church with de mission people, and would linger and linger until it was all quiet and dat was my time to run back to de Mastah's house," he said. "He was a bad man, he studied de law, and he was a big important mastah, but he was bad, he was swift to lift and swish der sjambok, dat is what it is called in Africa.

"Dat is a bad thing, that hide sjambok." Eden was eating his breakfast. The cold sharpened his appetite. "These eggs are good, man," he said. "Shall I bring Massah sme more?"

"No, my African friend, you will tell me more of your story. Your life story," and Eden made notes as the man spoke.

"Now, where was ah tellin' dat time?" he said.

"You were telling me your master Julios, who crossed the Sunday River, he used to use his damn sjambok, and was a bad man."

"Ah, yes, he told me to gather dem African men together so he could get them to work in fields in another land where dere was lots of work and good rewards. Ah god, one hundred and twenty-one men and three women, and den myself. So on dat boat on der high seas we came to dis land. All de woman survived, but many of de men were thrown into the water, stiff and dead. Dat lef' myself and 62 others, my massah would never see Swaarthaas no more.

"I helped a prisoner on der way and he gave me his hair and we stuck it onto my face with the gum of the pine tree to make a beard. I looked very old and white like an old lion, but I escaped and here I is. I too have no woman, I live by myself."

Eden looked up. "Was there no woman in your African master's house, then?"

'No Sir, Mastah Julios was not a woman's man. There was one woman once, a pretty woman with white hair, jus like yourself. She was an orphan chile, and she was good to Swaarthaas. He was dining her, an needin' her bad, my mastah, he was real sweet for her." Then Swaarthaas stopped speaking. He looked into space.

"Well, why didn't he make her his wife?"

"Dat is a sad and cruel story, Mastah McCabe," he said, "and it grieves Swarthaas to remember and not forget. It was in evening one Sunday, Mastah Julios says, 'Swarthaas, you can go to der church, when de sun goes down.' It was a hot Sunday, those African suns are very hot, and I went to the mission church, because this sweet lady's uncle was the preacher man. She lived with her preacher uncle, dis lady, she was a teacher, she done tol me dat. On dat night it was very hot, so hot, the church did not go the usual time and I did not brung a lamp light, so I ran home, in the moonlight. When I get to the massah's house, I saw dat sweet lady, got no protection, stumbling down the steps, an' onto the street. Her clothes were real torn all over, and she was a weeping real bad, her mouth was bleedin, bitten, mos' likely. The blood ran down her legs, maybe she was a virgin woman. She ran into the street crying and a weepin'. She went right on weepin' and sobbin' to her uncle's home beside de church, when she done get dere, she closed her sweet self inside. Ah ran after dis lady, because I was afraid I was to protect her, but when I saw dat she was in her room and closed the door, I ran back to my massah's home.

"He was in a bad black mood. 'Here, Swarthaas,' he growled to me, fix dis here place and burn dem clothes, do you hear me? And never must I hear one word from out of you or yer will never speak no more again. I will sever yer black tongue from yer body, hear?' And ah was very afraid he would do dat. So I done gathered up de clothes, pure white pantaloons and a petticoat and gloves, stained with her red blood were these laysee white underclothes, and I do not know why, I can't explain it, I did not burn those clothes. I done wrapped dem up and I tucked dem way out of sight, and ah hid dem in his house and kept dem. She was a pretty woman and after she went away I never got to see her no more. Maybe she died of de loss of blood or a broken heart. And ah scrubbed dat fine yellow wooden floor, which used to shine and shine with de wax from dem African bees. I did think of dat lady, and I never know why I was so compelled to hide her clothes. We were used to assaults, we slaves."

Eden was totally absorbed by the man's story. He gave him a guinea; that to him was a vast amount, and Swaarthaas was thrilled and very happy. "That, Mr. Swarthard, was a good breakfast." He had stopped eating.

He looked straight at Eden. "Yer sure yer not West Point?" He said this as though he was inviting Eden to disclose his origin. "No, Mr. Swarthaas," he said, "but I understand your name. I am profoundly intrigued by your story. You see, I am from Africa. I know the Sunday River, and I left for this country, probably from the very same port as you did before me. Do you recall the name Port Elizabeth? I, myself, came to study and learn in America, and perhaps see some of it."

Swaarthaas was stunned. "No, sir, ah does not recall, but some moments when I looks at you, I feel I have seen you before, some time, some place."

"I don't think I could be that man," said Eden, and he lightly laid his hand on the negro. He felt a kinship, an urge to keep his company. Swaarthaas turned around swiftly. "It was a long time on that slave runner ship, and like I said, many people died. Dem Blackbirders was very careful of how to dodge them. The Coast Patrols, they kinda know when ah got to my new Massah, after we cleared dat boat, I was glad to be on land. I kept my small bundle of Africa, and in the bundle I have dem clothes. I told Mistah Julios he never gonna see de face of his 'black bastard Swarthaas' no more. One day I gonna get me 40 acres and a mule and gonna find a woman. Ah want no child to be born to be a slave, no sir. Dem Jim Crow customs, dems are bad. Mr. Booker T. Washington, now he says not to try to be a white man. We must strive to be skilled business people." He rubbed his hands together and looked up to Eden. He was still a fine figure of a man, robust and very strong, but his eyes were weary, with the haunted look of mistrust.

Eden picked it up. "No one will ever harm you again, Swarthaas. You are a free man now. It is different in some ways between the north and the south, but it's free now. Tell me more of your life in Africa. Where was your master's home, and what was his lady's name?" "No sir, she were not his woman," he said, "she was a lady bird, she was, gentle and soft and white, with hair that shine like sunbeams and her eyes pretty and blue, like de summer sky. She turned away from his attentions, I surely did see that, but he done stole them from her with brutal force. I will not forget her sobbin' and sobbin'. He was a brutal man, yes sir, his name was Julius Jacobs or Jacobsen. I jest now recall."

He gazed at Eden, his face alight. "A man of the law," and he looked down on the floor, punching his left palm with his right fist. He seemed to have aggressive thoughts. "'Louisa,' he called her, yes sir, I do recall, her name was Louisa, but I do not recall her proper name," he said.

Eden was visibly shocked. He stared right at Swarthaas' face. He had learned that name from Kathy. Now the time had sped, the sun was struggling to emerge from behind the cold skies, through the day that soon passed away. Eden did not see Swaarthaas again during the day, but kept looking for him.

In the evening there was dancing on the deck, and a woman in a beautiful blue gown, with lace sleeves, made it obvious to Eden she wanted to dance. But dancing was not Eden's forte. He was not a faire with American dancers; nevertheless, he joined in the fun, dancing and flirting with being holiday jolly. All the time, he kept thinking of the negro's tale. He was quite certain the man was truthful. Finally, when it was nearly midnight, he ordered a milk and whisky to his cabin, and retired to bed. When he got to the cabin, there he stood, waiting in his black suit with the whisky and milk.

"I will be free till morning tea, Mr. McCabe sir," he said, "and no one can call me for a few hours." On the small table beside his trunk was a small parcel. "See dat," and he pointed to the wrapped parcel, "Now you'se gonna see that Swarthaas had good reason to jump that boat. Dat dirty slaverunner dat brought me here to dis here new land made false promises, Masser McCabe sir, Mr. Julius told them black men here was a place where there was opportunity, work and rich reward. He did not tell them they were all sold slaves. I was the spokesman and in view of dat, I had to suffer deeply. We still have no rights sir, the war is over, and slavery is abolished and the slaves are now working for a share of the crops. But the white people slow change really, sir, their hates for the black man is tolerated, and black people are still under the white peoples."

"Swarthaas, there are thousands of ten-acre farms that were once the feudal holdings of those big planters—the self elected great white aristocracy. At last you will be free to have your little farm, even if I have to see to it myself. I do not have much time left; when we return down the river, I will get on a ship and I am going home to Africa, where I have a mother. She is old now, but she is waiting for me to return. I have a father, a guardian, rather, do you know what a guardian is?" The negro frowned. "No, sir, is he perhaps a man who guards over you?"

"Yes, Swarthaas, I think one can call him that," he said. "He is a man I deeply love. He taught me to read the wind, recite the seasons, to feel the moods of the wilderness. He is a good human soul, inside an armor of strength, powerful and protective, generous and true. Swarthaas, he is all the father I have ever known, and his mother was from the Bushmen tribe. He is my own good fortune and together we ride on the wings of lady luck. I feel he is my father, but he has never told me so. His name is Lion. And as you know, the lion is the symbol of nobility. The name suits him, Swarthaas. I will tell you something now, and here's the mystery. He has an uncle, a lawyer, a very important person in the south of Africa whose name is the Hon. Julius Jacobsen. His mother is a Lady and his father was Sir Jules Jacobsen." He stared at Swarthaas. He waited for him to speak.

Swarthaas was strangely calm. "Gawd Arl Mighty, Missuh McCabe," he said, "your father's uncle was done surely my massah." He seemed bewildered, puzzled and devastated by this new revelation.

Eden sensed his desolation. He stood up, and clasped the man against his chest, rather like a mother would do. "Swarthaas," he said, "I always have believed, in fact, my beloved Lion had taught me, we get out of life much of what we earn. It is strange that fate has brought us together. I am perplexed myself. Of all the many people in New Orleans, is it not odd that I should come upon you? And is it not strange that you should find among the hundreds of people who tread the decks of this old river boat, the one person who fits into the segments of your broken life—that person is myself. Swarthaas, there is meaning in all this, it is hard to fathom among all this post-war chaos, this open dishonesty of profiteers, of shady politicians, and of the reapers of wartime harvests, the so-called carpetbaggers, fortune hunters, a great seed bed of moral laxity, speculation—no, our chance meeting seems pre-ordained," he said. "The one good thing though, see, is the relaxing, elastic loosening of political morality. Life will really change for you now, Swarthaas, but there are things we cannot explain."

There was a certain excitement in his episode on the river. Eden seemed to have stumbled upon something hidden, like a treasure, that he intended to take home to be unraveled. His journey home was on a large steam ship, and he felt the vibes of adventure. He wondered how long it would take. Lion had told him the Enterprise had taken 58 days from Falmouth to Table Bay. Lion had told him about that little wonder when everybody flocked to the beach to see the first steamship to Africa. Lion was six years old at the time. Now he would bid his tutor and friend William Maxwell farewell. William was very happy in New Orleans where the city hummed with trade and emigrants poured in from all parts of the world.

"I shall be leaving in 48 hours, Swarthaas," he said. He opened up one of his trunks carefully, pulling a collection of revolvers he had found for Lion. "This is a dragoon 1848," he said, "this is a Walker Colt, this is the Civil War Dragoon, and this is the Frontier Six Shooter." He turned the revolver over in his hand. "I bet some cowboy once carried this across the American frontier, trying to protect his herd, his hand on his holster as he sang to his cattle. Cowboy songs are just as much a part of the folklore as the songs the slaves sang of freedom in the South," he said. "But this is not what I'm looking for. What I'm taking out is good old greenback dollars," and he picked up a bundle of notes. "Swarthaas," he said, "I am going to give you a lot of money, and I want you to promise me you will buy yourself that piece of land, perhaps 10 acres out of one of those feudal holdings and there you will go and live with mules, and maybe with a woman. Maybe at last you will also have children."

Swarthaas held his hands out to receive the money. His mouth hung open revealing his white teeth. He was speechless, and then he sunk onto the bottom of Eden's bed, and he started to cry, and he cried and cried, his tears falling all over his shiny black cheeks and down the hollow beside his nose onto his chin. As he wiped his nostrils with the back of his hand he said, "You're so young yourself, Massah McCabe, sir." He caught hold of Eden's thighs and held onto him. His cheeks against Eden's body. "God bless you Massah Eden, God bless you," he sobbed, and Eden laid his hands upon his shoulders as he cried.

Eden left America for home that weekend, and Swarthaas came to help him carry his trunks when the time came. "Goodbye, Massah Eden, sir," he said. "If I should hae a son, would you allow me the honor to call him Eden, sir? I would like that," he said.

"Of course Mr. Swathard Hooper Lamont Hillstone," he said, and he held the man in a form of hug. He also was emotional and on the brink of tears. "You could come back to Africa with me if that would make you happy," he said. "No Sir, thank you Mr. Eden, I am happy to stay here in this America," he said. "We are free in this place, there are no slaves now. People have equal laws. I gonna change my name. I don't wanna keep my tribal name 'Ndlambe,' no sir, I wanna be Mr. Lamont Hillstone! Kinda important sound, don't you think? Or maybe, Mr. Black Hare Lamont: all the black people now use the names of the white peoples. Soon they will not remember their tribal names. I myself feel happy to be free. Happy I came to this land, and happy to meet with you. Maybe we may meet again?"

"Farewell then, Mr. Lamont Hillstone. I will never forget you."

He stood there waving his hand, his wide shoulders, velvet lapels and silken cravat blowing in the wind.

His hair blew in the sea breeze that blew against his face. He looked down at the Negro. He was also a fine, stately man, black-eyed and ebony skinned. And as the breeze blew tenderly between them, in a fleeting moment he read the message on the wind like Lion taught him. He and Lion, they knew how to read the wind: Thank the giver of all things!

Kathy looked from out of her wide open door. It was December and it was hot already. There had been no rain for a few days, and though the dust was settled and the yellow grasses had managed to turn to green, there had not yet been enough rain. The view from the open door was so beautiful, even if her sight was not so good. She knew what she was looking at, this spot that she and Jules had created, and improved till it became the show piece of the whole colony. Here, because the streams met on the sunny farm it was watered, thank the giver of all things, and the vlei down on the flats that spread before the hills were all mauve and blue in the distance. The trees were bursting with summer, new leaves in various colors and tat he small lake that Lion always called the dam. There on the vlei the butterflies flew like colored snowflakes and the brilliant plumage of the birds were a constant joy, their song the most wondrous of life's melodies. Ah, how she knew this beloved land, among the sheep, and cows and bulls and horses. Of course she had a hard life, filled with fear, uncertainty and threats of doom and assegai, but the sun always shone, the winds were always fresh and wild, then the summer rains. The almost torment, the unpredictable promise of an unknown quantity, was never without excitement, never uneventful.

There was no real water shortage. Sonnestroom had a spring, but other parts of the country had been dry at times, the surrounding farmers had to drive their cattle 20 to 25 miles and many died on the journey. They came in thousands, the strong cows up in front and the weak and seedy in the rear in long slow lines, they would wearily tread on until they smelled the water; then, even the weak found strength to hasten their movements in a rush to the water to drink and drink and then linger near the water, not wanting a return to their fear of thirst. This spring that bubbled in the center of the vlei, gurgling up cool water like a flattened gargoyle protruding from some crack deep down inside the entrails of the earth, this life-giving gift that saved these cattle. It was she and Jules who willingly gave to these men and beasts.

The vlei was always full of water, full of water lilies and flowers and long thin grasses which the cattle flattened in the drought. Once the drought broke, it righted itself once more. Those were horrible days when animals fell dead, and vultures followed in widening circles, sailing on motionless wings, way up in the cloudless skies, living symbols of impending death. Everything was waiting, and waiting, some for the rain, some for tomorrow, some for death.

Kathy was waiting for Eden who had graduated and was coming back home. Things had changed so greatly in a few years and his journey home would be much quicker and less hazardous. God almighty, when she thought of the first time she came to the shores of Africa; so much had improved. It would get better and better, but she would not know, her life was almost rounded now… sad that Jules had never known.

She wondered what it could be like. Sometimes it was an effort. She grew tired and begrudged not being able to witness more of this new unfolding world, this new rich Africa, over which so many people had already died. Now there were railways, new harbors, road construction and a rapid increase in population, diamonds and gold, immigrants and diggers. The feud between the English East and the Dutch West was still going strong and the British government regarded itself as the protector of all the black races in the Cape. England also maintained the upkeep of troops all over the Eastern frontier. Kathy's son in law was English and Kathy thought of her daughter in England. She had kept in touch with her child and had asked her to come out to Africa on several occasions, but she had never come again, despite the fact that Kathy had deposited money in England and actually arranged for her to draw money.

The press in England was critical of South Africa, and one writer who gave voice to rising ideas criticized the value of exploration. "Let us have instead conquest by bayonets and bullets directed by a civilized intelligence. It should be our aim," he said, to "extend education by the bullet. Clives were needed, and the civilization by the word of the sword of the whole valley of the Nile." God damned British civilization, they dared to call it. Moya's children were already young adults now and Kathy had never seen them. Of course, she also could have gone to England, but time had just flown away and though she always intended to do so, she had never made up her mind. She was too old now and the thought of a sea journey had lost its appeal. She lived well and she was not really alone, she had a good Scottish nurse-companion, hordes of servants, Elizabeth, Petra and Lion and, quite often, Julius. Petra's children were very charming, especially Kathleen, her namesake, but it was for Eden her heart ached, and for him or news of him, she waited each day.

Kathy got up and closed the door, for a breeze had started and was blowing through the house, this house that had grown and grown. There were more bathrooms now, and wash stands, with basins holding ceramic jugs filled with fresh water every day, Braam, God rest his soul, had made her a wonderful commode, it was a masterpiece of carving with a bucket neatly concealed inside. The house's first lavatory was outside, 15 or 20 yards from the house. Now there were three of them and because the house was so large, big, big bedrooms and wide yellowwood passages. Elizabeth had given her some innovative ideas.

Kathy felt sure Eden would love the turret-like room Liz had designed, a sort of view room, a prayer room, Elizabeth called it, for Kathy to go and puzzle God with questions. But Kathy's God was different, there were no puzzles, not for her God. God was all the world, God was everywhere. In every living thing. God was in her turret, over the hills, the fields, the sky, the oxen, the horses, the moths and beetles and frogs and flowers. Nature was the one perfect and almighty thing, that was for her, the only God.

She would never understand; no God surely ever would portray a God in the image of mere man. For all the evil on this wondrous earth, came from man. The destruction of all goodness and beauty, the fellers of trees and killers of fellow creatures, firemakers, murderers, plunderers, killers of children and creatures. Man, the brains of the language maker, worst of all God's creatures. No way could God be in this image. No, Kathy's turret was where she enjoyed the wonder and beauty of life, without mankind, where animals, birds and butterflies flew freely. Where she remembered beautiful people, like Eden and his own fragile mother, her own father, and Lion, Jules, Xosa, Marietje—yes there were plenty of good people, and plenty of evil people.

It was strange how one remembered the evil ones, the more one saw of people en masse, say, now hundreds of rough diggers were swarming over the land like ants in search of instant riches, doubling and tripling. Some horrible people who hunted and killed for ivory, calling themselves hunters, killing for money and often the sheer joy of killing. She imagined, God, in veldskoen and a mealie straw hat with a double-barreled flintlock muzzle loader and sharp, hand-smelted spurs on his veldskoens, spurring his horse. Now there was an image.

She smiled to herself. Life had spared her, had been good to her. She had been healthy and happy. She had reared her children and built a home. There was not much time left now. Jules, Xosa Braam, Louisa, Sannie, they had all gone. It was not fair, they deserved to have lived to enjoy and see fewer hardships. They were denied their three score and ten, yes, that's what the Boer's Bible promised! She stood in her turret room, and scanned the panorama of her surroundings. Indeed, it was lovely. Her eyesight was fairly good but she found reading difficult. She sat down in the carved wooden chair. One tended to reminisce in the past when one got older, perhaps because there was very little future left. She took a jug of water, and got up to water a plant. Plants were such tender things, and it was very hot this day. She watered the plant and sat down. Yes, she was alone and her own person, then, looking down from her window.

She thought she saw a moving dust trail. Yes, it was a horse kicking up the red and yellow dust, a Cape cart coming along at a swift pace. She knew it wasn't Lion because he had already called in the morning. She watched as it drew nearer and finally it came right up to the entrance. A uniformed person got out, a post office official. As swiftly as she could, she moved down the steps of her turret room out into the entrance where the man was waiting. "Message, ma'am," he said. "Lady Kathleen Jacobsen," he held out his book to receive her signature. She was among the first recipients of this new communication, the telegraph, in this area.

Telegraphs had only recently become acquired from private owners, and state ownership was established now. The man stood waiting. "Oh dear God, man," she said, "you must surely be exhausted. Please partake of some tea or refreshment."

"No thank you, ma'am, a cold drink of water, and I'll be on my way," he said. She summoned one of the servants to bring a tray with cold water from the stone jar in the larder. The telegraph message told her Eden expected to be in Port Elizabeth on December 29 or 30th on The City of New Orleans, end of year 1872.

They were all there to meet him: Kathy and Whitey, a footman, Elizabeth and Julius and their drivers, Petra, Lion and Kathy Junior. All the family had turned up to see Eden come home. The cruiser was still anchored in the bay, tossed by the waves and the usual winds that constantly swept the East coast, lashing the churned up waters to the shores and sloshing against the square stones that formed the base of the harbor quay wall. The harbor was under re-construction with a resident engineer from England who was in charge of harbor operations. Stones once broken by convict labor drawn on a track by oxen to the route of the proposed site were now crushed by a spectacular stone crusher, which upon its arrival from England was heralded with great excitement and enthusiasm, and even now a small crowd of people were watching it in action.

People walked up and down the wooden wharf, peering into the warehouse and into a ship with a huge mast, discharging cargo. Massive, thick ropes held the ship tied to the two ballards on the edge of the wharf. On the rocks on the East side of the bay was the stone lighthouse, approached by a hazardous sort of catwalk, about 75 feet long. The lighthouse lantern was visible for almost 11 miles and stood 55 feet above the high water, but during misty or heavy weather it appeared more as a feeble glimmer.

Right across the harbor was a similar lantern on an elevated point and these two lights defined the safe anchorage for all seafarers. The port captain's residence was just to the left of the lighthouse and the largest building was the Commissariat. Soldiers and officers went busily in and out, and a few hundred meters away was the clearing used for carriages and horses, wagons and tents. Oxen and mules grazed here and there, like it was a small commonage!

For her 72 years, Kathy was remarkably alert. She was not all bent like many persons her age. She was upright, she held a cane, her walking stick she called it, but as one looked at her, there were only traces of her once beautiful face. Her amber eyes, now only half their size, were hidden beneath hooded lids. Her lips were lined and her skin crinkled a little, but she had a sharp wit, and her eyes still twinkled with mirth or laughter or were serious and solemn with wisdom. She was impatient, but reasonably tolerant for one who was wise and far-seeing, above and beyond the average human mind. She was looking at a building, now empty and locked up, which read, "John Norton Ship Chandlery."

"Now there, was quite a man," she said. "He was a friend of my father, John Norton. A very clever Jewish settler. His son Joshua was one year old when he landed in Algoa Bay. Yes he had two sons, Lewis and Joshua. Lewis was the older son, a foundation pupil at Sacs, a very good college that opened in Cape Town in 1829, but Joshua worked for his father, who transferred his business, 'Ship's Chandlery' to Capetown. It went bankrupt and John Norton died in 1848. Joshua went to San Francisco, had some unfortunate business that affected his brain, I believe, and the poor deluded man developed great delusions of grandeur. Declared himself the Emperor of America. Do you know a newspaper, the San Francisco Bulletin, took up his story, and played him up for all it was worth. Destiny was gracious to Joshua Norton; instead of going to a lunatic asylum, his joke captured the American public, and he had risen to become quite a celebrity of international repute. He has contacts with very distinguished correspondents, Queen Victoria, Abraham Lincoln, Gambetta, Queen Isabella of Spain, Disraeli, and even the Czar of Russia. Stark, raving mad, he is, and he is now trying to invent legends concerning his lineage. Signs himself with a seal, Norton I, Emperor of the United States," she said. Everyone chuckled. "There were people here, when I was young," she said, "who were not strong enough to handle the trauma and stress, the triumph and disaster, of trying to tame these virgin lands, inside the frontier boundaries. Many of us deserted our locations, arid little plots, it is we valiant pioneers who have paved the way, together with all those gallant soldiers, and of course the Boers—the Boers who farm and love this land, who read the flight of the birds, and follow the spoor of beasts." She lapsed into thought.

Kathy traveled with her constant companion and nurse, a fine Scottish woman in her long frock and white apron, always carrying her forceps and scissors in a leather wallet hanging from her side. Now she was playing with Lion's children. "It is sad that Braam Piet is not here to see Eden return," said Petra. "Eden will feel sadness about that. He loved Braam Piet—there was a Boer that loved the earth!" The wind died down, and more people were gathering on the wharf. Eden's ship, "The City of New Orleans," was now moving in, flags were flying, and the ship let off a steamy hoot. Suddenly, there was an excitement in the air: a hum of conversation laced with laughter, neighing horses, barking dogs, whips and drivers, a quickening among the crowds and anticipation, as people hurried along to be part of the throng.

Slowly, "The New Orleans" steamed in, maneuvering until she came beside the wharf. There on the deck stood Eden. Big, wide-shouldered, his blonded hair falling upon his shoulders and his face alive with eagerness. The gangplank with wooden steps was attached to the side of the deck and passengers were beginning to get ready to make their descent. Eden was among the first to disembark. He clambered down the steps, an elegant man with American-style dress, silk necktie and driver's cape. He took off his hat and flung his arms about Kathy. "Mama Kathy," he said, hugging her to his strong young body, and Kathy held onto him, turning around as he lifted her off her feet. She was weeping with joy.

They all took turns in hugging Eden. Lion and Eden held each other like father and son. Julius also greeted him warmly. There was so much excitement, so much to say and tell. Horses were brought near, Whitey looking good in his black outfit and all the staff extending their hands in greeting. Collecting all the luggage, they packed it into the carriages and sent it towards the inn. After tea it would be quite a drive back to the farm. Eden wanted to see as much of it as he could in daylight. Petra remarked that the sight of Eden would cause much fluttering of hearts among the ladies of the frontier towns.

This was quite understandable. Eden was a magnificent young man, superbly dressed, with a noble face and rich, lustrous fair hair. Well built and athletic, with perfect charm and manners, he had clear blue eyes, flashing white teeth and a carefree, gentle bearing. He lifted his trunks as though they were weightless, and as he and Lion hoisted them onto the carriages they caught each other's eye.

It was a few days' trip, stopping at various inns to rest the horses and avoid night traveling and then quite suddenly, they were home. They stopped at the top of a hill, and Eden looked down onto his valley, tranquil and unspoiled, timeless in its life-giving beauty, ever constant, yet ever-changing from season to season. The children were laughing happily and one of the drivers sang a poignant African tune. Eden sat beside Kathy, silent. "This is our home, Mama," he said, "it's so lovely to just pause and ponder the beauty about us." The farm was full again for awhile; it was a happy homecoming. Even lugubrious Julius seemed to glimmer with a sparkle as they settled down to stay a few days. It was a happy time, only Braam Piet was missing. This was a good year, for responsible government was achieved, and ostrich feathers and diamonds had made the Cape self-supporting. The rich grew richer as 1872 passed quietly away, and 1873 began.

Breakfast the following morning had the feeling of celebration. The nurse was up first, only to find the cook had already baked fresh crusty bread, and hot scones and a jar of melted honey stood on the large warming iron. The aroma of coffee permeated the kitchen and a large pan filled with freshly sliced bacon stood above the iron stove, ready for cooking. A large can of fresh frothy milk stood on the table and the maids were already laying the tables. Nurse made tea for Lady Kathy and hardly had she prepared the tray when Eden came in with a wild dog rose. "I'll take her tea, Nurse," he said with a smile. "Allow me," and he took the tray and went towards Kathy's room. He tapped on the door, but she was already up and dressed.

Her face lit up. "Come in, my darling boy," she said. "Come join me for tea. Isn't it funny, I was about to go and bring tea to you."

"I beat you to it, Mama," Eden said, and sat down on a lovely chair. Kathy picked up the rose and pressed it to her cheek. "Eden darling, I cannot tell you how I missed you," she said. "You have grown into such a fine and handsome young man. I used to sit and wonder whether you were taller or broader, and sometimes when I was not well, I told myself, 'don't you dare be ill, nothing must happen to you until Eden comes back.' I was never going to die. Well, not until you had graduated and returned. Tell me Eden, did you love America?"

"I was lucky I had William Maxwell with me at first. Although I searched for adventure I must confess I was a little nervous," he said. "It was so strange to be so far across the oceans in another land. Maxwell started a school and is doing very well. He is a grand fellow, our William, and when I said goodbye to him, he was paying court to a southern belle whose father was a plantation owner. Most of his pupils were negroes. You see, the negroes are bewildered by their sudden freedom, and thousands of ex-slaves wander all over the south confused. Few of them owned land, and most of them are unskilled agricultural workers. Sharecropping provides a sort of substitute to the planters' supply of chattel labor.

"Of course, Mama," he said, "I was there during a drastic revision of American life, in the midst of a new sense of freedom. Although the North opposed slavery there is still a great prejudice against the negro. They all still consider one only useful as a simple laborer. Industry is now replacing agriculture. Self-help, they say, business leadership and beneficient industrialism is the idea of their lives at present. My life at the University was filled with interest, Mama. I have learned a lot over there in New Orleans, it's a growing city and although the south is devastated by war, its recovery is swift. Hundreds of miles of new rail lines have been relaid and all the harbors—Charleston, Norfolk, Savannah—are alive, busy, throbbing with a pulse of trade. Iron and coal are being produced, and instead of shipping the cotton north, the south has developed their own textile industry. Tobacco and lumber flourish, and the whole country is stimulated into a wild activity. New Orleans hums with trade. It reminds me of Africa in many ways. Not the people, but the land; it's a wealthy land, Mama, and wealth, as you know, is the key to any kind of success."

"But you've been extraordinarily lucky, Eden," Kathy said. "You're successful and wealthy and you are only a young man. When I'm gone, you'll also have this beautiful farm, I have seen to that."

"Why should you want me to have it, Mama?" Eden said. "Surely your son and daughter are the rightful heirs."

She swung around. "That's true Eden, but I have provided for Moya, my dear girl in England. Julius is a very wealthy person in his own right. He has two farms, a position of immense importance, a very expensive hobby in a collection of invaluable breeding horses with which no one can compare. Lion has a share in this farm, and it's up to him whether he would like to sell his share to you one day. The reason I'd like you to have it, Eden, is because in you I feel my blood. I see my father and you have an unquenchable love and bond with the earth. You love it as I do, and as I love you," she said. "I love you as my own precious son."

He put his arms around her. "Who is my father, Mama?" he asked, point blank. "And who is my real mother? Tell me Mama Kathy, I would like to hear it from you."

She was silent. She was vexed, indecisive. She had never said she was his mother, and she had never told him his mother's name. She held her hands together, looking for the right words. "Your mother was a very lovely, gentle, frail woman who also loved the earth, she loved everything that lived, all God's creatures. She loved me, and I her, but most of all she loved Lion. I never knew, nor did she ever tell me who was the father of her child. You are her son, she died giving birth to you and she named you Eden. It was so sad Eden, the grief engulfs me even now."

"Tell me her name then, Mama," he said.

"Yes, I will, Eden," she said. "Her name was Louisa, Louisa Shaw. She came as an orphan to Africa, she was a teacher, and her uncle was a missionary. He was all the family she had. For reasons of her uncle's own, he did not seem to be very grieved over her death, almost relieved, I'd say. He seemed to think she would be better off with God," she said. "We, Braam and I, buried her up in the hills, where the echoes are. That's what she wanted. She said her soul would be free, and we would hear her voice echo in the hills. She said she would leave only her echo and you. She hated to leave you." Kathy started to cry.

"I found this place, Eden," she said. "I found it long ago when I was young and often went there with my dear husband, I showed it to Lion and Louisa."

But Eden was not listening to her. He took her by the arm, "Come Mama, come Kathy," he said. "Come with me to my room," and they went in together. People were stirring all over the house now, and the children were already out on the dewy lawns. He sat her on the bottom of his unmade bed and opened his trunks. "Kathy," he said, as though suddenly he had found his mother, "Kathy, when I was on a riverboat on the Mississippi, I met a slave, a very fine, strong African. He was a slave to a man who bought him, he said, right here in Grahamstown. He hated this man, who also sold a whole shipload of slaves to a runner in America. In fact this man, his master, he said, had told him to collect a lot of desperate people, and this so-called master of his promised those people jobs in a new rich land. This slave never knew about the slave trade, and to escape, he disguised himself as an older man and boarded the slave ship to America. He went on the slave ship as a slave himself. It was a gruesome trip and many of the people died. He survived the journey only to be sold again, to another master. In New Orleans, he worked on this riverboat, and after slavery was abolished, he remained on the riverboat, because he knew nothing else."

She looked up at Eden. "Was his name Swarthaas?" Eden looked into her eyes. "Yes, Kathy," he said, "his name was Swarthaas, but because his American owner could not pronounce his name, he was called Swarthard Hooper. Mr. Hooper was the name of the Southerner who bought him."

Kathy stared in wonder. "Julius said he had run away," she said.

"Yes, Kathy," Eden said, "and there's something else. He told me that Julius sent him away to church on occasions, and on one of these occasions, when he, Swarthaas, was supposed to be in the church, he came home early. As he got near to Julius' house, this fair lady stumbled out into the street. She was crying hysterically. Her clothes were torn, and her mouth was bleeding. Also blood was running down her legs. It was a moonlit night, and he saw it all. Swarthaas followed her home, and she went into the house beside the church where Mr. Shaw once lived. She locked the door and he heard her sobbing. When he came home, Julius was drinking, and he grabbed him by the shoulder, and ordered him to clean the floor, and burn the clothes that lay on the floor. He slashed him with a sjambok, once or twice, and told him that if ever said a word to anyone, he would be sorry he was ever born. Swaarthaas then cleaned up the room, but for reasons he never understood, he did not burn the clothes, he rolled them up and placed them in a bundle of belongings he kept with him, and, almost as if fate had planned it all, he met me on the riverboat."

Eden unwrapped the little bundle, carefully he unfolded a pair of white lace pantaloons and a small white vest. The pantaloons still bore the bloodstains, now turned brown. "These clothes are the clothes my mother wore," he said, "and these brown stains are my mother's blood. I believe Julius raped my mother."

Kathy clasped her head. "Oh God, Eden," she said. "Now I know why Louisa was so scared and terrified when Julius came to Sonnestroom. Louisa came with her uncle when Jules died. He was appointed to deliver Jules' burial service. Jules had a state funeral. You know he was knighted for his duty to the country and England in the two Kaffir wars. Barnabas Shaw came to do the sermon, and he brought Louisa with him for the outing as she had been most unwell. She was unwell because she was with child, Eden, she was pregnant. So then she stayed with me; she needed a mother, she stayed with me until her death."

Kathy clasped her head, she grew visibly pale, her lips quivered. "Call Lion," she said, "call Lion."

Eden opened the door. He yelled, "Someone call Lion." He rushed back to Kathy. "Kathy, Mama Kathy," he said, "please don't be shocked, I only told you because you are my mama. Kathy, I wanted only to tell you."

Kathy looked gray and white. She clasped her heart and then her head. She felt for a place to be seated again. Lion rushed into the room. "Lion," she said, "Lion, please tell me now, please tell me, Lion, are you Eden's father?"

Lion was bewildered, but he could see that Kathy looked ill, her face was gray. "Tell me, Lion," she said. "I think I'm going to die, tell me Lion, before the nurse comes in."

"No Kathy," he said, "I am not Eden's father. Julius is Eden's father." They both reached out and they caught Kathy before she fell. She had no strength to fight this final truth. Lion picked her up.

"No Lion," said Eden, "give her to me," and he took her in his arms and carried her to her room and laid her on her bed.

The nurse was fussing with her pulse and wiping her forehead. "Send for the doctor, Mr. Lion," she said. "She's having difficulty with her breathing."

Eden laid her head back and untied her hair, long thick hair. Parts of the ends were still a little red-gold. Kathy reached out for him. "Eden," she said, "out of every sadness, something good always happens, especially in the morning, when the sun comes up so proudly. You are my grandson, you are my precious grandson. Only now I understand. You can trust Lion, he is all you could ever want in a father and a man. Your mother, Louisa, called out to him in her dying breath, 'You are better than God.' I will never forget that Eden, nor must you. Stay with me, Eden, I'm not ready to die."

He gave her a sip of brandy and she held onto his hand. He put his other hand over hers. "I love you, Kathy," he said. "You are a wonderful lady. I have only been home one day, please don't go away."

She smiled. "That's what I was thinking," she said. "Where is Julius?" and as she said it, a small child crept into the room. It was little Kathleen. "Uncle Julius is in Auntie Kathy's study looking at all of Auntie's books," she said. "Hello Auntie Kathy," little Kathleen said, and Lion lifted her up to kiss Kathy.

No one seemed to have attached any significance to Julius' whereabouts, for at that moment Elizabeth came in and opened wide the window. "Kathy my dear," she said, "the doctor will be here shortly. Whitey went with great speed, and we can rely on Whitey, you know that!" The nurse removed Eden's hand from Kathy's, apologizing, said she would only be a little while. She asked them all to leave the room while she removed Kathy's clothes. Eden returned to his room. He was shaken and felt his timing had been all wrong, and responsible for Kathy's shock. He was talking to himself. He folded up the faded pantaloons and kept talking. "My God, Mother," he said, "you have told us so much, you have guarded your things well. Mother, now keep Kathy well. You are here somewhere, I feel it, you have arranged it all. You don't care about time, you are with us Mother. I feel I know you, I wish I could have seen you."

He went to his window, and looked toward the hills, and he wondered why he had never been there. Carefully he wrapped the crumpled clothes, just as they were when Swarthaas gave them to him. He packed them back into his black-studded, brass-banded trunk carefully, as though he were laying them in a coffin. He closed the trunk and then his bedroom door, very quietly. As he passed Kathy's study and opened the door, he saw that Julius was not there. Slowly, he closed the door and returned to Kathy's room. The doctor was with her. "Well, well," he said, "how well you have grown! Give me your hand," he said. He looked keenly at Eden's right hand. "See those marks," he said. He pointed to a row of keloid scars. "When you were small, some person cutting hay or some such thing with a sickle was showing you how, and I believe you thought they were handing you the sickle and you reached out and took it. Just as they pulled the weapon to indicate how to cut, they caught all those fingers." He pointed to the scars. "Lady Kathy had a great shock," he said. "Then she thought you'd lose those fine fingers. She had a bad turn, Lady Kathy did."

Eden smiled. "I remember well," he said, "only it wasn't hay, doctor, and it wasn't a sickle, it was a shearing knife for sharing sheep." "Yes, well, it was some farm implement," said the doctor, letting loose Eden's hand. He looked at Eden. "Your mother has had a shock, she needs to be kept warm and calm," he said. "I have instructed the nurse with regards to her treatment. She's probably been overexcited about your return, you know." He looked Eden up and down. "I hear you're a fountain of knowledge in the discovery of gold," he said. "Well, you've come at the right time. First you fall upon a forest of diamonds and now you're hunting for gold, incredible! Some people traverse the world over and forget to look in their own back garden. The Boer trekkers all drove their trek oxen wagons and passed over the diamond fields of the veld, never even dreaming of what was there."

He shook his head. "Call me if Lady Kathy shows any signs of needing me." Whitey was waiting with fresh horses to take him back. Whitey looked elegant in an incongruous way. Here in the backwaters of Africa stood this stunning carriage, handsome horses and a black-clad driver that might have stepped from out of the deep south of America. The doctor climbed into the carriage and Whitey lithely turned the horses, and with a jingle of harness, the wheels, turning up the dust, he drove away.

There was silence inside the homestead over breakfast. Petra was helping the children. She was tying a napkin under the little boy's chin. He was a beautiful little boy. "I'm sure," she said, "you will look just like Eden. When Eden was small he looked just like you." She picked up his nut-brown curls. "See," she said, "your hair is like his, long and rich," she held his hair in her hands. The two little girls sat opposite the boy. "Daddy taught Eden to ride a big horse when he was still a small boy," said Kimberly. "Can we ride today, Mother?" Lion was drinking a cup of coffee. "That," he said, "is a good idea." He kept looking towards the passage. Recognition, money and status had totally changed Lion from the reckless farmer into a gentleman farmer, and the role suited him.

He had a fine, gentle bearing, and his charm and expressive stature made him stand out in a crowd. Though happy by nature, he was not gregarious and talkative. For the moment he was pensive and Petra did not intrude on his thoughts. He knew Julius would not enter the dining room while he and Petra were there, and he wondered where Julius had been during Kathy's trauma. He knew why Kathy went into shock, and now he knew Eden knew. The time had to come, but he did not expect it so soon. He was curious to know what had triggered it off. The children were talking about Eden's hair, of all things. Kimberly thought Eden's hair was the same color as the feathers around the red and gold rooster's neck. "But he hasn't got a red neck like the soldiers from England," said Kathleen. "Eden is very pretty, and when I get big, I am going to marry Eden." They all laughed merrily. "You are only ten years old, Miss Kathy McCabe," said Petra, "and a lady of very good taste!" The little girl was not smiling. She stood up and with small hands she dusted the front of her full-skirted little frock. "You will all see," she said, "I am going to marry Eden, and Eden is going to marry me."

In Sonnestroom, Eden was at the stables, checking his saddlery and tack, when Lion rode up. "Hello, Lion," he called, and Eden noticed Lion dismounted lithely, like a very young man. He was still lean and athletic, and Eden felt warmth and genuine affection. He spoke out at once. "You know, Lion, I always believed you were my father," he said. "It's sort of quite a shock to know that I'm a bastard, you know, born out of wedlock, that my poor mother died giving birth to a bastard. And I find it hard to accept that Julius did not do the honorable thing—I mean, marry her. It's Julius who is my father, and by the laws of the giver of all things, Lady Kathy is my grandmother. That means, Lion, that you are my uncle. But Lion," and he stepped forward and hugged him, "to me, you have been a friend, a tutor and a guide, but most of all, a father. I dearly love you and always will. We got rich together, man, we grew together, and nothing or anyone nothing will ever change that.

"There was an old Creole once who lived on an isolated island in the Indian Ocean, he chopped pieces of living coral from the sea, and placed them one on top of the other like bricks. He watered the blocks with seawater, kept the corals alive, and the coral bricks actually grew together, cemented together, by living coral. When I think of you Lion, I feel it's something like those coral bricks." They looked at each other with tears of emotion, but neither of them spoke for a few moments. Lion broke the silence as he fiddled with something on his bridle. "I always knew, Eden," he said, "that the right time would come to tell you, and answer all your questions. There are no bastard children, man, but there are some bastard parents. Your mother was my first sweet love; well, after Thombe, had she lived, we would have married, and I would have been even closer to you, perhaps you would have called me Father. She was so light, your mother. She danced, walked blithely like a spirit. She sang and laughed, which sounded like rippling water. She loved with a depth and a magic that dissolved all thought into nothingness. She bore you because she must have wanted to, she didn't try to be rid of you. When she finally gave birth to you she no longer had strength even to breathe, so she ceased to breathe.

She named you Eden, because she said you were born in heaven, and I promised her I would protect and guide you to manhood. How proud she would have been of you, Eden. She loved strength and you are strong and fine and handsome. You look like your grandfather, you know, and he was somewhat of a man among men, by God. By the way, how is Kathy, is she improved?" he said.

"She seems remarkably well again," Eden said, "but has now developed a nasty infection of the eyes and can't see well. Very irritable about that, she is. She tells me nature wants to be rid of her, so the young can get on with it."

"We must get back to her soon," said Lion. "Tell me Eden, have you said anything to Julius? He doesn't know anything about Louisa's wish. He knows she died, but he never knew, never dreamed, you were his son. He believes you are my son, which only makes him hate me more. He and I have never been anything but at drawn swords, you know. He hated me even when we were children."

Lion and Eden were quite at ease with each other, even in silence. They mounted their horses. "You know, Lion," Eden said, "you taught me that there was a time for everything. I'll tell Julius when the time comes. I don't feel ready now, now perhaps you will take me to my mother's final resting place. I'll tell you the time when it comes." he repeated. They rode on together across their valley. There it was, filled with creatures that lived in harmony with its moods in the ways that only nature in her infinite wisdom could devise.

Thirty-Two

The days were still hot, but the nights were icy. Eden had spent several months almost alone with Kathy. Though she was physically still quite frail, she was still alert and decisive, and in command of all her faculties. The nurse lived in the homestead and she seemed to have taken on the role of housekeeper as well. Eden supervised the wagons on their weekly trip to the town and rode miles all across the thousands and thousands of acres. Always he was looking for gold. In Lydenberg there among those dolomite quartz veins he would stake claims, but he was loath to leave Kathy.

He was enjoying his time with her, but in his free time he was examining stones all over the farm. He was restless, though ever filed with enthusiasm, and pondered for hours over stones and soil, testing and digging and scraping, placing specimen samples in little stone jars, flat little lids with sand, bring with the diamonds of mica sparks. Little black children in keen wonder also gathered sand and mica as though there was some sort of promise forthcoming from this strong, yellow-haired man who rode all the horses and who always seemed in a hurry to do it. Around their houses, some just single rooms with iron roofs and white-washed walls and a small square stoep in the front, stood little tin containers, just like Eden's.

Some days Eden would lift Kathy into the carriage or onto a Cape cart and take her across the farm on some soft, sandy track he had found. He would tell her where they were because her sight was poor since her eye infection, but she loved to be with him and treated each moment with contented, passionate gratitude. Her love for Eden was almost unnatural. He was careful to drive the horse on soft and, avoiding anthills and protruding rocks while she held onto the side of the seat. She had always taken such care of her hands, now they seemed a little stained with pigmentation. Her knuckles seemed bony. He looked at the thorn trees; like people, they also got gnarled. Their trunks were tortured and twisted, blackened by years of fires and sun, insects and droughts. How many years had they been there? People aged in a similar way, it seemed, but people had a short life span.

The hardships of Africa took its toll, even on Kathy, and he saw her draw her shawl about her shoulders. Once she was so strong and beautiful... but he saw her so, even now. He came to the top of a hill and drew the horses to a halt. He had never grown used to the wonder of the veld, his precious veld that spread like a golden canopy that climbed up into the purple cliffs, stately and copper-tinged before the blue, blue hills rising in the smoky distance, and there on the far right side, the green edged vlei, like an emerald, an oasis of green in a sea of savannah gold.

It looked small from this hill, but there inside that vlei, the gift, was a spring that gurgled into a stream, never ending, never dry, always running, even in the fiercest drought. The Boers had called it Sonnestroom. It was easy to be lost and confused around the vlei. It spread and wound and twisted all over the veld into little green crevices where marsh frogs made noises that sounded like birds. But presently it was quiet up here on the hill. "It's so beautiful, Mama Kathy," he said, "look at the copper lights upon the tree tops. It's big, this land. We'll never get to know the whole of it."

A red-necked francolin made a raucous cry, followed by the lovely song of the white browed robin. "He sings best in the spring," Eden said, "especially if he's near water. That's the songster of the veld, Mama. He sings a great repertoire. Different songs at different times of the year. Some say he's a cousin to the nightingale. Did you know that?"

"Yes, I did Eden," she said. "I grew to old age with the magical noises of the veld. The debonair drongo, black-collared barbets, shrikes and that wonderful Jacobean cuckoo called the rainbird. The African folk say if he sings only the first part of his call, the rains are far off, but if he adds his happy trill, the rains are very near. Yes, my boy, I know this land, and I know its birdsong. I still feed the birds in the garden. I don't recognize them, but I know their song. I was always enchanted by their silence in the midday hours, bird siesta!"

Eden took up the reins. The horses were getting restless and the air was getting cooler. "Alright, Mama Kathy," he said. "Time to go home."

"I love the way you still call me Mama Kathy," she said. "I prefer it to Grandmother or Ouma. I'm so glad to be your Ouma."

He stooped down and kissed her on the forehead. "You are the only mother I have ever known!" he said.

She smiled, a wistful smile. "And you will never forget me," she said. "I hope for that. This land, you so love, will be yours, and this land is part of me."

Three weeks later the weather changed. It became icy cold at night and misty and cold in the mornings. Perhaps it was the cold weather, no one really know, but Kathy contracted some sort of chest complaint, and the doctor predicted her life was very short, since the sickness had greatly weakened her heart. Over the weeks before, she and Eden were very close, and in these moments she had told him so much. She told him where her diaries in her desk were, her writings over the years, and also her last will and testament, which she carefully explained she had changed three times.

It was the latest one which was the last and final. It had been witnessed by Braam Piet and a lawyer from the Landrost's offices. The lawyer had been murdered, she had heard. She requested that when she died she should be buried near to, or beside, Jules. On one side of Jules' grave, Xosa was laid to rest and on the other was where she would like to rest. She insisted that Lion or Elizabeth or Petra be present during this conversation so that there would be no disputes afterwards. "Eden," she said, "I have made a codicil which tells you where I shall rest. Mr. Sheppard, attorney general of Grignaland, now deceased, arranged my final will. Julius was not meant to know, you see. Eden, Julius helped me with my first will, he was very clever with legal affairs. I thought a little too clever, perhaps. You have an uncle, your grandfather's brother, Jan. He is a fine man. He once showed me how to write my own documents. He started a newspaper in the Traanvaal. Such a clever man, a man of writing. You should find him, Eden."

Greatly weakened by her ailment, Kathy lost her appetite. She grew very thin and gray looking, and early in the morning on the 4th of July, 1873, she died. Kathleen Hora Jacobsen died in her large and lovely stone house, on the homestead of Sonnestroom. Eden, Lion and the servants, despondent and dejected, arranged for her burial. All the family had gathered. Lion's eldest child, Kathy Junior, found death inexplicable. Her questions were unanswered as she was ushered towards a melancholy nurse who softly closed the door without losing her expression, which clearly indicated children should be seen and not heard.

Julius came in, in full splendor, somber, elegant, never injudicious, but somewhat patronizing. Even here in this milieu of despondency his presence seemed to provoke a trace of prickled irascibility. Elizabeth put her arms about Eden and Lion. The funeral took place two days later and was one of the most imposing ever witnessed in the colony. Kathy's mortal remains were followed to her grave by a vast concourse of all classes of people, creeds and colors. Many preachers and ministers of different religions formed a processing, followed by a long train of Xosas and Fingoes and Zulus. Government officials attended the occasion in Cape carts, carriages, wagons and horses, all persons to whom Lady Kathy was well known and by whom her great character was duly appreciated.

After a short address by a Wesleyan Reverend and an army chaplain, Kathy was laid to rest in a polished coffin covered in flowers and herbs. Shots were fired in a salute, the minister who read the words in a long white robe withdrew, and the people, all in their best clothes, began shaking hands and offering their condolences. With her passing, it seemed a part of Africa was laid to rest.

Less than a week passed, and Julius was elected to read the will, which seemed the correct thing to do, so that each person knew what was going to happen to the farm. Julius, the man of the law, and well able to explain should the necessity arise, was the obvious choice, and of course Julius was Kathy's oldest son. It was a singular document that incorporated a declaration of her desires and aims to create a dynasty in Africa and her hopes that her family hereafter would endeavor to uphold the family name and its successes. She mentioned that her own father's will was a lengthy document of 200 pages and thus the chief reason for her own brevity.

She bequeathed the farm into a trust to her two children, Julius and Moya, and upon the demise of her son it was to pass to the eldest of his sons. She had arranged a monetary settlement upon her trusted and faithful servants, and a substantial amount of money to Eden McCabe together with all her private belongings, such as her stamps, diaries, musical instruments and carpets. To Lion, she left all her husband's guns, books, musical instruments and bric a brac that Lion would find useful. She also had given him all the imported horses. Nothing of the farm was to be sold, but was only to be passed from father to son, and to sons of sons. Her family were the trustees.

When the reading was over Eden was silent. He told Lion Kathy had told him about a codicil she had lately added. "It's strange, Lion," he said, "she kept telling me that she had done other things with this land. For one thing, you will remember," he was hesitant, afraid to appear grasping, "in your presence, Lion, once, she said, 'Eden, I'm so glad you love this land, for it is all yours when I die.'" Lion was perplexed. "You are quite correct, Eden," he said, "it *is* very odd. I know Kathy had made several wills; before she finally settled, there were two or three. I was quite certain she had made a new one after the death of Braam Piet. But here, I see this will was witnessed by old Piet."

Lion and Eden turned her writing bureau inside out, turning out all the drawers and piles of paper, and in the night, they read up on her diaries and the dates. It was quite clear that her last diary was not there. Her latest and final diary had been removed. They had troubled sleep. Something was wrong. In the meantime, Julius called all the staff together and informed them all things were to carry on as before, and despite the death of the "Inkoskas" there would be little change, just for a while. Julius and Elizabeth would move to Sonnestroom temporarily. Lion and his family left for their own farm, leaving Eden with Julius and Elizabeth. Kathy's nurse packed up and moved out and returned to a mission hospital in Uitenhage. Julius, at this time, had heard from his sister in England. Her husband was still in the Cavalry and her eldest son was also a professional soldier. She was saddened greatly by the news of her mother's illness; she had not yet heard the news of her mother's death.

Staying together gave Eden a chance to get to know Julius, this man, his father, and there was no doubt Julius liked Eden. He tried very hard to be pleasant and to be understanding. He expressed a desire to take a wagon and go and have a look at the Transvaal where according to attractive rumors there were gold discoveries every day. It was diamonds that appealed to him and it seemed diamonds were more profitable than gold. Eden began to make his plans. Somewhere inside of himself there was a deep disturbance. He was curious. He knew very well something was amiss, but there seemed no way he could pinpoint it. He loved the farm, the game, the hills, the vleis, the sheep and the yellow veld. It was a deep hurting love, and like when the drought came, he felt inside of him an insatiable ache. Then when the rains came and the drought broke, the agonies of the parched and tortured earth passed and his ache was also gone.

It was August now and the winds were starting. The winds could be fierce at Sonnestroom. It was exciting too, tucked up in bed at night, the winds would howl and whine through the rafters, trees would swish and creak and sometimes even crack and break, leaves and grass would go hurtling across the earth, up and away, lost and tossed away with the dust. The dust was unpleasant though. Africa was a thirsty, dusty land, sometimes especially around August. Kathy used to smile and say, "Ah, yes, now nature is going to sweep away the dry and tired leftovers of winter, and turn them into humus, so spring can sprout and burst into life." He was so small when she said that…he felt suddenly alone.

He remembered how it was to be tucked up and pampered with special foods, and morning tea. He moved to the hallstand, put on his hat, the hat Kathy gave him, and he went out into the path that led to the kopje where all the dead were buried. Her grave was still fresh, but all the wreaths of flowers had dried. However, one or two bunches of wild flowers laid by the Ingoes, that looked like edelweiss, a wild, everlasting bloom, still glowed with a little life, bright yellow and orange with little shiny satin petals. How the little cemetery had grown. There were so few graves when he was small. He wondered why he so seldom went there. People don't live long in this land, he thought; it's too damn harsh, the hot days, the bitter winds and cold nights, the dust and the dry. These things that make the lungs dry, and people cough. Each year, they cough more. Fears and wars, drought, ticks, and hard work, with little rest. They seem like nothing when one is young and strong, but they took a toll on people's lives, everyone had to pay. The price we pay for love is grief.

He looked at some of these stones. Some poor and pathetic, others painstakingly carved from the dolomite rocks chipped by hours and hours and hours of patient chiseling. The tall fir trees planted in a square seemed to guarantee them privacy and two large marula trees stood at each side of the gate. The kopje rose up behind it like a monument to them all, like a shelter from the wind. The birds were singing in this quiet place, filled with the smell of the gum, from the pines and firs, a loud hornbill called from the kopje. Eden looked across and noticed that on one of the graves, cape honeysuckle bloomed like a streak of fresh blood. Kathy used to say that life was just birth, life, reproduction and death, and after death, one's life's energy was sapped up by the next cycle as it began the new and constant, never-ending cycle. He wanted to pluck the flower and put it into Kathy's heap of earth, but when he got there, he couldn't pluck it.

He almost felt it would spurt blood. He went back to Kathy's mound. "God man, this is all there is when we die?" He began to walk back towards the farm. He was disappointed really. He would have loved to own this land, that was what Kathy kept telling him, over and over and over again, and Kathy never said any damn thing that was not true. He felt he could say nothing. He was a bastard, not an heir. The idea of talking about it, about inheriting, even to Lion, sounded impertinent and avaricious. What right had he? No, what he must do, and do right away, was to go to Kimberly or the Transvaal. He was lucky with finding things, and he and Lion lived well with what they found, a gift of God's on the muddy banks of the Orange River in a drift! He smiled as he thought of it.

He had not eaten since breakfast, but he felt no hunger. He felt disturbed somewhat. He went down to the stable, and took out the big bay. One of the grooms came running to saddle it, they did it together, he and the groom. He threw away the spurs; he hated spurs. He mounted the horse like a lithe athlete. He rode off down the winding road that led to the gate and the entrance, or exit of the farm. He got to be outside the farm boundary. When he was small it was just a track, but now it was a well-used road that led from town to town. and all over. He walked his horse, looking backwards. How much of the farm could one see from this road? It was a farm of hills and dales, so in the clearings on high ground one could see the sheep and the tall fir trees Kathy had planted. One could see how the vegetation grew darker as it went down into the hollows and creeks at the foot of the hills where the streams were.

He had that ache again. He walked his horse onwards, and he wondered why he was outside the farm boundary on a public road. As he walked his horse he noticed a wagon slap bang in the middle of the road. Several black men, as well as one of the Boer farmers were talking to a perky little man with a very tanned face, but the pink skin beneath his collar showed that he was European. He was a peddler; with four mules and two donkeys. He had a lot of stock, as he called it. He sold pots and pans, tin mugs jars and kettles. He had water jars filled with beads, knives, axes, bullets, skins, feathers and gunpowder. He had also farm implements, cotton, needles and many forms of medicine. He had sweets and candy, tea, coffee, sugar, salt and spices. He also carried boxes of seeds and several lengths of material and lace.

He was a bit of a bush doctor, a quack, and offered advice on various ailments. He came this way because he was coming to Sonnestroom with mail for a Lady Kathleen Hora Jacobsen that he had promised to deliver. It had come from an old gentleman in the Traansvaal, from where he, the peddler, had come.

"You may give me the letter," said Eden. "She was my grandmother."

He looked up at Eden. "You said she was your grandmother?"

"Yes, sir," said Eden. "You are two weeks too late. Some of the flowers on her grave are still blooming. Where might you be heading, then?" asked Eden.

"I am bound for Cape Town, sir," he said. "Well then," Eden said, "perhaps you'd like to ride to the farm, it's 35 minutes from here, and rest the night. If you will finish with your trade, you can follow me." Eden took the letter but did not open it, as he felt he had no right. He waited until the man had finished trading. He had a whole bundle of leopard skins, several large elephant tusks and lots of riems cut from the skins of animals, buffalo, hippo, and even rhino. His wagon was carpeted with zebra skins, and over the front were some fresh lion skins. The skins were not properly cured and bore the stench of the veld and vultures.

When he got to the homestead, the servants all gathered around him. He seemed to be known as he had passed this way once before. He had lots of news of the outside world, and seemed keen to tell it. But first the letter. Eden handed the letter to Julius, who broke the wax seal and started reading. It was from his uncle Jan, now, rather an aged man, who ran a newspaper in the Transvaal. He had sent, by various means, several letters over the years, but had never heard from his brother or sister in law down on the farm. "How can we tell him they are all dead, except us, the next generation?" Julius said.

The peddler, Goa Albassini, was of Italian stock. He had left Italy for political reasons and was an adventurer and merchant. He told of the feverish atmosphere in Kimberly, of the masses of black prostitutes, diggers, criminals and some scientific gentlemen who were fast becoming very important and rich with money from the digging of diamonds. Eden was enthused by this peddler's news, especially when he produced newspapers printed in England that told even more. First thing the next morning, before the peddler was hardly outside the farm boundary, Eden set off to Leeukraal to Lion. His fresh enthusiasm was almost overcome by his sorrow, disappointment and emotional turbulence. He took two horses, one on a lead. He was in a hurry, but didn't know why. He told Julius and Elizabeth he would stay overnight at Leeukraal.

Lion and Petra were happy to see him. It seemed they talked for hours. "If I were in your position, I think I would do the same," said Lion. Eden trusted Lion. He felt a security, a love that a man would expect from a father. Life had not seen fit for him to have both his parents, but kindness had not eluded him, and Lady Luck stood always at his shoulder. There was a lot he had to be thankful for. He asked Lion to store his trunks and belongings, telling him that one day, when he succeeded in his venture, he would return.

Before the New Year, 1874, Eden left with horses, his wagons and Cape carts. He crossed the high veld with his manservants and a cook, with digger's tools and a Greek lexicon and all his textbooks and scientific aids. Once at Kimberly he made several friends, set himself up in one of the local inns, camped his servants in a tent and his horses on the commenage. He met a man, Mr. Seppings Wright, with whom he became good friends. In only a short time, though gradually at first, Eden became an important man and a knowledge-able geologist, whose views and opinions were greatly respected.

In 1877, Sir Bartle Frere came to Capetown as High Commissioner on April 12th of that year and Shepstone issued the proclamationi annexing the Transvaal. Most of the petitioners in favor of this were English settlers. Bartle Frere directed his attention to affairs on the Eastern Frontier. He believed in a strong frontier force, in just rule of the tribes, and in taxation to encourage industry. In August, the 9th Kaffir War broke out. Sixty white Europeans were killed and the war cost the colony two million pounds. The British flag was hoisted at the Umzimvubu River and Port St. Johns was ceded to England for a thousand pounds. This was the last frontier war.

Julius Jacobsen was now an opulent and aggressive squire, wealthy, with three farms, all successful, exporting wool, skins and ostrich feathers. Frequently he went out hunting and took great pleasure in bringing down a graceful Gemsbok that had run free all its life at Sonnestroom, or a cerval or baboon. His attitude towards Elizabeth was brittle and cold, and Elizabeth, to escape him, had taken to pressing flowers from the veld and painting. Often he would go away on government affairs, leaving her alone. Once, when she complained, he insulted and deeply hurt her by saying she was barren and unproductive and deserved no company since she made no children.

In Kimberly, Eden soon settled. He was now well acquainted with a short, Jewish man, Barny Barnato, a well known kopje walloper who showed him how to buy stones from the tables. He met Leander S. Jameson, a quick witted doctor, and his friend Cecil G. Rhodes, an exuberant, bubbling, high-voiced and articulate man who had very little interest in women, and to whom business came first. Eden invested with both Rhodes and Barnato in the DeBeers Mining Co., and the Kimberly Mine. Rhodes did better business-wise, and hundreds and hundreds of diamonds were simply churned up from the tunnels. The bubbling, continuous vitality of Rhodes poured forth with his uncommon gift of subtle power, which had a way of driving his half-surprised, overcome listener into an attitude of conformity. Yet a stern and whim-sical rivalry existed between Barnato and Rhodes. Rhodes, with a vastly superior backing, emerged the winner. The diggings were so impetuous that rock falls occurred and many diggers lost their gamble with life.

Eden's gamble, fraught with undreamed of opportunity, paid him very well. A German Jew with an egg-shaped head, Alfred Beit, was a genius in financial warfare who backed the other giant who had feeble lungs and an overriding concept of money and reckless power. The Boer leader was Paul Kruger, 39, a real fighter and in the north Labengula was a fierce black leader of great cunning. All these men were part of the period of the awakening of the lightening of darkest Africa, a land once shrouded in mystery from which strange and fearless tales were told of stones and ivory, wild animals, feathers and skins. But the darkness was lifting to expose the glitter of gold and diamonds, and in search of her riches came adventurers and came wars and plunder and murder and the parched earth of Africa was darkened and stained with blood.

No sooner had the last Kaffir war ended than the Zulu war began, and a garrison of 832 soldiers was massacred with 491 Basutu allies. Of the 598 officers of the 24th Regiment only 6 privates escaped alive. Eleven Victoria Crosses were awarded to those who fought at Rorkes Drift and 3,000 Zulus were killed. Among the men killed in the skirmish was the Prince Imperial of France, the only son of Emperor Napoleon III serving Lord Chelmsford's staff. His death ruined the hopes of Bonapartists for regaining political power in France. P. Kruger went to London to protest about the annexation, unsuccessfully. On his return he was chosen as part of the triumvirate to form a provisional government and new hostilities. The 1st Anglo-Boer War began on December 16, 1880.

Though at all times Eden was in contact with Lion and Elizabeth in whatever way he could find to send mail, only now did he decide to return to the farm. He was, by this time, a fairly rich and powerful man, not only in financial terms, but also he was well versed in the government and politics of the whole country. He arrived at Leeukraal in a new and beautiful coach, made on the same lines as the state coach. He did not return directly to Sonnestroom, but first went to Leeukraal and to Lion. So often he had longed for the tranquility of the farm and for the unspoiled hills of his childhood. He felt an inner resentment towards Julius; whatever he did, it was there. He felt no fatherly love towards him now, though he knew this was his true father. Strangely though, when he was small he clearly remembered he was fond of him then. He also remembered Julius, the uncle, who galloped recklessly in the Cape carts, throwing them off their seats over the anthills and rough parts of the veld, the uncle with whom he had a lot of fun and happiness.

It was all forgotten and replaced by his anger when he heard the story from Swarthaas, and the poignant life of his mother was revealed. All the time he was away, especially when he lay in bed at night, thinking in the dark before being swept into the arms of sleep, there were always the thoughts that Kathy's wishes and his beloved Sonnestroom were amiss. No one was closer to Kathy than he, and he knew that her will was out of character. He had been to see Sheppard, but Sheppard had no copies of her will, and though he remembered Lady Kathy and the purpose of her visit, he could not recall the contents.

Now he was at Leeunkraal and what a pleasure it was to see Lion's smile. Petra and Kathy, Kimberly and Canaan were all there. Petra was still fiery in temperament, but seemed a little tired and quite a lot older. Africa did this to women. Too much sun seemed to dry up the bloom of their skins just as it took all the moisture from the earth and dried up the leaves that crackled and crunched under one's feet to a powder that went back into the soil. Kathleen, Lion's oldest child, was not there to receive him. She was inside and panned to make an entrance. In her mind was a maze of schemes and most of them involved Eden.

She had rehearsed her act in her room. "All women are actresses," her mother always said. She was preparing now, and here she stood, the embryo woman, a young girl with a woman's mind, as Eden came in. Her parents were quite nonplussed. Framed like a picture in the doorway, she had on her lemon frock with frothy lace and her long, nut-brown hair fell over her shoulders. Her childlike face was alight with wonder with flashing eyes, green that flashed brown. Petra said she had hazel eyes. Her small breasts were pushed out to show her budding womanhood, like an eagle owl that puffs its feathers out to double its size in a defense mechanism. Eden smiled, "Hello, Kathleen," he said, "what about a hug for Uncle Eden?" She flung her slim arms at him and held on a trifle too long. "You are not my uncle, Eden," she said, "you always said I could call you Eden, and Eden you are." She had grown into a lovely young woman, but was still just a girl. "It's so lovely to have you back," she said, "are you back forever and ever?" He never noticed her ripening womanhood the way she had hoped he would. Eden just saw a pretty young girl who was the daughter of the man he regarded as his father.

Eden settled down at Leeunkraal, and felt very much at ease. It was a calm and glorious July. They talked for hours and hours on end. He and Lion rode over to Sonnestroom and looked for his horse. He was looking old now, a little sway backed, and showed few signs of recognition after his long absence. Lion had cared for his horses very well, but two of them had died of the horse sickness. There had been a bad outbreak of ticks, hard-backed bont ticks. But for Lion it was a great pleasure to let Eden ride one of his stallions. He had many horses, brood mares and stallions and colts and fillies that raced across the meadow, tails up and flying, hooves thundering the earth, like a rain of cannon balls.

Lion's farm was full of animals, thousands of morgren of land filled with sheep, some with fat tails, but mostly merinos. "Ja Eden," said Lion, "a man needs capital to start a farm but you can stake your life and make a fortune. You do not require capital, you can be young and rich, you do not need years of work. No, my boy, guts, courage, brains and robust health, that's all it takes in this land, at this time. Ja, we have been lucky. You have been rich since your boyhood, a magnate, but thank God you do not smoke cigars!"

Sonnestroom was much the same, though Julius had placed a manager in the homestead, an English adventurer who had failed to find riches overnight. He had a wife whom Eden later discovered was once an English barmaid, who seemed uncomfortable and totally unused to the comforts that had befallen her. Old servants, one or two of whom were children when Kathy was alive, now were adults, and a few new families were engaged, including a half-cast Portuguese who was aggressively pedantic. He reminded Eden of Mexico. Lion and Eden rode through the farm, the trees, the tracks, all familiar and full of memories for them both. They got to the crest of a small kopje and they looked down at their valley.

"See those hills, those bluish ones covered with a cloud that lies around them like a silk scarf around a woman's throat," Lion said, "there's echoes in those hills, and there is a place where Kathy once took your mother and I, and in those hills is your mother's grave. Come, I'll take you there."

Eden looked at Lion and then up towards the sky. "Can we go there tomorrow, Lion?" he said. Lion could see Eden must have had a reason for not going there and then. "You know Lion," he said, "one's soul is part of the soil around you, the place where we live in childhood. Yes, tomorrow, Lion, you and me." They turned their horses. First they trotted, cantered and then with laughter, they galloped in a boyish race towards Leeunkraal.

Breakfast was always a hearty meal. The children left to have schooling, so they dined first; it was quiet and very pleasant, especially when it was served outside beneath the trees. Petra was a good hostess, and in true Dutch tradition there was always food aplenty, wholegrain bread made of wheat flour, sheep's entrails washed and cleaned and filled with liver and sweetmeats that looked like thick sausages, fresh eggs and milk and honey. "Liver," she said, "was what makes new blood, it is the part of the body that lions and vultures always eat first." She told them how when she was out hunting once, long ago with her brother, they saw a lion kill two buffaloes, pulling at their entrails, eating only their livers and leaving the whole of the carcass to rot or to be eaten by the asvoels (vultures).

Lion and Eden saddled up. Eden was riding a strong wonderful black stallion. Lion loved black horses, and this was one of his best. His coat shone like black satin, and his hooves were coated with a thick fatty grease right up to the hocks so they didn't collect ticks. The forge was going and a blacksmith was working with the shoes of another horse. He was an old Boer with a bent back and a broken leather apron. "He's a wonder with horses," said Lion, "I only hope he stays healthy and serves me for as long as possible. Oh yes, I've given him a nice cottage and the freedom of the farm. He can have whatever he likes, as long as he cares for my horses. He hates the British, old Van Reener, hated them from the time of the executions of Slagtersnek, then for the abolition of slavery. He hated paying taxes, and still wonders why in the name of God they should have been forced to pay taxes for land they themselves carved out of a hazardous wilderness. His family trekked, but he was held by the British and when he was freed, his whole family had gone to where the land was free of the verdamde English. They're a strange people, the real Boers, peaceful creatures who would rather give up all and move away, rather than fight. They

don't feel the need for laws and schools and police. Theirs is the law
of least resistance. Van Reemer, he's invaluable to me." He could
go onj, but he did not—yes valuable!

They mounted their horses and put on their hats. Eden
dismounted, went over to the tool house and extracted from a
pile of implements a short, stocky spade-like weapon. He put it in
his saddlebag, the handle sticking up like a small flat holder, then
remounted. The horse moved away as he mounted and he hopped
on one leg, his other in the stirrup, then flung his leg over. "You're
out of practice man," yelled Lion, laughing.

The hills seemed nearer than they actually were. After about
an hour's ride they still seemed distant. When they reached
Sonnestroom Lion took a track to the north west of the homestead. It was a beautiful ride. They bypassed the homestead,
stopping only to take a drink of water and to water the horses.
The track was wild, still full of large indigenous trees—even a
few yellowwoods still remained. Sakari hung with matted lichen
and the mimosa, acacia with white thorns and clusters of yellow
blossoms humming with bees, spread like a giant umbrella above
a thick trunk with patches of gray, hairy worms that look like flat
patches of living lichen, when he touched only one, the whole
mass as a group tumbled down, some of them on silver threads
like web-like spiders. Here and there a seedy domestic tree was
planted, some peaches and few oranges and a few colorful clusters
of hydrangeas, as though man had intruded with his own ideas
into nature's superb pattern.

They chatted as they walked along, the horses, snatching at
green clumps as they passed. Brambles tumbled haphazardly across
the scrub trees, leaves climbed up into the big trees, and there was
a wild fig with long strangling roots that ran all over clinging to the

rock gray and snakelike, then going down into the ground, rocky ground now with wildflowers here and there. And then, as they grew nearer the foot of the hills, it got greener. To the right was a vlei and pink-scented vlei lilies stood up like beauty queens, open trumpets proud and sure of their pink perfection, and there were butterflies. Lion came to a halt. It was the fluttering butterflies that reminded him of Louisa, his first love, delicate like a butterfly, and when they loved, the butterflies were all about them. He could almost hear her happy laughter. He saw some of the green buffalo grass that grew up from the edges of the vlei, and he saw her golden hair against the green and the blue summer sky in her eyes and he looked to the hills and he heard her voice. "Hello Lion, Louisa loves you."

Eden stood watching Lion. He felt the pregnant mood of memory and he did not intrude, but remained silent. So powerful were Lion's thoughts he did not hear Eden dismount. He tethered his horse to a tree and walked a little distance away. He leaned against a rock, protruding onto a small rock edge. Looking up into the hills Eden called, "Hello Lion," and the echo answered three times, fading on the third.

"God, Eden," Lion said, "that was like a blow beneath the belt. Come," he said, "we will walk towards that cliff side."

Eden returned to his horse, opened his saddlebag and took out the short-handled spade, and a small canvas bag. "We're going to my mother's grave, aren't we, Lion?" he said.

"That's it, Eden," Lion said, "I never understood why you never wanted to go before."

"Don't know myself, Lion," Eden said, "it was something private as though I was saving it for a very special occasion."

They walked towards the cliff, Eden following after Lion. "You see," said Lion, "She wanted to be partly up the cliff. She said that up here she would always hear the echoes. I bet she heard you call. She was a beautiful person, Eden, your mother. I feel such sadness that she is not able to see the son she left behind." He held out his hand. "Come," he said. After a few meters they came to her grave, a small level spot on the side of the cliff. Up on one end which was the head, was as slab of dolomite, the tombstone. On the left side was a patch of beeswax gum and chipped and carved into the stone was the head of a girl and a bunch of flowers, and underneath, carefully chiseled, was her name, "Louisa 1834-1854."

Eden stared at the grave. It seemed so strange, under this bundle of stones and the rough headstone, was his mother. He wondered what she looked like at the bottom of that hole. Was she just small bones and golden hair? He always imagined human hair never decayed.

Lion was pacing around the loose stones, balancing so he did not slip on the grave, and then loose stones were falling down. Eden took his small spade. "Lion," he said, "these clothes that Swarthaas gave me, I'd like to bury them here. I've wanted to do it ever since Kathy died, but I hung onto them. God knows why I could never bring myself to burn them." He removed some stones and rolled them down the hill. The clash as the stones hit other stones at the bottom made an echo in the hollow hills. An eagle called high up in the sky, eerie and wild and free. Lion looked up, but said nothing. He let Eden bury the little canvas bag, digging a deep hole nearly two feet deep, then carefully, like a child burying its beloved pet, he placed the little canvas bag into the hole, and closed it all up. "Dust to dust," he said, and Lion could see he was emotional and a little disturbed.

He pressed the earth with his hands and then stood up firmly, and with his shoe stood on it, pressing it down even firmer. He didn't seem to want to look at Lion. "Give me that spade, Eden," Lion said. Eden bent down and picked it up and then handed it to Lion. "You see this beeswax," he said, "I don't quite understand," he was saying as he prodded it with the spade. "You see, this is a built-in vase, I did it myself. It was meant to hold water and a bunch of flowers. Looks like the bees have sealed it up." He was digging off the gum and then he moved the wax and then he got inside the hole. "My God, look Eden," he said, "What is going on here?" The spade hit something. He scraped it clear and it was a small leather pouch wrapped inside a waterproof container with many pieces of bark of the camphor tree. Eden stooped down on his haunches, his knee on the grave. The pouch was sealed with wax, very tightly. They looked at each other. "Go on, man, open it, Lion," said Eden, and they opened it.

Inside was a document rolled into a neat scroll, in order to fit into its chosen place. Slowly they unrolled it. It was in Kathy's hand. Inside the roll was a single-page letter. "This letter will be found and read either by my dear half brother Lion, or by my very precious Eden. I had the feeling, or instinct, rather, when Eden was born, that he was my grandson. Be that as it may, he has been to me like my very own child. No mother and child were ever closer than Eden and myself. For those cherished years of caring and joy, I want to leave to Eden this land that he and I and Lion so dearly love. I am returning to Lion all money he has paid me for his share of the farm, this was also Braam Piet's idea. Why have I placed this bag in Louisa's grave? I shall not accuse nor shall I give reasons. I know this letter will be found, and with this letter is the original document of my last will and testament. I have also seen to it that it is legally correct so that there is no doubt or reason to question. I feel happy, now, that I know that

Louisa will see that my wishes are carried out. I cannot say I'm glad to leave this lovely earth; death must be very quiet and dull, but Eden will keep it beautiful."

It was signed "Kathleen Hora Jacobsen" and was dated 1871 and was co-signed by a lawyer in Grahamstown and three other persons Lion didn't know. They read it together over and over again. Their horses were tired of being tethered and were pawing the earth lower down the cliff where the grass was softer and greener, and large red aloes like orange-red spurts of flame in an olive candelabra stood stately to attention like a guard of honor. They picked an aloe and placed it in the empty hole on the headstone. They both stood looking at the little heap of stones, there all alone in the hills, yet this little heap of stones had unraveled a whole new era of light. Everything would change. Eden felt at ease, almost excited.

"My God, Lion," he said, "I've never felt happier. I shared too many years with Mama Kathy to feel happy about her will and wishes that Julius expressed. The way I see it, someone took Kathy's diaries and will, and replaced it with her old will made years ago when Moya was still at home. I'm going to take this land and I'm going to act right away. There's a lot to be put right." They mounted their horses and started down the track towards home. Suddenly, a shot rang out, then another. They galloped towards the direction from where the shots came from and saw the hunters. They had downed a gemsbok and were busy cutting it up.

"What in the name of God are you doing, you bounders," said Eden, and the hunter who was standing near a tree turned around while the other was busy cutting the animal, and they came face to face with Julius. Eden jumped down from his horse. The animal lay there, the sharp horns catching the glints of light, its eyes wide and staring. "For God's sake, Julius," Eden said, "these animals have been here for years, probably came up from the desert, they were almost tame. How dare you kill something that's almost a pet?"

"He has good experience with killing pets, Eden," said Lion.

"Your mother would turn in her grave," Eden said.

"My mother will never know," Julius said, "and even you can't tell her, and as for this land, this is my land, I will ask you to please get off it, remove yourselves, the both of you."

Lion said, "That's where you're wrong, Julius. This land belongs to Eden, and Eden's name is Jacobsen, just like yours. I do not need to tell you why or how, because you already know. Look it up and remind yourself by reading Lady Kathy's will, the copy you removed from her desk. You see, Julius, yours was not the latest original. Eden here has the original. I am glad we are out in the bush, it's the veld that shared most of our bitter moments. I do not wish my wife or children to know what sort of man you are, and I would like to spare Elizabeth the agony. Eden, tell you father how you found out about your mother."

Eden hesitated, looking for words and hung his head. Slowly he looked up at Julius who was staring at Eden with an expression of absolute defeat. "Remember Swarthaas?" Eden said, "He's in America. My mother was the beautiful Louisa, who was brutally raped by you. I do not feel able to tell the story, I'm afraid, but I was the child she bore, and died giving birth to. Look at me, Julius, your son! But all you will see in me is your own father. It is he I resemble, I've been told. I think I have no forgiveness for you. The two people in this world I love most are my grandmother, who has gone, and Lion. I lost my mother, and I've lost my grandmother, and I lost my father." He turned around. Lion had brought his horse. "Come Eden," he said, "come home."

In 1883 Paul Kruger was elected President of the Transvaal and a short time later left for England to discuss with the secretary of state for the colonies, the Earl of Derby, the total independence of the republic. He achieved a goodly amount, and the British government gave up its right to veto Transvaal legislation. All Europeans had full civil rights, no trade restrictions imposed on imported goods, and all Africans were given freedom of movement with a pass system. Rhodes was a member for Barklay West in the Cape Parliament with vast interests in the diamond fields and the gold mining industry of Witwatersrand. He was constantly driven by his ideal: "Africa, British, from Cape to Cairo." In exchange for mineral rights in Lobengula's territory which Rudd engineered, Lobengula was promised 1,200 pounds a year, 1,000 rifles, 100,000 cartridges and a small steamboat. All this led to the colonization of the territory north of the Limpopo River.

In 1883, Kathleen McCabe was 16 years old. She was a real beauty, but more than that, she was also a very bright and highly intelligent young woman. She had known what she wanted when she was six years old, and despite all the women in Eden's life, happily for her, he had not married. She had wanted Eden, she had always wanted Eden. She was a tall girl with long slim legs like a filly, even coltish, more than half grown up. She had firm breasts that turned upwards, big enough to fill a man's hand—a man with nice hands that is, a man's hands are very important to women and their fantasies of love.

Every time she saw herself she'd smile, flash her white teeth and pinch her cheeks until they were pink. Women were born with the ability to attract men, and by instinct knew how to be so that men understood. Well, she was tired of not being noticed in the way she wanted to be noticed, so she must now be a little braver, brazen perhaps. She was swaying to and fro, beautiful in her childish slimness, like a reed in the breeze, yet passionate. The pressure of time killed her girlish modesty.

Eden had been away, deeply involved in the control of the mines in the northern territories. He often wrote and told of Lobengula, immensely obese and getting old, who was being badgered, bluffed, flattered and deceived. No match was he for the agents of Rhodes and Beit, Rochford, Maguire Francis Thompson and, of course Mr. Rudd. He excluded the clergyman Moffat. They had so far managed to obtain the Rudd concession. Eden evaded the hard political issues but had obtained immense claims in the DeBeers diamond mines and had very great success in gold. There was a rapid growth of the English population in Johannesburg owing to the development of the mining industry and rumors were that the actual owners of the Transvaal soil would soon be an insignificant minority. The great horn of imperialist England was loudly sounding for political power to be shared by the masses of new white peoples.

Eden finally casually mentioned he would be coming home within the next fortnight, and wished to be at home before Christmas, in fact. The Cape Governor had taken over Walvis Bay and Port St. Johns from the British Governor. There seemed to be considerable peace beyond the kei, except for along the narrow strip of Tangoland and Kosi Bay. The whole Southern African coast from the Orange River in the west to Delagoa Bay in the east was under British control. Since the depression of 1873 there was no serious nor immediate investment despite the pull and the thrill of the discovery of the diamond fields. Diamonds were a risk for investors and bankers of London, Paris and Berlin, perhaps because there was no way of telling how long the mines would last.

A struggle for mastery existed between Rhodes and DeBeers and Kimberly. Barnato was going from strength to strength with a block of six central claims. Barnato was everywhere, he even held the purse strings of the Diamond Times. He had sold a group of claims to Rhodes who badly wanted them for their position, but there was no scheme for amalgamation and the struggle was fierce between Rhodes and Barnato. October came, with dense and gravid clouds and then in November the rains. In the middle of December, Eden headed for home, stopping at the inns and Boer farmhouses along the way. There was no meretricious glamour in Kimberly. The place was unpleasant. Hovels made of corrugated iron, tents, wagons, traps and carts, mules, donkeys and horses. Scattered among this melancholic spread were also solid buildings and more and more were being erected.

There was a distinct class between diggers and losers, and least pleasant of all was the grim life of black miners. Life was cheap and the death rate high. Only the rich insulated themselves from discomfort, dirt and disease. Only a small population of the many diggers were large mine shareholders. Many lingered in drinking bars, gambling among prostitutes, thieves and hosts of odd shady characters. Men gambled over anything—how many tusks an elephant hunter collected, diamonds good and diamonds bad, guns, horses, and even stupid things like how many flies would land on a lump of sugar. The mining life was the life of a gambler, a diamond dream, a gold rush. Man's thinking in the mining towns turned to simply gambling. However, towards the south and east, snatches of the quiet pastoral life of Africa still lived.

In the quartz vein of Brays golden quarry and the rich Sheba Reef, diamond and gold fever spread like wildfire in the mine leaving some men rich and others dead. Where there was money and men, there too, were women. In this year, February 27, 1884 the 3rd Anniversary of Majuba, a new convention had been signed: the British residents' supervision of native affairs and the right to march troops across the country was dropped. The Transvaal felt they had full sovereignty. No one seemed to be aware in England of how the 1884 Convention came to be signed at all. The moral effect of the concession was not very different to the Boers than that of the surrender of 1881. Mr. DuToit made a declaration at a banquet in Amsterdam, "The South African flag shall yet wave from Table Bay to the Zambezi, be that end accomplished by blood or by ink. If blood it is to be we shall not lack the men to spill it."

Bechunaland became infested by freebooters from the Transvaal, who rapidly became masterful whilst pretending to take sides in the quarrels. The Boers raided Bechunaland attacking Mafeking and murdering some Englishmen. Rhodes was just beginning to obtain political prominence, and urged the high commissioner not to led Bechuanland fall into the hands of a hostile state. He referred to Bechunaland as the "Suez Canal to Southern Central Africa." Despite the boom in "Kaffirs" which exhilarated the markets in London, hate was smoldering and brewing all over Africa. The Boers hated the British, the Uitlanders all had grievances against the Governor, Kruger still agitated against taxation on his people, was baked to the hilt by the backveld boers and their rifles. J. Porges and Co. formed a London firm to deal in diamonds and shares with Bert; the diamond age in Africa was a puzzling, mixed jumble of British colonies, Boer republics and African kingdoms, and the rand was waiting to be found.

Leenkraal was so beautiful. Lion had changed the living room into a tall cathedral ceiling with long beams of yellow stinkwood, stretching high up into a gable. It was an enormous living room

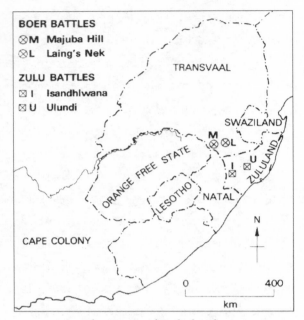

The Boer and Zulu battles

The British defeat at The Majuba Hill

and at its end he erected an elaborate semi-castellated tower with crenellated battlements and canceolate windows. The floors were laid with beautiful lengths of Knysna yellowwood and upon the yellowwood were sprinkled a few oriental rugs. Leuunkraal was a splendid haven, with tall trees and a rich orange grove. Large weirs on the little river conserved his water with narrow canals throughout the land, and where it was dry artesian wells were built.

Lion's greatest interest was his horses, large blood horses he had brought from England. He was proud of his farm, it was a model of success in fairly difficult terrain and conditions. It was soon to be Christmas again and having felled a small fir, Petra and her children were preparing the Christmas tree. Kathleen, now 17, was tall and lithesome. Her long brown hair shone in the sunlight like mica sparks, and her green-brown eyes flashed in happy laughter. Her sister Kimberly was similar, though not of the same slender mold. Canaan, her brother, was a quiet boy. He was full of compassion for most creatures, and even ants; he shifted, rather than stood, on them. His sisters loved him. They seemed to want to protect him, for he was such a gentle boy.

Laughing and happily placing little decorations upon the tree, they heard the crunching sound of iron wheels and they all rushed out to the yard where the driveway encircled a dolphin fountain. This fountain was Petra's pride and joy. It had come by ship from England. The driver of the carriage seemed to be sitting up high, his hands holding the reins that went through the harness of the collar; beautiful horses flexed their chins almost to their chests, breathing heavily and flaring this nostrils, streaked with salty white froth from their heated sweat and breathing a fast hoofbeat to a dusty halt.

The coachman, a colored man in a high hat, opened the carriage, and Eden stepped out. Lion clasped him like a loving son and Petra flung her arms about his neck, but Kathleen remained standing apart; she had brought her hair forward, and it blew gently in the breeze. She stood there, a composed child-woman, trying to use every talent of provocation. "Hello, Eden," she said softly, and waited for him to come over to her. She reached out her hand, and he took it to his lips. There were no hugs, but his eyes were upon her face. How beautiful she had become. Kathleen, the little girl that Petra once bore, the baby he well remembered, had burst from a cocoon and metamorphosed into a magnificent young woman. He felt a strange feeling as he looked at her. She held his gaze and he looked into her eyes. They were soft, like a doe's, like a quiet heifer's. There was also something like an animal about her that he had seen somewhere, a look he knew from somewhere in his life before. Christmas was a happy day. They feasted on lamb and chicken and pork, venison, guinea fowls and wild pheasant eggs. Petra made a stunning array of foods, with greens and fresh vegetables, and fruits and raisin puddings and brandy sauces. The wines flowed freely and the servants were singing and dancing noisily in their compounds. Bunches of dried onions hung up as a sign of plenty with corn bread, honey and homemade preserves, and they sang "Good King Wenceslaus" and folk songs that made them laugh.

Lion had drunk too much wine and sang with slurred words a melodious Irish lullaby. Petra wore a pointed cap that Canaan had made, tied with a green ribbon. She was especially devoted to Canaan, always touching him in a caressing way, his sensitive little hands often within hers. He was a different child from his sisters, he had smoldering dark blue eyes and golden brown hair that curled into shiny ringlets. She always pushed his curls up with her fingers, rolling them round her fingers.

Thirty - Three

God, there was something about women and their sons; Petra couldn't understand it, she just knew. She loved this child more than life itself. She hated herself for telling Lion, once, long ago, "You are touched with the tar brush, Lion McCabe." The Boers, they hated the thought of mixing their blood, or mixing it with the blood of the Kaffirs. No, her precious son, he was white-skinned, but his very being, his soul, his soft touches and his kindnesses, were almost supernatural, almighty to her. No matter what, he was pure, pure like the touch of angels. Not wild or dark stormy.

People change, she thought. Once she heard her mother tell about a woman who gave birth to an ugly, deformed son; at first she was so upset she couldn't look at him, but as he grew, she saw him as beautiful, no longer repulsive. She was blinded by her love for that sweet, ugly child she bore, who had slanty eyes and stubby fingers and thick lips. She was devoted to him like a little girl with her first big doll, and she never saw him as ugly for all of her life.

Canaan was different, and her son really was beautiful, inside and out. She and Lion, they had truly beautiful children. She was proud of their progeny. Her children, she boasted, were not just ordinary Boer children. Hers were schooled and clothed like, yes, rather like the best English, like all the aristocrats of the world. Today there was too much wine, they all grew tired, but not Canaan; he got a Boer pony for Christmas, a beautiful black pony. "Black Magic," he called him. It was love at first sight and they were already inseperable.

"I'll surprise Kathleen. I will bring her a diamond that one day will be able to buy a whole farm. This is the second time I feel that I really love these diamonds, Lion! Remember when we first found them at the drift?"

"I remember when you first found them," replied Lion.

Eden continued, "I was so happy to be able to be independent and then to have bought old Swaarthaas his little dream. This time, Lion, a diamond will be my expression of another dream. I have dreamed of a home and a family, of a beautiful loving wife. I must say I never thought it would be so sudden. But when your beautiful Kathleen stood there, haughtily, yet coquettishly, her hand extended, my fluttering, foolish heart missed several beats. Lion, you have beautiful children and I shall be fortunate to pluck the fruits from your marriage. The wondrous fresh ripening woman in full bloom of beauty and youth. Never fear Lion, I will always care for Kathleen."

He ran out towards the meadow. There was soft grass, and he left Lion standing beside the stable. The lantern stood ready as it was always placed there ready for use in the dark. Lion watched Eden playing on the grass with his shoes in his hands, and his feet on the soft wild oxalis that squeezed into life among the matted grass, succulent and green and sour if you broke off a leaf and tasted it. "Eden and Kathleen," he thought, "the boy, not in truth. But he is my son, that boy that Louisa gave to the world." He lit the lantern, it flickered into life, glowing unsteadily, like a little yellow leaf of orange light. He thought of Eden's mother. She used to frolic just like that, soft and light and silvery blithe, like a butterfly. She loved to frolic and dance barefoot in the soft undergrowth and wild violets.

He watched Eden, who was like her in spirit. There he was, the very life of her. He turned the flickering light down to low, then to nothing, and then it went out. "That's how it was," he thought, "her life went out like a lantern, only leaving behind this beautiful boy." Suddenly, like a crazy youth, he forgot he was 58. "Ah, Eden, it's good to be alive. Eden my boy," he said, dancing about in a foolish, playful manner. "We are jumping for joy, are we not?" And they looked at each other.

"Yes, Pa," said Eden, "we are foolish, but we are jumping for joy!" And they laughed and laughed all the way back to the house together, where the family were gathered in the large voorkamer (front room).

Thirty - Four

Lion emulated Braam. He always took heed of all Braam actually did. He loved his oxen, his span as he referred to them. He took his cue from Braam. They were now older men, but he knew each animal by name when they came in at evening time. He would wait at the gate of their kraals; once it was a rough kraal, surrounded by thorn bushes, but now, see how they lived? In the old days there were many more lions and leopards and serval cats sneaking about stealthily. It was very exciting and nerve wracking at night, yet wonderful to live among the kindred of the wilds. The cattle had strong stables now, protected from everything, and they obviously loved it, their mangers filled with hay, oats and Lucerne. No wonder they all looked so good! Braam taught him all about oxen, and he had patted each one as it passed. This was so gentlemanly. Braam could speak oxen, it seemed: Lion was quite satisfied.

He also said "Good night Vaalpens, good night, blesskop, Kaptein, good night Charlie," and so it went on till they were all inside. He always smiled in satisfaction; they had grown older together. Some had been replaced, others were old now. He loved them all and as long as he lived, so would they: lovely creatures with their long, spreading horns and intelligent expressions he so well understood. His friend, Sannie's husband, told him that he was always haunted by the faces of the oxen he had fed and fattened to sell to the butchers. "I tell you, Lion," he said, "those boys know they are going to their deaths, I could not stand it, you know. I want to sell them all, and go into the timber business. It's very haunting, those beasts' faces." Lion felt pleased; he never killed, but he did enjoy his lamb. There was no lamb that ever tasted as good as the lamb from the good old zuurveld.

Kathleen took Eden for a walk. "Come skat! You're far too young to have midday naps," she said, "what a waste of time, come let's go and see Canaan's pony." As they came near, there was a terrifying cacophony of neighing and snorting, noises so strange they sounded as though some wild animal had trapped itself inside the exercising ring. There was Lion's stallion and a stray mare, who, lured by the smell of a stallion, had found her way into the farmstead. It was an ordinary Boer mare, a cleverer animal than other horses, stocky and strong. She lifted both hind legs and kicked at the stallion. He approached her, smelled around her tail, raised his head into the lair, showed his long yellow teeth, lips uplifted off the gums, blowing and stomping up the red dust.

The mare was playing hard to get. Teasing him, it seemed. As he smelled her, she'd swing her backside around, kicking and swishing her tail as he bit at her mane. Finally, she stood beside him and he mounted her, clasping her body with his forelegs. He thrust his loins forward, her tail held high to the side, for a few seconds he sank with an ecstatic, painful groan upon her body. At that moment of surrender his huge body looked vulnerable. This creature held still in time, almost a poetic movement, and stood for a few ecstatic moments. Several minutes, and then as if their privacy was suddenly invaded, he lifted his forelegs and body, his eyes white and bulging, his legs dropped with a thud to the earth.

His shaft hung down, still rigid, and his tail whirled in sudden agitation. The terrifying snorting had ceased and his long mane lifted with the breeze against his powerfully set neck. Eden stood still: the smell of sweat, this pure and beautiful animal act of love and passion, caught their nostrils, trembling. Their heartbeats—breathing. They remained silent as they witnessed this fantastic stirring act of creation. Slowly the stallion recovered, lifted his powerful crest and gave a piercing scream of triumph.

Eden and Kathleen said not a word. They were both trembling, stirred by the scene of passion, emotion, excitement! Out of a daydream, Kathleen fell upon him. "Take me, Eden," she said, "take me, like he did. Did you see how tenderly he courted her? How gently? I grew up for you, waited for you. Take me, Eden," and she smothered his face with kisses, over and over, cheeks, chin, eyes and mouth. She kissed him full on the mouth and he held her in his arms and his blood raced through his veins. He kissed her and kissed her, standing as they were together. They were struggling for control. He called her name, "Kathy, Kathy." "No, no, Eden," she said, "I am a woman ready for your love." She held her hands on his shoulders and then held him as though she recovered, she held him at arms length. "Can't you see, Eden," she said, "can't you see that I have always loved you? I will never love anyone but you."

As he looked at her, she looked like the great Kathy I. It was as though Mama Kathy was there; she would have approved for him to love the daughter of Lion, her own namesake! Kathy! It seemed right. They loved each other. Kathleen McCabe and Eden Hora Jacobsen. They suddenly decided—and all the childish contacts seemed preliminary to this moment. They announced their love and as the days passed the talk was of their wedding—February 1885. Petra was very pleased, and immediately started to plan her daughter's wedding. Lion seemed dubious. "You know, Eden," he said, "of course you have my blessing, but it almost feels incestuous. I have always regarded you as a son, my own son." "That makes it very simple then, Lion," Eden said, "because I love you as a father, and now I can safely call you 'Pa,'" he smiled. "I went off to study geology, I've learned all about precious stones, and now, Lion, I have found myself a gem, even though I never knew it when I saw her born. I must find her a beautiful stone for our betrothal. Does it matter that I am older than her?"

Lion built a huge, high-ceilinged ballroom, mainly for his daughter's wedding. Dozens of extra workers were engaged to speed up the progress, for it had to be ready by February. The wedding plans were in full swing. The lawns were cut, the garden spring cleaned, the leathers looked new and the wagons were shining clean, with brass gleaming and wheels oiled. Lion's best team were going to bring the bride and what a show, with bells and brass and ostrich feathers, and a well-dressed footman.

"Ah Whitey," he said, "on Kathy's wedding day you will look like Paul Kruger himself." He pulled at Whitey's long white beard. "And you will wear a big black hat, a tall top hat, exactly like the Baas. You and I will drive the bride, Whitey," he said, hopping about, and his old faithful servant smiled broadly behind his beard, happily holding up his hands, waving his white palms. "And what about a black suit and a white collar?" "You shall have all that, Whitey!" Lion said, "You are very special in our family, and at this wedding of my first born. You shall be the gentleman you are, in a shirt like Cecil Rhodes, and a suit and hat like the Ou Baas! Just like the President!" and they laughed out heartily together.

The day of the wedding came so swiftly that Petra felt she could never have remembered everything. She and Lion were very proud of the large ballroom with its selected beams of stinkwood, and the yellowwood floors that gleamed and shone, polished with Petra's homemade shiner. She mixed beeswax and oil and lemon with herbs to make a scent. They were aromatic herbs that all the Boer women used to scent their homes, passing on their recipes to one another. Orange blossom soap, lemon leaves and paraffin wax, aloes with wattle dyes, and red ochre stain, taken from the pits that the natives use, pig fats, tallow, suet, bluegum leaves, potpourri from the frothy blossoms of spring and the yellow stinkwood leaves that stand against the silver blue eucalyptus.

The entire farm was intoxicated and bustling with excitement. This wedding was never going to be forgotten. It would be attended by people from far and wide, from Capetown to the banks of the Limpopo River, from Delagoa Bay right across to where the Orange River flows into the sea. When Lion McCabe gave a party it was one that would be remembered! And, of course, his party would have an outdoor barbeque—a Braaivleis where even whole oxen could be easily cooked in a pit, and the smell of crisp pork and succulent lamb titillated everyone's appetite. The house was reborn: white and clean, the doors and the brass doorknobs shone in the crimson welter of the early morning sunbeams. The stone columns were wound with palm leaves and ivy and the verandas were filled with flowers. Wooden tubs filled with wine were placed on little stone platforms to keep them cool, and some were put on the backs of the wagons at shoulder level for easy access.

Petra was fussing. Kimberly was Kathleen's bridesmaid, and Canaan was Eden's best man. Lion was to give his daughter away.

Guests started arriving a week before. "Why the whole country, including the frontier is here." The wide circling driveway, beyond the front entrance was filled with carriages, wagons and saddle horses, and shining black grooms were leading the animals to the barns to be unharnessed and unsaddled. The elders were seated in the large drawing room, very prim with fans and young officers in red and gold were bowing and grinning as they took the tall glasses handed to them on trays by the colored servants.

People thronged the polished stoep and the grand hall or ballroom was swarmed with people, young women in crinolines fluttering like blasts of soft color and landing on a small space like butterflies. The babbling of chatter and laughter was deafening, and the giggles and shrieks and screams and squeaks sounded strangely animal-like. The army band, on two wagons, was playing a crescendo of fanfares. When the trumpets started, four black men in knee-length breeches unrolled a long red carpet and from out of the crowd a priest in white lack smock, Bible in hand, stood waiting. Then along came the bridal carriage and behind the bridal carriage was Julius' carriage, bringing the best man and the bridesmaid and Petra and Elizabeth.

Eden was nowhere to be seen at first, but he suddenly emerged from the house. He was a calm, tall man, powerfully built, a man that turned heads and made people stare with admiration, his wide shoulders and muscled neck. Beneath his top hat, his shining golden hair and flashing white teeth were set off by his tanned face. He looked like an aristocrat, a man of blue blood, a quiet, elegant, awe-inspiring Bush aristocrat, confident and sure of himself. He moved up beside the priest and the band played on, with concertinas everywhere and piano, accordions, drums and cymbals, and Lion alighted from beside Whitey, who resembled a smallish Paul Kruger.

Lion opened the carriage door for his daughter as the horses in silvered harnesses jingled bells and ostrich feathers blew in the wind, like waving grasses that frolic, like wild herds, over the yellow ochre veld. It was all so breathtakingly magnificent. Kathy alighted as the vast crowd stood breathless. She was a vision in white silk and delicate sparkling translucent voile. Her long hair tumbled about her slim body and her slim hands rested on Lion's arm. She was followed by William Maxwell, then Elizabeth, Canaan and Petra, Julius and finally Marta in her voortrekker dress. Carried on a silken cushion was the ring. They all walked the full length of the red Eastern carpet, towards the priest through a sea of faces, which parted like a river in Jordan in the bible story, now beside the red carpet upon which they tread. Two African Chiefs attended in resplendent feathers, leopard skins, beads, bare feet rattling the bangles on their ankles. Absolute Africa—regal and royal!

The service was very brief. Lion gave his daughter to Eden, and the wedding went on and what a splendid wedding it was. It went on until the day was dazzled into obscurity by the crimson wake of the setting sun, losing its heat, dissolved and ebbed into a faint evening chill.

Eden and Kathy left in their carriage. The dancing was still full of life, the ballroom filled with brightly colored hooped dresses, some with lace petticoats peeping beneath. Shoulders bare and lace shawls, peacock-feathered fans, velvet and ear bobs that swung as they danced to the tireless Boer museek midst the smell of tea rose, and Cape jasmine garlands. There were many uniforms, resplendent British uniforms, with golden braid and shining buttons. Sabers glittered and gleamed, spurs jangled and deep-to-shrill voices laughed and sang in merriment, in English, Dutch, Welsh, and Scotch. Dozens of black warriors, resplendent in half naked African skins and feathers, wound their grinning ways, bowing, saluting and shaking hands among the crowds. Dressed in 3/4 white Indian-style outfits and scarlet fez were new Indian visitors in manner most gracious.

Congratulations, speeches, toasts made Lion a happier man. He was sure of one thing. Like should marry like, similar envions and background help create and make for happiness. Into the small hours when the dew dulled the embers and the servants still feasted on the cindered carcasses. The wagons, cape carts, buggies and carriages pounding of the horses hooves, ground and scattered the gravel with steel rims as they departed down the curved and winding drive. The floors were covered in flowers and rose petals. Here and there a piece of braid, some feathers. The ground was well trodden, flat, and the empty vessels only smelled of wine.

Thirty - Five

Bright and beautiful, Kimberly, Lion's second daughter, was a charmer, better looking and more lovely than his first girl, named after a diamond, all things being equal. She was also a clever creature, who loved fun and to write poetry. She adored her brother. She was a soft warm and lovely girl, full of human kindness and compassion, always singing quite roughly, barefoot, quick, rather a tomboy. In childhood, up in the trees with her brother in a little tree-house, they lived in a world of childhood fantasy. Such happy days! She told fairy stories and recited poems. She was seventeen and beautiful bud of early womanhood, then quite suddenly, she became aware of herself. All men notice beautiful women, especially young ones; within a few months a strikingly handsome financier met, and fell in love with her. Again Leeukraal (Lindnkeep/Kraal) went into the whole wedding. It rang with wedding bells. She had a beautiful wedding, almost the same as Kathy and Eden's. Perhaps a first wedding has the extra intoxication of firstness, the second, well, it's as though it has happened before, done before. Nevertheless it was happy, fun-filled and unforgettable. Kimberly and her capitalist financier rode off in their star-studded carriage to conquer all, aided of course by the gold law of the Transvaal, which helped with capital in the purchase of farms and claims. His name was Thomas Sandycroft, and his father made machinery and sold crushing mills made in England. He was a bright and alert young man, very English, rather a little sarcastic towards the Boers at times, which raised eyebrows and nice little tempers in Lion's home.

Lion and Petra were alone now with Canaan, youthful, neither child or man. It was difficult to know how they felt about their second son-in-law. They never expressed an opinion nor showed any resentment, yet one had the felling they were all too reserved about expressing their private feelings.

Kathy and Eden had come home for the wedding. Kathy was thrilled for Kimberly, and they all were happy to be part and parcel of this a handsome family. Canaan was wrestling with the trials of adolescence, hairs were growing on his upper lip. He had grown five inches since Kathy's wedding.

Kathy was pale, she seemed listless and without appetite. In the morning, Petra saw that she was nauseous. She sat on her bed with a chamber pot beside her.

"Kathy my kind," said Petra hesitantly, "you are pregnant, my love. Are you pregnant Kathy?" she asked.

"How do I know, Mamma?" said Kathy, and it dawned on Petra that she had never really discussed these things with her girls. The Boer people, they are very prudish about such personal things.

"No ja, my liefling (darling)," she said, "we must visit the physician, and we must see him as soon as we can."

That night she told Lion.

"My God Petra, have you never told your girls about all these woman's things?" he asked.

"It's not that easy, Lion," she said, "I'm not a person who can openly talk about these private things. You know I'm a very private person."

"What is private between the teachings of a mother and her child? Petra for God's sake woman, have you not outgrown that narrow way of thinking?" He sat down on the hassock at the foot of her chair and looked at her. Her face seemed florid and agitated.

"Lion, ag (oh) Lion, it's not necessary for a woman to tell another woman the processes of nature. I could see in Kathy's eyes the adoration, the wild happiness and tenderness of a grown woman which swept her very being like a flame, like a fierce wildfire into thoughtlessness, fanned by a south east wind to fan it. That's how love must consume a woman, and no one needs to teach."

He looked up at her pleading brown eyes, and he said no more.

The doctor confirmed Kathy was pregnant, and Lion and Petra felt a quiet joy.

"We are lucky, my skat," Petra told him, "Some of us will have our 'hereafter' like the Hebrew Bible says, our grandchildren! That's what the Bible means, by having a 'hereafter.' We are blessed really." And she smiled a contented happy smile.

In the middle of June Kathy gave birth to a beautiful blonde daughter. Eden was beside himself with joy and rushed about holding his hands above his head singing,

"I've got a little baby, her name is Katherine."

He had a wonderful party pouring wine over Lion's head.

"Lion, Dad, you must drink and be merry, you are a grand-father. Lion, the great man himself, you are a grandfather and your grandchild's name is Katherine Luisa the 3rd. This Kathy, Kathy the 3rd, brings us full circle." They looked at each other. "Katherine Luisa, the Luisa part is my mother's name." They both knew they could never forget her. Eden poured a mug of wine and then poured it on Lion's head, and for the first time he noticed how grey the great Lion's mane had grown; and thinner perhaps, like the fringe of an old horse's mane. In his heart suddenly, he felt a pang. *My God*, he laughed, *while I've been so busy how time had sped.* It was hard to think of the world, without Lion! He swallowed his morbid thought, and putting his arms about Lion he hugged him. "We are lucky to have each other hey? Shared lives?" "We have known closeness, Eden. If anything we are closer now," said Lion, "We have shared every secret and every new spring of growth, life has to offer. We have had fun too, lots of fun and daring adventure."

They clung to each other in a grip of love, of gratitude, an unspoken bond, unbreakable, except by death. A man's love! Yes, man love!

At about this time, young Canaan also got this feeling that he must make money. He felt he was a man now. He could ride and shoot; he could handle a carriage with a six-horse team almost as good as his father and better than his uncle Julius. He was not academically inclined; he hated Latin, disliked learning and his progress was not as good as his sisters. Petra tired so hard,

"It is very important for a man," she told him, "a woman can get married, easier and if she's good looking, one of the lucky ones, she can marry a man who can keep her well, and father her children. But a man has to support a wife and family. Ya a man is the breadwinner, Canaan, he must have education and knowledge. He has the responsibility of being the head of the house." She touched his hand, "Canaan you are so precious to me, I just want the best for you."

Canaan stood up.

"Mama," he said, "that's what I also want for you. I love you too Ma, you are so beautiful and so caring," he kissed her on the side of her face, and he got up and walked out down towards the stables. She put her hand on her cheek where his soft young lips had touched.

She couldn't understand herself why she loved this boy so deeply. Perhaps it was because of how he loved her. When he was a small child, brought her little bunches of wildflowers, how sweet it was. He worried himself into a state when she developed a cough, and pulled the burrs from her clothes when they walked together. He rode beside her like a man when he was only nine years old, a little man companion, warning her when he saw a hole or a low slung branch in the woods. No, this child was so special! Her son did something to her, she felt a fierce ache of love when she saw him return each day from school, or from a holiday. They were as close as Lion and Eden. She understood the feeling, she knew it well. She never felt the fire, that burning love, from Lion, there was no fire or passion. She loved Lion more than he loved her, and she knew that had Louisa not died, Lion would have followed Louisa to the ends of the earth to love her. It was as if Canaan was her very own; the intense fire that Lion lacked she felt for her son. She had made for herself a man of her own, from her very own womb had come this gentle sensitive child with his soft smile and a quiet forceful manner. She knew no one would break him once he made up his mind, nothing nor any person would change his attitude. Her father was like that; that is a trait of the Boers.

And so the day came that Canaan told his father he no longer wished to learn and he did not want to go to London to a university. He wanted to join his brother-in-law Eden. Eden had told him if ever he wanted to mine he must join him. Well he was going to make money and the sooner he started the better.

"But what about this farm, Canaan?" He bravely stated to Lion that he wanted to earn his living. His own living. "I had hoped you would take it over one day. Your dad is getting on now and I always felt you loved this land like I do. One's soul is part of the earth and soil around you, that one has grown upon, and to lose it is like a death in the family."

Canaan looked at his father,

"I love it here, Dad. I feel," and he paused to think, "I feel that the definition of heaven changes with the years for me. This place you have made, that's heaven, to me it's heaven, but I must spread my wings like people say, and fly from the nest like all fledglings do. My call to go is early perhaps, but it has come, and I must savor this urge to live my own life for a while. I will return."

So Canaan went to work with Eden, and Kathy was only too happy to have her brother in her home working together with her husband.

Kathy came home to Mamma to have her second child. After the birth, and it was not an easy birth, Kathy remained in Leeukraal for a while. Eden had found a new vein of gold, a thick vein that led down to the very core of the earth. He was glad to have Canaan to whom he gave the elevated position of advisor mine manager. After only verbal training, so young. He knew of course his youth but Canaan, trustworthy, bright, reliable, and loved, had made very swift progress. How often he looked at the white ridge, an odd strange dusty red-clouded sand dune, with layers of washed sand forming dunes full of ridges blown by the winds. The canteens were shabby and filled with a motley crowds of human rubble; there were newly erected general stores, storekeepers, traders and vendors, rugged transport riders, drunks, loafers, gamblers and losers, soldiers, Boers and a few toffee-nosed Toffs, they were named, who loomed through all this scum as self-styled aristocracy.

To this place Canaan had come but he soon understood why. He was in the right place for buying claims and dealing in the new stock market of Johannesburg. He was among the incoming new capitalists; capital accumulation had taken place, and soon he too was among men financially strong enough to swallow up a lot of small fry.

Kathy and Eden named their second child Godfrey. This one was dark haired and brown eyed. It took Kathy quite a while to get over the birth. She didn't enjoy her second pregnancy nor her maternal role, nor the midwives and doctors who attended her. She was so glad she had her mother with her. Petra nursed and bathed the child singing and cooing as though it was her own. Kathy stayed on a Leeukraal and extended her stay while Eden and Canaan floated a new estate, The Canaan Estates Gold Mining Company. Out of a total of two million 1 pound shares, 1½ million were 'vendors' interest'; all the shares were snapped up and soon began to rise. Canaan, like Eden as a very young man, had quickly made a vast amount of money. It seemed easy, close to Eden.

A couple of men called the Albu brothers bought a derelict mine, but this venture turned out to be a fantastic financial success. This gold reef city was certainly the place for a young entrepreneur to be. Eden enjoyed having the youth and freshness, exuberance, and enthusiasm that was Canaan's, and he arranged for Canaan to do all the managerial administration work on the mine to enable Eden to go with his carriage for Kathy. He felt he was quite able to leave it all to Canaan. As young as he was, Canaan always kept in contact with his mother. He had bought his mother a ring set with three diamonds of three different shades—yesterday, today, and tomorrow he called it—and he gave it to Eden to give it to her. He had spared neither patience nor cash to find them.

My future here seems limitless Ma, he wrote, *but I do miss you so.*

Eden was to leave with his carriage laden, as he had all sorts of things to take back to Sonnestroom and Leukraal. He left his maids behind, but his footman, coachman, and manservant all prepared to leave with him. He felt tired, and felt so happy and fortunate to have his brother-in-law to help him.

All set and about to go when suddenly a runner burst into his house.

"Come quickly, sir, come master come quickly! Quick masser, Canaan is hurt!"

There was no time to take the carriage. He sprang onto a horse and galloped over to the mine.

"Where is he?" he said, "for God's sake, where is he?"

And a group of miners and diggers stood above the mine entrance.

"He was going in the car, sir, he was going down to the guts of the mine, and the hawser snapped, sir. He's down there."

"Oh God almighty," said Eden.

It took more than a little while until they got him out of the mines. The doctor and nurses were there, but Canaan had died instantly. His neck had been clean broken. Someone came with a bottle of brandy and took Eden's hand and placed the bottle in his hand.

"Drink it, man," said a man with a Scots accent.

It was a non-stop ride. When Eden brought Canaan's body home to Lion, Petra stood there.

She whimpered a sad whine. "No," she said, "no it can't be. It can't be. This is not true. Lion tell me, tell me Lion." And then she

felt Lion's hands on her shoulder and around her and she screamed
and screamed and screamed. The doctor came and treated her but
she was totally out of the world uncontrollable. She called on God,
she admonished God. She said, "you can take me, or anything else,
but never my Canaan, my innocent good good Canaan. He's so
good, so good," then she stopped. "Canaan," she said, "I'm coming
with you. Canaan my beautiful boy, no one understands you like
your Mamma. Come to Mamma my boy. No, Canaan, you can't go
away." She started to be hysterical and Lion and Eden took a hold
of her. There was nothing they could do except watch Petra's life
squeezed out of her body like one wrings a wet towel.

"Bring the brandy."

"No," said the doctor, and he poured her a small amount of dark
liquid. She threw the medicine from her, sending the little phial
spinning across the floor where Canaan lay.

There was her Canaan, limp on a thin layer of canvas used
as a stretcher sewn across a wooden frame. His face was still and
smiling, his lips closed. His hair shone with the glow of youth and
his slim young hands were childishly fresh. He was hardly a man.
He was only a youth, a young man full of love and dreams, kindness
and compassion. Canaan would never grow old, life was denied
him, he had not lived even one score. His shaving years had hardly
begun and the fine growth of hairs of which he was so proud were
there on his upper lip. Petra kept screaming, her eyes fixed upon
her child. It was horror to witness.

"This is my boy, my Canaan. Eden you took my boy away, he
was so happy, Eden. Oh God I hate what you let happen. He'd
give mercy and life to an injured frog, you call a pestilence, but
you let the life of Canaan cease for no good reason. You let the
world be robbed of a good pure angel-like boy who does nothing

but good." She screamed and screamed. She fell down. Her body bent like a willow over the slim body of her son. She screamed out loud, "Canaan, Canaan my own precious Canaan, my deurbare liefling (beloved darling)" and she exhausted herself till it dwindled down to a painful whimper. Her eyes did not look normal, and when Eden picked her up and carried her to her bedroom, the doctor followed.

Lion put the bedsheet over his son, picked him up and carried him to his bedroom. He laid Canaan on his bed and covered him again. He drew up the riempie chair with cushions and stumblingly slumped into it.

"Just leave me Eden. For this night I must stay with my son, maybe his soul is not far away."

And the servants all staring and silent walked in and out wringing their hands. No one could speak. They all looked at Eden. He felt surrounded and was almost afraid. For it seemed they all looked at him accusingly. He thought "For Christ's sake," he said in a tremulous half emotional rage/weep, "it was a terrible, terrible accident," he held out his hands in despair, "a terrible, terrible accident," he repeated. His head fell upon his arms on the table. He felt lost. He breathed deeply, dredged out aches, sobbed, but all he saw in his mind's eye was that large glorified bucket they called a car, and that young eager virgin boy, Petra's precious son, crashing to his untimely, tragic death. He put his hands into his breast pocket to get a handkerchief and he found the letter from Canaan in which was the gift he had selected for his mother. He wondered what Canaan thought as he crashed through the air. He would wait for a better moment to give it to Petra. But for now, he was drained. The mine and all its gold had lost its charms, gone was the glitter, the claims, the whole damned thing, the whole reckless

God damned business. The good die young. He heard those words ringing in his head.

He fell into a depression. His wife fell ill with grief. As soon as he could he would sell it all. He crept into Kathy's room. He crept into her bed beside her. She had sobbed so the pillows were wet; he touched her heaving body. My God, they all made him feel guilty. A bottle of brandy stood on the small round table and he took the bottle and drank it to the last drops. He was alone and drowning in a deep sea of grief from which there seemed no escape. Outside all the dogs were howling, but there was no moon or distant echoes. Petra always said the dogs knew when death lurked.

What good is tomorrow, so filled with sorrow

Petra never recovered from the death of Canaan. She became mentally disturbed. Lion spent hours struggling to help her. He too had aged; everything at Leeukraal no longer seemed the same anymore. Also Kimberly was expecting child, but Petra seemed disinterested. She was always in her cape cart and driving down to the family cemetery at Sonnestroom where the kopje sheltered all those people who once lived, loved, and died. Priceless people, like her Canaan, now only a name on a granite slab of stone. Her beloved, he was no more! Canaan, who loved flowers; he brought little bunches of wildflowers in little fingers that placed them in hers with such love. Compelled and drawn by the grief of her loss, she would summon the horses to be harnessed and she'd go in her cape cart down to the cemetery before the sun rose. She'd set off then come back when day died, tired, wan, and drained.

Eden returned to Sonnestroom with Kathy and their two little children. There was comfort in knowing they were not too far away. Lion always had dependable trained horses. Often Elizabeth called, she was a very busy lady teaching little children, and taught mainly black children. She had started a little school on her farm. Julius was traveling a great deal and was involved in ships and shipping wool, which took him away to Port Elizabeth and every so often the Cape of Good Hope. He was totally disinterested in Elizabeth's life.

Some months had passed, and Eden had not yet given Canaan's letter and gift to his mother. He felt afraid of another hysterical destructive upset. As time passed he had hoped Petra would gradually accept the death of her only son, and adjust to life. Perhaps she was, he did not know, she was not prepared to even try and communicate with anyone. Lion eventually solved the problem.

"No, Eden, it's better to let it all happen now. Give her our boy's letter, they were so close. Eden, sometimes I thought it was unnatural, her love for Canaan. It was obsessive."

In the morning Eden tapped on Petra's door, but there was no answer. He tapped harder, and slowly opened the door. Petra was sitting in the window. It was a large old window that looked over the hills out onto the vlei on one side.

"Petra," he almost whispered, "It is Eden."

She slowly turned her head.

"Yes, my boy," she said, "come in." She sounded calm and almost normal. He put his arms about her.

"Ma," he said, "if I could only take your pain, I would do so gladly. What can we do? What is there to do?"

"I am not blaming you, Eden. Of course yes, it was your mine, but it was not you. I know you from a little boy. This tragedy is between God and I. I begged God each day and night and every hour, each time my son crossed the yellow veld to school: I will do all you ask dear Vader, I told him, only protect my son and keep him safe. You are the almighty. I always prayed, and I had faith, but now I see there is no God. No God could hurt a person so much, or crush a heart and such a soul into pulp, or to let so beautiful a human, perish in the dust and dirt of a goddamn mine. I will never be free of pain, Eden, never, and I have only memories left of my beloved boy. It is so empty." She bowed her head in absolute sorrw. She cried again, soft whispering cries, her lips trembling, totally helpless, bereft, and so very full of pain. She whispered, constant whispers. "I know now that religion is a myth. A total myth!" The weightless air felt strangely heavy.

"Ma, here, Ma," Eden said, "Canaan asked me to personally deliver this letter to you. This gift was bought from his first earnings. He was so very proud." His voice got tremulous. This is heavy grief, he had trouble stretching his arms. Words do not mean enough and pain is deep, very deep.

She took the letter in wet trembling hands. Her eyes were swollen and looked small. She tore the letter open with one finger, lest she should damage something, she felt was precious coming from Canaan. The ring fell onto the windowsill. She read the note.

"Eden, oh Eden, read to me, what does he say?"

And Eden read the note. She couldn't see through her tear-filled eyes, but the sun was rising, and a pink haze lighted the sky. Some clouds lay across the eastern horizon and a circle of bright silver and pink escaped like a lady's petticoat from behind the cloud. The light shone onto her ring.

"Yesterday, Today, and Tomorrow," she repeated, "Oh Christ, how lovely. Just so beautiful, just as beautiful as he was. Look Eden, he even knew the size of my fingers. Yesterday is the darkest one. Today is the pinkish one, and Tomorrow is the clearest blue white." Tears flowed, blinding out of control freely down over her face. A little river in a constant misery fall. "I now have some contact with my Canaan." She whispered, "Isn't it just like him to do this?" And she put her arms around Eden and she held onto him. "You must all forgive me, I know I am not well and I don't know how to handle this cruel terrible pain. Death is not so bad, I'm sure, Eden. Death must surely be less painful than this agony that's wrapped itself like a python around my body, squeezing out life, that is, myself. I will always suffer, Eden. How can one measure the years, the days, the hours, Eden? I only now realize the depth of love, only one love. How deep it ravages. Lion is so brave. He has suffered. He loved your mother Eden, and he watched her die while you were being born. Perhaps he also still has a pain like this. Ja-nee (yes-no) your grandmother once told me that just before your mother died, she screamed out 'Lion, you are better than God. This here our God is spiteful and without mercy,' and little Louisa died thinking that, Eden. That is now me. I love that man Lion, who is the father of your wife, our children. He once so loved a lion, so he has had double the pain I have had." She went silent, her face shone wet. She almost whispered, again "Yesterday, Today, and Tomorrow," she repeated softly, "Ja, my liefde (darling). And forever, and ever, and ever," she whispered as she hugged the ring to her heart with both wet hands. "Yesterday, today, and tomorrow, and for all eternity." She was looking at the skies, the tears stuck in her lashes, "like the sun, always will rise, today and tomorrow, and for always. For ever my liewe seuntjie (darling little son)."

The door closed softly as Eden left her, so miserable looking at the window and murmuring to her inner self. Petra had discarded her belief in God—almighty meant all good, all powerful—not cruel! Of this she was certain.

Eden, deeply affected by the great sorrow and grief over the death of Canaan. It left a flatness, naked and empty, like the wake of an earthquake, lifeless. It certainly took its toll. He seemed to lose interest in his gold mine. He was listless and fractious and too often impatient and intolerant. It was as if he was being constantly gnawed at, somewhere unreachable, deep within the labyrinthine channels of his mind. He himself could not retch it or understand it. Often he began to wonder whether he was losing his normal mind. It was affecting his thoughts!

He kept thinking of something he read once in his grandmother Kathy's diary.

This land, she wrote, *takes people. It's rich and wild. It gives and it takes, and it takes so many humans I wonder if perhaps it's a trifle odd. Across the Limpopo, towards the East is an African area—creepy this part of the land is named "Nyanga"—meaning the mists that take people. It is said that many people have disappeared in those mists of Nyanga.*

He kept thinking of those words, and then again when Canaan lay on his bed, cold, white, and silent, and Lion sat on the riempie chair, beside him all through the night. He talked in between his weeping.

"Eden," Lion said, "this is a strange country. It swallows many people, I've seen so many people disappear and die, and it's hard to see people die, it's so final and so truly, an end. Now it's the end of my only son. So pure…look at his face, Eden, full of goodness and innocence. He was a quiet boy, you know, always playing with butterflies and flowers and little mud cakes. He was a peaceful boy, devoted to his mother. I tried to teach him to shoot and ride, but he was gentle. He did not want a gun. He was warm, like a ray of sunshine on a cold day. He touched warm, and soft." And Lion wept, leaning forward his elbows on his knees and his head in his large rugged hands. "Only good was this boy. So tender. Not destructive!"

The strange thing he kept repeating. He was touching the young body, he picked up his hand. "This land takes people, my boy, and it has taken you. Yet you smile in death, might be that you are happy."

Eden kept remembering those words, he found them difficult to dispel.

He hoped, as time passed, his own depression would lift and he would become emotionally stable and physically strong again. Not burdened by this constant weight of impending decrepitude.

1821, Goldmining by the Transvaal

Thirty - Six

In July, Cecil John Rhodes became Prime Minister of the Cape Colony, and he seemingly enjoyed the Afrikaner bond support. J. Porges & Co. who had bought Eden's gold interests also returned and was succeeded by a partnership, Wernher Beit & Co. The weak fell at this time only to be absorbed by the almighty rich, who were able to afford the technical know-how of several imported American engineers. The development of Johannesburg's deep levels took place, Jonkers Deep, Village Deep, some of which were destined to become among the most famous mines of Johannesburg. Outlanders poured into the golden city and thousands of black miners rushed in and sought work in the mines. But there was fear these outlanders would soon outnumber the Boers. The Corner House, the godfather of the gold and diamond business with a division of spoils, spread unequally between London and Johannesburg, was the group to work for; the group way up at the top. The Rand Mines Ltd., a link with the Corner House, was Beit's cousin, and considered then the power behind the throne in Pretoria. He was Edward Lippert. He was also one of the losers in the crash of 1889, but he bounced back in this land of endless promise and unlimited gold, a devious obstreperous ruthless Lippert. He built one of the first mansions on the Rand and called it Sachenwald. Perhaps one good thing he did was to plant trees, even if most of them were used as mine props.

At this time also the Chamber of Mines was founded, and some of the questions that preoccupied this chamber were the dynamite monopoly, the railways, food supply, and native labour. One of their problems was that "the supply of Kaffirs for labour was inadequate." Wages also were in dispute, 63 shillings was considered too high a wage for labour and salaries were reduced to 40 shillings a month.

In the meantime railways were being constructed everywhere. A concession to build the railways had been granted to the Netherlands Railway Co. in 1884 and this company owned the Transvaal end of each of the lines from the coast.

Lands were continually being absorbed by Rhodes: Bechuanaland, Barotseleand, 200,000 square miles were purchased for two thousand pounds a year. Rhodes was prepared to sacrifice small, as long as he could achieve big. He was a many-faceted character, but the paramount trait that stood out above all else was his big thinking. He believed in the great. Big deals. The superior human, the elite, aristocrat above peasants; and his vast money was only a means to an end to achieve conquest and dictatorial overriding power. With his wealth he had power, as well as a devoted following. He had limitless credit. He had an Empire behind him and a close friendship with the English Queen. He was imperialist through and through.

Rhodes' dream was his triumphant trampling down of all and everything across South Africa onward towards the North. In 1890 the Pioneer Column pitched camp in what became Salisbury, and Rhodesia was born. Rhodes pursued his deluded dreams—political power in one hand and economic power in the other. He hoped for a Federation to be dominated by himself, but blocking his way in granite obstinacy and somber simplicity was Paul Kruger, Commandant-General of the Transvaal. The OFS of 1865, the zoutspansberg 1876, and now the political influence: the Kruger of the 90s in top hat, black suit, big Dutch pipe, hiding behind a scrappy fringe of grey beard. He was large, ominous, brooding, awkward, broad of shoulder, protruding lower lip, and pendulous lidded eyes, tyrannous in command. "Wees getrou maar vertran" remained in thunderous reliability. Nervous of educated men, never diplomatic, unable to quibble, of puritan faith, ill mannered, a nationalist and a die-hard. But he thought foundations and entire policy design rested upon the most respectable and venerable of traditions. Not lacking in shrewdness, his desires differed little from those of the imperialist counterpart, to whom it mattered little how he obtained control.

In Johannesburg, typhoid broke out and there developed a shortage of provisions. Workmen blew up the home of a mining manager. Dr. Sauer disclosed startling accusations implicating speculations of who went to England. Pretoria protested against the introduction of Arab labour by the imperial government and Rhodes met Kruger. The *Spectator* in England was asking if there was to be other wars in South Africa, and Rhodes' dream was deflated by failure to strike golden reefs in the north.

The Boers defending their "laager"

Thirty - Seven

Lion and Petra were grandparents to only three children. Kathy had two, one boy and one girl, and Kimberly one. Kimberly seldom came home, her life was among those of the new financial magnates. She was now planning to go to London to attend the "Cape Court." Her home was in Johannesburg in a new residential area called Parktown, which was being developed by a firm of which her husband had now become a director. Kathy was different. Kathy was devoted to her old home and her parents and though she and Eden now lived at Sonnestroom, they also traveled and kept a great interest in the golden city's future.

Elizabeth, Julius' wife, was devoted to teaching and had taken into her home, against the wishes of her husband, a small coloured orphan girl. Upon this child she seemed to give all the love she could not give to her husband. The child was the cause of continual irritation to Julius, who spent less and less time at his beautiful home and went more and more to the Cape.

Though she tried very hard to be a mother to her two girls, Petra failed as a wife to Lion. She became cool and distant, never ill-mannered, never disrespectful, but there was no contact, either bodily or mental. She lived in a world of her own, often spending weeks away at Sonnestroom with Kathy. She looked after Canaan's grave, her diamonds flashing in the sunlight as she tidied the weeds and touched and fiddled, pulling up imaginary weeds as though she was putting the finishing touches to some work of art. She was dutiful, Lion always had a good table. Her home was immaculate, and one day she moved out of Lion's bedroom into another room, filling it with growing plants and watering them, talking to them like children.

Lion was still a strong, broad-shouldered, handsome man, attractive, gregarious, and charming, so it was not surprising that he took notice of other interests. And new interest he found in the form of an English widow, still in her early 30s, a woman of seditious cunning whose husband had been shot in the back during a skirmish, accidentally, by one of his own battalion. Her husband, she said, was riding jauntily across the wild at the head of his staff when Boers opened fire on the troops. One ball hit him in the back and another cut through his stirrup leather and blew away part of his shin. It was actually the shot in his back that killed him, though. She had told Lion and put on a facial expression of deep sorrow.

Henrietta Brownlee was sly and stupid, but she was fun! It mattered not to her that a man had a wife and family. She was alone in Africa, living in a small shanty house. She knew too much of everyone's lives about her. She knew that men want women. Often even if they're married they don't get enough and go to tarts and even pay for them, but the one she had her eye on was different. He was a gentleman who lived in a mansion of a home, had servants and horses fit for a king, and a wife who was careless enough not to love him. She actually arranged a meeting with Lion and it just happened to be when Petra was away on one of her trips down to the Kopje, as she referred to it.

The meeting was a military occasion, and Lion had been asked to bring his team and demonstrated the working of his black horses in their silver harnesses. There were several officers wives, and quite a few adventuresses. She was one of these and she was going to prey on this handsome older man whom she knew to be among the men who were women-starved. Everywhere she looked were khaki clad soldiers and well-decorated officers, and then her eyes fell on Lion. The officers seemed aware of her plans; she was a good looking woman, dainty in stature, with small feet and hands. And women who have nothing know full well the charm that millionaires exude. She took him to the card room, she played, and she played her cards well. She excited Lion and she openly flattered him. She created a picture of herself of unsullied virtue, of caring, and she was careful to plant the seeds of anticipation. She was used to men in the cavalry, she talked of horses and openly invited him to call upon her. It happens!

It took a lot of thought, but Lion was excited by this cunning little woman. Like a pendulum his emotions swung to and fro till finally that powerful desire of body contact descended like a volition. So what if she bled him to death? For the moment it was wonderful, like submission to a glorious wine.

He did not relish this cheat. It stilled his desires, he did not feel guilty of doing anything particularly wrong in sleeping with another woman…but somewhere there was something about Henrietta he did not like. He was accustomed to wonderful women. Something false, totally selfish, seemed to vibrate through her soft clinging body she understood how to use very well. She understood men and understood their needs. She was younger and he was old. There was no love in it at all, just a bodily function of pleasure. Lion wondered if she enjoyed his body, which he scrupulously cared for, especially before his visits. Old people are different to the young, he knew that, but he did not feel enslaved by this pure animal desire. It made him feel a young man again, that life's core was still there, alive within him.

He wondered what he would do. He had always been truthful. So he would simply tell this woman he did not wish to continue. He thought of what an old farmer told him, when a rumor arose at school in the Cape. A teacher in her 42nd year of age had an affair with a young school boy—or so the rumor went; and the old Boer told Lion in Dutch; "Jy weet nooit hoe in Kooi n haas vang." Which means, "You never ever know how a cow can catch a hare." Well, it was amusing, but he would do the direct approach. He did not like his new behavior. It was not in his character, and so, forgiving himself his trespasses, he ended the relationship forthwith.

In May, responsible government was introduced in Natal. In July came war against Lobengula, Bulawago was taken, and on September 25th the British annexed Pondoland connecting the Cape Colony with Natal. In November, Rhodes met Kruger to try and amalgamate the customs union and in 1895 the land in the North was named Rhodesia after Rhodes. (It is presently Zimbabwe.)

The steam train chugged puffing up its smoke on its way around the edge of the rolling green hills. The hills looked like velvet when one was moving. They glided past, nothing stood still, hills after hills, light green and then dark in the ravines where the tall trees grew and the waters ran at the foothills. Mysterious and silent. In the open spaces were cattle herds and large flocks of merino sheep.

Eden looked out of the window. There on the road were little clouds of red dust with horses and carts. And how often had they all ridden across these roads, these roads of their lives, he thought, passing the little farms belonging to people he knew and people who knew him.

But things had all changed. He was going to war. He was going to fight against the English, many of them friends. He was fighting for his land, fighting on the side of the Boers. It was a strange feeling. He did not want to fight, and he was still not sure where to fight. But all the Burghers expected him to be, to do, to advise, to lead. They felt he was, one of them, one of the men of "OnsLand." A great brain, a great rider, an unbelievable spy, a wise and cunning, invincable leader!

Kathy opened a basket of food, giving each one of them a hand-embroidered serviette. Then cut up a roast chicken and served them. She was nervous and jittery but she put on a brave face. Godfrey ate nothing. He watched his father eating. When his father turned away he put his chicken leg on his father's platter.

The train steamed on, an hour passed, and conversation seemed stiff and unwarranted. The children had a sense of fear. Finally the train got to River Station. Eden was quiet, said goodbye to his family and told them he would be returning home on the train in two or three days. Kathy and the children had to now change trains and return home. After all, they were on the train to be with their Pappa, and to enjoy a ride on the train.

On the journey back, Kathy tried to make happy conversation, but there was fear in her heart. She was going to be somewhere in a war, but Eden said she and the children would be safe at Sonnestroom. He wanted to send Kimberly home, as she would be in the war area. There was much to do in two or three days, and then he would return home and join his commando unit.

All the way back through every station, at every dorp (little town), Kathy saw the men gathering. Sons and fathers, grandfathers and boys, groups of young burghers, riding on their own horses, without uniforms and carrying their own guns, all forming into groups, the commandos.

What is to happen, she wondered. Everywhere men were riding away, some grimfaced, some smiling, all heading towards the commando assembly points, riding over the wild onto tracks and roads. They were burgher men, Boers, fighting for their land. This was their land and they were preparing for its defense.

But Kathy didn't understand war. She was a child so protected, so loved and cared for, she did not know the fears of her parents, they who had faced this danger. She listened to goodbyes at the stations, the winging, watching and flags flying. Children seemed excited by this thing they called war. Whitey was waiting at the station with four horses. Lion always sent Whitey rather than Eden's own coachmen on important missions. She looked at him sitting up on the carriage. My God, while she was growing up how old Whitey had grown. He was white all over now, like an old dog all white and whiskered and watery eyed. How wonderful he looked on her wedding day. She came nearer and his fever-bright eyes with baggy circles beneath, lit up.

"Masser Lion said to fetch you right off the train, Mizz Kathy." He was very well cared for and was family now. "I ken take yer to the house quick sharp."

They didn't have much luggage and he called to the other coachmen to pack it away. Kathy sat the children up first and leaped in. Whitey gave the lead horses a jerk and a call and they sprang forward with a start.

The children were chatty and laughing, but Kathy was silent. Wasn't it so strange? So many Boers wives had told her how they stayed home and looked after their farms and livestock when their

men fought the English in '80. Some of their husbands never
came back. How brave they were to have faced the Kaffir raids
and survived their dangers and fears. She thought of all this and
wondered if she would ever survive a raid of assegais or stock theft.
She looked over the veld from the road, the trees, the wild veld, the
krantzes that jutted out of the Kopjes, the aloes stretching out like
little red tongues. This also was her land. This was where Eden and
Lion grew up into men. Where Jules and Lady Kathy, and all the
people who built homes, lived and died, and then their children lived
in them with the workers. Were they all going to war? Or would they
stay and help her on the farm? There was a railway line now, and on
the sides of the line all day she saw soldiers in little camps and tents
dotted across the veld. There were one or two laagers and one with
a flag flying half-hearted because of the slight breeze.

She wished Eden was home already, and she longed for the
sweet comfort of her parents, and the safe security of her home.
It was so strange, this feeling; she could never feel free and independent. At the slightest discord, disharmony, or fear, her fight
thoughts were for her home, her mama and pappa. They were
always so strong and protective and she felt so secure on the long
rolling green stretches of lawns of home under the big trees with
her dogs and horses and the chickens, scratching and pecking like
a purring cat, as they happily picked their way freely everywhere.
And Ma's pet birds and the feisty little bantams who seemed well
respected in the old chicken hok, with the rusty wire on the door.
She used to love to collect the eggs, sometimes still warm from
the hen's body.

They passed Moorplaats' beautiful dwelling. Eden had a
manager in there, well he was not too far from Sonnestroom, but
she wished Leeukraal were not so far. It was thirty miles north

towards the town called Tarkastad. The nearest town to Sonnestroom was Cradoek, a goodly distance by horse and trap, however.

True to his word, Eden came back in two days.

"No Kathy, my darling," he said, "I have definitely decided. I
must go to war if it's war. I do not want to join another commando.
Where Lion goes, I go, he will come with me."

"But my father is an old man, Eden."

"Not if you look at him, no one would know he was a grandfather.
Lion is powerful. He can handle horses like a boy in his 20s. He is a
fantastic leader. Such a great leader. All the Boer leaders look to Lion."

"It's wrong, Eden. He must not go, really."

'He can ride, woman. He knows how to ride right beneath the
very noses of the English enemy. Only he can do that. He's only
afraid the commandos will take his precious blood horses, he says
he'll take them and go himself. Even if he has to take a wagon to
war—Jesus to war in a wagon."

"That's the real reason, Eden? It's his horses?"

"Kathy, I'll feel double strength with Lion. There is no one in
this wild world who knows the land better than he. He speaks the
language of the wilderness, the earth like God himself, your father.
He is born to be an earth leader. We cannot remain on the lands
like women, this war is man's business. Your Pappa and I will ride
together. We may even die together. He has been a father to me,
my darling. We will each take eight to ten days rations and care for
each other, along with all our men."

"Eden, Mamma and Kimberly should come and stay with me.
We will feel stronger if we stay together."

Lion arrived with new guns—ugly German mausers. They
were going to load the horses onto the train and travel towards
Standerton. Suddenly they were ready to go.

"Oh, Pappa," said Kathy, "you have had your share of wars. You are mad to go to this war with the English."

Lion was upright and jovial,

"Kathy, my sweet child, your Pappa has experience, he has knowledge of war, of tactics." He repeated, "tactics and strategy, he understands horsemanship and all the uses of weaponry. No one is safe in war. But when you understand your business you are a little safer. I will look after Eden and you will feel less afraid. All soldiers do not die so easily. It's the very brave who die." He said loudly, "Yes, the very brave and daring. They die bloody useless."

It was not easy to overcome the strain of parting. Kathy tried to settle down with her two children. Kimberly remained at Leeukraal with Petra for another week, and then, they harnessed in all remaining horses and moved in at Sonnestroom. Whitey and the workers remained at Leukraal, though Kathy felt remorse. She trusted Whitey, he seemed to have assimilated Lion's characteristics over the years, and one felt safe and comfortable in the knowledge that he knew full well whatever he was doing. He had a deep belly laugh, "No problem," he would say, "desa no problem." He had a lovely accent that belongs only to Africa. She wondered if she could arrange something with her mother, and perhaps bring Whitey to Sonnestroom.

She was afraid for her mother. The death of her brother had been too much for her mother to bear. She used to think about these things often, before she was grown up. She and her sister were quite aware of her mother's devotion to Canaan. They had watched their mother's nervousness when Canaan was not home at twilight, and once when Mr. Petzer took him away on a hunt and they stayed away two days. Or when he did not feel well, or even had a headache. They knew he was their mother's favoured child. She had hoped that nothing terrifying or dreadful would ever happen to Canaan, her quiet, loving, thoughtful brother. She had to admit he was a good brother, full of fun, always with some fresh item of discovery or knowledge, teasing a solitary wasp, sticking a brown house snake in Whitey's saddle bag. He always tucked his hand into his mother's or brought her unusual plants from the bush, and little bundles of wild flowers. His little "tok tokkie," (live beetles on a string tied up by their legs with very thin thread. Fly them round and round in circles) and numerous collections of insects and animals. Then when he went away and lived with Eden and Kimberly. They had such fun, he was so full of enthusiasm and life, until that goddamn horrible, horrible accident happened. For her mother life had taken a dreamlike quality, she seemed to live and hover in a limbo of disbelief, her, yes her dream was too horrible to be real. Who would have dreamed that the quiet tenor of life was so completely changed. They had been through Kaffir raids, cattle raids, sickness, burning silos, and wildfires. They knew the horror of an almost invisible bush war, of droughts, locusts and floods, and immeasurable losses. They knew the dangers of fears of not surviving. But this untimely unexpected accident, for that is what it was, a horrifying accident, was unreal. It was grotesquely unreal, that's what it was, and with this death her mother's very soul, the essence of her life was totally squeezed out of her. There was no hope, she drifted from day to day, like an empty shell squashed and battered sadness, by hopelessness; that was her mother!

Now she, Kathy, would have to come for them all. She was not brave, but nature makes for us a merciful adjustment when what cannot be cured must be endured.

No, Kathy was not so brave, she had never had reason to be, because of the men in her life. Her father, really he was too old to go to war. He agreed he was too old to march, but not too old to ride and shoot. Was he a Boer? No, he would rather have gone to war than allow his horses to be taken by any of the commandos. He would go to war in a wagon; he had in mind one of his plans.

She wondered where Eden was and she hoped that he would stay close to her father. She thought of them cantering along, their rifles over their shoulders, their hats down over their faces, and hair sticking out above their collars. Her father's silver mane and her husband's golden blonde that shone in the sun like the purest of the gold that he dug from the veins that came from the very heart of the earth, deep down into the bowels of his beloved Africa!

Two men, father and son, riding to war, with the Boers, because, like the Boers, all they wanted was their precious land, and to be left alone in peace to be upon it. They felt no consequence fighting against the British, the very source from whence they came. They were not uitlanders, they were like pathfinders, the makers of this land, the preservers of all that it bore; they were not its rapists. They were the seekers, bypassing the bad land, finding the good rich red soils, ever advancing their settling in the wild and wondrous valleys that lay between the start of the mountains where water was plentiful and where the pastures were sweet. Where the wild game of Africa, alert, jittering, were crammed full, sharing the yellow-green wild and retreating into the bush. The Krantzes were never sure when life would be blasted suddenly away into nothingness from this place that for millions of years was free and wild and belonged to no one.

She suddenly put her thoughts all together. My God, she should have paid more attention to the guns. Did she understand how to use them all? Yes, well, she had her mother, and women get very brave when they defend their young.

"Here," she used the Dutch word for God, "my Here," she said to herself, "if anyone enters and threatens my children, I shall shoot to kill. But Eden, my darling, Eden, brave, kind and strong. He said, this was not a war zone area so maybe we'll be safe, plus there is Petra, powder and shot." The children were laughing somewhere in the house. Such happy laughter, it was like music, children's laughter always filled the atmosphere and changed the ambiance. A crow cawed in a hoarse croaking sound. Why, even that sounded good.

And the days passed in tranquility and the nights came and went with only the African magic that was music to their ears. Nevertheless their guns were always at their sides, the doors all strongly locked and old Whitey slept inside again. Petra gave Kathy a feeling of security, Petra, her grieving mother; she feelingly could forgave her her grief. Her mother, her strong Boer mother, who had trekked for new land and peace, who also knew the perils and dangers of the land almost as well as her father, the great grey Lion with his four-pounder and finger on the trigger, ever ready. His mind was alert to every snap of a twig, imprint in the sand, aware of the circling aasvoel, the moods and plans of both Boer and Redcoat, of clinking spurs, rattling sabers, who knew the beat of heart, and thud of hoof of every horse that breathed. A great man he had to be, for he understood the most powerful and almighty of all. He understood almighty Nature. It was no surprise to Kathy to know now why her childhood was so secure. Who would know fear with parents like hers? It was only now she understood…She also understood fear.

She picked up her gun. "Always point it upwards to discharge" Eden had said, but once or twice she nearly scared them all by forgetting to point upwards.

Once the peddler came around, or the smous (beggar/vaga-bond/rag & bone man) as he was called, she fired and caused his horse to bolt.

Petra, dressed in her black silk dress, and wearing a white lace cap, constantly nurtured the plants. She wanted to ride to Leukraal, but Kathy said she should stay at the house Sonnestroom, as Eden and Lion had instructed. She sat down with a slump,

"Ya," she said, "my mother and father trekked with us on the Great Northern trek, always retreating we were, from the British power. My Ma told me how she hid in the reeds waist deep in water with leeches and harsh stabbing grasses, hiding from murderous Kaffirs." She watched the leeches sucking her blood, she had to remain motionless. "And now, Kathy, as I grow old, I have lost my son, in such a needless way, my heart aches even more. Instead of the fear of Kaffirs and beasts, we have people of our own kind wanting to kill each other. It is a sad disgrace against the human race.

"My Here, Kathy, this now is a war, its blood against one's own blood will be shed. There is so much intermarriage between the English and Dutch. If Lion fights against the Engels, he will be called a traitor, and if he fights with the Engels, he will be called a renegade by the Boers. So our men, our loyal wonderful men, what is to be?

In October 1899 the Boers fired their first shot at the British, fired by the Doornberg Commando. Even though Rhodes had said "there was not the slightest chance of war" Kruger was seventy-four and had also hoped for a negotiated peace. He had trained artillery, he had guns, and volunteers from all over the world. The Boers also hoped for a change of government in England. If Chamberlain went out and a liberal government got in, they would probably get what they wanted. But it was not to be, and the Boer War began. It has been described as a gentleman's war. It was remarkable, for it was not so filled with atrocities or sadism. But war is war, men are killed, and people suffer. Some of the Boer sons fighting for their land were thirteen years old and some were deep into the last decade of life. Brave, hardy, and foolishly fired by a strange belief in God with keen faces and no sign of fear nor wavering. There were also Boers against the war, like De La Rey who denounced the Boers for making war.

And at once time there was a period when Boers had the opportunity to win, but sadly it was lost. This was when the British forces and Dundee and Ladysmith fled in disarray after some skirmishes. Janbert should have pursued them in a mounted blitzkrieg—a warfare the British did not understand—till they reached the sea. With the Cape Colony neutral, all Africa behind them, world opinion on their side, plenty of supplies and provisions, the Brits would not have been able to land enough troops to capture the country.

This Boer War was a religious and political war, a civil rebellion, and some of the Boer actions were those of gentlemen. Perhaps "the gentlemen" were mainly Boers. But war continued in great billowing clouds of dust across the wilds among soldiers and horsemen. Perhaps because of the Boers' decent character, they lost the chance to win in the first few months of this strange war. When defeated, the British were infuriated by their defeats (the prestige of the Empire!). Six thousand of the Brits were killed a Spion Kop and perhaps from here the war changed by sheer force of numbers and reinforcements. Also the British resorted to foul methods of destruction. Cattle, sheep, and horses were lifted, crops destroyed and women and children were rounded up and put into camps while men and boys were sent away as prisoners. Thousands of women and children perished through cruel neglect. The British gave some puerile excuse, blaming the Kaffirs instead of Roberts' scorched earth tactics. Roberts and Kitchener! Kitchener, an evil British runt, could not outfight the Boers, so he started to capture their women and children. He was a foul-minded butcherboy.

Thirty - Eight

In February 27, 1884, the Convention of London defined further the relations of the S.A. Republic to Great Britain. In May there were fears of German expansion eastward. Guided by Cecil Rhodes, the British concluded treaties with the native chiefs of Bechuanaland about protection. In August the Boers, under Joubert, attempted to establish a republic in Zululand in order to secure access to the sea in the East. In December the British annexed St. Lucia Bay to Natal. And so the years passed.

Christmas came again. Eden and Kathleen had been away most of the year, but word had come that they would be coming to visit. They were not sure exactly when. Lion and Petra were very happy and beside themselves. Christmas came and went. Eden and Kathy were unable to make the visit. She wrote to her mother. "I am so happy, Ma and Pa. I have a beautiful husband and a big diamond ring that all the diggers and people stare at, and sometimes I wear it on a chain around my neck to hide it. I just feel it's so big and showy. I do miss our home, though life is very busy. We travel a lot and Eden's gold mine is prosperous. Eden is now using dynamite, it's a mixture of nitroglycerine and clay and this blasting does away with the long hours of digging. He has also made a new discovery at this town called Barbenton. He really has struck a rich gold vein. It is for this reason we cannot come home. Sometimes I feel I love Leeunkraal beyond all natural explanation."

Her letter was full of news of Eden's friends, but there was a distinct feeling that she was living a nomadic sort of life, to which she was unaccustomed, especially on one trip when they were near the southernmost part of Portuguese territory, in savage bushlands and a veld that was raw and wild, filled with animals, tsetse flies and horrible mosquitoes. "Many of the diggers who had come in from Delagoa Bay crossed these mountains and came through this treacherous veld, but never made it," she wrote. "Others set up little camps. There was this man, a transport rider on the new road, James Percy Fitzpatrick, and he tells wonderful tales of the veld, of snakes and wild animals, that makes one's hair rise," she ended by telling her Mama and Papa, "he wrote an acclaimed book entitled Jock of the Bashveld." Kathleen wrote expressing she was so homesick, "so very homesick."

In 1885, more than 100 different shares were quoted on the Barbenton Stock exchange. Commissions came from London and Paris and shares went higher and higher. But Barbenton was not a great builder of public confidence or in SA mines. Thousands of people had shared certificates that were worthless because most of the mines did not produce gold. Of course some went on producing gold, and these shares paid good dividends. Barbenton faded into obscurity. Sammy Marks, a friend of Paul Kruger, did very well. On the farm Kromdraai, a digging was proclaimed in 1885 on the west Rand. Petronella Francina, a widow, lived on that farm, Langlaagte, and on this farm the outcrop of the main reef was discovered.

Paul Kruger

This discovery was almost entirely Eden's. The state declared that private land could be thrown open, with compensation in financial inducement—the mynpacht was staked all along the aterop. Amalgamation took place swiftly on the rand, mainly by a few persons who had already vast fortunes—Robinson (rumor had it) seduced widow Francina before buying her farm. He'd ended up with seven farms, 40,000 acres and the Robinson Gold Mining Co. Here was a nasty, cunning man, successfully ensconced, though he was never liked by anyone. His capital increased from 50,000 to 2.34 million pounds. Rudd and Rhodes were not so happy in gold as in diamonds, and Rhodes found the Rand a wild country full of snakes of which he had great fears.

It was also at this time that Rhodes' friend, his beloved companion Neville Pickering, died. But despite his misgivings he had bought a farm that gave him a basis for gold mining. Rhodes, at this time, was an enormously wealthy man. The standards of financial morality on the diamond fields was notoriously low. Streetlights were installed in Kimberly in 1885 and horse drawn trams. In July 1886, Kimberly had its railway station. Labor of every form was very cheap. While Eden grew richer, a battle raged between other giants. 1886 was the year of great gold discovery. Johannesburg was laid out. Rhodes and his associates were greatly involved in financing and organizing industry and soon they controlled a very large share.

Rhodes, who considered all things British, to be the first and finest, was also concerned with human pigmentation. He was a misogynist who disliked women, was unmarried and childless and hated loafers. He was a stocky, thickset male with a double chin, a soft, sensual mouth, ice blue eyes some referred to as "cold", large and square, with large hands and an odd high-pitched voice. Perhaps the best thing said about him was that he was not religious and leaned towards Charles Darwin. He would have liked to believe that the English, and this included the Colonials and Americans, were God's chosen and the best human product, and in his ethnocentric opinion, they should rule the world. He was inexhaustibly energetic, a megalomaniac who thought big—bit mountains, big orchards, big spaces. He thought in thousands when others thought in tens. He had wealth and he had power. His money was only a means to achieve his ambitions. He had no conception of money as money. He was greatly angered that they could not win America. He kept harping on this loss of power.

Eden was fairly well acquainted with Mr. Rhodes, Mr. Beit, Doctor Jim, Mr. Rudd, and of course the engineer John Hammond from America. Rhodes was already nervous as his health started to fail in 1894. His face was swollen and blotched. People know when one's body starts failing. Rhodes dream was to unite the whole country and have a great commonwealth. He had a scheme for a telegraph system from Cape to Cairo as well as a railroad. It vexed him greatly when Swaziland passed into the control of the SA Republic, and it annoyed him that German intervention prevented the purchase of Laurenco Marques from the Portuguese, but most of all, he wanted Kruger's gold in the Transvaal that lay richly embedded beneath the ridge of white water, the Witwatersrand. He resented it was not in his newly acquired north, nor in the Cape Colony. He was frustrated Kruger was not a man who could be intimidated, could not be bribed and could not be threatened.

But he stood like a rock from Alladin's cave, blocking the fulfillment of Imperialism, Rhodes' dream. Kruger was a squat, stubborn man, solid as a rock, smoking his pipe, with his rifle in one hand and his Bible in the other. Old Kruger was described as "a shepherd peasant leader" behind his ragged beard, rugged face and eyes sharp and cunning and wiry hair swept up like a wild horse's mane, a large nose, and a hard stiff mouth. He carried himself inside a massive frame of granite-like physical strength that lasted even into his dotage. While Rhodes saw the British as dominant, the superior white race, the finest civilization, the masters who should have and control all whites, also, he deeply lamented the loss of America. His wealth and ambition grew beyond all the realms of rational proportion, and as the dense and gravid clouds of October grew darker, conspiracy, rebellion, revolt and war hung like a blacker rain cloud, gathering and growing.

On January 1895 on the border of 14 streams, Rhodes met Kruger and agreed to meet. The boundary was provided by the London Convention. Rhodes' English were the masters who should control all—especially this rich gold-filled fantastic land, which was also filled with "the most despicable of human beings." This was how he described the black folk. Rhodes and Beit conspired to take over the Transvaal—a cunning, power-hungry, money man Rand Lors from 1870 which brought the diamond rush, in Kimberly situated on the borders of the Cape Colony. Rhodes became prime minister of the Cape.

In 1886 came the great gold rush to the Witwatersrand. This made fortunes. Rhodes, together with Beit precipitated a collusion between Uitlanders and Boers. The Boers would not give them political rights (the Uitlanders). Jameson was C. Rhodes' right hand man, a small, arrogant person, smooth talking and not adverse to a little duplicity. He had a column of African servants and mule carts, and men from the Welsh Fusiliers, the horse guards and Innis Killings. He planned to invade the Transvaal. He only had 600 men and planned a three-day dash for Johannesburg, hoping he could do it before the Boers could mobilize. His visions of glory overcame reason, so into the Transvaal for 170 miles rode Jameson and his 600.

The Boers were downwind of Jameson's plans, sadly for him, and like the old British Justice long ago, one of Jameson's men got drunk and cut a fence instead of the telegraph wires. Poor Jameson, he was barred by this brilliant invisible enemy who disarmed the British, seized their baggage and helped the wounded. They laughed at Jameson's white flag made from the apron of a servant girl. A weeping Jameson was taken to a Pretoria gaol to dream in safety of his madcap ride across the African veld that resulted in dismal failure.

The failed mission was a cause of tremendous embarrassment, even to Rhodes. He and his rich backer, Beit, underestimated quite hopelessly Kruger and the Uitlanders (the Uitlanders here were

Germans, French and Americans who were all making good money on the gold fields). They were not in a hurry to overthrow the Kruger government. Rhodes himself cut a poor figure in the witness box it was said, and he sent a message to Jameson to "take the blame." Jameson was referred to as an idiot. Kruger was re-elected four times and Rhodes was forced to resign at the outcome of a parliamentary inquiry. Milner lost trust in Rhodes and Beit, but, of course, this was not meant to be heard by the ears of the world.

Meanwhile, British soldiers, who were paid a shilling a day, were landing at all ports. Landsdown was preparing for war. Oom Paul (Uncle Paul), as he was fondly called, was a heroic survivor from the Great Trek. Who could forget Oom Paul crushing Dingaan at Blood River! In 1898, a very young handsome Boer who had achieved a double first in law at Cambridge, opposed the state attorney: at this time the Uitlanders did not have the vote. His name was Mr. Jan Smutz. Milner lost trust, it was said, in both Rhodes and Beit, and replaced Rhodes as chairman of the Charter Company. He was a troublemaker, was Milner, and Jan Smutz accused England of interfering in the country' internal affairs by breaking the London Convention of 1884. So Kruger reluctantly decided war was inevitable. He actually wanted a deal with the Uitlanders and October 2nd saw mobilization of Boer troops in the OFS.

It was their Goddamned War; they wanted supremacy, they wanted the land, the strategic key to the imperial route to India. They despised the peoples of South Africa whose territory brought no power to England. Here these people came into the Boers' land opened and developed by earth's real people into farms; the Boers were now turning up at the frontiers of the Cape and Natal.

After the rains, the earth was verdant, and all over wild daisies were out. Near Valksrust at Sand Spruit (Spring) the Boers were waiting. Troop trains emptied their loads of carriages filled with men and boys wearing their Sunday clothes and carrying Mausers. Cattle trucks were loaded with creosote, artillery wagons, oxen, wives and servants. The plains were dotted with ponies, oxen and covered wagons. Bearded burghers from Pretoria and the Rand, a large marquee was Jauberts HO. Jaubert also wondered if this war was necessary at all. The men had no raincoats, the mules were not strong, wagon wheels were broken, and the whole thing seemed undernourished. This people's army and their elated leaders were made commanders.

So at Sandsprint on October 10th, 1899 at 3 p.m., the Boers received Kruger's ultimatum. They stood up in their stirrups. The Boers formed a crescent of 15,000 Transvalers and 6,000 OFS divided into four groups to try and trap two forward positions and Ladysmith and Dundee to seal off Mafekey and Kimberly from the South. Sir George White waited on Natal's frontier. The *Times* in England called Kruger's ultimatum of war "an infatuated step." The Globe denounced the war, the little state, and its impudent burghers," but the Victorian life in England was not over ruffled by the war. "The War in the tea cup" they called it. Butler left on the Dunottar Castle as the English people yelled, "give it to the Boers." Remember Majuba, or "Bring back Kruger's whiskers."

Little indeed did they know, the silly fools.

There were the Imperial light horse, the SA light horse and the 60th Rifles in their scarlet and green uniforms financed by the Rand Lords, and 400 Yorkshire arrived from Mauritius. But wherever the Boers passed, they left no contact. All telegraph wires were cut. The Boers had 75 mm field guns that outranged the English 15 pounders. Trainloads of men in cattle trucks were led by armored trains. The slate-colored funnels and a new thick Boulin, and increased size, carried squadrons of 1st Devons Natal Mounted Rifles, natal Artillery, the 1st Manchesters, 5th Dragoon guards with the Imperial Light Horse ride beside the trains and 10,000 troops went to Natal to Sir Pim Symonds GOC. Chamberlain thought it may precipitate war but Silbourne formulated this idea, Milner confirmed it and so did Rhodes, Beit and Fitzpatrick: the best way to avoid war was to make preparations for it.

Chamberlain found it difficult to deal with Kruger, but they believed he would climb down. Some were even cheerful. They expected a small war even before Butler landed; all would be over by Christmas. But the Boer armies turned up in large numbers on the frontiers. Kruger, with plenty of defects, was a statesman. Sadly, he put more trust in God than in the Mauser. The brave and God-fearing Boers tired of the greedy and power hungry British. They declared war on the English. It was expected, though, that it would soon be over…or so the English surmised.

It took 2 ¾ years of horrible, bloody fighting. 22,000 British soldiers lost their lives and 25,000 Boers. It was a lesson to the English and it was very humiliating. Wars are all stupid, cruel and revolting. The Boers had to protect what was theirs, but it was Milner who was damned; it was he who was responsible. He, an over-egotistic megalomaniac, was responsible for making war. Two factors in the British army, Roberts, Ray and Wolsely fought each other (over army reform, etc.). Perhaps it was the usual human greed. Gold, all was the reflection of gold!

Butler, with his mishaps and mistakes, in the end tried new tactics. Blacks served as laborers, drivers and guides. In Mafeking, 2,000 blacks under Baden Powell* were left to starve and were shot

---

* Founded the Boy Scouts—Baden Powell.

by the Boers. Boer families were caught up in the guerrilla war. Kitchener, the vile butcher, ordered the British "to sweep the veld clean." It was not a gentleman's war. Wars are ugly, cruel and vile, the word gentle cannot be used in the same breath.

Into a useless, unnecessary war, these two men, pioneers, makers, creators, torn between double loyalties, neither wanting to fight or kill, were now going to war. Riding away to where, they were not even sure. Maybe they would not even return to their precious woonpleks (dwellings)—no, there was no reason for negative thoughts, they were always winners. They did not lag or lose, they never thought like losers, yet they all were weeping. Of course men wept, war did this to men, uprooted and forced to defend. Here was a call, all men 16 to 80. Neither wanted to fight, neither wanted to kill.

"Are you nervous, Eden?" asked Lion.

"With you I have courage, Lion," Eden said. "I'm just pleased we are together. There is always danger in times like this. We will join a Commando, or we will form a little group."

They had 8 days' rations. They rode on until suddenly before them they saw a field of horses and men as far as the eye stretched. Guns were being distributed and Lion refused to hand over his Mausers. Practice shots were popping everywhere. Stallions (Boers hated to geld their horses) were whinnying and neighing, fighting, shuffling, a sea of movement, waves of restless men. Lion and Eden's horses were trained to come with a whistle.

They were swept up with Botha. It was the 15th of September, the night of the great rain. Riders were sliding down the slopes, bullets hissed everywhere. The horses were sick looking and hungry. Khaki uniforms were stolen from dead soldiers, and raided from English store tents. Botha had raided two British camps, captured

180 Lie Metfords, 30,000 rounds of ammo and 200 horses. Sadly, the horses were also worn out and useless. In the Dongas were dead men, and some were shot to pieces and dying. There was no dignity in death, in open mouths and upturned bodies and bodily fluids. For what were people killing each other? Savage and uncivilized. Within this useless, unnecessary war went two powerful men torn between loyalties that tore them apart. Neither wished to fight or kill.

But they were needed. It was their land. All men from 16 to 80, men of the earth, mothers who had passed their years from earliest childhood through the University of life itself, here drawn into a conflict between Rhodes and Kruger, two men typifying the British and the Boer! The Boer who opened and built the land and the ailing Brit who had come to conquer. Rhodes came to Natal as a young, sickly man and became a millionaire, and a gold bagger. In Kimberly, in 1880, he founded DeBeers Mining Company. He believed England was the Master Race. He was a misogynist who disliked women, and who wanted all the world to be ruled under the English crown, a man able to resort to duplicity, using his position for his own ends.

People do not change, really, but the dormant and dominant slices of personality often swap positions through the tollgates of life. Paul Kruger farmed in Rustenberg. He was 45 in 1870. Lobengula was a young chief of the Matabele tribes. Charles Darwin upset religion with his "origin of the species," aristocracy was attacked and undermined by Labour, and the whole cog of movement started in Africa. The railways were running amidst conflict, bikes were the rage, so were bloomers, motor cars, electric lights, phones, private carriages, Huxley, Kipling, Oscar Wilde, Freud…and Eugene Marais was digging deep down for termites. Not only had the tide turned against the Boers. Devilish rains fell.

Keitz, short of ammo, threw away his gun and took a dead soldier's Lee Metford, killing 12-14 men at "handshake range." Men were cold and hungry. Men were dying in trenches, some half blown up, blood pouring, groaning, clutching, rolling in agony. A lot of dead were just buried in a donga (a ditch or empty hole).

It was the suffering of their families, their women and children, typhus, dysentery and fever that demoralized the Commandos: Kitchener. A revolting, bloodthirsty, murderous creature, he executed 51 Boers as war criminals. The "burned home" policy, his internment of women and children, destruction of stock, was his own cruel idea. It was this that brought the war to an end.

Time lessons the brooding. The joys the sorrows of mankind. We survive.

Petra got word of the horrors of overcrowded tents, no water or soap, no beds, and wanted to set off in her wagon—with murderous Kitchner's permission—to inspect and bring comforts. She knew what to do, she said. There was no love lost between Milner and Kitchner, a merciless couple of killers. Milner was resplendent in his villa in Johannesburg with its red-tiled roof overlooking the magnificent rolling hills of the Magaliesberg. Meanwhile epidemics had broken out in Kitchner's camps and spread death with terrifying speed. Emily Hobhouse, a brave lady did a lot to expose these lethal blunders to the eyes of the world, but it was Millicent Fawcett who faced Milner and Kitchner, quoting figures with deadly accuracy.

As the rains continued, dams were polluted with rotting slaughtered animals strewn like straw across the veld. The whole country an indescribable horror. This was the British war! Kitchner's sweep, mangled with dynamite! Their humiliation from Botha towards Gough was a little nightmare to these khaki-clad Brits. Shortage of horses presented a problem, but what caused the misery to all the Boers was the terror, the death rate and suffering in the concentration camps. Kitchener wrote with woe that after a year under his command, the war still continued. His thoughts mingled strongly with extermination and he sought more troops.

Wools Lawson, an eccentric Uitlander, gold miner, ex-commander of the ILH who used Black and colored men to follow spoors, caused the discovery of the Boers in their laagers. An ugly hunt resulted in losses of thousands of cattle carts and wagons. For this, the turncoat was given credit. Rawlins exalted in hunting down Boers like game and springing upon their laagers at night. On Christmas Day, de Wet returned from his version breathtaking hunt when the Brits were negligent perhaps, despite Spion Kop and Majuba, from which they did not learn a lesson, despite the Kopjes and urged on by bully beef and cases of rum that looked so good to hungry Boers. They mutilated a camp in the tangled chasms of Tiger Kloof, never to be forgotten! Kitchner brewed extermination.

Kitchner learned to arm the African and they were dangerous scouts, and twenty thousand strong. Masterful de la Rey in Boer style further humiliated Kitchner's army. He attacked Metheun, whose men fled into the dust. Metheun was wounded in the hip, and was forced to surrender. He was the last of the British generals to be captured by the Boers. When Kitchner heard this news, his nerves were totally shattered, and he heard that a six man delegation were about to ride into Pretoria to talk about peace.

Milner was aggravated, but considered peace terms a compromise. He would have preferred wrestling the Boers, forever obsessed with the dream of imperial Supremacy over all South Africa. Together, of course, with more avaricious peoples pirating gold, Rhodes, Wernher, Beit, and the blundering British army.

Thirty - Nine

Milner became High Commissioner. Ever aggravated by the siege of Mafeking and British defeats at Colenzo, Stromberg and Majuba, Roberts instructed that Boer houses should be blown up. Boers were punished for any possible reason. Roberts handed the scorched earth policy over to Kitchner (who had visions of becoming Viceroy of India). He was an evil, nasty man. He ordered Block Houses, barbed wire and farm destruction, horses and all domestic animals destroyed.

An eleven-year-old girl was raped and a woman who had given birth was carried off and her newborn child was left to die. These were the men who conducted so much of the "gentleman's war." The British armed 30,000 black men that brought about increased cattle smugglings (African Riches) they built camps near the railway lines, put up tens and crammed 11 people into one tent, women and children, in extreme temperatures with no beds, no toilets, incredible degradation, according to Emily Hobhouse of Suffragette fame, who offered help to the women. Each tent had only one bucket of water per day, enough for one pot of tea!

These so-called "gentlemen" inflicted terrible suffering (run by the military). It was the diabolical punishment of innocents. Kitchener was strongly suspected of poisoning foods. Measles and typhoid broke out and the English media made the Boer look primitive and ugly. But a war is not a war when conducted by methods of barbarism and cruelty. The scorched earth devastated the lands painfully created by the Boers and settlers. The English wanted a Boer genocide. It was their ugly policy of deliberate extermination. History proved, and the legend lives on, that the small group of Boers taught millions of British "a bloody good lesson."

Germanic Milner and Butcher Kitchener were both keen on Kitchener's barbed wire blockhouses and strong columns. But there was the clash of personality and principle?

Botha and de la Rey then began to talk peace terms with Kitchener. Around May 19, 1902 (Milner hoped they would fail), there was an odd atmosphere of adverse opinions among the leaders. Hamilton actually declared the Boer leaders "the best men in South Africa," casting quite a sneer at the Royalists, and he also realized Milner was doing his best to block peace talks. Milner seethed with an urge to destroy the Boers as a political force. Jan Smutz, a young, brainy Boer offered to draft the peace plan. What really brought things to a head was not only their long suffering, but also it was found that some of their own people had turned against them. The condition of the country then seemed hopeless—beaten now by blockhouses and food burning and women constantly threatened by the kaffirs.

All the Boer commandos came together exchanging information and on Saturday May 31st in Vereeniging came the bitter end, the Boers voted for Kitchener's peace. It was all over in five minutes, 20,000 bitter Uitlanders emerged into visibility, threw in their guns (mostly British) they had captured and with their pride intact, and their heads held high, they rode off and sought their homes and families.

The gates to Sonnestroom, once large, stone-built and imposing, seemed neglected, forlorn and overgrown. Lion and Eden had been away with Botha and seldom had word some to the farm. His family had lived through fears and fires. Many of their sheep had been killed and stolen, their cattle driven away. But the stone house was a refuge, strong and well fortified with a slate roof, and stood proud and regal like a king's palace in the veld. Marta and Kathy had survived through it all. Petra felt old and tired, the fire in her soul was burned out like the fields. There were rumors of peace and a ceasefire. Botha had gone to Pretoria. It was time the gunfire was silent now and Lion and Eden rode with Botha. Lion had told the women it was better to remain on the farm, but it was fearful and difficult. Food was available but not easily obtained. They had so many sheep when Lion went to the war, but thousands were killed and the little lambs, left when their mothers were killed, bleating helplessly, were taken inside and nurtured. Sadly they had to slaughter some, killing a pet and the children having to eat them, cooked with water Blometjies to make Mealie pap (porridge) for breakfast.

Petra was so clever. She filled the wagons with mealies and there was always a little mealie bread, and a vet-koek* Marta knew how to make. It was Marta and Whitey and their little isolated family and cabbages and a few eggs and sacks of flour behind closed doors. In May, and the air was cool and the nights were cold. Kathy had spent all her days teaching children. They had remained

---

* vet-koek = fried dough in oil.

standing together, a mixed little group, they knew of the horrors of the camps and the dreadful tales of Intombe. Marta told how a nurse had told one of the coloreds that there was a big trench where people who died were thrown into, and just covered with a little sand. Few people survived Intombe.

They were lucky, in fact. Petra and Whitey had built an underground henhouse, large enough to house some sheep, and it was there the lambs were reared with cows' milk and honey. Up in the trees were the honey boxes, with empty boxes especially made for new swarms always available. The English had never looked up or they'd have shot or shelled them. Kathy regretted deeply the loss of Lion's sheep. The sheep not stolen or driven off were shot, and the stench of their rotting bodies lay in the meadows till only a ball of wool remained. The veld had an alien scent. This was a different smell, something odd, dissolved and distilled by the heavy summer rains. It was a hard rain and the ravines were thick with growth. The stream trickled musically on its moss bed, murmuring as it always did. Summer was handing over to winter. It seemed normal for a while, and life settled and it felt peaceful. The new year quietly came promptly, and delivered a new set of challenges. There had been no fearsome marauders, the vines hung heavy with frosted bunches of grapes, cattle multiplied and a few new calves had dropped. Though ever on guard, life at Sonnestroom went along again at Africa's ox pace.

It was pleasant, and with Eden's gift of brilliance in geology and business flourished, his fame was widespread. He and Kathy had two children. His eldest child, a son, was proving A grade and bright, and his daughter was as pretty as a picture. Lion loved his horses and practiced racing his team of six blacks. Eden prospered, he was so busy with constant consultations, night and day, messages arriving daily by horse riders and carriage mail. The gold bugs were obsessed by the lure of gold, and scrambling across the untamed land were diamond prospectors from every corner of the world. They were Rhodes, Beit, Milner and those greedy gold baggers, even Col. Baden-Powell among them all. In dealing with black men he, Baden-Powell, said one had to be fair but firm. He executed by firing squad some hungry Africans for stealing food; also he had 115 others flogged. Indeed, many a good deed was matched by many a bad one.

Behind the British Union Jack were Matabile Spears. One bad move Baden-Powell made was "Black Boxing Day." Perhaps Baden-Powell felt he'd like to show the Boers how good he was. It was a beautiful clear day. "The Protectorate Regiment" as shot at point black range, returning with a white flag blowing in the wind. Casualties numbered 96, one-tenth of the White garrison at Game Tree Fort. In all directions on swift Boer horses were the Boers, strong, healthy men with an air of triumph. Interesting to note Baden-Powell used black labor paid with promises of food to dig their trenches for defense works. He used black runners as messengers both in and out of Mafeking. The black watch were threatened with flogging if they did not fight the Boers. Kruger's gransdson, Sarel Elof, a daring young man, attempted to capture Mafeking and succeeded on his first attempt, of course, by burning a cluster of huts down, he awoke.

Thus he awoke the garrison, and triggered war. Many men and women died and the British behaved as though they had beaten Napoleon, though not many thanks went to the majority of the garrison, The Africans. Baden-Powell founded the Boy Scouts movement as one of the most famous of Englishmen of all time. Roberts considered this to be a gentleman's war that he had won.

Lion was an old man. Hiding and night riding and war were taking their toll. Eden could take over. He was young but he was damned if he would let him encounter any danger. He loved this boy. Eden was a brilliant geologist, a consultant of acclaim, he was also a farmer, taught by life and guided by the seasons. Lion was bonded to Eden, inseparably close like father and son. He was a born leader and the commandos needed his wisdom. Never mind about him being of British blood. He was just a mixed breed. It mattered not how old he was, age was not important to him. He never thought about his age. It was his cunning, his wisdom and his leadership and experience they needed. His reputation extraordinary, but he chose not to speak of Majuba. He had protected his farm and his family. He felt they would be fairly safe, for he felt this raid would be a short one. What did it matter, he was the son of the great Frederick McCabe. He could ride under the Union Jack or he could ride with the "vier Kleur." He was prepared to do the right thing, and to him the right was with the Boers. After all, he was a farmer. That is what Jules would do. He mounted his horse in one fluid movement, like an athlete. He didn't think. Look how he led us at Majuba: His reputation went before him like a zephyr. He knew it was useless to ask Eden to remain. And the commandos came. Lion was their commandant, whatever his age or status. He was their leader at Majube, and their leader now. He and Eden rode valiently into war!

Forty

The old colored man was leaning against the post. These days he preferred light duties. He never thought he'd lose his power but it happens as one gets old. For many years he'd worked on this farm, then he worked at Leeunkraal with his master. That's what they all call the heads of the home: Master, the man who taught him how to live, the man who gave him life and wages, and a home. They had come through lots of wars but he couldn't understand what this present war was all about. White men, white men were fighting each other now it seemed to him. The redcoats were jealous of the earthy Boers.

Now that he felt older, he didn't even want to think of fighting. He wished to see his master come home. It would be a happy moment to see the great Lion come riding down the dusty road into this beautiful place where his daughter Kathy, her mother and Kathy's two children were living. Somehow he felt he was their guardian, and he always slept inside the house, so that he was there when it was dark. Women were always afraid of the dark. He looked down at the fields. The horses were all grays, gray like he. Lion, his master, had said gray horses were not for war, too visible!

So they remained at home. "Whitey, they belong at home," he said, "It's the dark horses that go to fight!" Ya, where was his master, Lion? He shook his head. He wondered if he were safe for they had no word or news, and missus Petra and Missus Kathy were dulled out and quiet, like lonely doves who have no mate.

He stuck his forefinger into his ear and shook it vigorously, as though he were trying to reach a deep down itch. So much had taken place at this lovely place, so much that was happy…and now so much that was sad. He supposed he should also hate these pale men in their red coats that rode through the country like a moving red cloud with shining silver steel. They seemed and looked like the 'voetgangers'* (a ground locust), that come to eat and destroy, but they burned the crops and killed the cattle and ate the sheep and slipped through the red dust and then moved on. Just like colored locusts that hop and don't fly. He would sit here at the post and hold his guns and powder and shot, it didn't matter how long, and at night he'd keep vigil inside the house.

He enjoyed the smell of the kraals, the smell of manure that drifted through the air. Something always happened like a hawk after the chickens with feathers flying and leopard, or a wild cat or Leguaan scattering all the sheep over the fields like little white blobs of fleecy clouds. There'd been so much rain, and now the shooting, here at the tables, of the English soldier, a young man who had blue eyes and light hair. Maybe he was lost? Petra and he took him down to a shallow grave near where the Baas lay. He hoped the jackals or hyenas would not dig it up. He and Petra put heavy stones on top, but first they covered his pale face with a clean cloth and they rolled the stones down on top of the earth. There

---

* voetganger: red/green locust, does not fly.

was something disturbing about that soldier: Still, Whitey was the man of this home and he had to be unafraid. This was what Lion expected of him and he dismissed his thoughts of the English, and of ending his life on a hangman's rope.

When December came, it was nice time; everybody got presents and people from the Kerk came to sing and brought gifts of konfyt and homemade sweets. Workers had a holiday when all the chores are over. But even on holidays cows had to be milked, which reminded him that he had to de-tick the animals from that bont blue boere tick, then just take them off and drop them into boiling water and put grease into the ears. Where had all the cows gone? Had all the families trekked? He'd been hearing strange stories. Some people put their precious possessions in crates and secretly hung them under the bottom of the belly of the wagons. Missus Kathy and Petra, Engels, and a Boer, so to speak, they didn't trek. Here on this farm, they were off the roads and hiding the special things every day.

His old leather trousers were semi-threadbare and his feet, with cracked and crusted heels, hung over the soles of what remained from very old boots, too small for his feet. To allow him some comfort the toes of the boots were severed and his big toes protruded from one end and the heels from another. The skin of his ankles were dry and scaly, as were his elbows, gnarled and calloused like an old dog, but he managed to stay alive all through these terrible days, through the horrors of a strange guerilla war of an unprecedented kind. Black armies marauded and murdered, then dissolved and moved back into the busy, driving their loot and bloody spears before them. Kathy's stone structures and thick stone walls kept them alive. The old Boer leader, Mr. Stockenstorrom, he knew how to drive the kaffirs back. Now he himself was a traitor. This war was different. This war was with the English, a murderous big gun war. It seemed all about taking the land from the farmers.

He and Missus Petra and Kathy, they were quiet. They had to hide the horses, and they still had chickens and cows left. How many sheep did the English kill and burn, and carry away? There was no way he could stop them. He hid in the house behind the heavy doors that locked all of them in. They were safe in their stone house. The old bull was still in fair condition. The children had milk, and servants were fed. Petra was thin from fear and worry. Strange how the bull seemed to know how to survive—that was good because there was a new calf and that meant extra milk.

Whitey ventured out towards the track, where a group of black men carrying bundles on their heads had passed. He spent a few moments there then suddenly turned and came back towards his gates. He went to the farmhouse and looked inside the half-open kitchen entrance. "Miss Kathy," he said, "there's no more war! Some people are dancing and some are in the broken kerk. The farm near Sannie has brought back children and their mothers from the English camp. They are back on the farm." Kathy stared at the old man. "Where did you hear this story?" she said. "It is what the people have told me, Miss Kathy," he said, and she called Petra and the two children. He was at ease with her son. "We will wait for tomorrow and we will take the wagon and ride to Sannie again," she said. "It is true Petra, that there have been no sounds of guns and shells. Maybe we can move outside the gates and Lion and Eden will come home."

In the morning, before the sunrays were warming, the gong near the gate aroused them at breakfast. Kathy dashed to the window. Two men in khaki, who looked like soldiers, rode in. One had dismounted and the other remained on his horse. Petra loaded her gun, but Whitey had already confronted them. He was bringing them to the door. Petra stood behind Kathy. "Madam, are you Mrs. McCabe?" he asked. "I am," she said, and then, before the man said another word, she was overcome with fear and emotion. She yelled, "I hate you British plunderers! You've brought this stinking death-filled war, you careless, greedy murderers, like the rest of your bloody forebears, like all your bloody history and all your bloody red necks and your bloody red eyes! Get out of my sight or I may not be responsible for my actions. Get away now!" She tried to slam the door. The soldier put his boot inside.

Her face wet and her hair wild, tears rolling down her cheeks, she leaned against the door and let her body slide down upon her haunches. She wept aloud, in uncontrollable anguish. Petra stepped forward. The man saluted. "Madam, Mevron, I am from General Botha's army. We are just wearing the British soldier's uniforms! We are here to tell you your husband has been injured. The war is over, peace was signed on May 31st. There is no more war! Here is where your man is sheltering, you will need transport to bring him home." He mounted his thin and bony horse, and Whitey led him away. Petra watched them go. Then Whitey halted them both near the stables and in an old bucket brought their horses some food. She watched them take the bridles off as they fed the hungry Boer horses. The emotion was too much for Petra and Kathy. Their emotions were spent, it was all they could handle. Today was now, yesterday was gone, tomorrow was on its way. Both McCabes were coming home.

Forty-One

All through the war Kathy and Petra had no word from Lion or Eden. They lived each day in stress and in anticipation of news, perhaps even of their deaths.

Then one morning, almost at first light, the cocks were crowing, and the night jar was still singing, when the dogs attacked something or someone near the stables. Petra was up near the windows, gun in hand, as Kathy came to her own window. They could see the dogs had cornered something. They suddenly they saw a saber, and, sure enough, the brass helmet and red flash of the British tunic.

"My Gott," Kathy said. Petra ran into the living room where the light seemed slightly better.

"I saw it Kathy, it's a rooi baatjiie (red jacket). A red coat armed, a sniper."

"Where, where."

They looked out together and the Redcoat was clearly visible, back to their window, warding off the dogs. Kathy looked.

"It's a young man, Ma, a British soldier, let's talk to him first."

"No, Kathy, he is an officer, I can see that, and any moment now he will shoot the dogs."

But he was turning around, his saber in hand, trying to ward off the dogs. The horses were making a fuss and stomping and neighing noises came from the stable.

"My god, Kathy. You know what these British have been doing? They must have been destroying our horses, our cattle." She took her gun and ran towards the door. "You stay here, Kathy, let Ma go, through, I know these people. You stay inside and keep your gun loaded." Whitey was now awake and also ready with his gun. "Stay, Whitey," said Petra. Like an experienced snooper she shot out the door, hiding behind tree trunks. Suddenly she shot, and then she reloaded, and shot again. The two shots echoed into the hills. There was silence. She reloaded, and carefully moved stealthily. There was a groan, an agonizing gurgle.

"Why did you shoot, man?" he was trying to say. He lay there crumpled on the ground, the dogs pouncing around him. Petra screamed at the dogs.

"Weg met jou voetsak" (away with you footbag), she yelled, and they backed off.

The man was bleeding profusely; his scarlet tunic was blackening all across the chest, and blood ran in between his fingers. Red smooth and thick like rich dark velvet.

"I'm not a foe," he croaked, and he looked up to Petra. He was so young and he looked familiar, very fair and handsome. His brass helmet was on the grounds and beads of perspiration had wetted his face and neck, his blonde hair stuck to his forehead.

Suddenly Petra seemed aware of what she had done. She had killed a young man, some mother's son, who was very little older than her own precious Canaan. He was rattling in his chest, she knew the sound, she had heard it before many times, that was a rattle of death. She knelt down beside him, and Kathy and Whitey were out there now.

"Oh my God, mother, it's just a young man, alone on a horse. See, there's his horse tied to the wheels of the cart, that's why the horses were making all the noise."

Whitey stole around, gun in hand.

"No, Missy, there is nobody. Nobody at all. Just a strange horse with silver pistols beside the saddle."

Pistols were in the saddle bays not even unstrapped. Kathy looked at Petra.

"Oh my God, mother, what have we done?"

The man's hand, with the blood between the fingers, fell and lay limp beside him and his blue young eyes were staring. Staring at Petra.

"What did he want here, Kathy? Why was he alone at the stables? We know what happened to our landswomen, put into camps, with children under terrible conditions, and all their livestock destroyed along with their crops," as she said that she picked up his hand and felt for a heartbeat. The rattling noise had ceased. "The heart is no longer beating, Kath. Whitey, now what shall we do?" she was nervous and trembling, they all looked at each other. "No ja, before the children wake, we must get this soldier to the cemetery. Whitey, we have to be careful to be rid of this rooi baagtjie (red jacket)." Kathy was staring at the man.

"Mama," she said, "that man's face reminds me of someone." She knelt down, opened his tunic and took from inside his breast pocket his wallet. It was crammed full of pictures and papers and his own identification saying his name and rank number. He was Captain James Austin Armstrong. There was also a letter Kathy read.

My cousins live at Sonnestroom, it said, *and my uncle is called Lion. My uncle Julius is a lawyer* and the letter went on to describe the route and all about grandmother Lady Hora Jacobsen.

"Oh Jesus, Mama, do you know what we've done? This Redcoat we have killed is our English relation. This young soldier is the son of Moya, who is grandma Cathy's daughter, who married Armstrong, had her wedding at Sonnestroom, she then went to England. Oh dear God," she got up and flung her arms about Petra. "Moya," she said, "Moya was Uncle Julius' sister."

The horror of what they had done was paralyzing. They were crying, and while they wept, they talked.

"He must have been looking for us, Ma, he was family. Our own family. Oh Mama. Oh Mama."

Petra seemed stunned. Life seemed to have drained from her, life was always draining from her. Why was she being punished?

"Kathy," she said, she sank down, "I'm going to faint. Why does God see fit to punish me always, already my heart is burdened with grief too heavy to bear. Why then should I be so punished? Why then did I not be given some sign? If he had a chance he would have shouted, 'Don't shoot, I'm family,' but he couldn't see me, he was warding off the dogs, and I, slyly creeping up on him...I murdered him. Maybe I have to pay for all the sins of everyone, so they are all free, maybe that's God's way."

Whitey brought an old horse, "Bloiepens" an old grey that they used, to turn a pug mill that mixed the mud from which they made bricks. He was in a harness and drew a sled also used for carrying wood and felled trees.

"Hold him, Missy," he said to Kathy. "Missus and me, we will put the soldaat onto the sled and take him to the cemetery."

They pulled him by his boots which were shiny and bright, and then wrapped him in a blanket and rolled him onto the sledge.

"Go, Whitey, you and Blowpens go down to the graveyard. We must bury this man and we must not say a word. If we do, Whitey, the British will hang us. They will not know it was all a horrible mistake. Go Whitey, to the graveyard."

Kathy took all the soldier's papers, removed the ring from his little finger, took his pocket watch and his saber, and the silver pistols from the holsters on each side of his saddle. She put them all into her skirt, gathered it up like a large basket and walked with her mother on one side, the saber handle in her skirt, and the long blade pointing skywards to the back of her. What was there to think? Who ever could answer all the curious riddles of life? Dead was dead. It was the end. No one can restore life into death. And why in God's name should war find its way into the very heart of her home life? She felt like a tornado had swept through her mind and soul. Her thinking was flattened. Her mother, so brave, so burdened by grief, had yet another weight to bear. Dear God, they killed their own flesh and blood? So young, so handsome a man, only started into the prime of his life.

"Ma," she said, "come, Mama, I will make you some coffee. We must be strong for each other, we do not want that the children should know what has just happened."

Despondently they sat down and neither of them spoke. Bunches of tied up onions hung from protruding nails, sticking out from the rafters and the skins of animals were spread across the floor. The stone shone with beeswax between the skins. A tray was constantly laid for coffee, and the big oven was already warm. The servants came early to kindle the stove then went back awhile, returned later, when it was all hot and ready, to prepare breakfast.

Kathy put the big black kettle onto the big stone and the fireplace which was by now already warm. They sat there together, morose and silent. Neither spoke a word and the birds were everywhere. The day was well started. Outside on the veranda, a swallow was building a little mud nest; it darted in and out, plugging together little lumps of mud in a corner. As Petra looked, it seemed as though the mud was dampened, perhaps made wet, mixed with blood. She knew that sand. She knew the look of blood on the sands of Africa. She'd seen so much. Maybe it was that wet patch where the body lay? It was all so useless.

"Oh Jesus," she wailed aloud, "Please give me some strength, some courage."

And the Rand was filling with British soldiers, everywhere.

Forty - Two

There are different versions of what actually triggered off the Boer War in 1877: the following incident is said to be the truth. A Boer farmer did not have money to pay the taxes, demanded by the British, who threw him off his land. He lost his home and 300 Boers took up arms. The same time, the British annexed the Transvaal. No Boer could accept such interference. They did not care about the British fighting Bapedi. "Let them fight," they said, but to annex their land (approved by Disraeli in England) brought absolute anger and resentment. The Boers had taught them a good lesson at Majuba! Humiliation rather than war! It was this incident that sparked the war fires.

All land greatly increased in value. There was growing European interest. They thought diamonds were everywhere, gold in the Transvaal, diamonds in the Cape. Banks refused loans if taxes were not paid. Black people swarmed into the land to come and work in the mines, Indians came to grow sugar, and tea plantations developed. Many came in from railway construction and mining. The Cape grew suspicious of the British and did not accept their interferences. Kimberly became the 2nd largest settlement. And the Cape because, it was the strongest for organizing the diamond fields economically! It was also an incentive to bring about the union of four areas.

It has been suggested by some sources that this is what triggered off the Boer War, and the Boers looked to Paul Kruger for leadership. He was elected president four times. He was an experienced commando leader.

With an English father and an African mother, and a wild and cunning Bushman's brain, Lion went to war and with him, Eden. Two and three quarter years of a humiliating, devastating, infamous imperialist war.

AFTER THE WAR

Lion and Eden climbed out of the trench. Neither knew who had dug the damn trench. There were a great deal of shooting and explosions, so it seemed the right place to be. They had come through a storm, a torrential downpouring that never seemed to end. When morning came, it was like the land had become a vlei. The spruits were filled with rushing little flash floods and when he found the wagon it had sunk 1/2 way up to his wheels. Lion laughed, had his own private joke. This place seemed out of the shooting zone, where it was strewn with empty tins, bullet shells and cigarette packets. It smelled of war. Even rain had not washed away the rattle of musketry he imagined he heard, but birds were singing, doves and shrikes and drongas. Somewhere a dog was barking.

He exhaled. "I've had enough. Come Eden, we move," Lion said.

"Don't touch Bully Beef tins, Brits make them into bombs with gunpowder." He gave a weary sigh. He paused, looking skywards. He muttered, "Some men enjoy war. Not me, Eden, war is not for me. I really dislike everything about it, it's hateful. We do it because we have to, both for our family and for our land, to survive: Gold, diamonds, money, vineyards, the British want all of it. I can't say I don't like that myself, they gave me much to be thankful for." He chuckled away.

"I should think so, Lion," Eden said, "they gave you more than that—they made you a rich man. It takes all kinds of people to make the world, and all kinds of ways to be allowed to live in it. I'm not sure about wars."

There was a volley of gunfire, a Dutch voice was speaking to his son, "Jy moet n man wees," (you must be a man). They looked at each other and supposed it was a father talking to his frightened young son. They looked down the slope. Someone was searching the saddlebag of a horse that had been shot. "The soldiers are moving," they heard in Dutch, and then something about rednecks and the sun. Suddenly, Eden said, "Tell me, Pa, why do you hate your brother?"

Lion turned. "I did not know you noticed."

"Everyone noticed, Pa! Not only I."

"Julius is not my brother." Just then there was more firing, so their conversation ceased.

Suddenly out of nowhere, as he was looking at his horses, there stood Ndoda, who had come out of hiding. They looked about warily, then heartily greeted. They hugged each other like blood brothers. Lion was truly so happy to see Ndoda. "The horses were grazing up near the spring, Mr. Lion, and those English, they found me," Ndoda said. "They looked at the horses and asked a lot of questions, they did not shoot, no sir, they were good horses. The captain told the soldier to do nothing, nothing to me and nothing, no harm to the horses. I thought today we would meet in heaven. They just rode away, just like that!"

A laager

"What do you think Ndoda?" Lion said.

"Don't know, Sir, the Captain was a good man, maybe it was our English Head Collars? That stopped them. Don't know sir, we are here, they did us no harm."

"Is that a laager? Come, follow me, we will go and join them," said Lion.

"No sir, those men are not a laager. Those men are deserters, that is what the farmers said. Myself, I don't know what deserters means, but I heard that spoken. Come, we will help them fix the wagon and harness up and then we go home."

"What good luck, Ndoda, that you come here at this time," Lion said.

"Oh yes, my chief. It is not luck! We know the busheld. It's me that is lucky? Do you know that black people have guns and fight for these British?" said Ndoda.

"It has been reported to us, Ndoda," Lion said. "Come, we move now. It is lucky we have the wagon."

"Yes, and very lucky I have you." Ndoda cut graze and stacked it into the graze links. He did his job well, he always did. "Shall I make us a drink?"

"Hold these leads, Masser Lion." He took a three-legged pot. He saw there was venison in the read box and a bottle of pork fat. He needed the fat to grease the axels and also the barrels of the guns. He moved the bandoliers away from the fire. He took Lion's mauser, the old Takhaar. They had coffee together.

Lion, touching his neck, asked Eden what it was. "It's a Goddamned Bont tick." There was no actual road, but they knew the direction homewards. They came eventually upon a deserted homestead, hardly visible in the trees. "We will go in there, Ndoda. I think the clouds are gathering for another storm. Put our horses in that cow shed and we will put the wagon sideways across what was the door. The English sods have burned the doors." Lightning flashed.

"Oh, the sky is angry," said Ndoda.

"Angry and disgusted at wanton killing I saw. Men killing each other and destroying food and animals," said Lion. "It is no wonder the skies roar and rumble so violently."

And then it rained like a solid fall of water. They sat, the three of them, water splashed through the burned out window, beating upon the zinc roof. They were pleased the horses had shelter. Holes were filled with water running everywhere, rushing down towards the slope. Spring clean, a good washing will do our land good.

They heard a frightened goat bleating. Eden jumped out into the rain and brought it in, a distressed mother seeking desperately for her kid, probably eaten by a British soldier. She was full of milk. They pulled it in. They gave her mealies and some graze. They squeezed milk from both her teats. Ndoda had warm milk from her body. He loved it. "Two teats on the hoof, Ndoda," said Eden. Ndoda said it made him think of his childhood. Lion did not feel too well. "I will take you home, Baasie," he said. When the rain ceased they again traveled. "Tell me, Ndoda," said Lion, "do you know when a man is dead?"

"I know Baas Lion, all peoples know when a man is dead, 'no beating heart.' Haat! You, Baasie, have teached me."

"So tell me, how will you know?"

"I got it in my head, Baasie." He patted his head. "Kidney," he said, patting his head knowingly.

Eden gave a chuckle. They all laughed. "Brains, man, you have brains up there."

"Oh, yes," he said, "I have brens."

In a good mood again, Eden broached the subject. "Tell me about Julius," he said.

"I'm not dying yet, Eden," Lion said. "It's only a bloody tick bite. True, I don't feel too good though." The further they went from the goat's house, the less mud they encountered, and the worse they felt. Strange, Africa, a few miles back it was stormy and wet, mud was deep and now it was dry. "Ndoda, where's your famous Muti? You have brens, and you are also a very good Bushman. Where's your medicine man?"

"Ah, Mr. Lion, that tree does not grow in this area, where the dust blows. But I shall find trees."

"Yes, I suppose he knows what he's talking about. What would we do if there were no trees?" Lion said. "Did you know, Eden," he said, "that the Bayobab tree is hollow from the fork down? Do you know why? Because it stores water there, for times of drought. It's not exactly a desert tree, it's a wise tree."

"Whatever made you think of that?"

"Just that, I said, there are all kinds of ways to live in our world." They both felt peculiar; unused to not being well, they did not know how to handle it .They both felt that something was wrong in their bodies.

Whitey at home, the home guard, tells the children a story:

Whitey was standing at the farm entrance, where there hung a round steel plough disc on a post. He picked up an iron rod and smote the gong. The gong was used for herders, ox-wagon drivers, etc. It was truck in the morning and again at lunchtime, then again in the evening. It was like a time giver, time to start and time to knock off, time to break for lunch. If a stranger called, they also struck the gong.

The children came running up to him. "Why did you strike the gong, Whitey?"

"I don't know," he said, "like old times for your grandfather, no, for your great grandfather. He was a very strong man, do you know about his story?"

"No Whitey, we don't," they said.

"Ekskuus, (Excuse me) I will tell you one day."

"Tell us now, Whitey, please tell? My daddy brought us a book from the grammar school, and it has some stories, lots of stores. Tell us Whitey."

He paused, getting his facts right before he told them. "Yes," he said, "your great grandfather was plowing the field. He used one ox and his English plough. He had one ox of the span who was his favorite. While he was plowing—do you know how to plough?"

"Yes, Whitey, we know how to plough."

"This farmer was busy plowing, his ox was pulling and he was pushing to guide the plough and keeping straight lines. Down that road came a lost traveler and his horse was overloaded. He called to your grandfather to ask which track he should go to get to his destination. Well, Mr. McCabe, he knows all things, he stopped the ox and he picks up the plough in his right hand and he points the direction. Did he just pick up the plough as a pointer to point the way? That is what he did. Not for showing off, you see, just because he was so strong." The children listened quite absorbed, then ran off laughing to the cowshed to examine the old iron and the old steel plough.

At home the women waited. People passed on horseback and runners who knew the footpaths, or short cuts as they called them. It was amazing how fast news traveled. Farmers called it the bush telegraph. The settler community had changed; pressures forced upon settlers were more powerful than arbitrary agreements. Lives were made difficult. The black people pressed south and settlers north. Albany settlers moved into the wilder world of Africa, but among trekkers was dissension, bitter conflict, uneasy peace.

Kathy was of two minds. She wanted to get into a cart and go and look for her family—well, Eden and Lion. And where was Ndoda? Looking across the valley and distant houses, she imagined she saw smoke coming from chimneys. She wondered where all the stolen cattle went. The bush seemed formidable! Once there was a Hottentot, handcuffed to one of the black men on their way to arbitrate: they were set upon by marauders. Unable to unlock the handcuffs, the marauders chopped off the Hottentot's arm, then they shot him, and completely disappeared into the bush. On the slopes, the bush was thick, also filled with cactus Euphorbia and spiky aloes. Enemies were invisible, and now they had guns; she watched for dust in the distance.

She called Whitey. "Let's go, Whitey, and meet our men," she said. "You know they took a wagon with them."

"No, Miss Kathy," he said, "better we wait. We do not know what is outside of our lands, nor inside, Miss Kathy! There is war and there is peace. That is what I understand."

Kathy wondered how she would tell her father that she did not save all his sheep. He was so proud of his merinos. Had he not gone to fight they would all still be there. Mind, she and Whitey and all who could help, they did save a lot—all the lambs, some of the sheep, all the rams except one, and while they were closing them in, some of the chickens were bagged and carried off. Thank goodness the horses and the bull were safe. It was such a thrill after two days the big rooster named "Careful Hans," came through the bushes back home. He had lost a lot of feathers, but there he was: a survivor or escapee who found his way home.

The shelter Petra had the foresight to make really was the thing that saved them all. That big hole where once all the earth was taken and used for building with, like plaster between stones and brick, she made it into a huge fenced and covered shelter. She had them place the ploughs and harrows and sleds and zinc in front where the entrance was. And so, many were well hidden and thus saved: the British had changed their brilliant uniforms to a far less conscious kit, they were in khaki now, which had almost fooled the Boers. It was confusing, but the Boers are a slim, alert people. They could outmaneuver anyone in the bush, the women and children as well, women kept the home fires burning, as the saying goes.

The succession of numerous wars had toughened the settlers, and scattered them. Ruined by deprivation they spread out, founded new towns, new harbors, new roads and pioneered trails into the hinterland. They brought also news, manners and customs: exercised influence in many ways to a rising new nation. Imagine the joy and relief when the men finally arrived home?

They were home! Lion and Eden and Ndoda were home, thankfully. When they returned after Majuba, some of Lion's commandos celebrated. This homecoming was so wonderful there was that celebratory atmosphere, but celebration was never Lion's inclination. Coming home was a rare and wonderful pleasure. They wee just so glad to be home. Lion always claimed his bed was his refuge! Who goes to war in a wagon? They all said, but no one cared to explain. Lion's thinking was always way way ahead. He knew what they were doing, why, when and how. He was home now, whole with Eden. Ndoda and his horses, that was enough. The battles were over.

There was a loud knock on the door, Marta was there instantly. Marta was always there. Marta, who lives forever, reported it was Ndoda. Whenever Lion was not in good health, he would jokingly call Ndoda, who unjokingly applied his wild African remedies. "Come in Ndoda," they both called.

"I have found the medicine," Ndoda said. It was obvious he had been running. "I want to speak to Mr. Lion." He was panting and had not yet found his normal breathing. "This muti will cure you, sir," he said. "I went out to search for the tree and I am very pleased I find one. It is a bad taste. Please come outside." They both did not yet feel well and were somewhat wary. He got two small stools upon which to sit. He then dug a hole about a foot or two deep and placed the stools beside the holes. "Sit down," he said. Both Lion and Eden obeyed. He threw the spade aside and ordered Marta to bring him a jar of boiling water. He crushed up the leaves and twigs and poured on the boiling water. "I have made you a good health tea. When it has been brewing you will have tea from the forest which has been teached to me by the bushman. When you have swallowed this tea your blood will be clean and your stomach very empty." Lion did not hesitate, but Eden was wary.

"Perhaps you're sick from the ticks?"

"Come now, Sir, you drink," he said. Lion threw it back in his throat, and swallowed. It was ghastly. Eden did not fancy to drink it.

"Come on Eden," Lion said, "Don't be a sissy, man, knock it back." So with a sputtering struggle, he swallowed it. Ndoda pulled their legs astride. A few moments passed. Then suddenly Lion heaved and threw up, dredging his guts, purging and contorting like a nauseous animal. Then Eden followed. They retched and vomited until they both thought they would die, while Ndoda looked on. Finally they could vomit no more. They were exhausted. Ndoda summoned Marta for more boiled water, boiled but not boiling, he said. So they both drank hot water. "After you finish," Ndoda said, "you go to bed." Ndoda covered the holes, washed his hands and picked up the spade. He seemed satisfied. He had run a long way and he too was tired. It was time to rest himself now. He said his medicine was "la-tie-le" (La-tea-LE) as in Egg. Only a self-respecting "Nganga," or medicine man, knew of this tree and its healing powers. Of course they were both right as rain the following day, never having doubted Ndoda's medicine for a single moment. They had become devoted believers in Ndoda's remedies. Nature's 'cure all,' and he sure did have cures.

Lion was also devoted to his span, Braam Piet had known each animal by name. When they came home, Braam used to wait. No matter what bad or inclement weather, he waited at the gate, and patting each ox he wished them all good night by name. Lion wanted his spans to be like Braam's. His oxen were one of his greatest loves, and he succeeded. Despite advancement and progress, Lion really loved his spans, just like Braam used to love his span. He knew each animal and he also waited, like Braam, at the gate to their stable—once it was a kraal, a circle of land surrounded by thornbush. One could hardly forget the old kraal, Yessis. How it was all changed. There were lions then, and leopards and so many animals stealthily sneaking wherever fowls or lambs were. It took years, but his span were trained, affectionate and safe, protected, their mangers filled with hay and oats, and didn't his oxen look so beautiful?

He patted them as they passed, so gentle as they avoided hurting him with their big horns. "Goodnight Vaalpens, Goodnight Kaptein," and so it went until they were all inside. Yes, he really felt deep love for his oxen. They had grown old together and he felt thwarted if he could not be there to greet them every evening. As long as he lived, so would they! He understood those boys; they were seldom understood, so often sent to an abbatoir.

Time melted away, swiftly passed the years, children grew up, and parents grew older. But life was good. Lion looked around. "There's a time for everything," he thought. It would be nice to retire and enjoy what he worked to achieve. He could not call himself self-made, no, no, he remembered his good fortune every day of his life. He thought of his little mother, the little blithe spirit of Sonnestroom, flitting about, struggling to learn English properly, like a little brown butterfly. A Monarch maybe? His father, the brave Englishman, and Kathy, his true friend. She gave him "Tombe." He had a rush of emotion, the thought of Tombe always made him sad. But finding those stones in the drift made him glad. He smiled. Yes, he loved Tombe. The name suited her, "young girl." What a sweet love, unconditional like a dog rather than a cat. He smiled, remembering how, when the ewes had twins, he fed one to Tombe. They had such fun. He thought he felt a pain somewhere in his body. It happened sometimes, when he thought of Tombe, when he dreamed of Louisa.

A beautiful white flower that blooms in the night, trumpet-like, slowly unfolded. The moths would visit; it was one flower one could actually watch opening up. Damned if he could remember its name. Twilight brought melancholia to a man's soul: a patch of time, the ending day, a quiet spell, and the arrival of night. Night, like a soft, beautiful, dusky shroud across the whole wide earth.

Julius sat at his desk, neat and elegant in a dark English suit. He wore a diamond pin in his stock, and a rose in his buttonhole. He was pondering. He was a hybrid, part Uitlander and part Imperialist. An elegant speaker, he was a self-made man, highly respected. He was deeply impressed with the tremendous success of this young man calling himself Eden McCabe. His mother often told him that Eden distinctly looked like him. That was alright, it pleased him, but never would he accept his father's half-caste son, Lion. He hated him for as long as he could remember. Nobody tells Julius H.J. what to do, or when to do something. Conceited, narcissistic, alone. A monied man—a lone monied man.

Kruger's reputation had lessened after Mjuba. The veld had bred in him fine qualities of leadership—strong yet flexible, human cunning and self-reliance. He had told Joubert to order thousands of Mausers from Krupp, because the Martin Henry Single Shots were not as good. Paul Kruger considered Rhodes a plotter and a traitor. Julius was interested in politics, as well as gold shares and land investments. The Boers regarded him as slim (clever). Chamberlain waited for Milner, a frustrated man, bearing the weights of lost dreams and aspirations of being England's prime minister. He was offered two choices, Treasury and War Office. He chose the colonies to make Britain greater. He believed that the new Imperialism demanded expansion. An Uitlander coup was expected. As with Jameson, failure was one of the "war jokes" of history.

Julius came to visit in all his splendor, looking quite regal. All were whispering, glancing sideways, eager to hear what his mission would be. Eden welcomed him. The whole family was seated in the large, comfortable living room. Petra was ever wary. Lion, a proud grandfather, was most attentive to the children. Julius requested a private conversation with Eden.

"Eden, please do so in the study which you know is our office," Lion said. "This, after all, was your father's office."

Lion rose from where he was seated and Kathy sprang, "Pappa, please, just tell Julius to truth, please do that for me, I do not believe in family skeletons and secrets," she said.

Eden joined Julius and there was no more privacy. Eden put his arms around Lion.

"Julius has just offered me a most fantastic proposition," he said, "but I have given him my answer. I do not wish to accept." There was a pause. Lion stood tall.

He looked tawny and strong. He still rode a horse like a youth. "This day had to come, Julius. I think Providence saw to it. You and I have the same blood, but I am not your brother. I'm a half-caste, born of Marietje, the servant girl who worked for Willem de Swart. I have no illusions. My father is Frederick McCabe. Your uncle, is who I am. That's all we have in common."

Julius started to speak, but Lion held up his hand.

"We are worlds apart. You are evil man, and it's a problem to my mind how the beautiful Kathy could have given birth to you. You are the real bastard here, Julius. You are untouchable, ugly. If there is a God, you sure have a great deal of explaining. Remember when you brutally shot my precious loving pet, the beautiful Tombe. I still hurt for her. Did you think I did not know, that you killed her? Or that you would escape your filthy deed?"

Julius tried to speak. "No, no, no!"

Lion held up his hand, indicating he should not speak.

"Let me speak. I come now to Louisa." It was hard to speak. He looked away. "Another gentle creature," he swallowed hard. "You raped that lady, in your own home, you rotten bastard! She died because of you. We have her clothes. You ordered Swaarthaas to burn them, but we had them here. It was only because of Mrs. Kathy and our father that you did not go to trial. There is no forgiveness, nor desire that you are any part of us or this family!"

He sat down in the big chair. Eden and he looked deeply at each other.

Julius spoke. "I am your father, Eden."

There was an uncomfortable silence.

"No sir, I have only one father, best friend and confidante!" He moved over to Lion and the fear passed away from Lion's face. "This is my father, whom I love and honor. Till only death do us part." Lion gave an audible laugh. "Happiness is not all about money and prestige, you have just given me, sweet satisfaction, like Xosa loved a revenge." This was the day Lion had long awaited. This was sweet satisfaction ,revenge! He swung around, picked Eden up and planted him beside himself.

"You have set my soul free."

Julius picked up his attaché case. His bitter face showed both hate and a proud pale disdain as he elegangtly, he made his exit.

Forty-Three

U p on the slope was a dug out shelf, an almost level patch of greenery. It was special, this place—one could feel it, and automatically straightened one's clothes and wiped one's hands clean, the little graveyard. Below the grave of Xosa was a new mound of earth, pretty fresh flowers among the wild flowers. White arums, some open, some still spiked lily buds, clusters of happy lily buds. They seemed to always bloom. It was special. Petra stood, her eyes searching, wandering with her thoughts. She used to be such a happy, fiery girl, but she became a sad, hurting woman. Her face lit up.

"Well, at least the men came home safe!" she said out loud.

She looked around. Yes, they had all helped to save this lovely place. She almost felt like crying. Crying does sometimes wash away an engulfing emotion but she had little enthusiasm these days.

"Maar, Here die wereld is so mooi" ("But God, the world is so pretty.")

At 5 a.m., the roosters crowed and the early birds were out already. Whitey heard a single shot. Ja, it came from their place. He let himself out and trundled down in that direction. The smell of gunsmoke was hanging in the air. This air was fresh like all new mornings. He took his time, yawning and blinking his eyes. He looked around, smelling the sweet smell of jasmine and then also the smell of gun smoke. He liked both smells. Lots of his friends liked the smell of gunpowder. The dew was on the grass. He took a shortcut toward the smell. Ja, it was in the graveyard. He stopped and looked all around, blinking again; there she was, so small on the rugged ground, lying on the grave of Canaan. Part of her head was blown away.

He saw the gun Lion had taught him to use, that she also used so well herself. He felt great pity. Sometimes tragedy is so great, the human mind can become bewildered. There is no nemesis, no destiny, no hope: caught in a net of misery, the hurt beyond endurance! She never ceased grieving for her son. Her hands had relaxed and had opened, and the gun had fallen from her grasp. He wondered what he must do, and how would he tell them at the house? The morning sun had broken and beams of light were sharp in the sky. What was the hurry? No one had risen. Everything seemed half asleep till the sun came out. It silently, brightly shone a beam across her body, upon her face and upon her hands, shining with a million prisms; on her finger was her three-stone ring. He stood gazing at it. She was a good woman, so tired of sadness that made her suffer. Look at that ring, young Canaan made it for her. Yesterday, today, tomorrow. How that child loved his mother. Yes, and she, him.

Today. He was not sure whether or not she was right to end her life in such sadness. Such a clever, strong woman. Maybe she'd be glad and maybe find the spirit of Canaan. He suddenly saw an end. Such a good worker, full of ideas. He was sad. Who will collect the seeds and feed the birds, and keep the garden? He was silent, there was no one to speak to. So quiet. He felt no shock, and there was no need to hurry. Tomorrow will come, as it always does.

He straightened up, staring at those sparkling diamonds. He paused, staring at the ring, looking or thinking. Then, slowly, he walked away. He loved living in his house and his own life with these people. It was his family as well. How important they made him when Mr. Eden got married, exactly the same like Paul Kruger! He looked. It was an important day. So now where will he work? And will they bury him in this graveyard? He would think about that, but for now he was still the man inside the Big House. He must pull himself together, he would soon know what to say. Be like the Big Baas, be along now, there are many things to be done.

Lion and Eden seemed ever at arms. Funny thing, they both behaved older now, but eternally on guard, always alert. Some of the men in the Commandos were well into their 70s. In war it's all the same.

"Mind," they vowed vehemently, "No rooinek would touch our farms or harm our family and friends."

That's how it was!

It was a mystery how they always were there when danger lurked. The British did not get their roasts "on the hoof" as they bragged. Not near their farms, and if they camped or settled near their farms, well that was something else, under cover of darkness they disappeared. However, few ventured nearer to discover. Lion, Ndoda, Eden and Whitey—a little great Commando. Whitey rode a horse like a cripple, but never made a single mistake. Ndoda learned to enjoy riding, and he was a warrior. Under cover of darkness, in the African bush, they were invincible, and now it was time to measure one's good fortune. The fighting had ended.

There were groups of soldiers returning, riding across the land, some who had actually been hiding and others believing they were triumphant, still wearing weapons.

"Keep out of reach," Lion ordered.

These half informed chaps could and would make bad mistakes.

"Yes, well, they were going home, it's so damn nice to have a home to go to."

The men were grateful for their good fortune. To hell with Vereeniging, yet somehow the air felt cleaner. Losses in life were a horror; the aftermath, after the toll it has taken, leaves little consolation. People's minds, bodies and emotions. It was confusing, the fears and insecurity. If a man shot and killed murderers or robbers, he could be charged for murder, but soldiers who killed innocents get rewards, even medals for distinguished services. If we follow the laws of nature we are better by far. After all, nature is also a mother, and understood the consequences of the interferences and the mistakes of man. This was an unfair war. There should never have been any bloody war, or winners, losers, or conquerors.

How magical, though, that against great odds, one man reigned over his lands? Not only did he preserve the land, but he rescued horses, drove sheep from enemy, extinguished fires, saved the herds (some of them) and even the zinc stayed on the roofs of many houses! There were large gatherings of people around now, church parades and long church services. Lion and his family were not church people, never entered a church, not even for their children's weddings. In fact, the cross, to them, was a symbol of cruelty. Many helpless souls had died that way, long ago, crucified and nailed to a goddamned cross. Long ago, that was the method of execution, equally as cruel, evil, ugly and merciless as being stoned to death. At least there was mercy in a bullet or even the hangman's noose. Some men are protectors—leaders. Clever enough to go to war, even in a wagon. Yet still able enough to divert and save, rather than kill. Across the Cape of Good Hope "quiet" fell.

Peace reigned. Years of levelling took place which sped on in rebirth and repair. War made the embittered people more conscious of life's values, property, and possessions, not to mention time.

It resurrected everywhere, even the neglected vines covering the old crooked wooden pagodas made large dewry benches that hung underneath. Ant hills grew taller, and swallows returned. Nights again filled with magical night-time yowels, cricket shreiks, skunks and barks, and the distant beat of the African drum.

250,000 British troops disbanded to be sent home, and also black troops. There were 7,000 Boers dead, not to mention the destruction of their herds and stock and homes, etc. Of course, it was the seizure of their families that decided them, to sign for peace. Men dispersed, some just rode away. There seemed to be no law and order.

Forty-Four

"You know, Eden, I would like to ride through our lands, I'd like to sort of sweep away any debris or reminders of this time. You and I and Ndoda will fix a clean up programme!" Swiftly the days passed. It was quiet, though Vereeniging still buzzed. It was a rare pleasure for Lion to be with his family in peace. War had made them more conscious of life, of living, of family, the joy of life—especially regarding their wishes in regard to property and possessions.

"We will check for campsites and shoot the Bully Beef tins, and keep in touch and in sight of each other. We'll take food with us and have a day in the veld. Make sure we are armed." One never knows what lurks in unreachable places.

They rested, lived and loved and laughed. Happy days pass more quickly.

Hard work resumed. Horse riding and games, hen houses and repairs. Hard work and order saw the farms resurrect. Pigs made bigger litters, heifers gave more heifers—hen houses and chickens—flowers came and went with the seasons, zealously in refurbishing. Lambs were dropping, strangely out of season. The earth seemed to be shedding the horrors of ugly, in every corner, rocks or cliffs. The rebirth was infectious.

Roasted lamb and good wines made the women merry. Beswipsed (lightly drunk) and full of amazing nonsense talk. People loosen up after a trifle too much wine. Uninhibited, less inhibited. Vino Veritas, it is said. Yes, nothing wrong with free speech—freedom. And unburdening fears. Whatever peace had come—it was gratefully and graciously lived. Life was good—life was better than before. Healing happened. Time passed.

Lion decided he, Eden and Ndoda should do a clean up and check ride across the land. Ndoda brought the horses.

Lion sprang like an athlete into the saddle.

"Such alacrity," said Eden, and he and Ndoda did the same.

"Here, Ndoda, take your gun and put extra ammo in your pockets. We must keep together and in touch. And if any of us encounter anything wrong or if we separate, shoot twice into the air."

"Come Eden," said Lion. "There is no hurry, no urgency. We can walk. I was thinking last night about all the Boer leaders, Joubert, Cronje, and Botha."

"And what about the fiery de Witt," said Eden.

"Ja, he gave us many a good laugh. They were all big thinkers, Eden, but what about us? You and I are half British, hey?" They laughed out loud.

"We fought as Boers, fighting for our rights, our land," said Eden. "Strange, our family, don't you think?"

"We had a little crown land, part given, part purchased. We bought, we amalgamated, we got ourselves quite a lot of territory. Sailor, farmer, worker, soldier, leader." Eden was muttering, seemed to be turning things about in his mind.

"No Pappa, we have done our duty, especially you. 'Lion's Law,' I called it!"

They laughed at themselves like the ponderous Boers often do. Eden spoke softly now, like he was thinking rather than talking.

"We were forced to kill, Pop."

"Ja, or be killed," Lion replied, "But remember, we avoided it many times. We are alike, Eden, you and I. You will need to know things, EED, like I have provided for Jules' girl Moya, she's in England, as you know. It was such a sadness. Poor Petra unknowingly killed her young son. Poor Petra, was struggling to handle the death of Canaan. Then this other mistake. Don't ask me why, but I always felt that Canaan was too tender a human. I could not fathom his destiny. He was sort of too good to be true. Too gentle. A tender child. You know my lioness Thombe. She also was too tender to be a lion."

Eden did not want to intrude on his musings.

"That boy was too gentle. Once, I found myself feeling he was the reincarnation of Louisa. The way I see it all, you, Eden, must take the family, our children, yourself, and all you hold dear. Go away, dissolve into anonymity, a renaissance, anomalous. I cannot think of enough words. Go into a new beginning where no one at all knows you, where there is no knowledge, reflection or trace—a rebirth! That way you will survive and live on. Peace. Acts of war are not ever completely swept away. There will always be someone or something—retribution, hate, revenge, history—lurking. Escape boy, you will survive. In the rich valleys, vines grow well, earth and rainfall are plentiful."

"I have nothing to hide, Pop."

"Oh yes, you do, Eden," said Lion, "Forgiving is possible, but never, is forgetting. You understand what I mean."

They came to the little spring oozing out. Nice clear water. Lion palled his horse.

"We escaped death by a whisker several times, but here we are, alive. Where did these soldiers camp? I don't see many signs. Another thing, Eden, when I die, don't bring a predikant or any of that, you know, the religious things! No hollow show, my boy, I have told you before where I'd like to go. Do you remember? I have shown you, there were the echo lives, among the beautiful wild flowers in our special place."

Eden listened, but didn't say much. They dismounted. He never felt closer to any creature or human. Just deep love for this Lion! So whistling for Ndoda, they chatted and joked and laughed the day away. They had lunch where the water trickled, and the three men happily talked. Somehow when the subject got on to spirits and ancestral beliefs, Ndoda explained how they put a dish of food on the graves of those that die, so their spirits can dine before they go away.

"You believe in spirits Ndoda?"

"Yes, I do," Ndoda said. "We all become spirits."

"Who knows, Ndoda, maybe you are right. I have thought about it. I wonder what happens to all the energy, all what humans are?" said Lion.

"Me too, Pop," said Eden.

"Well, tell you what, if we do get to be spirits, mine will be there to guide you," and he touched Eden's shoulder affectionately.

"I don't want to be a pussy, Pop, but give me a hug!"

Mingling emotions flowed between them. These strong men, ruled by the sun, they were men in tune to the earth, in rhythm with the song of life. They laughed out loud.

"The way we love, Pop, people would think we are a bit queer."

"See how time has gone. Next week we will ride again, wherever we missed today," said Lion.

After their lunch they checked behind large rocks, caves in the kloof, on the slopes and around the dam area. They found one old vacated camp, some trails and a dugout, old cigarette stompies, and yes, Bully Beef tins. It seemed as though whoever had stopped there made a safe getaway. The lands, so far, were pretty well cleared. In fact, their farms had certainly not suffered badly, comparatively speaking. The slate roof and stone walls were fireproof and a great advantage. They rode on, in fun and laughter. Ndoda took a trail southwards. Eden and Lion got into another serious conversation. Eden, with a little fun had a little gallop. Lion could still ride like a young man. They had a fun race, and heard the sounds of cattle lowing somewhere, perhaps nearby. On a trail that had been used quite a lot by the cattle, they raced. The trail was wide enough. No one won, it was a tie, so they rode back up again. "Hey Ndoda!"

"Where is Ndoda? Hey, Ndoda! Where is he? Where has he gone?" They headed for home.

Playing childishly, they had overlooked their third man. They got home and called out loudly. No one had seen him. They went outside to the stables. Jesus, there was Ndoda's horse, the horse breathing as though he had just run a hefty race. He had obviously escaped, the stirrups dangling. Nervous now, Lion picked up the horse's hoof.

"This horse has come near a dam. See this mud?"

Suddenly two shots rang out from the direction of the dam not more than ten to fifteen minutes away. Whitey was very concerned. He pointed north.

"Heavy bush," he said.

"Whitey, see the cattle in, we must go!"

How careless of them to have lost touch with Ndoda. They loaded guns, strapped on a revolver. Both armed, they galloped in the direction of the shots.

"We will circle, Eden, you go that way and I will take this one."

There was an opening in the thick bush, and Lion felt sure, as he got in, that he heard Ndoda scream.

"Don't shoot, Mr. Lion! Don't shoot!"

"What is it, Ndoda?"

"Zulu warriors, Sir. They are armed, but unable to speak English."

Lion rode in. One man stood holding his spear in the throwing position.

"They want cattle, Mr. Lion. They say you have a bucket of diamonds, they say they know about it. You brought them to your home long back from the river. They want cattle, and that bucket."

Lion answered in a very loud voice. He shouted, "My cattle are on another farm."

He knew Eden would hear.

"They will kill both myself and you. They have stolen guns from the British. It's no use talking, Mr. Lion. These men are killers."

Hardly had Ndoda finished speaking when Eden emerged, from the unexpected side, he instantly mowed them down at lightning speed, firing straight into the group. "Lie low Ndoda!" At the very same instant, Lion fired into the man who was holding Ndoda, who was not yet tied up. They all fell, except Ndoda and Eden.

"This man is alive, Mr. Eden. He has been hit in his hips or backside. What shall I do with him?"

"Take his weapons, smash his spear, and let him go. Lion, for God's sake! Have you been hurt? Lion! Lion! Lion!" His voice was full of fear.

He fell down upon his father.

"Oh my God Ndoda! Check that these men are dead and come and help me!"

There was no time to waste.

"Lion," he called repeatedly. Lion had fallen.

Eden was in a desperate state. He loosened Lion's shirt.

"I can't see any wounds, but he is smiling, Sir. Is he joking?"

"Come, Ndoda, check. Oh, God, what's happened to you. I can't see a wound." No bloody wounds.

He felt for Lion's pulse and turned him over. No blood anywhere. He leaned over and listened to his heart beat, grappling at his throat, trying to find a pulse.

"Come Lion! Ndoda, help me! Help me Ndoda!"

He was shaking and nervous. They both were nervous. Ndoda put his head down against Lion's heart.

"Is he breathing, Ndoda, tell me? Tell me man!"

"Maybe the heart has failed, Mr. Eden? There is no beat, and no wounds, and see how strangely he smiles."

"Ndoda, he can't be dead," cried Eden. "No Ndoda, let me press his heart and lungs, we can start it again. God check all those others' guns, heartbeats, breathing."

Eden was on his haunches beside Lion. He was calling for help from any source. He even called God. In desperation he got up and Ndoda held him. What now? They both seemed stunned, speechless.

"Jesus, Ndoda, we have come through the jaws of death and living hell together. What now?" he wept. "I do not know, I cannot understand." His voice was trembling.

Suddenly, Lion's horse half reared and then galloped away, empty saddled, stirrups flying. Ndoda wiped his nose on his sleeve, and his eyes wide, stared as though in shock.

"Mr. Lion has gone home, Sir. I know well how he rides." He had taken his horse and gone home.

They watched the horse gallop out of sight.

"Go, Ndoda, ride my horse, bring back help, a wagon. I will stay with my father."

He sat down again beside Lion and stared at his happy, smiling face. Then, with his arm open in a questioning manner, he talked out loud.

"Tell me, Mother, did you call Lion away? Did you fetch him as you promised Kathy? You would."

It was eerie and helpless transcendent. A mystic man in a spiritual apprehension of truth beyond understanding. He placed his head upon Lion's abdomen. He wept as he waited. It took what seemed like hours.

Finally Lion was brought home and was carried to his room. It was dark now. There was no moon. They were all silent, bewildered. No one seemed to understand. Energy deserted them. No one remembered the terrifying experience Ndoda had undergone. Ndoda said not a word: he sank to the earth. Eden found a bottle of brandy and poured some into a container he found in the carriage and handed it to Ndoda who drank it all. They sat there together silent. They both were thinking, and wondered how much emotional distress one man can suffer? Eden drank some brandy from the bottle.

No news travels faster than the bush telegraph! News had spread. It was the new month starting, also a new moon. Not only the frontier, but the entire Cape got the news. The following day the press had front page news. From the Limpopo to the sea. Jan's paper got the news, and made him a glorious Leader Lost. It was on every tongue. Wagons, trains and horses started moving towards the Stone House.

Lion lay on his bed, still smiling. He looked happy and healthy. The truth is, he did not look like a dead man. The doctor arrived. After his examination was over he requested other doctors. He was unsure and soon there were four doctors in attendance. They could not find any reason for his death. They were all quiet.

"His body is sound, but his soul has fled," the first doctor remarked.

Telephones, carriages, dispatches and runners, thousands of mourners arrived, women made weird outbursts. Some in a strange attitude questioned if it were some hoax or mistake.

"Why is the man smiling? Is he dead?"

Many openly wept. Various sayings overheard everywhere.

"Hy het my plaas gered" ("He saved my farm")

"The man is alive."

"Uncapturable, undefeated, invincible!"

"Slim" ("Clever")

Overwhelming admiration was only surpassed by sorrow and mourning. A horse drawn carriage arrived with a footman and, the Union Jack flying high, it drove up to the house. In a full uniform decorated with masses of ribbon and medals and pips of brass and plumes, an officer respectfully removed his hat, and humbly requested to look at this man named Lion he had heard so much about. He wanted to look at him. Col. Aubrey Wools Sampson bid Lion, the mighty Lion, farewell. Thousands filed past in endless sorrow and saw Lion lay there, unchanged, for five days. It was as if he were the President of the land. Ever Boer from every nook and corner of the Cape of Good Hope stood to attention, some in tears. At a given time they fired 21 shots in respect of a unique human being, whose departure, like him, was unique. A Boer, smiling to the bitter end.

On the day of Lion's burial the news broke out in every paper across the land that Julius Hora Jacobsen, the uncle of Lion, while on a voyage to England, had been swept from the deck of the "Spirit of the Sea" during a violent storm and sad to say was never seen again. Rescue was impossible, having occurred at midnight when he was washed overboard into the dark marine depths.

Lion was not buried. No one would lift his coffin. No one could bring themselves to cover his body with earth. He was alive, they said. A stone vault was then erected—an odd imposing impromptu vault—built by many helpers purring words of love and affection and strange consolation, dripping constant tears. There he lay inside his vault. He remained smiling where the winds blow, and wild violets and lilies grow.

There are snatches of truth in stories and tales, and this is what happened and can truthfully be told with impunity. In fact, on that very day, the family was still reeling in shock. There came from outside a strange, almost musical lowing of cattle, a continual mournful lowing of cattle, all 36 service oxen. The span leader, who was always Lion's leader over the years, the front animal, for he had exceptionally large horns, was in front. Behind him followed all the span, circled the vault, and some scratched with their hooves like bulls do before they fight. They all circled the lion's grave continuing with mournful lowing, and every ox participated, beautiful, amazing, mournfully sad.

Both Whitey and Ndoda stood to attention, unmoving, erect as a soldier on parade, or military training; they stood there until every ox did his visit of farewell. It was totally spellbinding, stirring, weird beyond belief and all speech: If it were not witnessed it would never have been believed. When it was over, they came as usual to the kraal gate. Eden sprang quickly into position, exactly where Lion usually had stood.

"Goodnight, Bless, Goodnight Vaalpens. Goodnight Charlie."

Until he saw them all to kraal, he touched them all as they passed, until the last ox was in, as he closed the gate. He was startled by a loud roar of a lion.

"Do you hear that?" Eden said to the two men, still standing to attention.

"Yes, sir," they both said. "Yes Sir."

"Ingomyama."

They repeated the word until the roars faded away into nothingness. Truth is stranger than fiction, Eden said to himself, as he too, simply repeated:

"Ingomyama!"

Epilogue

Mystery still surrounds the stone house. Algoa Bay is Port Elizabeth today, named after Rufane Donkin's wife Elizabeth who died very young in childbirth; he never overcome his grief. He committed suicide. Sonnestroom/Moorplaats was bequeathed to the state, to remain forever a memorial to the valiant pioneers and robbed solid Boers. In some of the old buildings that were once painted with clay, sand and milk (a mixture used by settlers) are many old implements. Inside the old historical museum is a painting that hangs above, quite high, of an old English plough. It's a picture of a big smiling English farmer, pointing with his plough up in the air with his right arm and holding the ox with his left. "It's not to show off, see. It's just because he was so strong."

About the bucket of diamonds—the marauders were wrong. It was not a full bucket, it was a little less than half a bucket of diamonds. Mind, it was an old fashioned large bucket.

Katherine, Kathleen, Kathy—Always regarded as an honored name often held in awe! In Afrikaans, it's "Katrina." It's a regal name.

Lion—Lion the symbol of nobility and strength. Lion was an extraordinary man, equally so was his extraordinary death, but befitting it was. Many people believed he was buried alive, or had a paralytic fit. Six doctors were called to verify his demise. They concluded: no impaired defenses, no traumatic injury, no chronic conditions of the liver, lungs, kidneys. Cause of death was unknown. Could he have gotten into a trance? What about witchcraft? Why was he buried on the 6th day after death? He was smiling. It was difficult to close his casket and put him under the earth. No one wanted to throw the first spade of earth atop his casket. So they built a vault without doors—hurriedly. So stone upon stone, with a small opening to allow his spirit to be free.

Elizabeth—Founded an orphanage for children who lost parents in the wars. She expanded on this later.

Julius—He was sailing to England on a smallish ship called "The Spirit of the Sea." He was consumed with frustration and hate for Lion mainly because he felt that Lion had ribbed him of his only child, Eden. Cautioned by the Captain for some simple offense. There was a heavy storm, enraged, he went on deck at night. He was washed overboard and lost forever in the dark marine. Many years later, Eden was supposed to have inherited considerably, both in property and finances—an amount came from one of the first accounts held by the Standard Bank of South Africa which opened during the Diamond Rush, all correct legally, clearly stating it was from his "biological father."

Xosa—His tombstone still stands. Cared for by unknown somebodies. His name is honored, and the legend still lives. Words do not convey their sibilance nor the depth of meaning. He was a true warrior. This man exemplified the spirit of man. He lived unconquered by the tragedy inflicted upon him, very close to the environs. He demonstrated no signs of subjugation. Despised sham and withered the hard rough earth beneath his calloused heels. He could not tolerate a hypocrite and earned ungrudging respect for his courage, kindness and honesty. He met and faced life straight on, considered it "man's business". He was powerful, yet he was able to be as gentle as a woman. He cried. He stood apart, he belonged yet he did not. Alone and leaned upon though unprotected by the hazards of civilization's advances. Must be forever acclaimed, forever in an amnesis. A humble great man.

Ndoda—Furthered his education. Bought a shop and became the most well known and respected farrier in all the Cape. He also trained horses and his opinion in selecting a prospective racehorse was greatly desired. He was well spoken and behaved like the gentleman he was.

Whitey—He lived on and went into pig farming and breeding. He had his own house, sold suckling pigs for "braais" and wished to be buried where his family was.

Marta—Remained at home until she died.

Swarthaas—Remained in America as an African-American. He claimed, eventually, another name of his choice. He fancied to be Mr. Lamont Hillstone-Hare, but he never forgot his tribal name. He felt the new other name sounded important! Most African-Americans took Caucasian names.

Willem and Piet—Willem and Piet became extremely successful and developed their shipping into a fleet. They were the leading shippers of the Cape of Good Hope. They returned to Moorplaats and erected a grand headstone to their parents who were murdered at the same place where they were laid to rest. Willem also erected a tombstone for "*Marietjie.*" A beautiful poetic headstone—and an Afrikaans poem.

Boseman—Went to Steven's Grammar School with Julius, Moya and Lion, and became a captain of the biggest vessel in their fleet. He married an Italian opera singer from Italy.

Braam Piet Retief and Jan Hora-Jacobsen—Best friends that used to travel by wagon for fun and adventure. Jan established a classy paper for the time, became a prominent citizen. Braam fell madly in love with Jules' widow Kathy, always, but Kathy was a one man woman. An ox wagon, very old, was placed as a memorial upon Braam's grave.

Eden—Among the beautiful rich valleys of Stellenbosch, French Hoek and Paarl, there are many wonderful, magnificent homes. Most of them are vintners and of a vinous ambience, many of the wines from this area are prizewinners on the international wine markets. Some of the families can trace their family back 12 generations. A particularly fine wine is "Riis to Vrede" (Rest and Be Satisfied), a marvelous selected red Sauvignon. The farm's name is "Eden Vale," a lovely estate, very private, with good people, very art conscious too. Near the entrance are three life-size stone statues, two black and one gray, a paler metal, it is said. The writings are obscure, but at the bottom of one, clearly visible, is "Xosa!" already eroded. The English ploughman features on all the letterheads gaily pointing his plow skyward. There is the old saying that says, "Every picture tells a story." It is sad that in the times of the frontier and the early settlers it was so filled with sadness and sorrow. It was a very sad time full of tragedy, as well as adventure.

Canaan—A carving of an angel that seems to evoke tears. The graveyard small, almost dainty, if one can say that of a cemetery. It's on a levelled green that goes up a slope, serene and extremely beautiful. Not too far from the Stone House. It is mysteriously maintained even to this day. If one calls a name, there's a triple reply—a graphite on a rock says "Valley of the Echoes." All graveyards have a tinge of sad atmosphere, but here among the echoes one distinctly feels sorrow. Great long slabs of natural rock, buried deeply, like stakes in the rugged ground, are headstones gone with the harsh wind, long gone but still standing, even against the power of the south east trade winds. Some are no longer able to be read, eroded and bleached and battered by the ravages of time. Hard as they are, there's a tenderness. Strangely triumphant they stand, tall and proud, heads high above the natural and glorious wild lilies.

Glossary

There are experiences people have in near death. Perhaps Lion McCabe fled from his earthly body when he faced death. Louise, the woman he loved, had promised him she would fetch him when he died. At the moment when his soul did an "out of body" flight, he saw Louisa and smiled happily. He went towards her and overstepped the spiritual boundary. He then could not return. This is referred to by Sigmund Freud, also Ernest Hemingway, in "For Whom the Bell Tolls," during combat. Another reference is Charles Dickens' in "The Christmas Carol."

Life After Life—Dr. R. Moodie.

Glimpses of Eternity—Dr. Moodie.

Evidence of Afterlife—Dr. J. Long, Paul Perry.

SOME LEGENDARY AFRIKAANS WORDS

How do you explain the word "sommer" to an Australian or an Engelsman or to anyone else, for that matter. It's not only a foreign word, it's a foreign concept. Perhaps the English never do anything "just sommer." But when you've explained it, it's been adopted enthusiastically. Although there's no equivalent either, they sommer take to the idea. "Why are you laughing? Just sommer."

"Bakkie" is another one of those useful "portmanteau" words (see-English doesn't have a word for that, either), very useful around the house, for all sizes and shapes of containers and dishes. Also used for what they call "utes" in OZ. I find it an indispensable word.

We all know "voetstoots" of course. It's been officially adopted into South African English. There's no concise, one-word equivalent in English. "As is" just doesn't hack it. And it's such a humorous word, conjuring up images of pushing that brand new car home...

There's no good English word for "dwaal". It doesn't mean dream, or daze. It's close to absent-mindedness, but that's not quite it. Being in one so often myself, I'm not likely to stop using it.

I think "gogga" is the most delightful word for insect I've ever heard. Children all over the world should use it. "Insect" just doesn't stand a chance.

And I think "moffie" is a far better word than all those embarrassed English attempts at defining a homosexual: gay, queer, poofter, etc. aren't half as expressive. Somehow "moffie" doesn't sound as derogatory either.

And then there's "gatvol". Ok, I know it's very rude. But it's so very expressive, NE? "Fed up" doesn't have half the impact. It's like Blancmange in comparison. "Gatvol" is a word used more frequently than ever in the workplace these days, with increasing intensity.

While we're on the subject, another phrase which outstrips any English attempt is "Hy sal sy gat sien". (also rude). "He'll get his com-uppance" is like milquetoast in comparison. It definitely lacks the relish.

"Donder" is another very useful word, used as an all-purpose swearword, which again has no good English translation. Used as a verb, it can express any degree of roughing up. As a noun, it is a pejorative, as they politely say in dictionaries, to mean whatever you want it to mean. And there's no good translation for "skiet-en-donder" either. (Shoot and Thunder)

It says something about the English that they have no word for "jol". Probably the dictionary compilers regard it as slang, but it's widely used for "Going out on the town, kicking up your heels, enjoying yourself…" Not just getting PISSED out of your Skull (See, there's no English translation) although curiously, the word "Yule" in Yuletide is related to "jol" and derived from Old English. So somewhere along the line, the English forgot how to "jol".

I've yet to meet a South African over the age of two who doesn't use the word "muti". Translation is impossible—"witches potion" is about the nearest I can get. It needs a long cultural historical explanation. Between "muti" and the pedantic "medication", there's simply no contest.

And of course, my personal favorite "Kak en betaal", which just says it all, doesn't it? A bland and effete English translation would be "Cough up and pay", or "Breathe and pay". But it just doesn't cut it, does it? Not by a long drop.

How do you explain the passion of "LEKKER!"? Wow last night was a "lekker jol".

Dudu or doeks. Telling your infant to go to bed is just not the same as: "Go dudu now my baby!"

How about "bliksem"—I'm going to bliksem you or ek gaan jou donder!

Both wonderful Afrikaans expressions with nothing to compare in the English language, at least nothing that gives the same satisfaction.

Trapsuutjies ..... the way certain maids and others work. Slow-coach just doesn't do it, hey So first—Mielie pap—there is no word like pap here, ... they have porridge, and when they say porridge, they mean oats.

There's no Maltabela, no Tasty Wheat, no Creamy Meal, no Putu pap. In other words, there's no pap!

Mislik—such a "lekker" word, and one that my kids are familiar with. "Why are you so mislik, you little skelm?

Do you want a snot-klap? Vulgar, but very expressive.

Which brings us to skelm—here you just get "baddies", but that doesn't have the same sneaky connotation of a proper skelm, does it? And snot-klap ... fabulous word! How would you say that in English? "I'll slap you so hard the snot will fly?" Yuk! Just not the same.

Loskop is another favorite. The English just don't understand when I say "Sorry, I forgot—I'm such a Loskop!" Ha ha.

Finally, moer! There simply isn't a word here that denotes the feeling behind "If you don't clean your room, I'll moer you!" (It actually means murder.)

AND WHAT ABOUT "VUILGAT" or "poephol"?

Africa has a different definition of color. A person of mixed blood is called a colored. The word Caffre means disbeliever, all the wars were called Kaffir Wars, the Afrikaans spelling for Caffre.

The expression "bitterend" is derived from the cucumber. All the housewives know the end of the cucumber where it joins the growing stem is slightly bitter, and if you cut off a piece, rub it against the body of the cucumber until it makes a froth, it dispels the bitter.

Cultures—ways of life and living.

Monopolies—control by a single person of trade, etc.

Puritanical—of being strict in matters religious or behaving.

Liberty—freedom of speech, movement, etc.

Fraternity—recognition of brotherhood of man.

Aristocratie—belonging to noble or privileged classes—upper class.

Middle class—middle band of peoples.

Squatting—living on properties of others.

Bliksem—ugly word used in slang.

Wag or bietjie—wait a little bit.

Nie so hastig nie—not so quickly.

Just nono—in a minute or so.

Sakkie Sakkie—music.

Ja-nee—How are you? No I'm fine thanks.

Grond Vet—means rich ground

Rinder pest—1881 Disease of cattle (fatal)

VolksRaad—supreme authority legislative power—12 members.

Termites built anthills always forward west.

Bayobab tree grows all over Africa northwards.

Ama—Xosa word for people.

Sekumi—Chief of Bapedi—1861

Trek Chains—Chains used to tie wagons together.

Bathurst—30 miles from Grahamstown.

Kudu—Antelope natives cut off its legs while it is alive to keep its meat fresh as it slowly bleeds to death. (Their living fridge!)

Tuma—wild sweet potato.

Moshesh—Chief African, lived East of Caledon.

Atherstone—First surgeon (1828).

Pretoria—Seat of government.

Pretorious—1853, Potgieter—1848—Boer Leaders.

Grond Vet—means rich ground.

Rinder pest—1881 Disease of cattle (fatal).

Diamond Rush—1870, Judicial power by Landrost. Drosdy authority (Roman Dutch Law)

Slave ship—1854

VolksRaad—Supreme Authority Legislative Power—12 members.

Termites build anthills always forward west.

Bayobab tree grows all over Africa northwards.

Ama—Xosa word for people.

Sekumi—Chief of Bapedi—1861.

Imgomyama—means Lion in Xosa language.

Sigmund Freud was a cocaine addict.

1819	5th Kaffir War
1820	Albany Settlers
1834	Freedom of all slaves
	6th Kaffir War
1836	Great trek
1838	Death—Piet Retief
	(Blood River 16th Dec.)
1846	7th Kaffir War
1848	Boer Leaders
1850	English Kaffir War
1853	Pretorius—Potgieter
1854	Slave Ship
1865	Kaffaria annexation to Cape
1870	Diamond Rush—Judicial power by Landrost. Drosdy authority (Roman Dutch Law)
1877	Transvaal annexed.
1881	Magaba Hill 'Majuba'
1885	Gold—Rand
1893	Jameson Raid
1899	Boer War
1902	Peace finally

Tail Piece

A visit to the fairest Cape in all the world will be unforgettable for any human being, from anywhere. Visit the Cape.

Stop, have tea, real bushman brews—Rooibos or Honeybush. Enjoy a cold Lion Lager beer or maybe dine where the magnificient Cape wines are served. Love the sheer beauty of the valleys and the coast: If you are tempted to have a bunch of grapes that grow freely on the road sides, ask a Vintagers. He will teach you how to steal a bunch properly. Farmers don't like any destruction. Try some wonderful, original foods. Kingklip fish and Koeksusters! Africa will hunt you foreever.

The wind from the south east is commonly known as "The Cape Doctor." Exhale and let it blow you away.

About the Author

Sheena Summerfield was born to a Danish
mother and a British/South African father,
somewhere on the wild coast of Africa.
It was written in her mother's diary that the
town was "Butterworth" in the Transkei. The
mother sat up and pulled her out, delivering
with the help of the kitchen maid, a sort of self
delivery—the maid could hardly speak English
and there was never a birth record.

During the Second World War, her father went away with the
Sappers engineering core and she and her siblings were placed in
a German community boarding school in the countryside.

For pocket money Sheena wrote all the other students composi-
tions—"10 bob a compo." 10 shillings was half a British pound in
those days. The Principal was an Afrikaans gentleman. When she
left school he told her she had a talent for writing and that she
should consider it as a career. Instead she went into beauty and
fashion and became a well-known model. Wed to an English
gentleman who had settled in Africa in the 60's the couple settled

in Rhodesia, now known as Zimbabwe. When her daughters were of age they were sent on a trip around the world in lieu of the usual coming of age party. They both married Americans and settled in California. Another love of Sheena's life was her garden and every day, when the garden staff went to lunch, for 2 1/2 hours she took to writing a story from her imagination—and germinated a seed of a different kind, "Where the wild lilies grow."

The wonderful country of Rhodesia was smothered by a sad, cruel and wicked bush war. Despite the fact that it was nominated the bread basket of Africa, during this bush war: guns shot through windows, AK47's, dogs poisoned, children killed, horses with hooves slashed off left bleeding to death, boy soldiers, farmers murdered, barbed wire and high walls... People fled. No doctors, no equipped hospitals, no law and order, bank accounts emptied, and finally no food. Aids and disease rampant. Politics changed everyone's lives.

Gerald, her loving husband, succumbed to cancer and what remained of the family moved to America, leaving her beloved garden and most of the family possessions behind. Sheena was packing up in the library, lying on the floor, where the little pile of black school exercise books, her lunchtime writings, hand written, caught her eye... throw those books into the container security, she said—the container for America!